GARY L. HOLLEMAN

DEMON FIRE

Quinn Ramsey couldn't believe his good fortune. As the nephew and sole surviving relative of recently deceased Bernard Ramsey, Quinn had inherited a massive fortune and an exquisite estate in the lush Hawaiian Islands. But terror lurked in the deepest shadows of the palatial structure, and Quinn found his dream home was really a house of horror. Soon he had to gamble his very life to rid himself and his home of the maniacal evil that burned in the flames of the demon fire.

GARY L. HOLLEMAN

DEMON FIRE

LEISURE BOOKS **NEW YORK CITY**

To my wife Kathleen.

A LEISURE BOOK®

July 1995

Published by

Dorchester Publishing Co., Inc.
276 Fifth Avenue
New York, NY 10001

Printed in the United States of America.

DEMON FIRE

PROLOGUE

September

Bernard Ramsey locked the door of his Mercedes sedan, flipped up the collar on his trench coat to protect his neck from the windblown rain and waited for his eyes to adjust to the gloom.

The clouds over Mauna Kea were heavy and low, obscuring the volcano's snowy peak. Bernard had parked in the visitor's lot at the state recreation area, near a field of volcanic rubble. The rain made the rocks look black and slick as if they had been dipped in dirty petroleum. Once he could see, he walked to the edge of the pavement and gazed up the dark slope. Mauna Kea was sleeping, with little chance that rain or the restlessness of rattling palm fronds would wake her.

He looked at the gold Rolex on his wrist: 11:22. "Shit!"

Bernard was 56, but most people thought he was forty. Six feet tall, he had a treadmill-trim body and a narrow face. Thin eyebrows rose over cold gray eyes that resembled wet concrete. It was not a face anyone would call warm.

Restless, Bernard stooped and picked up a chunk of lava about the size of a baseball. He tossed it in the air and caught it. Hearing the clatter of rocks at his back, he whirled around, his right hand instinctively seeking the fetish inside the raincoat.

A bandy-legged mountain sheep stood precariously on the rocks, shivering and staring at him indignantly. Its pointed ears drooped dejectedly and water cascaded from its dirty white coat.

"A bad night to be out, my friend." Bernard chuckled nervously. He checked the wristwatch again. "Fuck it."

He marched back to the car, fumbling in his pocket for the keys. Then he heard another sharp clatter in the rocks behind him. Before he could turn around, his body was engulfed in a ball of white-hot flame. There was no pain or time for fear. Before he could even blink, his body was a smoldering hunk of charcoal. When the police found the remains the next morning, they pried opened Bernard's fist and found the piece of lava.

Chapter One

October

The sound of a belligerent female voice jolted Quinn Ramsey out of a sound sleep. His knuckles began to throb as they always did when he heard that particular tone, a legacy of 12 years with the nuns. He opened his eyes and saw the flight attendant dabbing his son with a towel. Quinn Junior was squirming and casting anxious looks at his father.

"What did you do, Q?" Quinn asked.

"Nothing, honest."

Quinn looked up at the stewardess. Her face was flushed and her jaw was clenched so tightly he thought her teeth might crack.

"I'm sorry," Quinn said. "What did he do?"

The woman was Asian or maybe Polynesian, and she would have been pretty if she hadn't been so an-

9

gry. She gave Quinn a canned smile and said, "He tried to take a glass of champagne from my tray and spilled it all over himself and the passenger across the aisle."

The seat across the aisle was empty. Quinn decided the man was probably in the lavatory, and he made a mental note to apologize later. He smiled at his son, but it didn't fool anybody. It was the reflexive baring of teeth that prehistoric parents had developed to keep from strangling their young, thus putting an untimely end to the human race.

"He's nine," Quinn said. "But my son doesn't believe in age discrimination. Did he apologize?"

The stewardess leaned across the boy and whispered, "I don't think so. He said I have awesome tits."

She pushed herself up and marched back into the coach section of the jumbo jet. Quinn mulled the situation over. What was he supposed to do? It wouldn't be fair to yell at the kid for lying—the woman's breasts were incredible. She proved that while leaning across the seat. But he couldn't very well give the boy a raise in his allowance either.

"What did you think you were doing?"

"The stuff is free, isn't it? I just wanted to see what it tasted like."

This whole flying business was new to the boy—especially flying all the way from Florida to Hawaii. And maybe going first class had been a bad idea too. Quinn probably should have cashed in the tickets the lawyer had sent and flown coach. Heaven knew he and his son could have used the difference.

"Next time, ask."

"You would have said no."

"Exactly."

They were quiet for a few minutes, Q swinging his feet and Quinn looking out the window.

Why couldn't Q want the window seat like every other kid in the world? Quinn wondered. He was nine. Was that too early to be rebellious? Quinn couldn't remember being nine. Hell, he couldn't remember being rebellious either. His father had been a big Irish cop, not the kind to tolerate boyish exuberance.

"Dad, what are we going to do when we get to Hawaii?"

"Like I told you. First we go to the lawyer's office for the reading of the will; then we can go to the beach or do whatever you want."

"This guy was your uncle?"

"Yes, my father's brother."

"So how come he never came to visit?"

"What can I tell you? Uncle Bernard was a recluse. Pop only mentioned him twice my whole life. I don't know much about him except that he never married."

"What was he? A homo?"

Quinn counted silently to ten. "The word is homosexual, or gay. And I'd like to point out that the world is rapidly changing. Someday you're going to wise off to some guy just because he looks or acts differently, and he's going haul off and clean your clock. You get my drift?"

"Don't call people homos?"

"You're not supposed to call them anything. That's why their mommies and daddies went to all the trouble of giving them names."

"Geez, Dad, chill out. I didn't say you were a homo."

The stewardess made another pass down the aisle with the champagne tray. She tried to give the Ramseys a wide berth, but Quinn held up his hand to stop her, took a faux long-stem glass from her tray and downed the contents in three gulps. He smacked his lips and looked down at his son.

"Mmmmm. Good stuff."

"I feel like a dork."

Quinn had forced his son's bony frame into a pair of navy slacks and a short-sleeved oxford shirt. The outfit reminded Quinn of his Catholic school uniforms, but the boy did look cute.

"Don't be silly. You look like a young gentleman."

"Isn't that what I just said? And you look like a lawyer."

"I'll get you for that later."

Quinn had on his best suit, a slightly out-of-date navy polyester with a thin maroon pinstripe. When he'd taken it out of the suit bag, it had so many frazzled threads that Q had asked if he'd chased a perp through a barbed-wire fence.

Q was perched on the edge of a green leather bergere chair, scoping out the lawyer's office, while Quinn looked out the window at the hoards of tourists combing Waikiki Beach in Bermuda shorts and floppy straw hats.

"Where do they get those shirts?" Quinn muttered to himself.

The offices of Block, Growe, Peterson, Smythe & Rynd reeked of money: floor-to-ceiling Chinese bookcases, an aquarium full of salt water fish and a bank of windows facing the ocean. You could play table tennis on the desk, and the executive chair behind it looked as if it operated with hydraulics. The books on the shelves were bound in thick leather and their rich aroma helped cut the odor of cigars and Old Spice.

"Where is everybody?" Q asked.

"Beats me."

"I thought the relatives would be circling to pick over the carcass."

Quinn looked over his shoulder. "Where do you get this stuff?"

The door opened and the lawyer came in.

The man was immense, and he tried to hide it in a pair of loose silk slacks and a busy red-and-white Hawaiian shirt that covered his bulk like a circus tent. He appeared to be suffering through the latter stages of male pattern baldness; his remaining hairs were held in place by something that smelled remarkably like shellac. Quinn saw the glint in Q's eyes and silenced him with a look before the boy had a chance to open his mouth.

"Mr. Ramsey." The man offered his hand across the desk. Quinn took it, shook it and let it go. It felt like the tail of a tuna. "Have a seat. We'll try to get through this legal stuff as painlessly as possible."

After pulling a thick manilla folder from the top drawer of the desk and spreading it out on the blotter, the man separated the papers into three precise piles. He saw the boy's expression and glanced down at his shirt.

"Oh, I guess you're wondering about my shirt. It's

Aloha Friday. Everybody wears one of these to work. Bank presidents, lawyers, doctors—everybody." Q didn't know what he was expected to say, so he just smiled. The man pushed the papers across the desk, placed his burgundy Mont Blanc on the center stack and said to Quinn, "If you'll just sign the last page on all three copies, I think we can be on our way."

Quinn picked up the first pile and hefted it. It was at least three inches thick.

"Mr. Peterson. What is this? What am I supposed to sign? Where is everybody?"

The man's face went blank for a moment. "I'm so sorry. I thought someone told you. Mr. Peterson is over on Maui today. I'm Randall Stalkins, his paralegal. I prepared all the papers though, and I can answer any questions you may have."

Quinn flipped through the papers and saw his name—Quinn Booth Ramsey—typed on the last page under a black line.

"I condensed everything into one document," Stalkins said. "Its a transfer of ownership for your late uncle's property and a preliminary tax return for the estate. Just as soon as I get your signature on those, I'll have some signature cards for your checking, savings and credit card accounts. The stocks, bonds and T-bills will take a while longer."

Quinn saw the man's lips moving, but the words didn't make any sense. It must have showed.

"Mr. Ramsey, who contacted you?"

"I got a letter with a pair of airline tickets. The letter said my uncle had died and I was in the will. That's it."

"Do you have the letter?"

Quinn produced the envelope and handed it over. The paralegal unfolded the letter and read with minute movements of his lips. After a moment he muttered, "Tisk-tisk, Ms. Van Dreelan." Then two minutes later looked up.

"Do you have some form of identification?"

Quinn handed over his Florida driver's license with his photograph and a credit card used so often that the numbers were almost illegible. Stalkins squinted at the likeness on the license and at Quinn. He saw a man in his early forties with an angular face and mouth that looked as if it had forgotten how to smile.

"You are Quinn Booth Ramsey of Delray Beach, Florida?"

Quinn nodded.

"Your father was Barton Ramsey and your mother was Phyllis Booth Ramsey, both deceased? Mrs. Kathleen Ramsey died in an automobile accident in 1987 and you are currently employed by the Palm Beach County Sheriff's Department?"

"That's me."

"Mr. Ramsey, I feel like the guy in that old television show *The Millionaire*." Stalkins stood and held out his hand again. "You are the sole heir to Bernard Ramsey's estate. According to our audit, the estate includes a house on Maui, land on the big island and Kauai, several cars, office buildings in Honolulu, Lahaina and Hilo and liquid assets, cash, CDs, stocks, bonds and treasury certificates in the amount of"— Stalkins checked the post-it note on the folder— "thirty-four million, seven hundred eighty thousand, forty dollars and fifty-seven cents."

Quinn looked at Stalkins's clammy hand, then down at his own knees and thought about putting his head between them. Q tapped him on the shoulder.

"Dad, does this mean I can have my own room?"

Ten Days Later

"This is the most god-awful excuse for a highway I've ever seen," Quinn said as he fought the Mercedes's steering wheel. Q was belted into the passenger seat, dividing his time between the car owner's manual and the blur of exotic vegetation rushing by the window. They were following a stretch of Highway 360 that, if they survived the hairpin curves, would take them to the city of Hana on the east coast of Maui.

"Dad, was that a weasel?" Q asked suddenly.

"Weasel? I don't know. What does a weasel look like?"

"Wow! Another waterfall."

"Yeah, yeah. This friggin' road has more twists and turns than a kyphotic snake." Quinn had been unable to find ten feet of straight highway since they passed the third mile marker.

"What'd you tell Capt. Johnson when you called?" Q asked.

Quinn slammed on the brakes on his side of a one-lane bridge to keep from front ending a geriatric couple driving a battered Geo Storm held together by Avis bumper stickers. "Damned tourists."

Q gave his dad an amused glance before returning his attention to the jungle.

"I told him I got a better offer: being rich."

They rode for another mile. Then Quinn pulled off

onto a wide shoulder in front of another waterfall to give the circulation a chance to return to his knuckles.

Q was out the door before the car stopped rolling, and he sprinted across a small footbridge to the edge of a deep green pool under a canopy of thick trees. Quinn caught up in time to keep his son from trying to walk the moss-covered rocks to the falls.

"How come they have so many waterfalls?" Q asked.

"I'm glad you asked," Quinn said, mimicking W.C. Fields. He had been up half the night studying tourist books on Hawaii in general and Maui in particular. "You'll be interested to know that this end of the island is one of the wettest places on earth. In some spots, forty feet of rain fall every year."

"Forty feet! Crud! I'll never be able to skateboard."

"Don't be so negative. Over on the other coast, around Lahaina, it almost never rains, so you've got one of the wettest spots in the world here on the same island with one of the driest."

The waterfall looked like a set designed and built by the chamber of commerce. One side was framed with a thicket of thin bamboo stalks and the other by a massive rubber tree with dozens of thin roots that hung down from the limbs like locks of stringy hair. White, blue and pale yellow orchids and pink protea grew around the rocks at the base of the falls. The air was damp and softly perfumed.

"Mom would have loved this," Q whispered, giving his dad a sideways glance.

Quinn squatted on his heels, ostensibly to examine a bed of red heart-shaped anthuriums, but in reality to hide his expression. The mention of his dead wife brought back memories of cinnamon freckles and auburn hair, of cool eyes as green as creme de menthe and the warmth of her touch. Kathleen O'Riley Ramsey, dead at twenty-nine.

"Yeah, she would've."

"What are we going to do, Dad? Are we going to stay here? Do I have to go to school?"

Quinn studied the boy's face. It was a lot like looking into a mirror: clear blue eyes, dark hair that refused to submit to a comb, a slim face with full lips that were too often compressed in anticipation of bad news.

But Kathy was there too—in Q's smile, in the high cheekbones and small ears and especially in the tiny, straight nose. Sometimes just looking at the boy made Quinn feel like crying.

"Why don't we take a look at the house before we decide? But wherever we live, you'll have to go to school."

"How come? We're rich, right? Why can't I work for you?"

"Yeah? What can you do for me? I don't think I'm gonna need a skateboarder or a third baseman. And I definitely don't think you could be my decorator. I've seen how you keep your room."

"I could teach you about music, so you'd quit listening to that old stuff."

"My God! What old stuff?" Quinn said, aghast. "Credence? The Stones? Did I ever tell you your mom and I went to Jimmy Buffet concerts at Gussman Hall?"

Q picked one of the heart-shaped flowers and

18

sniffed it. "Only about a million times."

The boy dug the toes of his Nikes in the damp soil and picked at the sides of his jeans. The tail of his T-shirt was out again, hanging down almost to his knees.

"First thing we do is get you some clothes that fit—some new shorts and shoes. What do you say?"

Q looked at the ragged tennis shoes and shrugged. "Can I get those high tops with the pump?"

"If you think you can keep them tied. I don't want to see you walking around with the laces loose. You'll fall and break something."

"Okay. And, Dad, I know something I can do for you."

"What?"

"I can be your numba one son," Q said in his best Charlie Chan accent.

Quinn picked up his son by the back of his baggy jeans and threw him over his shoulder. "That you can."

"Where is the Ramsey file?" Randall Stalkins demanded. "It was on my desk yesterday and now it's gone!"

"Calm down, Randall. It's right here," Corine Van Dreelan said. The executive secretary tossed the thick file across the top of her desk.

Randall hurriedly flipped through it.

"It's all there. Scout's honor," Corine said dryly, holding up three fingers in the Boy Scout salute.

"What are you doing with it?"

Corine's nostrils flared as if she had just found something foul on the bottom of one of her expensive pumps.

"I have access to everything Mr. Peterson is working on. Someone stopped by with some questions and I took the file. Now take it and run back to your cubbyhole. I have important things to do."

Randall Stalkins did a slow burn. He would give anything to have the woman at one of the coven's initiation ceremonies. She'd quickly lose that haughty attitude.

"Who stopped by? What questions?"

Corine was already lost in her word processor. She spoke idly as her fingers flew over the keys. "Some woman. Another paralegal, I think."

Randall looked as if the folder had suddenly become radioactive. "What woman? What did she look like? What did she want?"

The nimble fingers stopped and briefly became claws. Then Corine turned and gave Randall a sugary smile. "I don't remember, Randall. She said she was from another firm. The will is through probate. It's public record so I didn't see a problem."

"But, there are other papers in the file beside the will."

For the first time, Corine looked concerned. "What papers?"

Randall hugged the file to his chest. "Never mind. But you can be sure Mr. Peterson will hear about this."

Feeling much better at having the last word, Randall scurried back to his tiny office.

"What a moron," Corine muttered as she turned back to her typing.

* * *

Hana was small and remote enough to qualify for end-of-the-earth status—so secluded, in fact, that Charles Lindbergh, a man no one would ever accuse of being a party animal, picked the area for his final resting place. And yet for all its brooding isolation, Hana was as easy on the eyes as any town in the islands.

It started as a sugar plantation town in the mid-1800s. When sugar took a nosedive in the 1940s, the town put on its cowboy hat and chaps and became a ranching town after San Francisco industrialist Paul Fagan purchased 14,000 acres and imported Hereford cattle. It survived tidal waves and waves of tourists and Hollywood types, and thanks to its singular highway that rivals the Burma Road in switchbacks, it was still relatively free of glitz.

Quinn breathed a sigh of relief as he drove past the medical center at the edge of town. His neck and shoulders felt like steel bands after three hours on a 30-mile road.

"I think I know what happened to Uncle Bernard," he whispered conspiratorially. "He committed suicide rather than drive over that road one more time."

"How did he die?" Q asked.

Since Kathy's accident, Quinn had shied away from any mention of death. But Q was growing up, and he couldn't ignore the subject forever.

"Everybody is real careful about that. All the letter said was he died over on the big island and Stalkins either didn't know or wouldn't say. I guess we'll find out sooner or later."

"Has he already been buried?"

Quinn wondered if his son had memories of his

mother's funeral. Q had only been three and a half, but you never knew what kids remember.

"Yeah, before we were contacted. Cremated, I think."

They came to a fork in the road and steered to the right to stay on the main highway. The traffic was light, predominated by American-made convertibles with young couples who were looking everywhere but at the road. On their left was a police substation, and just as they drove past, a copper-colored sedan fell in behind them. Quinn cut his eyes to the speedometer and then glanced in the rear view mirror.

"Why do they call those things unmarked cars?" Q asked. "They might as well paint fuzz all over 'em with dayglo paint."

"We don't say fuzz, son. We say guardians of the American way of life."

"I forgot."

The blue light on the Plymouth's dash started winking in the mirror.

"Now what?" Quinn pulled to the side of the road and shut off the engine. The police cruiser parked a car-length behind.

"Shouldn't speed, Dad. Speed kills."

"Just what I need, a junior advertising executive. Besides I wasn't speeding."

"That's what they all say."

"It's a good thing I'm getting you out of Florida. You've been hanging out with Kerry and Tim too much."

Carl Kerry was Quinn's partner. They had been driving together for seven years, and he was one of only two people in the entire Sunshine State that

Quinn would miss. The other was Tim Wolinsky. Wolinsky had been a cat burglar, gun runner and part-time con man before butting heads with Quinn and Kerry.

"What's he waiting on?" Quinn muttered.

The cop was still sitting behind the wheel. A moment later the door opened and a slight Asian woman wearing a lime-green pantsuit climbed out and began walking toward the Mercedes.

"Great. They give meter maids unmarked cars in this town," Quinn grumbled.

While he watched the woman's reflection, his organic cop computer began to catalogue and file her description: Long black hair, oval face and full lips with pale pink lipstick. Slim, about five-six and a hundred pounds. She wore mirrored sunglasses, but he figured she'd have brown eyes. He didn't see a sidearm, but her brown leather purse hung heavy from her right shoulder.

Quinn pushed the button and enjoyed the way the tinted glass whispered out of sight.

"Good afternoon, sir," the police officer said.

Nice soft emphasis on sir. He liked that too.

They waited for the diesel roar of a truck loaded with pineapples to recede. The oily taste of truck guano filled the car.

A leather case appeared out of the bag and the woman flipped it open with practiced ease.

"Sgt. Okata, state police. Could I see your license and registration please?"

Quinn fished his wallet from the pocket of his cut-offs and took out the Florida license and a letter from the law firm stating that the car's title was in the process of being transferred. Okata took her time checking the photo and then the letter. Quinn got the distinct impression that, behind the reflective lenses, she was sizing him up.

She bent over and looked at Q. "Afternoon, son."

"Hello, ma'am."

"Mr. Ramsey, would you mind following me to the station? It will only take a few minutes."

"May I ask why?"

"It's about the death of Bernard Ramsey."

The woman's eyes gave away nothing, but her manner was way too casual—as if statie sergeants had nothing better to do than greet every car that survived that tortuous road. Quinn had used the technique himself and it made him wonder.

"Why not? Maybe you can give me directions to my house when we're through."

Okata turned to go back to her car. She had barely made it to the rear bumper when Q said, "Some meter maid."

As police substations went, it wasn't much: half-a-dozen offices; chrome-and-glass partitions; desks cluttered with file folders and Styrofoam cups half full of coffee and cigarette butts. The crackle of hand radios, the smell of unwashed bodies and Binaca. Several male cops were sitting around doing paperwork or shooting the breeze when Okata led Quinn and Q through the room. Okata acted as if the men were invisible, her face set in stone as they watched her pass. Some watched her walk, zeroing in on her hips as she moved down the aisle. Some watched her face. One or two averted their eyes.

On the other side of a glass wall, Q studied wanted posters while Quinn faced Okata across an institutional metal conference table in the station's lone interrogation room. The table had been worked on with everything from cigarettes to hunting knives, and the jumble of initials and profanity looked like hieroglyphics on the wall of an Egyptian tomb.

"Coffee okay?" Okata asked.

Quinn nodded. It was the mud-brown police blend that tasted like burnt tires.

"Mr. Ramsey, where were you on September twelfth of this year?"

Quinn tapped on the glass and waved Q to the door. "Run out to the car and get my filofax out of the glove compartment."

He let Okata's question hang in the air until the boy returned.

"We gonna be long? I'm hungry," Q said.

Quinn gave the boy a dollar. "Get a candy bar."

Q held the bill like a dead mouse. "A whole dollar? I hope I don't go into a sugar coma."

Quinn jerked two more singles out of the wallet and handed them over. "It's bad form to hold up your father in a police station."

Quinn reclaimed his seat and flipped through the calendar. "What time?"

"About midnight here."

"That would be about what? Six a.m. in Florida? I was driving around Palm Beach."

"At six in the morning? Can anyone verify that?"

Quinn flipped through his notes. "Yeah, my partner, two nickel-and-dime pushers we arrested at five o'clock and my watch commander."

Okata tapped the tabletop with her long finger-nails. She didn't look pleased. "You're a cop?"

Quinn smiled. "Was. For nine years."

"Why didn't you just say that right off?"

"I wanted to know what this was about. You mentioned my uncle."

"Your uncle was murdered, Mr. Ramsey."

Quinn nodded, finally understanding the questions. "Round here? How?"

"No, over on the big island. The how part is giving us a few problems. The investigating officer is betting on a flamethrower, but the M.E. says no. No trace of gas or any other combustible."

"He was burned?"

"To a crisp."

Quinn looked down at the table for a moment, then up into Okata's flinty eyes. He'd been correct. They were brown.

"You don't seem terribly upset." She said.

Quinn allowed himself a grim half smile. "Sarge, I didn't even know the man."

"Yet you're driving his car."

"And living in his house and spending his money—my money now. He left it all to me."

"Kind of strange, you not knowing him and all."

Being on the other side of an interrogation was a new and rather unpleasant experience for Quinn and Okata's tone wasn't helping matters much. "No stranger than you not knowing I was his heir. What were you going to do? Sit out on the highway and stop every Mercedes that drove by?"

Okata frowned. "You think we only have one homicide going? This may not be Palm Beach, but we

sure have our share of lowlifes. And as far as you
being the heir, we didn't even know there was an heir
until the impound yard called this morning to tell us
you had picked up the Mercedes. I've been trying to
find out about the will for weeks, but getting information out of that thousand-dollar-an-hour mouth-
piece of yours is like trying to pull teeth from a
buzzard. At first, he wouldn't even admit being your
lawyer. Then he wouldn't return calls. He would only
promise to reply to our questions by messenger and
didn't. On top of that, your late uncle wasn't exactly
a social butterfly. He didn't go to parties or get his
picture in the society pages. Nobody in town knew
where he came from or could even remember when
he moved here. When we sent his prints to the FBI,
all we got was a question mark. Was he a spy?"

Quinn shrugged. "So it's the same old thing, right?
Love or money, who gets the gravy?"

She leaned back in the stiff vinyl chair. "You know
the drill."

"Look. He left his estate to me because as far as I
know there are no other relatives."

Okata made a few notes in a folder. "So where's
the wife? She didn't happen to be visiting out this
way last month, did she?"

Quinn felt his ears start to burn. "My wife is dead.
Years ago. Sorry I'm not making this easy for you."

Okata bristled at his tone. "Mr. Ramsey, you
haven't made this easy from the start."

Her rage was so sudden and unexpected that it
frightened him. Quinn did what he normally did when
he was scared, he lashed out. "Gee, Sarge, life's a bitch.
I guess it must be a bad time of the month, huh?"

Okata started out of the chair, then stopped and visibly took hold of herself. "Nine years, huh? And you weren't even a sergeant. Why not?"

Quinn's mind was a tricky beast. Just when he thought a memory was safely locked away in the old gray matter, something clicked: a name, a place, an old hurt. Quinn flashed back to the night he and Kerry had caught up with the bastard who had crashed into Kathy's car and then driven away, leaving her to strangle slowly in her own blood. What he'd done to that guy made what happened to Rodney King look like a fraternity prank: three broken ribs, a fractured radius and a concussion. If Kerry hadn't pulled him off and then covered for him, Quinn would have been the one in jail.

Then had come the long months sucking on the bourbon bottle, the binges, the fights. Q's babysitters refused to work for Quinn because every now and then he forgot to come home. That was when he'd lost his stripes. He'd gone to work once too often smelling like a distillery. When the case worker told Quinn social services was about to take his son, AA had started looking pretty good. After attending 90 meetings in 90 days, he'd received a clean bill of health from social services. But he still managed to sneak a cold one every now and then.

He noted Okata's neutral expression. She was good, and a good cop knew exactly which buttons to push. He decided to try a button of his own. "I didn't have the benefit of affirmative action."

This time Okata did come out of the chair, bracing herself on stiff arms and firing volleys of sparks from those hypnotic eyes. "Get out of here, you arrogant son-of-a-bitch."

Quinn slowly got to his feet. "I won't mention this little tantrum to anyone. I have too much respect for the badge."

He went out the door, careful not to slam it, and led Q to the front door. He found a patrolman at the desk and asked directions to his new home.

The town of Hana was fronted by a bay that looked from the air like the profile of a human head with its mouth open in a never ending scream. Modern brick, wood and plaster homes sprouted like mushrooms among the ancient cabernet-colored lava-rock dwellings, all of which were designed more to withstand the elements than from any sense of aesthetics. The low, lavish homes of the well-to-do were on a hillside with a breathtaking view. The citadels of the truly rich lined the rocky coast.

Quinn had to backtrack to the fork in the highway and take a narrow branch to Waikoloa Road. Then he headed over a wide stream, along the edge of the picture-postcard bay, to a jutting neck of land between Kainalimu Bay and Hana Bay—a place called Nanualele Point. The land on one side of the road was a patchwork of green-and-tan pineapple fields; the other side was rugged cliffs. Across Hana Bay, on a rocky island no bigger than a two-car garage, the rotating cyclopean eye of a lighthouse circled lethargically.

The road started out well enough, but after a mile turned into an obstacle course of potholes and dust that rolled behind the sedan like the train on a bridal gown. It twisted as it climbed, forcing Quinn to slow the car to navigate an endless series of sharp turns.

"Nobody in this friggin' state knows how to build a straight road," he muttered.

"Want me to drive?" Q asked.

"You'll be driving soon enough. Let's not rush it."

Q sat with his head hanging out the window, watching the surf smash against the rocks. "This is neat."

"Hard to beat the ocean."

"It's not like back home. It's wild. You know, rough."

Immense waves crashed onto black boulders at the base of the cliff, sending emerald geysers laced with rays of sunlight all the way to the top. The air was ripe with salt water and the odor of rotting seaweed, yet softened by spicy fragipani trees that grew wild along the rocky promontory. The sun had ducked behind the red hill that dominated Hana Bay and the palm trees striped the road with long fingers of shadow.

The Ramseys rounded another curve and took a steep grade through a grove of swaying coconut palms. A minute later they lost sight of the ocean.

"Where is this place?" Q asked. "I'm hungry."

"You have a tapeworm."

"You always say that. I might have to trade you in for a dad with some new lines."

"We're just going to find the house. Then we can go back into town and eat."

"That was a town?"

"Well it isn't Miami, thank goodness. You've never spent any time in a small town. Give it a chance. No drug dealers, no muggers, no boomboxes."

"Aw, Dad, come on. No malls, no movies, no fun."

They passed a sign for Nanualele Point and a moment later rounded a bend and saw an eight-foot lava wall accessed through a solid wrought-iron gate. Quinn slowed at the mailbox. The name Ramsey was painted in flowing script on the side of the box.

"Dis must be de place."

Quinn pushed one of the two infrared garage door openers that hung from the sedan's visor, but nothing happened. He pushed the other button and the gate slowly swung inward.

"Cool," Q said, trying to mask his excitement with a kid's bored indifference.

Quinn steered up the asphalt drive, through trees and shrubs that looked as if they had been manicured with fingernail scissors, past flower gardens and topiary in fanciful shapes: dragons, squat ogres, a wolf and a giant gargoyle.

"What is this place? Fantasyland?" Q asked.

"Looks like Vincent Price was the gardener."

"Who?"

"Why do you do that to me?" Quinn asked.

The driveway ended in a parking circle with a fountain in the middle and a five-car garage at the far side. Quinn slowed to a stop and stared at the house.

The main house was a one-story, Spanish Gothic structure done in dark woods and chiseled lava. It covered the whole end of the peninsula. A pair of four-story, pentagonal towers stood like glowering stone sentinels at either end. The entrance was a set of wide steps and double doors that Quinn could have driven the Mercedes through. The high arched windows in the front were filled with leaded glass and the tiered roof was covered with red Moorish tiles.

"I bet Emily Bronte slept here," Quinn said.

"Who?"

Quinn stepped out into unexpectedly cool air and watched the water in the fountain shooting out of the flute of a stone satyr. The feeling of unreality was like a fantastic LSD trip. He had grown up in a series of rental houses from South Miami to Lantana as his father chased the ever elusive promotion out of uniform. His mother had never had a washing machine or a stove with four working burners. She had never had a car, a color television or more than two pairs of decent shoes. This was the antithesis of his life. Things like this didn't happen to him.

Q opened his door, but Quinn called, "Sit tight! I'm just going to make sure the keys work and then we'll go eat. From the looks of this place, we might starve before we find the kitchen."

"Can we get pizza?"

"I saw a seafood place back on the highway."

"Yuck!"

At the front door, Quinn took out a piece of paper with the alarm code and tried the key. It turned easily, allowing him access into the foyer. It was dark. The light from the faux candles in the cut-glass chandelier didn't do much to penetrate the gloom. There was a pair of sturdy Mediterranean tables—one with a heavy brass lamp—and a pair of oil paintings that faced each other across the corridor. The walls were covered with dark grass paper and the floor tiles with a long Persian carpet runner. The understated opulence made him feel like an intruder.

He followed a muted beeping sound to the coat closet just to his right. Inside, he pushed aside several dark overcoats and punched in the four-digit code to disarm the security system. Q was doubtlessly fidgeting in the car, but what man could resist taking a quick look around his new house?

Quinn ran his fingers over the glossy tabletop and stared, somewhat taken aback. What, no dust? The place must have been closed for almost a month and yet it was spotless. He glanced down at the Italian marble floor, which gleamed like new dentures; then he looked out the door at the fountain. The grass was cut and hedges were trimmed. Quinn half expected a maid or a gardener to jump out and yell. "Welcome!" But the place was quiet. Besides, nobody but that pain-in-the-ass Okata knew he was coming.

"Oh, well." Quinn sighed. His uncle must have had a maid. He made a mental note to thank her later, then gave his attention to the painting on the wall behind the table. There was a windswept hill surrounded by dark clouds. On its summit, a naked woman was bound to a pole with tongues of flame licking her body. A crowd of people in black clothing and button boots stood watching. The expression on the woman's face was somehow erotic and Quinn figured a painting that disturbing had to be worth a fortune.

"Heavy," he muttered to himself.

He had always told people that he wasn't into possessions, he didn't care about things. But then, he'd never had any possessions worth caring about.

When the Mercedes's horn blared, Quinn reset the

alarm, locked the front door and strolled back to the shiny sedan feeling very smug.

"Be it ever so humble . . ." Quinn said and raced back to the car. Then his son and he headed off in search of dinner.

As the sound of the Mercedes's engine faded, quiet once more roamed the dark corridors. It was a cloying silence that would have felt harsh to human ears. Then, the door to the wine cellar creaked. And the needle on the wall thermostat began creeping down until it struck the bottom of the gauge.

The robes gave the proceedings a comic opera appearance, but there was nothing funny about the intent. Three people had gathered on the patio of the penthouse apartment. Despite the fact that they knew each other intimately, they hid their faces behind grotesque stone masks.

The trio faced the raging storm with upraised arms, chanting in a tongue that was already old when the megaliths of Stonehenge were new.

"Mighty Lucifuge Rofocale, Prime Minister of the Infernal Kingdom, heed the pleas of your servants.

"Great Fleurety, Lieutenant-Commander of Gehenna, keeper of the flame, worker of miracles of the night, grant your subjects power. Grant our requests so we may spread your glory."

The storm answered with waves of rain that chased the trio inside the penthouse, where their disciples waited.

The sunken living room was packed with men and women in conservative suits and dazzling evening gowns. The mood was festive and the crowd could easily be mistaken for revelers at a post-theater cock-tail party. There was even a servant in a tuxedo making the rounds with a tray of drinks, only the glasses weren't filled with martinis or Manhattans.

All conversation stopped when the trinity came through the sliding glass doors.

"The signs are favorable," the red-robed woman called in a loud voice, holding up a large emerald with an ancient letter inscribed on the flat surface. "We have reason to believe, if our sacrifice is accepted, Lord Astaroth will assist our cause."

The group began to whisper among themselves. A few nervous giggles and a smattering of applause broke out but quickly died when two bulky men in silk suits led a filthy street urchin into their midst. The little girl was wearing her whole world: tattered jeans that fit her like hand-me-downs from a line-backer and a grimy Bart Simpson T-shirt. She smiled shyly at all the beautiful jewels and silks as she chewed happily on a microwave corndog. The smartly dressed people recoiled in horror. The child was so encrusted with grime that, if it hadn't been for her eyes, it would have been impossible to guess her age. But even the sad orbs were misleading. They were flat and dead from seeing things no child was ever meant to witness: gnawing hunger, poverty, degradation of the soul. They made her appear as old as the emerald in the hand of the leader.

"Clean her up!" a tall priest in a black robe snapped, and the child was whisked away. "Prepare yourselves."

The crowd hurried to drain their glasses. The potions had been specially prepared by the subpriests.

A concoction of rocket seed, pepper, cumin, purslane, honey, the gizzard of an ostrich, the powdered left testicle of a fox and, to make the mess palatable, strong red wine.

They began to fling the expensive clothing into the corners of the room. When they were nude, they used special red, blue and black acrylics to paint ancient runes on each other, giggling and fondling, working themselves into a fever of anticipation as the aphrodisiac worked its magic. A few couples and trios began to kiss and rub each other, but before things could get out of hand, the leader called out, "Make way!"

The attendants, nude and showing off an impressive array of exotic tattoos, led the little girl into the room. Behind them, a short man shuffled along on bare feet. He had a bald head and a belly that nearly covered his genitals. The child had been bathed and her silky black hair washed and combed. She stood nervously with her hands trying to cover her hairless pubic mound.

"She is pure?" the red-robed woman demanded.

The fat man, a noted gynecologist in Honolulu, scratched his hairy belly and nodded.

"You know what will happen if you are mistaken?" the red-robed woman asked, and the doctor blanched, but nodded once more.

Outside the penthouse the storm continued its fury. Rain pounded, wind blew hard enough to rattle the glass and the lightning had become a constant explosion of celestial light. The robed trio led the mass of pink and black bodies down a narrow hall and into a wide room at the back of the condo that was inappropriately called the game room.

The walls were adorned with the stuffed heads of so-called game animals: deer, lion, antelope, bison and a tiger. Each pair of dead eyes watched with stoic anticipation from the wall-mounted gallery.

The people pushed in close, the women exerting their newfound equality by shoving and elbowing their way to the front. They mobbed the little girl, touching and pulling at her hair as if she were a rabbit's foot. For the first time, the child showed fear. Tiny tears trickled down her cheeks, but she went quietly where she was lead. The priests stood on a raised platform behind a billiard table that had been covered with a thin rock slab. The walls had been temporarily redecorated with posters containing the signs of the zodiac, the five-pointed Seal of Solomon and banners with runes and hellish incantations. The attendants lifted the little girl up and eased her down onto her back. She stared at the masks with wide, frightened eyes. Even after everything life had thrown at her during her brief time on earth, this was a new experience.

The leader stepped to the side of the table. She held a stone knife gingerly behind the folds of her robe. The dagger or athame had once belonged to the patron saint of the black arts, Gilles de Laval, the Baron de Retz. The double-edged blade had been tempered in the blood of a hundred children, then etched with ancient runes. The pommel had been carved from the yellowed leg bone of a Catholic bishop. Its history was a chronicle of violent death, for it had been used to pierce the hearts of both clerics and witches throughout the centuries. Its power over life was an almost visible force.

"Quiet now, honey," the leader said in a soothing tone of voice. "It's just a game."

The onlookers were all but panting, straining to see and surreptitiously stroking a breast or penis. A subpriest held up an ancient book bound in human skin, a medieval collection of incantations and spells of conjuration.

"Let us pray," the leader said and expectation stilled the wagging tongues. "O, Astaroth, I conjure thee. O, all ye demons of power and wealth, of blood and pain, dwelling in the air or in the night or in the nether regions, I conjure thee.

"Emperor Lucifer, master of all spirits in revolt, I entreat thee: Send unto your servants the commander of your mighty legions. Send unto us the mighty Moloch that we may make a pact. I entreat that he manifest himself in any form which he so desires. In payment, we offer up this pure soul for your feast."

With no little apprehension, the coven's grim reaper carefully raised the athame high overhead and completed the invocation.

"Lord Astaroth, send your minion. Let him wade through the blood of innocence and strengthen himself on the heart of the pure."

With that, the de Laval athame flashed down.

Chapter Two

November

When the doorbell rang, Quinn was in the library with his nose buried in one of his uncle's books. It was a room where Edgar Allan Poe would have felt at home: hundreds of dusty old books and manu-scripts on the most bizarre subjects imaginable, bookcases that reached up into the dark recesses of the domed ceiling, an exquisite French Provincial writing desk, and furniture that was both massive and comfortable. Most of the interior wall was taken up by a huge fireplace that burned small trees, yet never seemed quite to cut the lingering chill.

After marking his place, Quinn trekked down the hall in his bare feet and opened the front door. The man on the steps wore faded jeans and a black T-shirt; he had the same close-cropped cop's haircut and cynical, lopsided grin that Quinn wore. He could have been Quinn's twin except that his skin was the color of hot tar.

"There goes the neighborhood. I move six thousand fucking miles and I still can't get away from you?" Quinn threw his arms around his old partner, Carl Kerry.

After they finished hugging each other, Kerry held Quinn at arm's length. Three weeks in Hawaii had deepened Quinn's tan and smoothed five years' worth of worry lines from his face.

"What kind of joint is this with the lord of the manner opening his own damned door?" Kerry asked.

Quinn looked past Kerry and saw the taillights of a copper-colored Plymouth disappearing around the bend in the driveway. Kerry's battered suitcase was on the steps.

"How'd you get here?" Quinn asked.

"Lady cop gave me a lift. Some looker, huh? I tried to talk her into moving to Florida."

Quinn grabbed Kerry's bag. "Come on. I won't make you go to the back door this time."

He led Kerry through the hall, where his friend did a fast double take at the gallery of macabre art before racing to catch up. They passed vast, high-ceilinged rooms sparsely furnished with heavy Mediterranean pieces. Then they went down another short hall and up an open spiral staircase with a banister of thick, rich mahogany. Finally, they arrived at one of the nine bedrooms in the south tower. Spacious and cold, the room had five neutral gray walls and dark Moorish furniture. A black marble bath was reached through a cavernous walk-through closet.

Quinn tossed the suitcase on top of the bed and grinned as he watched Kerry walk around the room like a kid on his first visit to F.A.O. Schwartz.

"Unfucking believable," Kerry said.

The framed oil paintings, the ornate furniture—Kerry touched everything. He walked to the window opposite the door with its view of the driveway, the fountain and the front gardens, with their strange and unusually lifelike collection of hedge animals. After nodding that he was impressed, he crossed to the arched double windows that looked out on the bay and a fleet of toy sailboats with their crews resplendent in yellow-and-black rain slickers.

He turned around, threw out his arms and shrugged. "What can I say? It's a fucking castle. How many rooms?"

"Would you believe I don't know?" Quinn replied. "I haven't been in all of them yet. There's a tennis court out back—"

"Tennis court? Since when do you play tennis?"

"I don't." Quinn laughed. "The garage you saw. There's a greenhouse, an indoor swimming pool and sauna, a wine cellar that I haven't had the nerve to set foot in yet"—Quinn smiled as Kerry gave him an understanding nod—"a miniature observatory on the top floor of the other tower—"

"Observatory?"

"You know, telescope, stars, all that astronomy crap."

Kerry shook his head as he threw open his suitcase, moved stuff around and pulled out his nine millimeter. After he put the gun in the night table drawer he seemed to really relax. He was home.

41

"You got an extra bathing suit?" Kerry asked.

"What if I did? You couldn't fit into it."

"What do you mean?" Kerry slapped his belly. "Like a rock."

"So's your head. I hate to be the one to break it to you, but you lost your girlish figure a few thousand beers ago."

They laughed at each other, the house, and their friendship and sobered.

"How did you get here?" Quinn asked.

"I flew over to sponge off my old partner. Be glad I ain't got a wife and kiddies."

"Why didn't you call? I'd have sent you a ticket."

"Well, you did, sort of. You gave me all that shit out of your apartment. I kept the TV and sold mine for enough to pay for half the airfare. Your old Toyota went for the other half."

"How long you got?"

"Two weeks."

"All right! What do you want to do first? Beach? Bikinis? What?"

"You left out the most important B."

"Beer!" they said in unison.

As they retraced their path through the house, Kerry stopped at the wall with the paintings. "What the hell is that supposed to be?"

"The gallery de art."

The oil was a grim illustration of a naked woman with long red hair and bulky black wings tipped with red claws. She was squatting on the chest of a screaming man. Each painting had a tiny brass plaque engraved with the title and artist. That painting was called *The Evil One* by Frank Pape. The next frame was a pale red etching of two naked crones wrestling on a flat rock with two raging panthers for an audience. The title: *Witches in Combat* by Francisco Jose de Goya y Lucientes.

"Goya?" Kerry said. "Have I heard of him? Is that expensive?"

Quinn took his friend's arm and steered him toward the kitchen. "How the hell am I supposed to know? I don't share my late uncle's taste in art."

"I know. Velvet Elvises are more your speed."

They kept going, passing an office with a desk, two IBM computers, and three file cabinets, and paused at the door of a large room covered with mirrors.

"Gym," Quinn said needlessly.

The room was a shrine to chrome and iron. In addition to enough free weights to sink a luxury liner, there were Nautilus and Keiser Machines, treadmills and stairclimbers. There was even a gizmo that resembled a giant gyroscope. A man could strap himself in and spin himself silly.

"Jesus!" Kerry said, turning sideways and smoothing his hand down over his stomach. "I am getting fat."

They continued past a formal dining room with a long table made of almost black wood, then down a hall with more grotesque paintings and a glass display case full of pre-Colombian figurines. Finally, they headed into the kitchen. Quinn went to a restaurant-size, double-door refrigerator and took out two tall brown bottles of Mexican beer. He didn't bother with glasses.

"I thought you quit?" Kerry asked with a smile.

Quinn shrugged. "I have a beer every now and

then. I don't have the problem with the stuff I had a couple years ago."

Not wanting to dredge up Quinn's painful past, Kerry changed the subject. "Where's the maids and butlers and shit?"

"It's funny." Quinn replied. "My uncle was a bachelor, and as far as I have been able to tell, he didn't have a steady lady. So you'd think he'd have a bunch of maids and stuff. But so far I haven't found anybody in town who ever worked here or knows anybody who worked here. So far nobody has shown up in one of those little black maid uniforms."

Kerry looked around the gleaming kitchen and sipped the beer. The place was yards of butcher-block counter space with a cooking island in the middle of the floor. A rectangular, cast-iron rack for dozens of pots and pans floated on black chains above the island. The cupboards were made to match the dark dining table. If it hadn't been for the double-wide window over the sink and the planter full of African Violets, the room would have been gloomy.

"Place looks pretty good. Maybe you should hire out."

"Naw, that's weird too. I haven't picked up a sponge since we moved in, but every morning the place is spotless."

Kerry arched his eyebrows.

"I think it's Q," Quinn said. "I don't know why all of a sudden he'd want to do it, but he's been acting weird lately. I know he isn't sleeping well."

"Where is Qujo?"

"Round somewhere."

"Why would he clean up? I don't recall him being particularly neat."

"Buddy, he's having a tough time adjusting."

"To what? Being rich?"

"Don't laugh. I jerked the kid out of school in the middle of the year and moved him six thousand miles away from everything he knew. Thank God, he wasn't chasing girls yet. I'm trying to find a tutor for him to give him time to adjust, at least until next year."

Kerry finished the beer, gulping the last few drops from the long neck with his Adam's apple bobbing like a pile driver. Quinn pulled out another. Kerry nodded his thanks and used one thumb to flip the cap into the sink, a trick he had learned from one of his bodybuilding friends.

"So why not move back to Florida? Money obviously ain't a problem. You could get a house next door to the Kennedys."

Quinn killed his beer and tossed his and Kerry's empty bottles in the garbage. He looked up and saw the reflection of his son's face peeking around the door behind him in one of the stainless Revere Ware lids.

Quinn spoke without turning. "I'm gonna tell you something, buddy, and you better not laugh. In my entire life I've only had two jobs. From junior high through junior college, I sold shoes. After I got out of school, I went to work for the sheriff's department." Quinn glanced up to make sure his son was listening. "Kathy and I met on the job. I took one look at that red hair and those freckles and fell like the Great Wallenda. Then, the second day we were partnered, she took down that three-hundred-pound scuzball who was flying on PCP"

"Yeah, she was a pistol." Kerry nodded in agreement.

"After that, it took me three months to work up the nerve to ask her out." Quinn looked at his old partner to see how he would take the last remark.

"No shit?" Carl Kerry was an imposing man, but he was also a man of few words.

"Two years later we got married. The next five years we worked our asses off and saved almost every penny. We wanted our own home, but you know what houses cost in south Florida. When Kathy got pregnant wc agrccd shc would quit the department and stay home with Q. I took the sergeant's exam and passed. In another few years I was going to push for lieutenant. Then Dickerson plowed into our Toyota when she was on the way home from the grocery.

"Florida has a lot of bad memories for me. I think it has a few for Q too. And I own something here: land, buildings. I want to try my hand at running a business."

He saw Kerry roll his eyes and said, "I know. But I can learn. I learned how to tell when a junkie was holding and when he was trying to get me to make a fool out of myself, didn't I? I learned to keep one hot load in front of the five regulation loads. I can do this.

"My uncle's lawyer wants me to sell some of the land over on the big island. He called the second day I was here with an offer from some Japanese cartel, but I turned him down flat. I'm gonna learn how to do this shit." Quinn turned around in time to see the boy's head disappear. "My uncle handed me a gift, but when I turn everything over to Q, I want there to be more than there is now. I want him to know that the work is as important as the money."

Kerry tossed the second empty in the garbage and stuck his head in the ice box. "You having a party?"

"No." Quinn laughed as Kerry came out with another beer. "Most of that stuff was there when we moved in."

Kerry walked around the kitchen, lifting the cover on the rectangular skillet that was built into the island.

"What's going on with Tim?" Quinn asked. "I'm surprised he didn't come with you."

"Wolinsky? He's as bad as you. I asked him to come, but the state is being overrun with snow birds and he's determined to sell an alarm system to every damn one of them. Me, I just want to put in my twenty and get a nice cushy night job guarding a liquor warehouse."

"Right. That's why you take all those accounting courses at F.A.U."

Kerry switched to his phony South Alabama field-hand patois. "Aw, shucks, boss, you all knows de depat'ment. Dey give us poor minorities all kind of perks for taking dem dere classes."

"So Tim's too busy to come, huh?"

"Well."

"He's not fooling around with anything funny, is he?" Quinn asked, dropping the grin.

Kerry took the opportunity to drain the bottle, then shrugged. "You know Tim."

"He isn't?"

"Oh, no. I don't think so. I think it may be guns."

"Guns?"

"It's south Florida. Alpha 66. The Jamaicans. The Haitians. We got more revolutionary groups than the Middle East."

"Christ!" Quinn muttered running his fingers through his hair. "Doesn't he realize that every other guy down there with a Spanish accent and a beret works for ATF?"

When Kerry shrugged again, Quinn threw up his hands, then decided to change the subject. "How did you happen to catch a ride with Okata?"

Kerry chuckled and shook his head. "Johnson called. He goes to some big meeting out here once a year and he knows Okata's boss."

"Johnson? Capt. Johnson? He hates my guts. Why would he do us a favor?"

"That was the old Johnson. Before you became Donald Trump. I think he wants to be your friend now. Matter of fact, I think every cop from Orlando to Key West is planning on coming out for a visit."

Quinn realized how much he had missed Kerry. It would be good to have him around. Good for Q too.

"Guess I'd better start locking the front gate."

"What'd you do to her anyway?"

"Who?" Quinn asked. "Okata?"

"Yeah. Man, she sure has a hard on for you. At first I thought she just hate us po' black folks, but on the way up here I got the distinct impression you are not here favorite millionaire."

"Don't sweat it, the nip bitch."

"She ain't a Jap, you insensitive redneck. She's Polynesian."

"And how do you know that?"

"I'm a trained investigator. I asked."

Quinn started laughing again just as the doorbell sounded. He motioned for Kerry to follow. "What'd you say? 'Hey, baby! Are you a slope? Wanna fuck?' "

The doorbell sounded a second time, saving Quinn from Kerry's retort. They looked at each other and took off running. Quinn grasped the knob just ahead of his friend. When he jerked the door open, a slim, conservatively dressed young woman was smiling at him.

Her blouse was white, with a frilly but feminine collar that revealed just a hint of a long white neck and part of a gold chain that dipped out of sight. Her hair was shiny, autumn red and coiled into a tight bun at her neck. She wore stylish gold-frame glasses and carried a thin briefcase. Quinn checked her fingers for rings and then for other ornaments, but decided jewelry would most definitely have been redundant.

"Mr. Ramsey?" the woman asked, taking stock of his disheveled clothing. It was reasonable to assume that he was the handyman.

Quinn stuck out his hand. "Quinn Ramsey."

She placed an embossed business card in his palm. It was made of textured paper, printed in plain, block letters and read, "Adar Sydelle." Below the name was a telephone number in Boston and a post office box in California.

"What can I do for you, Ms. Sydelle?"

" 'Scuse me," Kerry said. "I'm going to wrestle another long neck. If I'm not back in two days, call out the rangers."

Adar Sydelle waited until Kerry had vanished down the hall, then said, "You inquired about a tutor for your son. The agency in Honolulu sent me."

Quinn slapped his forehead. "Right, right. They called. Please come in."

He decided to use the office for the interview on the assumption that the computers would impress her. After pointing to one of the high-backed leather armchairs, he took a seat behind the desk and tried to look at home in the space-age executive chair. Everything started out fine. She noticed the computers immediately.

"Oh, IBM. Are they four-eighty-sixes?"

Totally at a loss, Quinn cleared his throat and presented her with a vacuous smile. "Would you like something to drink?"

She shook her head, pulled a folder from the briefcase and pushed it across the top of the desk. Quinn picked it up and tried to lean back but the chair wouldn't cooperate. He groped around the sides for a release lever until he felt like a complete fool. In desperation, he slapped the folder on the desk and framed it with his elbows. It was her resume.

Adar M. Sydelle was 34 years old and single. She had a degree from UCLA in primary education, and a master's in educational theory from USC. She had taught both elementary school and high school in California and had a stack of teaching references as thick as a phone book, but a surprising lack of personal references.

"Ms. Sydelle, help me out here. Have you done private tutoring before?"

Her eyes were maddeningly serene. They reminded Quinn of the deep green cenotes of the Yucatan Peninsula. She was so relaxed that Quinn was beginning to feel like he was being interviewed.

"No," she said.

"You're from California?"

"I have lived in California, but I was born in Massachusetts."

"No accent," Quinn said, but she just smiled.

Quinn's hand brushed a button on the underside of the arm, and he was finally able to get into a comfortable position. He made a tent out of his fingers, a gesture he had seen his watch commander do a million times.

"You understand I'm looking for someone to live here? Not just teach Q, uh, Quinn Junior, but to spend time with him?"

Adar Sydelle nodded once, so he asked, "Where are you staying?"

"I have a room at the Hotel Chana-Maui."

"That's here in Hana, right?"

"Yes."

Quinn tried to disregard the woman's looks and concentrate on her credentials, but he kept sneaking a peak at her. He couldn't think of any reason why a tutor couldn't look like a fashion model, but he was disturbed because her hair was the same color as Kathy's.

"Mr. Ramsey, maybe I could meet your son?"

God, I am an idiot, he fumed silently.

"Of course."

*   *   *

Q tiptoed to the spiral stairway that led down to the wine cellar. He was torn between the desire to see his father's old friend Carl Kerry and the need to return to his secret place. His hand traveled the black iron handrail as he went down and down into the icy darkness. He didn't bother turning on the light. The cellar had already become familiar territory.

His third night in the new house, after Quinn was asleep, Q had wandered the mansion's strange halls, looking into the cold rooms, exploring the garage, sitting in the cars, climbing up to the observatory, then staring at the macabre paintings and hideous statues. He had been having a bad night, which happened occasionally. He had nights he dreamed of a mother without a face. Naturally he had photographs of his mother. But in his nightmares, his mom always had beautiful red hair and a black hole where her face should have been. Normally he'd go back to sleep after a while, but for some reason that night he couldn't lie still and had finally rolled out of bed.

Eventually he'd found his way to the wine cellar and strolled past rows of dusty bottles, taking a few down to look at the labels. Q didn't recognize any of them except for the one green bottle of champagne. It had been bitterly cold. He remembered his dad telling him that wine had to be stored at a constant temperature, but the place had been like the bottom of an Alaskan lake. He'd shivered until his bones had ached, and he had been ready to return to his room when he'd heard the voice. Soft, a whisper really, but familiar. Q had searched the maze of racks, sneezing from the dust, the dank concrete floor turning his feet blue, but he couldn't stop.

"Over here, Q," the voice had called.

His mother had been the first to call him Q. She'd refused to call him Junior and insisted that two Quinns was too confusing.

"Pull down the long bottle."

The boy had stood on tiptoes to reach the skinny red bottle standing up in the end of the rack. When he pulled, only the top moved and the rack and the whole section of wall it was attached to had moved inward. In total darkness, he had fumbled inside the door until his hand found the light switch and so much more!

Now the boy knelt on icy flagstones at the edge of a painted rectangle. Within the rectangle, the four points of the compass had been inscribed in great detail. At the bottom, five daggers pointed directly toward his body and at the top were five circles with writing that Q couldn't read. Between the daggers and the circles were three progressively smaller rectangles followed by a circle around two squares. There was a lot of the strange lettering all around as well as eight five-pointed stars alternating with eight misshapen crosses. Facing him, high on the back wall, was a massive red-and-gold pentagram with more scribbling. The other walls were covered with thick, black velvet drapes. Underneath the pentagram, on a raised dais, was a flat-topped stone table.

Q was comfortable. His knees were numb, so he didn't feel the floor. Nor did he feel the icy air emanating from the glowing star. He was lost in the voice.

"You were not wise to come here in the daylight!"

"I'm sorry, Mother. I couldn't help it. I miss you so much."

"If you want me to return, you must do everything I tell you."

His eyes were puffy slits. Climbing out of bed at the crack of dawn to keep his father happy coupled with his nightly conferences in the cellar had pushed the boy to the edge of exhaustion and allowed him to fall into a semisomnambulistic state with little effort.

"But, Mother, I—"

"Q! Are you down there?"

The intruding voice sounded very far away, but it was as distracting as a mosquito buzzing in his ear. His mother's presence dimmed.

"Q!"

"You must go," the voice commanded. "Come back tonight."

The boy shook his head and climbed stiffly to his feet. His eyes fluttered and he looked around. As he did each time he visited the cellar, he had forgotten where he was.

"Quinn Junior!"

Brushing the dust from his new shorts, Q scampered through the door, careful to close the portal behind him. Once outside, his head seemed to clear and he ran up the spiral staircase.

The grill of a dark-green Jaguar XJ12 stopped inches short of Quinn's driveway. Behind the tinted windows, the driver nervously drummed the wheel with fingers that resembled sausage links.

"This is crazy, Tammy. What if he comes out and

see us skulking around his driveway? Ramsey knows me!"

"So what?" the woman replied. "I need to obtain something of his. And I need to see the place and I want to feel for emanations." She closed her dark eyes, which slanted like those of a cat. "Can you feel it, Randall?"

Randall Stalkins fingered the bone-and-feather fetish under his starched white shirt. "Uh, yeah, I feel something."

Her laugh was a slap in his face. "You feel nothing. If occult power was the west wind, you couldn't blow out a match."

Suddenly, all pretense at humor was gone from the woman's face. She closed her eyes and hissed, "Wait! You said Ramsey and the child were alone."

"They are," Stalkins said. "We've watched them for the last week."

"I sense two others—and something else."

Sweat began to run down Stalkins's face. "Honest, Tammy—"

"Silence, you slug."

The woman was quiet for several seconds before opening her eyes and snapping. "We will have to come back later. Drive me back. I have to talk to my daughter."

As Q stomped out of the solarium, Adar Sydelle turned to Quinn. "Has he been sick?"

Quinn stared at the doorway. They had moved to the sun room so that Q could meet the tutor, but in the sterile light the boy's eyes had looked haunted. What was worse, in spite of taking the wooden stairway down the rocky cliff to the beach almost every day, his son was as pale as a ghost.

"Since my wife died, he's suffered periods of insomnia," Quinn replied lamely.

There was an uncomfortable silence. Adar pulled nervously at a strange pendant around her neck while taking a moment to admire the room.

Perched on the edge of the cliff, the solarium was surrounded with glass panels that gave breathtaking views of the open Pacific, Hana Bay, and the estate's tropical gardens and greenhouse. In the corners, strange but beautiful macrame holders contained delicate tropical plants and flowers that filled the room with the musky aroma of orchids and wet earth. Quinn found the combination very stimulating.

"I'm sorry to hear that," Adar said.

Adar's voice was husky, but soft. It set Quinn's thoughts spinning off in unexpected directions. She looked remarkably like his dead wife, which made him wonder if he could stand having her around. He just might end up making a fool of himself. How would Q react? The boy appeared not to notice the resemblance, but that could have been shyness on his part. The woman was qualified, she was poised, and she was probably perfect for the job. Quinn made one of his infamous snap decisions.

"Do you want the job?"

Adar looked startled. "Won't you need time to check my references?"

Quinn stood and went to the wall of glass. "Here's my offer," he said as he turned. "I'll pay what you asked if you can move in tomorrow. I'll pay all your moving expenses and give you two days off each week—your choice. But I want Q's nose in his books the rest of the time. He has to take the state achievement test in May, and if he does well, the job is yours for as long as you like."

Adar opened her mouth, then closed it.

"Ms. Sydelle, don't get me wrong," Quinn said. "I will check every one of those references. If I find anything funny, I'll have to ask you to leave. The truth is, I'm trying to learn a business and I'm in way over my head. Q is alone too much. If you're willing to accept the job under these conditions, it's yours."

Adar stood and held out her hand. "I'll be here in the morning at eight o'clock. And my name is Adar."

A few minutes later Quinn found Kerry in the library, a thick, leather-bound book in one hand, a cold beer in the other. He had changed into a pair of cutoffs and a torn jersey with the words F.A.U. Owls across the chest.

"When does she start?" Kerry asked.

Quinn glanced at the stack of references in his right hand. "How do you know I hired her?"

"Get real. With that body?"

Quinn considered getting mad, but it was too much trouble.

"Were you reading this?" Kerry asked as he held up Ashdown's *Ke Alaloa o Maui*.

"Yeah."

"Jesus, Quinn. Some of this stuff is pretty gruesome."

"I know."

"I mean, weird gods, human sacrifice. I thought it

57

was all grass skirts and surfboards. Why are you reading it?"

Quinn went to the window and stared down the driveway. "It was on my uncle's bedside table when I moved in. I find it interesting. Everyone thinks of Hawaii as paradise because of the weather and scenery. Now developers have turned a lot of it into Miami Beach with mountains. But the place has history. Tourists think the natives are cute. But they had serious wars here. One army threw another entire army off a mountain right there on Oahu. Thousands of people one minute. Then poof! buzzard food."

"Makes me want to take a native to lunch."

"Their gods were cruel, but fair," Quinn said as if Kerry hadn't spoken. "They had a good thing going until the missionaries showed up to teach them the error of their ways."

"Good thing? I wouldn't call getting tossed into a volcano a lot of fun."

"Show me a religion that didn't have human sacrifice at one time or other."

"Ha! I'm a Christian."

"Shows how much you know. Anyway, until the Christians showed up, these people had a good way of life. They worshiped their gods. Their gods took care of them."

"Don't tell me you believe that shit."

Quinn grinned and shrugged. "Doesn't matter what I believe. Only matters that they believe."

"What's that?" Kerry asked, nodding toward the roll of papers in Quinn's hand.

Quinn dropped the reference letters in the trash can in the corner. "Nothing."

Randall Stalkins parked in the garage under his high-rise condo on Waikiki and waited, listening to the hot ticking of the engine as it cooled.

Strange, he thought, where was everybody?

He checked the rearview mirror and the side mirrors, then turned his head and looked, but the garage was deserted. Grabbing his briefcase, he climbed out, opened the trunk, took out his Monday-Wednesday-Friday raincoat, then set the alarm.

He shuffled slowly past the long row of silent automobiles, barely picking up his feet as if to make a noise could be fatal. But it *was* creepy the way the garage was so still. Even after midnight, somebody was usually around. He chuckled, nervously peering into the narrow islands of deep darkness between cars. Black holes breached only here and there by anemic 60-watt cones of light. Jesus, he thought, an entire army could be hiding in here.

Randall normally hated people. But truth be told, this night he wouldn't have minded a little company.

At last he reached the elevator, jabbed the call button and paused, pushed it again and stood muttering with his back to the door so he could watch the garage.

"Come on. Come on."

The muted whine of elevator gears sounded too loud in his ears. When it stopped, he glanced over his shoulder. The thirty-ninth floor indicator was lit. A moment later the elevator started again. Going up.

"Shit!"

59

He jabbed the call button four times, but the elevator ignored him and climbed mindlessly toward the penthouse.

A soft clopping sound came from the back of the garage. His head snapped around as if it were spring loaded, but he couldn't see a bloody thing.

Like a horse walking on concrete, he thought. That was what it sounded like. A horse walking on concrete.

Randall stepped back, caught his foot on a mottled drop cloth and kicked over a large can of paint thinner that some asshole had left next to the elevator. He crinkled his nose as the astringent liquid washed over the floor.

The strange clopping noise came again.

Clop! *Clop*! Stop. *Clop*! Stop. Nothing.

Randall forgot about saving his shoes and scanned the garage again. If anything, the shadows appeared deeper. Dark rents in the fabric of the cosmos that seemed to pulse with menace.

"You're a paralegal, for God's sake, and paralegals do not let their imaginations run amuck."

The up arrow bonged and when the doors opened his heart almost stopped. Randall stepped quickly into the faux pine interior, hastily stabbing at the button for the twenty-third floor, but nothing happened.

"Give me a fucking break."

The paint thinner oozed into the elevator like a tide of clear congealing blood.

"What is going on tonight?"

He stabbed the button again and stepped back into the corner. The elevator gave a tired groan and the recessed bulb in the ceiling dimmed, but it still re-fused to move.

The thought of climbing 23 flights of stairs made Randall slightly nauseous. In frustration, he made a fist and went to attack the control panel. But then that odd noise came again and he started seeing him-self as the butt of somebody's sick sense of humor.

"Who's out there? If you don't stop fooling around, I'm calling security." He picked up the emergency phone and held it up to the empty garage like a cru-cifix.

Over the reek of paint thinner, his gourmet nose suddenly detected another odor. Something pungent and sulfuric. He stuck his head out of the elevator, looked both ways and was almost decapitated when the doors whooshed together. Before he could get his breath, the elevator began to climb.

Randall collapsed against the back rail with a hand over his heart. "By God, those cocksuckers in main-tenance are going to hear about this tomorrow."

He rode the first five floors lifting first one foot and then the other to see if the thinner had stained his shoes. Just before the elevator reached the tenth floor, the ceiling light flared like a star about to go nova. A microsecond later the bulb exploded and the inside of the elevator became an inferno.

A 70-year-old lady waiting with her toy poodle on the twentieth floor fainted when Randall's smolder-ing body fell out of the elevator at her feet.

Chapter Three

December

Three Weeks Before Christmas

Quinn stood at the edge of the cliff behind the house, watching Adar and Q share a yellow beach towel on the black sand. Everything else in his field of vision was either green or blue, except the orange ball that burned in the sky like the head of a giant kitchen match.

Adar was reading aloud, her hands providing rhythm to the story like digital metronomes. Quinn was a little surprised to discover that he envied Q's proximity to the woman. He was also amazed at how much progress the tutor had made in such a short time. Q seemed to be sleeping and eating better, and he was spending part of every morning doing laps in the indoor pool. Having Adar around brought home just how much the boy had missed a woman's touch.

The staccato drone of a lawnmower broke Quinn's concentration. Carl Kerry came zipping around the corner of the house, cutting the steering wheel on the big John Deere as if he were making the home turn at the Brickyard. He had on an old pair of coveralls with the legs cut off and his bare upper body glistened like ice crystals on asphalt. Quinn scratched his head. Kerry was harder to figure out than a Rubic's Cube. Within a day of his friend's arrival, Quinn had offered Kerry a job as security analyst and executive assistant at double what the sheriff's department paid. Kerry was single and had no family to speak of, so he'd jumped at the opportunity. What Quinn couldn't understand was the man's compulsion to cut grass and dig in the garden.

"I lived in apartments all my life," Kerry had said when Quinn had asked about it. "I never had a chance to mess with all this lawn shit. Leave me alone."

Kerry surprised Quinn in other ways too. One day, when he came home with a stack of books on Hawaiian law, real estate, economics, banking, and mortgage financing, he'd looked at Quinn with uncharacteristic gravity and said, "This job may be a joke to you, old buddy. But I'm not laughing."

Kerry borrowed enough money to send for his belongings and to buy a few things: two new suits, toiletries, some dress shirts and shoes. And he had driven to an office-supply store in Lahaina for a blank promissory note form. After diligently filling out the amount he had borrowed, he'd added the going interest at the local bank and the term of the loan. Then, after signing the note, he'd had it notarized and presented it to Quinn.

"What's this?" Quinn had asked.

"If you don't recognize a promissory note, you'd better consider another field."

Back on the cliff, Quinn ignored the rattle of the mower and shifted his attention once again to the beach. Adar had finished the lesson and she was walking across the sand toward the water. She tested the temperature with a foot before diving in, cleaving the water with strong, crisp strokes.

Q was still on the towel, lying on his stomach, his chin resting on his upturned palms as he slowly turned the pages of a book.

Quinn decided to join them, and he started down the long flight of steps. Before taking this break, he had been in the library, dividing his time between the accounting reports he had just received from the management company and another book from his uncle's extensive occult library.

The books were beginning to trouble him. The tomes on the ancient Hawaiian gods seemed benign enough, even with Ku, the sky father who doubled as the god of war. A patient fellow, he wasn't beyond demanding a human sacrifice or two to get the young men primed for combat. His ceremonies went on for days and anyone caught napping could wind up as the entree at the next luau. Kane, along with Ku and Lono, was the father of mankind. A pacifist god, he eschewed all forms of human sacrifice, which put him at odds with Kanaloa or the great squid, who was king of the dead and one heck of a black magician. Then there was Pele, the goddess of fire, who lived in a volcano and was said to curse any tourist who dared take a single piece of lava from her enchanted islands.

Pele's life had been the stuff of soap operas. After being raped by the pig god Kama pua'a, she got into a brawl with her sister over one of the local hunks. The sister ambushed Pele at a spot on the coast of Hana called Kaiwi o Pele, or the Bones of Pele, and beat her to a pulp. Bruised but unbowed, Pele pulled her bones back together and proceeded to build a neat little love nest for herself and her beau inside a volcano. She was reported to be a kind of chameleon with the ability to change form and temper at the drop of a hat, and the natives bought her off by tossing ohelo berries into the volcanoes. A patroness of the upper class, Pele was fiercely loyal to the chiefs and kahuna who worshiped her.

In sharp contrast, the volumes on witchcraft and demonology both fascinated and repelled Quinn. The local divinities were flower children next to black gods who organized themselves like armies. There was nothing haphazard about witchcraft. Every hour of the day, every day of the week and every week of the year had meaning and was detailed in the witch's bible, something called *The Grand Grimoire*. Where the Hawaiian deities at least pretended to be fond of mankind, the dark lords' sole ambition was to torment and terrorize their human neighbors from the next dimension in the most abhorrent and painful ways possible. Yet as much as these books disgusted Quinn, several times he had picked one up, intending just to read a chapter or two, and found himself closing it as the sun came up over the eastern sea.

Quinn stepped down onto the hot sand just as Adar emerged from the surf, slinging the water out of her hair the way a field hand would shoulder a bag of cotton. She walked stiff legged through the waves, her face glowing. She wasn't breathing hard at all after her vigorous swim. Her bathing suit was conservative—a black two-piece with white piping—but it didn't conceal her high breasts and flat stomach. The suit was a pleasant change after the business clothes that, while tasteful and attractive, always made her look somehow frumpish.

Neither Q nor Adar saw Quinn until he called out, "Hey! How's it going?"

Q looked back over his shoulder and gave his father a halfhearted wave. Adar paused to pick up a black robe and fumbled with it as if unsure whether to put it on or just hide behind it.

Quinn nudged the boy with his toe. "You better put some oil on that back before you start to sizzle."

"I won't burn," Q replied without looking up.

"Oh? And may your poor ignorant father be so bold as to ask why you are suddenly immune to the sun's rays."

Pointing to a leather pouch around his neck he replied with the strained forbearance of youth, "Adar gave me something to prevent burning." Then he went back to his reading.

Quinn arched his eyebrows at Adar.

"It's nothing much," she replied, but blushed fiercely under her tan. "Something I learned in one of my holistic ecology courses."

"Okay," he said, eyeing the strange brass amulet she wore. "But if either of you burns, don't expect any sympathy from me."

Q ignored his father's attempt at humor and Adar studied her feet. Quinn didn't realize it, but he was studying her.

Without makeup, she looked like a teenager. The sea had washed away any perfume she might have worn, leaving her body smelling clean and musky. Other than the amulet, she didn't wear jewelry, but Quinn thought the freckles that dotted her chest and shoulders were more attractive than gold rings or bracelets.

Adar looked up at last. "Mr. Ramsey, you're staring."

It was his turn to blush. "I'm terribly sorry. I was just admiring your amulet. What is it?"

She held the brass disk in her palm and said, "A good-luck charm my mother gave me."

The brass was graved with curious letters and symbols, and despite being shinny, it gave the impression of age.

"You haven't said much about your family. Do your mother and father still live in Massachusetts?"

Adar let the necklace fall back between her breasts. "No. They passed away several years ago."

"I'm sorry."

She smiled into his eyes.

"You don't have any family?"

"Yes, sisters, a brother, a great-aunt and a bunch of cousins. We stay in touch."

He moved closer to her and his skin began to tingle

as if he were standing under a bank of high-tension wires.

"Dad, Carl's yelling at you," Q said.

"What?"

Q was still lost in the book, which at any other time would have seemed odd. The boy replied, again without turning his head, "Carl is yelling at you."

Quinn looked up at the top of the cliff. Kerry was waving. A woman with long black hair was standing beside him.

"Shit!" Quinn said and waved his acknowledgment.

"Excuse me?" Adar said.

"Sorry. How long are you two going to be down here?"

"Another hour or so. I want Q to finish this chapter, and then I'll give him an oral exam."

"Okay. I may be gone for a while, but I'll be back before five."

On impulse, Quinn took her arm and pulled her a few feet away. Touching her made his fingers tingle too.

"Listen. I'm going into Lahaina tonight to do some Christmas shopping. Since I still haven't found a cook, I was wondering if you'd like to come? We could grab a bite to eat."

Adar thought for a moment. "That would be nice. Thank you."

Quinn nodded and then started up the stairs. He paused on the bottom step. Adar had gone back to the sea, swimming past the breakers before raising her legs straight up and letting their weight drive her body under in a perfect surface dive. As Quinn climbed, he kept his eye on the spot where she had gone under, but by the time he reached the resting platform halfway up, Adar still had not surfaced. He slowed down and then stopped. It had been at least five minutes. After giving it another 30 seconds, he started back, taking the steps two at a time.

Suddenly, Adar's head broke through the surf. She saw him, waved and began a slow crawl back to shore

"Christ," he muttered as he resumed his climb. "What is she? A fucking fish?"

Quinn and Kerry had been putting in an hour in the gym each morning, but by the time he reached the top of the stairs, he was panting like a dog. With one hand on his chest, he said, "Don't let me have a heart attack and I'll put in more time on the treadmill."

Okata and Kerry were sitting around a wrought-iron table in the shade of an ancient breadfruit tree. The wind couldn't penetrate the thick foliage and insects were buzzing happily around Kerry's sweaty face. Okata, cool as an ice sculpture, had on pale orange lipstick that made her eyes look as if they were flecked with gold. She wore another pantsuit and a matching navy purse was on the table by her right hand. Quinn could almost feel the gun in there next to her badge.

As he approached, Okata laughed at something Kerry had said. Quinn pulled out a chair and took a seat next to his friend.

"Hello, Sergeant."

"Good morning, Mr. Ramsey."

"What's so funny?"

"Tim called," Kerry replied. "He's really pissed. Swears we moved out here just to get away from him."

Quinn smiled. "I moved to get away from both of you. What else does Master Wolinsky have to say."

"That he misses Q and that crime is running rampant since we left."

Quinn's laugh was restrained because of Okata's presence. "He should know."

Kerry stood. "Want a beer, Sarge? Or would you rather have tea?"

"Tea will be fine."

Kerry cocked an eyebrow at Quinn, then retreated toward the house.

"Beautiful place you have," Okata said, inhaling and letting her eyes roam over the gardens.

The backyard was as serenely beautiful as a convent courtyard. Tropical plants abounded: red and yellow hibiscus, yellow allamanda vines, protea, and creamy plumeria. The beds were interspersed with clumps of Queen Emma Lilies with wide green leaves growing next to bright orange, yellow and purple bird of paradise plants. The grass was the color and texture of a putting green and the tropical motif extended to the trees: breadfruit, huge Banyan trees with dangling, hairlike roots, and several varieties of palms. A lily pond and fountain were in the middle of the yard and lacy tree ferns softened the corners of the house. Every few seconds a hummingbird zoomed in from the thicket, snatched a bit of nectar and zoomed away again. On one such trip, the hummingbird suddenly veered over to the table and hovered a few inches in front of Okata's face. The lady cop smiled and stared at the bird for a few seconds.

"Friend of yours?" Quinn asked.

"Oh, yes," Okata replied dreamily. But the spell was broken and the little bird went back to his flowers.

"I don't mean to be impolite, Sergeant, but is this visit business or were you just in the neighborhood?"

Nodding as if the question had settled something in her mind, Okata took a notebook out of her purse. "You know a paralegal on Oahu named Randall Stalkins?"

"Yeah, we met the first day I arrived in the islands. He works for my uncle's attorney, a guy named Peterson."

"He was killed two weeks ago."

"Stalkins? Really?"

"You didn't know?"

"No, why should I?"

"It was in the papers. He was burned alive in an elevator."

Quinn was quiet for a moment. "Burned? Like my uncle?"

"Not exactly. Somehow or other, paint thinner got spilled in the elevator, and while he was riding up to his apartment, something set it off."

Quinn shivered. "Damn. How awful."

"You've had no contact with Mr. Stalkins since that first day?"

"I talked to him a couple of times on the phone."

"May I ask what about?"

"The first time he called to tell me his boss, Peterson, had been contacted by some Japanese group about one of my properties. He tried to talk me into selling. I refused. The last time he said the Japs had upped their offer. I refused again and that was it."

Okata scribbled some notes.

"How did you happen to come to me?" Quinn asked.

"The department was going through the list of clients in his briefcase. His notebook survived the fire. Honolulu just got around to your name and called me this morning."

"So you figured since I'm the local torch you'd better rush right over to make sure I wasn't turning any of our tourists over a slow spit?"

Okata kept writing for a moment, then put the notebook away. Before she could reply, Kerry came back with a pitcher of iced tea and three glasses. He placed the tray on the table and poured.

"Thanks," Okata said.

Kerry took his seat and grinned for no apparent reason.

Okata leaned forward to keep the condensation on the glass from spotting her suit. She took several swallows and sighed. Then she stood and nodded to Kerry. "Well, I'll be on my way. Thanks for the tea."

Kerry bounced up. "I'll show you out." He gave Quinn a puzzled look, then ran to catch up.

"Two people burn up a few months apart," Quinn muttered, like a cop puzzled by a difficult case. "Two people connected to me. What are the odds of that?"

He pursed his lips and went back to the library. "Let's see what the books have to say about fire."

Quinn and Adar faced each other over a candle flame in one of the better restaurants on Front Street in Lahaina, the one-time whaling center turned tourist Mecca. The tables were made from the refinished hatches of old three-masted schooners, and the chandeliers from wooden ship wheels. The waiters wore tight britches that ended just below the knee and striped socks and hats with little forked tassels in back. In the center of the room was a large aquarium with dozens of brick-red Maine lobsters staring morosely through the glass like inmates on crustacean death row. The restaurant's unused chairs were loaded with shopping bags overflowing with gaily wrapped presents.

Correctly anticipating that the evening breeze off the harbor would be cool, Adar had worn a forest-green wrap-around dress that fastened with three large gold buttons on the bodice and reached to mid-calf. The way the linen dress parted when she was distracted kept Quinn's attention away from the menu.

"Did I tell you how nice you look?" he asked.

"Thank you. And you look quite handsome. Is that a new jacket?"

In the last month, Quinn had spent a day in Waikiki buying the new jeans, shirts and sneakers his son had begged for. He had also spent several hours selecting new things for himself.

"This old thing?"

His sports jacket was charcoal-gray cashmere worn over navy slacks and a light gray shirt with a tiny flower pattern. The salesman had shown him a photo of it in *GQ*.

"Have you decided?" Adar asked.

Eyeing the aquarium, he said, "Anything but lobster."

"I agree."

Quinn concentrated on the menu. "Maybe veal, wok fried in picante salsa. Or the Asian prawns with cream sauce. What do you suggest?"

She pulled absentmindedly at one of her half-moon earrings. "How about the Dungeness crab and clams. It's in a black-bean sauce and we can split it."

Quinn passed the instructions along to the waiter and was debating whether to order wine, but his inexperience inhibited him.

Adar must have read his thoughts. "Could I have a glass of the house wine? They serve a nice Mondavi Reisling."

"Sure," Quinn said.

They relaxed over a serving of spicy onion rings, conversing easily in the intimacy of the candlelight. Quinn started out asking the usual parent questions, but when he tried to work the subject around to her past, he found himself up against a brick wall. Adar was more than willing to talk about her life in California or at college, but if he tried to go beyond that she turned the conversation as deftly as a Castilian matador performing the faena.

After a few minutes of poorly disguised interrogation, all he had learned was that she loved the ocean. When asked about her swim that afternoon, Adar launched into an animated description of the colorful fish and coral in the waters off his beach.

"Have you ever been scuba diving?" she asked.

"I thought about it a couple of times in Florida, but I never had the time. I like to snorkel."

"So do I, but it isn't the same."

Once she got going, Adar was like a juggernaut: hands flying, eyes wide and glistening, her voice finally coming out so Quinn didn't have to strain to hear. A few minutes later the waiter set up a tray and served their food.

They were so engrossed in the culinary delights that neither of them noticed the two brawny men on the padded stools at the bar. The men had been sitting quietly for half an hour, glancing at their watches and every now and then sneaking a peak at Quinn. When one man slid off the stool to make a phone call, the other turned to order coffee, quickly closing his jacket over the large knife in his belt.

That same evening, Carl Kerry watched a string of mindless sitcoms on the big screen TV in the living room until the ten o'clock news came on. After the first ten seconds of the President's speech he switched it off, trying to figure out why the guy didn't do something about his hair.

"Two hundred bucks for a haircut—why doesn't he just dye it?"

He decided hanging out with the rich and famous was boring and he wished he'd invited himself to dinner with Quinn and Adar. But somebody had to stay home with the kid. Besides, Quinn would have shot him if he had so much as looked hungry.

Speaking of children, Kerry thought, he hadn't seen Q all evening.

He launched himself off the couch and strolled down the hall, past the door to the garage, and he looked through the glass wall at the pool. The boy wasn't there.

"Probably in his room watching TV," Kerry muttered.

The pool looked inviting and he gave a passing thought to going for a swim. Then he briefly considered going for a moonlight dip in the ocean instead.

"Nope, all the grouper you ate, don't want no shark getting payback."

Kerry trotted upstairs to the third floor of the north·tower, the larger of the twin towers that held both Q and Quinn's bedrooms. The boy's door was open, but the room was empty, the bed made, the place spotless.

"Where the devil is he?" Kerry remembered how Q had kept his room in Florida. "Being rich must make you neat."

He climbed all the way to the huge pentagonal observatory at the top of the tower and looked around. When Quinn had told him about the observatory, Kerry had pictured one of those little brass telescopes people put in their offices to spy on their neighbors. The thing was real brass, but it was about 15 feet long and must have weighed close to a ton. He peeked into the eyepiece.

"Shazam!"

He looked up. The walls were papered with star charts and strange, psychedelic posters. In the corner was a blackboard full of Latin phrases and math. Kerry looked closely at a poster beside the door. It had a series of concentric stars and triangles drawn on yellowed parchment. There was a handwritten note in the corner: *The Great Seal of Dr. Dee*.

Shaking his head, Kerry retraced his steps to the ground floor. "Man, the rich really are different."

Walking through dark halls he realized that the night had crept up on him, and without lights the big old house was pretty damned spooky. He rounded the corner near the front door and put on the brakes.

The waves of icy air washing over his ankles made him feel as if he were wading through a cold stream. The house was cold, too damned cold to be just Btu's.

Kerry's grandma used to say that people were walking on her grave, and for the first time he knew exactly what she'd meant. The draft frightened him, but he couldn't say why. The hall behind him was dark but empty. The house was quiet. But the hairs on his neck were standing straight up, and for no good reason, he thought about Quinn and wished his old partner were there.

At the far end of the corridor, past the display case, the door to the wine cellar swung open without a sound. It was only a couple of inches, but in a house that was otherwise pathologically neat, the incongruity was unmistakable.

Kerry flattened himself against the wall, slipped his arm through the gap and flipped the wall switch.

The light was dim and all he could see was a very uninviting set of steep steps that spiraled down to dark rows of dusty wine racks. He paused on the landing to listen.

What was that? It didn't sound like voices—more like the soft moan of an animal in great pain.

The telephone was right down at the other end of the hall. He gave it a long look, but figured if Quinn came home and found Okata and a house full of cops waiting, he'd have a cat.

"Fuck it!"

Kerry placed his hand on the handrail, then jerked back, leaving an inch of black skin frozen to the steel.

"This is ridiculous!" Kerry stared at the bleeding palm. "What the fuck is he keeping down here anyway?"

With each step Kerry took, the temperature seemed to drop another degree. By the time he reached the bottom, the cellar was like a meat locker at a morgue. He picked up the first wine bottle he came to and discovered the label was spotted with ice crystals. If Kerry had known about wine and wine cellars, he would have realized how wrong the temperature was. But he just thought cold wine was as good as cold beer and kept shivering in his thin T-shirt as he searched for the source of that eerie keening sound.

The far wall was standing open like the mouth of a cave. As he crept closer, the moaning stopped and he heard voices coming from inside the hidden room. Low, sinister voices, like furtive whispers in an adult theater. His hand instinctively went to his hip, but of course his gun was in the drawer of his night table.

Cops who lived to collect their pensions had built-in survival computers that told them when to stay in the car and when to chase the perp down the alley. Every instinct told Kerry that something monstrous was going on and to get the gun, yet he couldn't go until he knew for sure the kid was okay.

Kerry forced himself to the opening and moved

aside the thick drape. He stood there, speechless, for all of ten seconds, then turned and ran as fast as he ever had in his life.

Quinn lingered over his dessert, spooning silky chocolate mousse into his mouth and letting the wine and soft candlelight work their magic on his tongue. He found himself telling Adar about his life as a cop and as a single father.

"So there we were, sitting on the couch, watching the Dolphins. I had a can of beer in one hand and the remote in the other. Sally was the dispatcher at the station and we had a running bet. She was from Buffalo originally, and it seemed natural to invite her over to watch the game. I mean, I knew she was divorced. She had mentioned it a couple of times."

Adar's coffee went down wrong and she covered her mouth with the napkin. "She mentioned it?"

"Well, yeah. So we were sitting there and Buffalo scores. I make some remark about the Dolphin secondary not being able to tackle a Girl Scout carrying a box of cookies and the next thing I know her tongue is halfway down my throat."

Adar laughed, using the napkin to stop the tears, as Quinn took another sip of wine, amazed to discover he was so witty.

"So I'm sliding off the couch, trying to keep from spilling my beer, and Sally has a death grip on my belt buckle. I hit the floor, look past her nose and see Q standing there in his *Star Wars* jammies. Somehow her blouse had come unbuttoned and her—you know—breasts were kind of out."

"Somehow?"

"I swear," Quinn said raising his hand. "I never laid a hand on her. Anyway, I got up so fast that I dropped Sally and knocked the coffee table over. Q looks at us, takes his thumb out of his mouth and asks, 'Is this my new mommy?' And I started bawling like a baby."

Adar smiled sympathetically and patted his hand. "Sounds like something I once saw on *America's Funniest Home Videos*."

Quinn nodded and reached for the wineglass. "You ever been married?"

Adar drained her coffee cup and looked around the restaurant. "I think they're waiting for us to leave."

"Come on. It's a simple question."

"It has a simple answer. No."

"A woman with your brains?"

"At least you didn't say a woman with your looks." Adar smiled.

"Thanks. What's the matter with the men in California—or is it Boston?"

"Come on, Quinn. It's getting late."

"Geez, Dar, you'd never make it as a cop. You don't know the first thing about sucking up to the boss."

She laughed again, this time with real appreciation.

Quinn looked around. Other than two businessmen sitting at the bar, and the waiters hovering around their table like a flock of vultures, the place was deserted.

"Golly gee, it's almost midnight," he said and signaled to the relieved waiter. "Why didn't you say something?"

Adar's hand sought Quinn's arm as they walked

down the restaurant steps. It was a cold night, with a breeze off the ocean that had teeth. The stars shone down like diamonds scattered on a black-velvet jeweler's cloth. There were a few couples wandering about, staring in the shop windows as if mesmerized. Adar released Quinn's arm to help him carry the presents he'd bought earlier.

"Thanks," he said.

They strolled down Papelekane Street, pausing to look at the *Carthaginian II*, a restored two-masted schooner that the city used as a museum. The old girl shimmied in the swells and her rigging creaked like old bones.

"Can you imagine living on that thing for years at a time?" Quinn asked. "No showers, up to your armpits in whale blubber."

Shaking her head, Adar sighed. "There are worse things."

"Such as?"

"Oh, lots of things." She turned around and walked backward in front of him, grinning. "Scary things." She raised her eyebrows dramatically and lowered her voice to a whisper. "Things that go bump in the night."

They moved down Wharf Street, making their way past the stadium-size Banyan tree behind the old Lahaina Court House, and headed for the public parking lot.

"You believe in stuff like that?" he asked.

"You don't?"

"Boy, my uncle sure did. Witches, werewolves, ghosts, demons. He has books on all of them. He must have been a charter member of Kooks R Us."

"But not you? Not even one little spook? Not even Casper?"

Later, Quinn would wonder if his instincts had been dulled by too much wine or his proximity to Adar, but his antennae finally picked up the rush of whispering feet. Adar had just opened her mouth to ask another question when her eyes suddenly flew open in alarm. He dropped the packages and spun on his heel. His arm went up to block the tire iron even before he saw it. The other hand shot out like a bolt of lightning, striking the bulky shadow in the throat.

The man choked, dropped the iron bar and clutched his battered voice box. Quinn went down on his heel, ripping the seat of his new trousers. He swept the man's feet out from under him with an extended leg and bounced back up before the guy hit the sidewalk.

Adar grabbed Quinn's arm and tried to pull him to the car, but he was too busy congratulating himself on his quick reflexes. He didn't realize there was a second man until the sky rockets went off inside his head.

Kerry blew through the door to the garage, grabbed the first set of keys on the board, and began trying the locks on the cars. The Jeep didn't have doors and the red Porsche wouldn't accept the double-edged key in his hand. So that left the van.

He unlocked the door and jumped into the high-backed bucket seat, twisting the key in the ignition so hard that it nearly snapped off in his hand. Then he shifted into reverse and pressed down hard on the pedal, nearly demolishing the garage door.

"Shit! Shit! Shit!"

Quickly pulling forward, Kerry found the electronic garage door opener and sat there, gunning the engine as he waited for the door to grind its way up. The second it hit the stops, he screeched backward into the night, made the loop around the fountain on two wheels and laid rubber all the way down the winding drive.

"Oh, man. Oh, man. Got to get help," he mumbled, his eyes glued to the rearview mirror. Kerry wasn't sure what he expected to see, but he thanked God it wasn't there.

The speedometer needle was pushing 60 when he shot through the gate, but as soon as he cleared the jungle at the edge of the cliff and could see the lights of Hana, he eased up on the accelerator pedal.

"Oh, God!"

What was he going to tell the cops when he got to the substation? How was he going to keep them from locking him up and make them believe the unbelievable? His eyes were wild and he was afraid the pounding of his heart might break a rib, but his mind was gradually starting to work again. He glanced at the speedometer and let up some more.

"They'll say I've lost my fucking mind."

Then, in the soft green glow of the dashboard lights, Kerry caught a flicker of movement from the corner of his eye. He glanced at the seat beside him and saw a ragged four-inch rip in the leather. The road broke sharply to the right, and he jerked his eyes back just in time to keep the rear wheels from slipping over the edge of the cliff.

"Slow down, dickhead!" he said to himself.

This time he felt more than saw the furtive wiggling and again gave a quick flick of eyes to the passenger seat. A black spider that was as big as a softball and hairy enough to walk on a leash had pulled itself through the split in the leather.

"Gross!" Kerry said as he looked around for a club.

The second he took his eyes off the road, it swerved to the left and he had to use both hands to keep from driving into the vegetation. When he looked back, the spider had disappeared.

The skin at the back of his neck began to creep like cold fingers inching up under his hairline. "Ugh!" He shivered. "I fucking hate bugs."

He checked the floor, then the rip in the passenger seat, and right in front of his eyes, another of the hairy monstrosities crawled through the gap. This one was more disgusting than the first with a swollen red belly and fangs the size of ice tongs.

Kerry tried to convince himself that it was the same spider, but when he glanced in the mirror, the first one was on the back of the headrest, reaching for his neck with two bristly legs.

"Shit!"

His hand flew up and batted the thing into the back of the van. It felt as if he'd hit a wire-haired cat.

There was no place to pull over. The road had narrowed and he was still going downhill at a prodigious clip. Besides, he was really more afraid of what might be behind him than he was of a couple of fuzzy arachnids.

The road curved again and Kerry fought for control, watching the edge of the cliff whiz by right below his window. In spite of the murderous road, he couldn't keep his eyes from wandering to the passenger seat again.

"Oh, Christ."

Two more spiders, smaller but just as ugly, squeezed through the hole and scurried up the back of the seat faster than eight legs should be able to move.

"That's it, hair balls."

He reached for the button on the glove compartment. A baseball bat would have been preferable, but he'd settle for an owner's manual or a map or anything he could roll up and use as a spider swatter.

The door swung open and a boiling mass of spiders spilled out onto the floor, running up and under the seats, filling the compartment with the fetor of their digestive enzymes. When Kerry felt the first of many pairs of venomous fangs sink into his ankle, he released the wheel and screamed.

The van crashed through the guardrail and soared gracefully for about four seconds before it exploded on impact with the rocks.

Quinn's eyes popped open and he immediately tried to sit up. When he did, nausea and vertigo almost made him pass out again.

As his head stopped spinning, he saw he was still on the sidewalk outside the park. A few feet away, two clean-cut, well-dressed men were busy taking a nap.

"What happened?"

"We have to go," Adar said, pulling him gently to his feet.

"We have to call the police."

"Can't we just go? I'm scared."

Quinn checked to make sure the men were still breathing, then pulled a handkerchief from his pocket and dabbed the back of his head. It came away red. He looked down at the unconscious muggers sprawled across the concrete and seriously considered kicking their asses into the bay. However, with Adar standing there and it being their first date, he was afraid to appear less than chivalrous. Later, he'd remember to ask about her views on the rehabilitation of violent criminal types in view of recent Supreme Court decisions. Right then, he handed her the keys and asked her to lead him to the car.

After noting his bloody handkerchief she said, "I'll treat that when we get back."

They drove down Front to Prison, then to Wainee on the way to the highway. The houses they passed were the restored homes of old-time seamen and whalers—or someone had gone to a great deal of trouble to make them look that way. The houses were quaint and touristy, but Quinn didn't care. His head was keeping time with the tires as they thumped over the blacktop, and a blinding red pain was making his eyes feel as if they were about to pop out.

"Here," Adar said, holding out a dried plant leaf. "Put this in your mouth."

"What is it?" Quinn asked, twirling the leaf by its stem.

"Tacamahac leaf."

"What's it for?"

"Your head. You think it could hurt?"

Quinn popped it in his mouth.

"Don't"—she waved with one hand as he bit down—"chew it!"

"Ugh! It tastes like my gym shorts."

"Just swallow," Adar said.

They drove through Wailuku and then they passed the airport at Kahului, where cascading runway lights beckoned toward black ocean. By the time they started on the highway, Quinn's head was feeling better.

"Why don't you try to get some sleep?" Adar said. "By the time we get to the house, you should be okay."

"That stuff beats the hell out of Tylenol."

The rode in silence for a few minutes. The radio was tuned to an oldie's station in Honolulu, but the volume was so low that it sounded as if spirits were sighing softly in the void.

"What happened back there?" Quinn asked eventually.

"Those men? You knocked them out, I guess."

Quinn pulled the handkerchief down. The bleeding had stopped. "I hit one, but I don't think he was out, and then the other guy coldcocked me."

"The other man came out of the shadows and hit you, but before you fell you hit him with some kind of karate chop or something and he fell down."

"I did?"

"I was impressed."

Quinn was feeling a lot better. He felt better until they pulled into the driveway and saw the flashing blue lights. When he saw Okata standing under the porch light in her latest pant ensemble, he felt positively rotten.

Chapter Four

Two Weeks Before Christmas

Every time Quinn looked up and saw Okata's Plymouth in the rearview mirror, he felt as if he had a needle in his eye. After waiting a week for the postmortem, Quinn had just buried his best friend, and he was in no mood to answer questions. Adar was slumped against the passenger door, crying so hard that Quinn's monogrammed handkerchief was almost transparent. Q was sprawled across the backseat, staring with vacant eyes at the passing greenery. They were dressed to match the weather: dark and gloomy.

"Sgt. Okata was very considerate to put off her questions until after the funeral," Adar said.

"She put them off until after the autopsy. I'm telling you, that woman looks at me and sees a promotion. She's not going to be happy until she's staring at me from the other side of steel bars."

"I don't believe that. I think she's as upset as we are about Carl."

Quinn made the next curve and slowed to open the gate.

"Come on, Quinn," Adar said as she handed back his handkerchief. "What's really bugging you?"

He pulled in and waited. "I don't know. I guess when I inherited all this stuff I thought I was going to be the captain of my own fate. Now I feel more like the captain of the *Titanic*."

They parked near the front door and Quinn waited for Okata while Q and Adar went directly into the house. Quinn watched his son's face as he walked past. The shock of the accident had driven the kid back into his shell and he hadn't said two words since the night Carl Kerry had died—as if anyone could blame him for what happened. On top of everything, Kerry died while in a car, just like Q's mother. It was a wonder the boy would go anywhere near an automobile.

Okata came up the walk, pulling down the hem of her skirt. Quinn thought it was too short for a funeral, but he shrugged and led the way into the house. She paused, as Kerry had, to stare at the paintings with a quizzical expression.

"Don't ask," Quinn snapped. "My uncle didn't go in for Disney lithographs. So what?"

They went into the office and he pointed to the armchair. Since he had mastered the controls on the executive chair, he took his seat and leaned back.

"Okay, Sergeant, I know you've been chomping at the bit for days. Shoot."

Okata managed to look somehow hurt and embarrassed, but the act didn't fool Quinn. He knew the games cops played.

The police officer took out her notes. "The autopsy didn't tell us much. Mr. Kerry had a little alcohol in his blood, but not enough to make him drunk. He also had a minute amount of venom in his system. The pathologist thought he detected bites on his legs and ankles, but the fire. . . . Mr. Kerry was in good health otherwise."

"I could have told you that. Carl could bench press 400 pounds. As for the bites, he liked to work around the yard. He was always getting stung by something."

Okata nodded noncommittally. "The marks on the road indicate he was traveling at a high rate of speed. There were skid marks on the drive, on the road at the end of the drive, and all the way down the road to the barrier. It looks as if someone was chasing him."

Quinn had been studying the woman, and he decided most people would probably find her attractive. She had a set of cheekbones that any movie star would kill for; her eyes were deceptively soft, with an endearing tilt at the corners—except when she got angry. Then they took on a strange reddish glow that Quinn found a bit unnerving. But all in all, it would be easy for most people to forget she was a cop.

"That's nuts," Quinn said at last.

"What about the garage door? He was in such a hurry he crashed into it."

That bothered Quinn too. Kerry had been a careful

driver. He always used the seat belt and the shoulder harness. According to the police, he hadn't wearing either when he'd died.

"And your son doesn't remember anything?" Okata asked.

Quinn shook his head. "Q was asleep."

"And Mr. Kerry would go off and leave the boy alone in the house while he was sleeping?"

Quinn shot out of the chair and began stalking the floor in front of the windows like a madman. He turned and pounded his fist on the desk. "No fucking way! That's the part that's driving me crazy."

"Then something made him leave in an awful hurry," Okata said.

"Okay. Something made him leave. But what? Your people went over the house. There was no sign of an intruder, no sign that anyone had tried to break in. Nothing."

"What if someone called and said they were holding you? Would that have made him take off like that?"

Quinn pulled out the damp handkerchief that Adar had used earlier and began to twist it. "No, he would have called the cops. But Carl would never have left Q alone."

Okata crossed her legs and rested the notebook on her knee while she jotted more notes. Quinn noticed that she had nice legs and then mentally kicked himself.

"One last question. What happened to your head that night?"

Once again, Okata had managed to catch him off guard. Quinn blinked like a startled lizard and dropped the handkerchief on the desk. "My head?"

"Mr. Ramsey, I know you don't think much of my abilities, but I'm not blind. The back of your head and the collar of your shirt were covered with dried blood. What happened?"

"Look, Sergeant, you know where I had been. You have Ms. Sydelle's statement and I'm sure that by now you've checked with the restaurant."

Okata watched him squirm for a moment. She never seemed to blink. "When you were a policeman and someone started dancing around your questions, what did you think?"

Quinn fell back into the chair and rested his head in the palms of his hands. "Okay, you win. We were mugged in Lahaina. One of them hit me in the head."

Okata started scribbling furiously. "Did you report it?"

"No. It was late, my head was killing me and I managed to chase them off. All I wanted to do was to go home and climb into a tall Scotch."

She shook her head. "Sorry. I don't buy it. You were a cop, and you just let them go?"

It galled him to admit it, but she was good.

"Sarge, you know how things are today. I knocked the two guys around a little. If it got into the papers that I have money, I would've been in court until I was ninety. My head hurt. I wasn't thinking clearly. At the time it made more sense to just walk away."

She studied his face through eyes as thin and cold as dimes, then nodded. "All right. I'll let it go for now. But I'm going to make inquiries." She saw his expression and hurried on. "Your name will be kept out of it. I'll just check the hospitals. See if anybody came in to get their lumps patched up that night."

She pushed out of the chair and he got up with her. "I'm sorry about Mr. Kerry. I liked him."

They went to the front door, reaching the steps just as a black Lincoln sedan pulled up behind the Plymouth. The driver jumped out and ran around to open the back door, practically standing at attention as a man with flowing white hair and a Saville Row suit climbed out.

"He's a lawyer or an undertaker," Quinn remarked dryly. "Nobody else can afford a suit like that."

When the man saw Okata, he paused for a beat, but quickly recovered and strode to the steps. "Hello, I am Marcus Peterson."

Quinn shook Peterson's leathery hand and introduced Okata. Then he invited the lawyer inside.

"I have to be going," Okata said.

Quinn watched Okata as she opened the Plymouth's door. When she paused and looked back over the roof of the car, Quinn turned to show the lawyer into the house, but something about the way she was staring at Peterson made him pause. Maybe it was the position of the sun or his imagination, but her eyes looked like tiny balls of fire. When she noticed his scrutiny, Okata gave Quinn a half smile and a wave, then climbed into the car and drove away.

"You know Sgt. Okata?" Quinn asked.

Peterson shook his head. "Never had the pleasure. Why?"

"No reason."

In his office, Quinn offered Peterson a drink, which the lawyer accepted. The lawyer sat carefully so as not to cut himself on the creases in his slacks.

They wasted a few minutes wading through small talk, then got down to the purpose of the visit.

"Quinn, I know Randall spoke with you about your property over on the big island before his accident."

"Yes, he called twice."

"He was authorized to go as high as fifteen million."

"Well, yes. First he offered ten million, and the second time he upped it to fifteen."

We must be talking about beans here, Quinn thought, trying to keep a straight face. The idea that anyone, much less Quinn Ramsey, would be calmly tossing about eight-digit sums of money seemed utterly preposterous.

Peterson pushed out of the chair with a tiny smile and a crafty sideways glance. He put the empty glass down next to Quinn's handkerchief and began picking his way around the office, examining the books and knickknacks with feigned interest. His fingers were quick and nervous as blow flies.

"What would you say to twenty-nine million?" Peterson said with sudden gravity.

Quinn let the numbers bounce around inside his skull for a moment. Twenty-nine million would almost double his cash.

"I happen to know that Bernard only paid seven million a year or so ago," Peterson added.

To a guy with Quinn's background, a 29 with that many zeros behind it sounded like all the money in the world. He had to force himself to think and not let the numbers blind him.

"Who's making the offer, Marcus?"

Peterson raised his eyebrows. He shouldn't have.

They drew attention to the network of red veins running through the whites of his eyes.

"You know I can't tell you that. All I can say is that it's a Japanese group and that they have asked to remain anonymous."

"Then tell me what they plan to do with the land."

Peterson looked down his nose at Quinn's obvious naivete. Another bad move. The nose had as many ruptured capillaries as the eyes.

"That isn't the kind of question one asks. These are businessmen. Whether it's another hotel, a golf course, or condos, what does it matter?"

Quinn had been a cop most of his life, and he wasn't without experience with the legal profession. He had been a deputy in Palm Beach County, the Great Barrier Reef for every sleazy legal shark from New York to Timbuktu. He had been on the stand dozens of times, facing high-priced hired guns for dope dealers, psychopaths and con men. Quinn knew that when a lawyer got up on his high horse, he'd better keep one hand on his wallet.

"Where exactly is this land?" Quinn asked.

"On the south side of Mauna Kea. Between Hilo and the crest of the volcano."

"How soon do they need an answer?"

"As soon as possible," Peterson said. "These are not the type of men to wait around. There are other properties available."

"So you think I should sell?"

"Definitely. It isn't often one has a chance to quadruple his money in such a short time."

Quinn was quiet as he considered the offer. "I need a couple of weeks," he said finally. "I'll give you my answer the day after Christmas."

Peterson held out his hands, palms up. They were soft and white, the nails clean and perfect. "But why so long? It's a simple proposition."

"I'm going to look at the land before I make up my mind."

"But why?"

Quinn opened his mouth to answer and then realized he didn't have an answer. "I really don't know, Marcus."

That afternoon, Quinn called Adar into the office. He watched as she picked a place on the leather couch, forcing him to come out from behind the protection of the desk. When she crossed her legs, dark hose peeked out from beneath her skirt.

He asked himself what was different about her. The severe business suits had gradually been replaced by soft-colored knits and flattering double-breasted jackets, but it was more than that. It was the way she walked, the way she held her head—especially the way she looked at him. He could feel her eyes even when she wasn't in the room.

His wardrobe hadn't changed: another pair of ratty cutoffs and a T-shirt with Palm Beach Sheriff's Department Boy's Ranch stenciled across the front. She made him feel like a bumpkin.

"I'm flying to the big island tomorrow morning."

Something akin to fear flashed across her face, but it could have been the shadow of a cloud passing outside the window.

"All right," she replied slowly. "I'll keep Q busy."

"Adar, I was wondering if the two of you would come with me?"

Her expression brightened. "Sure."

"Will it upset his schedule? It'll only be for a day or so."

"It shouldn't. We've been studying Hawaiian history. This will give me a chance to put some places with the names I've been throwing at him."

"But will the trip screw—I mean, I don't want to upset any of your plans. It's going to be over the weekend."

"I don't mind."

"Okay, then. Let's get him in and give him the glad tidings." Quinn said and Adar bounced up and practically skipped out of the room.

Quinn was a little disappointed. As much as he enjoyed the woman's company, something in him had wanted her to beg off. He couldn't quite put his finger on why, but since the day she'd moved in, Adar had hardly left the house. She spent her days off either relaxing on the beach with Q, swimming laps in the pool or working out in the gym. A couple of times, after Quinn had thought everyone was asleep, he'd looked up from a book and found her staring at him. The intensity of her gaze had made him feel decidedly self-conscious.

"Why doesn't she have any friends?" he mumbled. "What's the matter with the men on this island?"

Quinn sneaked a peek at the framed portrait on the desk. His dead wife's smiling eyes mocked him. "Don't give me that look."

A moment later, Adar trailed Q into the room. The boy looked sullen, an expression Quinn was becoming accustomed to seeing on his son's face.

"Good news, kiddo. We're flying over to the big island for a couple of days. I have some business, but we'll have time to swim and see the sights."

"No!" The shout hung in the air like a bad smell.

"What do you mean?" Quinn asked, genuinely perplexed.

"No, I'm not going."

"You have to go. I can't leave you here by yourself."

When the boy replied by clenching his fists at his side, Quinn asked, "Why don't you want to go?"

"Don't act like you care whether or not I go. You don't care about anybody but yourself and what you want."

Quinn was too stunned to utter a word.

"You're not sorry mom's dead! She told me. You're glad 'cause now you can go away with her"—Q pointed an accusing finger at Adar—"and fuck!"

Quinn's lower jaw almost hit the floor. "Where? What? Who on earth told you such a thing?"

"She told me everything!" Q screamed and ran from the room.

Quinn had never heard his son speak like that to anyone. Adar patted his shoulder and said, "Give me your handkerchief. He may need it."

Quinn felt around his pockets, then looked around the room. "I don't know what I did with the damned thing. Did you give it back to me?"

She nodded, then ran down the hall.

"She?" Quinn mumbled. "She who?"

The air was charged like the inside of a generator shed from the approaching storm. Quinn stood at his favorite spot at the edge of the cliff and watched the whale-watching boats coming in from another profitable day of pestering the harmless humpbacks. Down below, angry waves pounded his little private beach, and he could feel their booming vibrations through the soles of his shoes like Godzilla's footsteps. Lightning ripped the sky and a second later the clouds cleared their throats. The wind brought the smell of ozone, salt, rain and a spate of bittersweet memories.

Quinn was living the story of the "Monkey's Paw." What had been given with one hand was being taken away with the other. Q was born and Kathy was killed. His uncle died, leaving him a fortune, and his best friend ran off a cliff—and it looked as if his son was losing his mind.

Quinn glared at the steely curtain of rain sweeping toward him and shook his fist. "Goddamn it, quit fucking with me!"

The sky peppered his head with fat drops of ice water, but he refused to move. With the rain came more wind, whipping his clothing and lashing the trees. Forcing every natural thing to bow to its will.

"Damn you! What did I do wrong?" he bellowed into the gale. "You can't have him too!"

Suddenly his head was covered. Adar had slipped into a simple white blouse and jeans that hugged her hips like a surgeon's glove, and she had come to his rescue with a golf umbrella. It was the first time he had seen her in jeans.

She stood at his side for a time without speaking, evidently lost in the light show. Finally she shouted over the wind, "Having fun? You'd better come in before you catch pneumonia."

The lightning exploded again, and for that frozen moment, he stared into eyes that danced with unearthly green light. Like St. Elmo's Fire running the rigging of the old clippers. But it was over so quickly and the darkness afterward was so complete that he thought he'd imagined the whole thing.

"I'm sorry, Dar—about what he said."

"Don't you think I know that?"

"Did he say anything else?"

"Nothing that made any sense. He's mad at you, me, the world. He's very upset."

"It's my fault. I've been so wrapped up playing tycoon that I forgot he's my kid."

As the sky ripped itself apart, firing electrical fusillades that turned night into day, Adar moved closer. Her warmth bridged the gap between them and seeped through the skin of his arms. He noticed how the soggy fabric of her blouse clung to the mounds of her breasts and desire filled his mouth like bitter acid. Mercifully the lightning faded and the moment passed. He began to shiver.

Her hand gripped his belt and tugged. "Come on."

They made for the protection of the solarium. Then Quinn paused with his hand on the doorknob. "I'm sorry, but I can't take you this trip."

Adar allowed a bitter chuckle. "I figured that. Don't worry, I'll try to get him to open up about what's bothering him."

They stepped into the stillness of the glass room. Adar shook the water out of the umbrella and stood it against the door. Quinn's eyes were still on the storm. The rain poured down the glass and, with each burst of light, made the world look sinister and warped.

"It's like an aquarium," he whispered. "Only the water is on the outside, and we're the little fish trapped on the inside."

"I love storms," Adar replied. "It's when the gods fight over mankind. The good fight to protect, the evil to destroy and the battle has raged since the beginning of time."

Quinn looked at his digital wristwatch and was surprised to discover it was 11 o'clock. "I'd better hit the sack. The flight's at ten in the morning."

"Come with me for a minute," Adar said.

He followed her to the south tower, then up the stairs to the second floor. Her room was just below the room that had briefly belonged to Carl Kerry. Once Quinn realized where they were going, his mind began to race. Q's accusation, as crazy as it was, was still fresh in his mind. What if she asked him into her room? He wasn't sure how he would react.

"Wait here," Adar said when they reached her door.

He breathed a sigh of relief, then wondered why he was so relieved.

She came back in a moment, holding a small leather pouch decorated with three tiny blue-and-white feathers. "Do me a favor and wear this."

Quinn held it up with two fingers. "What is it?"

"A good-luck charm."

"Like the one your mother gave you?"

Adar smiled. "Kind of." He started to untie the thread that kept the pouch sealed, but she stopped his hand. "No, don't. It mustn't be opened."

"So what do I do? Wear it around my neck?"

"Yes. Promise you'll wear it till you get home."

Quinn's eyebrows inched up toward his hairline. "Aren't you carrying this holistic hocus-pocus a bit far?"

She took the necklace from him and shook it in front of his eyes. "I know you think I'm quaint, but humor me, okay?"

As she slipped the charm over his head, Adar looked deeply into his eyes. Her lips moved silently as she arranged the pouch directly over his heart. Quinn felt foolish, but he grinned. He was just about to make one of his remarkably stupid male comments when she stopped him with a finger to his lips. She went up on her toes and kissed him demurely on the cheek.

"Be careful."

Chapter Five

Thirteen Days Before Christmas

The Aloha Airlines DC-10 came in low over the flat gray water of Puhi Bay, leveled out and touched down on the rain-slick runway of Gen. Lyman Field. Quinn Ramsey, in pressed jeans and his favorite plaid L.L. Bean shirt, carried a change of clothing in a faded green duffel bag. He was the first down the rolling ladder. He made a beeline for the Avis counter and, just as the sun came out, drove away from the airport in a shiny new jeep.

As near as he could judge, navigating the streets of Hilo was akin to driving inside a greenhouse packed with women and small children. Several streets had been turned into dark tunnels by giant Banyan trees, and everywhere he looked, the buildings and thoroughfares were sprouting tropical flowers and baby strollers. After stopping twice for directions, he located Waianuenue Avenue, which, according to the auto-club map, would take him to Saddle Road. He stopped at a coffeehouse across from the Y.W.C.A. for an excellent hamburger and home fries and asked for more detailed directions.

"You got a four-wheel drive, hon?" the blue-haired waitress asked. "You gonna need it."

After his meal, Quinn sat in the jeep studying the map and letting the sun warm his shoulders. Before moving to the islands, he had always believed that Florida had the highest skies on earth. Yet right in front of him the brooding black-and-green cone of Mauna Kea squatted under layers of cottonball clouds. The trees around the parking lot, the streets and all the flowers wore diamond-studded cloaks of dew under a sky so clean and blue that it made him squint through the dark lenses of his sunglasses. He didn't seem to notice the black Nissan Pathfinder that had followed him into the parking lot before lunch.

Taking an extra second to readjust his glasses, Quinn pulled back onto Waianuenue, following the avenue until it turned into the highway. The black Nissan was three cars back. Quinn ignored the turn-off for Rainbow Falls and enjoyed the isolated beauty of the rain forest along Saddle Road. He whistled an off-key rendition of "Sympathy for the Devil" as he tooled past huge ferns and high grass. Every mile or so he glanced in the side mirror, catching the sun's black glint off the top of the Pathfinder.

Quinn had spotted the tail as soon as he pulled out of the airport, but he wasn't sure what to do about it. The only person he could think of that would want him tailed was Okata, but the guys in the Nissan were too clumsy to be cops.

The road twisted as it climbed. In some places, Quinn had to hit the gas to get around small convoys of trucks from Pohakuloa Military Camp. In other places the road was a muddy washboard and he was forced to creep along, the jeep and his teeth rattling like rocks in a tin wagon. But the Nissan kept its distance.

According to the map, the road that would take him up the side of the volcano to his property was coming up in less than a mile, and the closer he got, the less the idea of driving over an unfamiliar stretch of road, unarmed, with that mysterious Nissan dogging his bumper appealed to him. He'd have to be Amish not to have heard of the bandits that preyed on Florida tourists driving rental cars. He felt safe in assuming that Hawaii had its share of vultures too.

A sign on the side of the road alerted travelers to a photo opportunity a hundred yards up the road. Without thinking, Quinn switched on his blinker to keep the VW bus behind him from creaming his rear end, then pulled off. The hippies in the van pulled off right behind him, and as he rolled to a stop in front of the guardrail overlooking an exquisite emerald valley, the Nissan parked at the far end of the crescent-shaped lot.

Quinn removed his sunglasses, climbed down from the jeep and went to the rail, shading his eyes with his hand as he gazed out over the slope of the volcano. The east side was green jungle and black volcanic rock. Above that, covering the top like melted vanilla ice cream, was a glittering cap of white snow. If his calculations were correct, a good part of that slope belonged to him.

Careful to keep his head still, Quinn shifted his eyes to the right. Two men the size of Arnold Schwarzenegger had taken up positions at the rail. Their clothes were struggling to contain 50 inches of beef in 40 inches of Gold's Gym T-shirts and shorts and it made them look like a couple of burr-headed Polish sausages. Professional wrestlers, maybe, Quinn thought, but no way were those two cops.

The men made little pretense of admiring the view as they worked their way down the rail toward him. At his rear, three rowdy, long-haired college kids from the van were horse-playing their way up the rail from the opposite direction. Their flowered shirts and baggy surf shorts were almost as loud as their antics. As long as those surfers were nearby, Quinn didn't think the musclemen would try anything, so when the kids stopped to take pictures, Quinn decided it was time to leave.

As he hurried toward the jeep, one of the hulks, the shorter one with a reddish-blond crew cut, turned and stepped in front of him.

"Hey, dude! You know how to get to Waimea?"

Before Quinn had a chance to reply, the man lunged forward, shoving a map in his face. At the same instant, the side window of the Volkswagen van exploded and the man spun around, grabbing a bloody shoulder and yelling at the top of his lungs.

Experience had taught Quinn that a sensible man ducked when he heard loud noises, so he dropped flat and tried to become one with the asphalt.

There was another explosion and bystanders started running around like turkeys in November, shouting and generally becoming pain-in-the-ass civilians. Another gun went off, followed by a god-awful screaming, more shouting, then the unmistakable blast of a riot gun. Finally, everything was quiet.

Feeling no qualms about lying on his belly in the middle of a parking lot, Quinn clasped his hands protectively over his head and waited. He figured he was caught in the midst of a skirmish between rival factions of the fashion handicapped, and he had no desire to become a casualty of the clothing wars. In a moment he heard the tap-tap-tap of a woman's heels, then felt something poke him in the ribs.

"You can get up now." Okata was in jeans and a sweatshirt. "The fun's over."

Quinn pushed himself slowly to his knees. "What the hell happened?"

When she crooked her finger at him, he trailed her to the front of the jeep. One of the weight lifters was lying facedown in a spreading pool of blood. The man had ragged holes in his shoulder and back that looked like massive splotches of tomato paste. Beside his outstretched hand was the folded map. Okata kicked it open, revealing a .380 automatic fitted with an evil-looking sound suppressor.

Quinn glanced down the sidewalk at the flowered shirts standing in a circle around the second man. Each of the surfers was carrying a gun.

"They're cops?" Quinn asked.

"State."

"They shot these guys?"

"They got the other one," Okata replied and pointed to the van. "Andy bagged this one."

Quinn looked past her shoulder at a man wearing a black protective vest leaning against the van. A rifle fitted with a scope was resting casually across his knee as he blew a puff of blue cigarette smoke toward the sky. Quinn looked back at the silenced .380.

"God bless Andy. Who were these guys?"

"You don't recognize them?" Okata asked. "Help me."

They turned the man over. His eyes were obsidian chips staring blindly at the high sun. Across his throat was a narrow purple bruise.

"Son of a bitch," Quinn mumbled.

One of the cops in the psychedelic shirts came over to Okata. "You think that's something, come take a look at this other bird."

They trooped across the lot and parted the crowd of laughing men. Quinn remembered times like this, times after a shoot-out when cops would stand around making bad jokes while they waited for their hands to stop shaking and the adrenaline to flush out of their systems.

The second man was already on his back. It was hard to tell what color his T-shirt had been. The shotgun hadn't left much. Under the blast damage, the skin appeared to be covered with bizarre tattoos: some kind of blue reptilian scales, red spider webs, and something that looked like a giant lizard, only now where its head had been was an oozing red crater.

"What's that?" Okata asked indicating a strange round scar on the man's forehead.

Above the vacant eyes was a circle of raw skin that

looked like it had been burned with a branding iron. Quinn thought that the circle and the faint letters inside it looked an awful lot like Adar's amulet.

"So?" Okata said.

"So what?" he asked.

"You know these two?" she asked, but Quinn shook his head emphatically.

One of the surfers had been on his knees, going through the corpse's pockets. He fished out a piece of paper and handed it to Okata. She read it, raised her eyebrows and handed the note to Quinn. He heard the sound of a siren approaching as he read the words aloud. "Ramsey. Flight 210. 11:00"

"Who knew you were coming?"

"Nobody. My son. His—"

"Yes?"

"Nobody."

Q pressed his ear to Adar's door. He was as patient as he was silent, but after five minutes he still couldn't hear a thing. In frustration, he eased the door open and peeked inside. Adar was sitting cross-legged on a tiny rug in the middle of the floor. Her back was to the door, but the boy's extraordinarily sharp ears picked up the sound of her soft chanting. He closed the door, tiptoed down the stairs and then ran through the house to the wine cellar.

At first it appeared that nothing had changed. The large rectangle, the black drapes and the stone table were just as he remembered. But the pentagram that had always glowed with ethereal radiance was obscured by an icy haze. Q dropped to his knees and stared in awe as the cloud pulsed with alien life.

"Mother, I am here."

The mist churned and swirled. Wiry tentacles of mist curled back upon themselves like arthritic fingers forming into claws. Lights flashed and sparked inside like the signal flares of a doomed ship in frozen fog. In moments the haze began to solidify, elongating into a vaguely humanoid gel. The temperature in the hidden vault, already at the freezing mark, plummeted. At last, the pale naked form of a woman stood before the boy. Her head was a mass of soft auburn hair that matched the curly thatch on her pubis. High pink-tipped breasts jutted proudly from the slim, comely body. But looking into the eyes was like gazing into blazing red pits.

"What is it, my son?"

Q's eyes fluttered as his mind labored to form words. "I have come as you told me to."

"The whore, where is she?"

"She is sitting on the floor of her room. I think she's chanting."

The image flickered like a television screen on a stormy night. "Your father has gone?"

"Yes, he left this morning."

"Then you know what you must do?"

Q was silent. His face twisted as he forced a thought to the front of his mind. "Mother, isn't it wrong?"

The white form became tinged with red, and the eyes seemed to grow. "How dare you? The whore works against us. I have felt strange forces at work in the ether. She must die."

Q was at a loss. He was only nine years old, ten in two months, and his father had been a policeman all of the boy's life. His mother had been a policewoman before his birth. Murder! Cold-blooded murder was wrong. Wasn't it? But this was his *mother*. Didn't he *have* to obey her?

The voice dropped to a soft purr that seemed to caress his skin like a silk boa. "Son, do you want us to be together again?"

"More than anything, Mother," he replied, tears staining his cheeks.

"I cannot return as long as this woman lives."

The boy bowed his head to hide his fear.

"Will you do as I say?"

"Yes, Mother."

"Come then. Give Mother a kiss."

The mountain road was over 6,000 feet above sea level. It was little more than crushed volcanic rock mixed with rich red loam and ruts. The jeep tossed them about like crash dummies, and Okata was clinging to the roll bar for dear life. If they shouted loud enough, they could hear each other over the roar of the engine.

"So how come you were following me?" Quinn yelled.

Since he had refused to forgo the inspection trip and Okata had flatly refused to allow him to go alone, she had invited herself along. "Would you believe an anonymous tip?"

"No."

"It's the truth. We got a call last night from some old woman."

"What old woman?" Quinn laughed.

"She didn't say. That's what anonymous means. I

listened to the tape and it sounded like some old woman saying an attempt would be made on your life today. After what happened to your uncle and Mr. Kerry, I couldn't afford just to blow it off."

"Old woman." Quinn was truly puzzled. "I don't know any old women."

The high air was cool and damp. Wisps of cloud crept down from the summit, leaving trails of glistening fingerprints on everything they touched. To their right, the valley was a rolling sea of small Koa trees, Fiddlehead ferns, and rocks wrapped with velvety moss. Up slope to their left, the altitude had fashioned the trees and high grass into an avant-garde lava meadow teeming with wild white mountain sheep and strange-looking geese wearing black skullcaps.

"What are those funny-looking birds?" Quinn asked to break the silence.

"That's our state bird, the Nene. Some people call it the Hawaiian goose."

"You know a lot about Hawaii. Were you born here?"

"On Kauai."

"You're Hawaiian? I mean, you know, your people were Hawaiian?"

"On my mother's side. All the way back to Liliuokalani."

Okata stared at the volcano's summit as she spoke. The sun beat down through the mist, spotlighting the snow and turning the peak into a field of blue-and-white glitter.

"How much do you know about volcanoes?" Okata asked.

Quinn let his eyes dart to the summit, but quickly

pulled them back to the treacherous road. "They erupt at the most inconvenient times. They can barbecue your butt if you aren't careful, and they're a lousy place to look for virgins."

Okata laughed ruefully and nodded. She pointed to the patch of dirty ice. "Did you know that Mauna Kea has the only glacial ice in the tropics?"

Quinn took another quick peek. "I didn't know that."

"Our people believe it's the home of Poliahu, the goddess of snow and ice. She fights an eternal battle with Pele, the fire goddess, who lives across on Mauna Loa. They battle over the love of a man, if you can believe that."

"Why not." Quinn laughed. "Let me tell you a story.

"Once upon a time there was a topless joint in Boynton Beach. In it worked a pair of fairy mud wrestlers. Every Thursday night, two women would get in a pit full of slop and rip each other's clothes off, pull hair, kick, bite and try to bury each other's head in the mud. They went at it so hard a couple of times Kerry and I ran them in for simple assault. The third time we hauled them in, we cuffed them to opposite doors in the back of the car to keep them from killing each other. Kerry had hosed them down before he'd let them in the car, and they looked like a couple of drowned cats. By this time we'd felt like old friends, so Kerry had asked why the women hated each other so much.

"As it turns out they were sisters. Kerry asked them why they fought all the time. One of them—the oldest, long, stringy blonde hair and a hard face—said, "Cause that bitch stole my husband.'

"Kerry looked at the other woman—her name was Cindy or Candy, I think. Candy, and I'm quoting Kerry here, was about as appealing as the hazardous waste from a gynecologist's office. He asked her why she wanted to mess with her sister's husband. Candy said that the three of them shared an apartment and that the husband had the hots for both of them, but he thought she was a better lay. So they started screaming at each other and Kerry told them to shut up or he was going to empty the mace can on them. Finally they shut up and I asked why they did this thing with the mud every Thursday. Why not just move away from each other? The blonde said they couldn't afford it. So I asked if they were tearing each other's clothes off in front of a bunch of drunks for the money.

"Blondie said, 'No. We need the money to bail Paul out of jail. He got busted for fighting with Teddy.'

" 'Teddy?' Kerry said. 'Who the fuck's Teddy?' Seemed Teddy was their cousin and old Paul had been making it with the cousin's wife too."

Okata laughed so hard she lost her grip on the roll bar and almost wound up in the road.

"Love or money," Quinn said. "It's always one or the other."

When she sobered, Okata said, "This land is sacred to our people. For years it was protected. It couldn't be sold. Many of our old people believe the souls of our ancestors live on the sides of the volcanoes. Then one day a judge signed a paper and your uncle owned it."

"I guess that makes me the greedy landlord. But I promise, Sarge, I won't evict your relatives."

"What are you going to do with it?"

When the jeep hit a pothole and almost tossed them both into the high grass, Quinn said, "First thing I ought to do is pave it."

"No, really."

"I don't know. The reason I came over here was to take a look at it. There's a group of Japanese businessmen that want to buy it."

"What do they want to do with it?"

"Beats me. Probably build another golf course."

The dirt road ended in a split-rail fence with a lop-sided gate and a sign that said the land was posted and belonged to Ramsey International. Trespassing was prohibited.

Quinn hopped out, kicked the kinks out of his legs and opened the gate. As soon as they drove through, the trees closed in, casting the muddy trail into a strange, premature twilight. In addition to sunlight, the jungle blocked the breeze and made the humidity unbearable.

"Pele. I've been reading about her," Quinn said after a moment.

"Oh?"

"Yeah, my uncle has all these books in his library on Hawaiian gods as well as a bunch on witchcraft."

"A little light reading?"

"Some are." Quinn nodded as the jeep slewed in the mud. "She sounds like a pretty hot number."

Okata glanced at him sideways and muttered, "Boo."

"Any of your people still believe in that stuff? Or is it all just part of the bull they feed the tourists?"

Okata was quiet for a minute, taking in the natural beauty of the forest. "You'd be surprised how many people still live the old ways. In the hills, they still sit under the Koa trees and listen to the *moolelo*, our oral history told by the elders. Many still pray to their family gods, the *aumakua*, to keep them safe. And in some areas, hardly a day goes by without someone saying they saw a *kupua*, one of the gods' children. Waterfalls are very special to my people and many worship the *aku li'i*, the spirits of trees and waterfalls."

"Yeah, I read some of that. But do you mean it goes on today? I mean, I thought the Hawaiians were Christians."

Okata smiled sadly. "Did you know that, when the Catholic Church converted many of the African tribes, the natives merely changed the names of their ancient gods to the names of the saints and kept following the old ways? While the priests were patting each other on the back, the natives were still making effigies and casting spells."

Quinn chuckled. "I get you. Beats the hell out of the rack."

They came to a wide muddy hole in the middle of the road and had to skim along the trees to keep from getting stuck. Most of the tree limbs supported a variety of parasitic orchids, and when Okata went into another of her quiet spells Quinn said, "It's beautiful here."

"Yes, it is."

The road had been reduced to parallel ruts by the oversize tires of four-wheel drive vehicles. It crossed a narrow stream and snaked through a maze of trees, coming to an abrupt halt in a tiny glade. Quinn shut off the engine and sat for a second listening to the birds and the sound of falling water.

"Let's take a look around," he said.

Okata slipped off her pumps and rolled up the legs of her stretch jeans. She saw Quinn watching as she debated taking the purse, then shrugged off his amused look, shoved the pistol into her waistband and tossed the bag behind the passenger seat.

"You never know," she said defensively.

She's really a good-looking woman, he thought, when she isn't making a career out of being a pain in the ass.

They followed a path through grass gone silver with dew, past a thick grove of swaybacked coconut palms to a tower of water that dropped eighty feet from the top of a sheer cliff. To their right, against another wall of solid rock, were stacks of loose building materials surrounding the skeleton of a half-completed house. The walls and roof beams were unpainted and had weathered to gray. There was a front porch with missing boards like gaps in a mouthful of teeth and dark squares for windows that looked like vacant eye sockets. In the distance, they heard the barking of a dog.

"I didn't expect this," Quinn said, indicating the waterfall. Butterflies landed on silky cattails at the edge of the pond, working their wings as if trying to get the stiffness out. "It's beautiful. And so peaceful."

"Yeah, but that doesn't fit," Okata said, nodding toward the abandoned house. "Let's take a look."

They waded through a sea of tall weeds, avoiding a few overgrown two-by-fours and stacks of molding strips. At the porch, Quinn rested a foot on the front steps to test the build.

"Seems sturdy enough. Wonder what it was going to be?"

117

"Let's go inside," Okata said.

The front door hung by a single brass hinge at the top, and it had a rough hole for a knob. Across the header and down both jambs, someone had scratched lines of comical-looking stick men. Quinn ran his fingers over the strange glyphs.

"What do you think they're supposed to be?" Okata asked.

Quinn shrugged. "How about an Egyptian mezuzah?"

The living room was unusually large with wide windows on both sides of the door that gave excellent views of the falls. Across from the entrance was a stone fireplace wide and deep enough to cook a steer. The ceiling had been installed and the sheetrock was up, but the electrical wiring and switches were dangling from holes in the plasterboard like dead worms. With each step, the plywood floor groaned like it had arthritis.

"Big place," Okata said.

"It's not that old."

Okata went down on one knee and picked up one of the cigarette butts that littered the floor, working it between her finger and thumb.

"This is fresh."

Quinn wasn't paying attention. His head was back, sniffing the air. As he stepped through the doorway into the hall it got stronger, that cloying, sickly sweet odor that tied his stomach into a knot and made his body break out in a sweat.

"Jesus!" he whispered and glanced over his shoulder.

Okata was still on her knees sleuthing. He took

another step, giving his eyes time to adjust, following the smell and remembering a day three years earlier when he and Carl Kerry had answered a call at one of the ocean-side condominiums on Delray Beach.

Several tenants had complained about an awful stench emanating from an apartment on the third floor. After letting themselves in with the super's pass-key, he and Kerry had discovered the body of an old woman sitting in her rocker, surrounded by empty Twinkie wrappers and soft drink cans. The super told them the old girl had been depressed and lonely, and the way it looked, one night she simply plopped down in front of the tube, pigged out for a while on her fa-vorite junk food and then opened her veins with a steak knife while watching *The Price is Right*. Blood had splattered onto everything in a six-foot radius, and in that stifling apartment, it smelled like heated copper pennies. Quinn never forgot the odor.

Now, using his fingers as eyes, Quinn inched deeper into the dim recesses of the hall. With each step, the odor intensified, clogging his lungs until it felt as if he were breathing the halitosis of the dead. At every door, he paused to run his hands over the frame. Each was decorated with those strange figures. At the end of the corridor he came to a wide door. When he reached for the knob, Quinn was amazed to discover that his hand was shaking. The thought of calling for Okata crossed his mind, but he was afraid that if he did, he would never live it down.

"Quit being a wuss."

He jerked the door open and was blinded by the brilliant sunlight that flooded down through the ex-posed rafters. He closed his eyes until they adjusted, then cautiously checked his surroundings.

It was a wide, open room. The walls were simple concrete blocks; the floor was sculpted concrete set in a wide diamond pattern and in the middle was an Olympic-size swimming pool. As he crossed the threshold, his ears picked up a new sound: the high-pitched buzzing of flies.

"Gail!" he called, his voice little more than a dry whisper. "Gail!"

He walked woodenly across to the concrete pit. It was a thousand times worse than the old woman in the condo. The little girl had been stripped of her clothing and dumped into the deep end of the unfinished swimming pool like a sack of garbage. Her sadly undernourished body had been slit from navel to neck and strings of rubbery intestines dangled like thin gray ropes from the gaping wound.

Quinn's first reaction was to turn away, to pretend this atrocity had nothing to do with him, but it wasn't going to be that easy. Next to the corpse, someone had written the word sell on the floor with bloody fingers.

Quinn's professional eye took over. It ignored the human tragedy and took in the bruises on the thin arms and the horribly discolored lesions on the insides of the scrawny thighs. One leg had snapped on impact, and a splinter of bone jutted through the skin like an objecting finger. Her face was chalk white and he wondered what color her eyes had been, for now the sockets were empty and dry, crawling with bloated flies and their offspring. The last thing he noticed was the one detail that would haunt him for years. Her tiny toenails were painted with bright red polish.

He heard movement behind him and spun around. It was just Okata. She walked to the edge of the pool and stared at the sad little body and whispered, "Goddamned, cocksucking motherfuckers."

"Well said."

"She's been here a while," Okata said. "God, what did they do to her eyes?" In the child's raped expression was all the pain and horror of her last few minutes on Earth. "What are those marks on her thighs?"

"Somebody's teeth."

After squandering half an hour searching for a gun, Q slammed the last drawer in his father's dresser and muttered, "Shit! What now?"

The answer came into his head like a laser beam: "The library!"

He scurried down the stairs, slipping into the library and locking the door. Unsure where to begin, he searched everywhere: in the drawers of the small desk, behind the scary paintings, under the couch cushions. He even ransacked the bar, pulling out and then carefully replacing each bottle. As he contemplated the rows of books, staring at what to a nine year old looked like shelves that reached all the way to the moon, he finally threw up his hands.

"This is impossible!"

On his way to try the next room, he spotted the display cabinet mounted on the wall behind the door. In seconds he had the doors open, gazing in wonder at the collection of exotic cutlery: ornamental swords in jeweled scabbards, bayonets from a host of foreign countries and several medieval poniards and daggers. Off to the side, the ugly stepchild next to all the sleek steel, was a stone knife. Its blade was eight inches long and curved; it looked as if it were made of black glass. The hilt was covered in red velvet with the face of a demon carved on the pommel.

Q took the knife down and waved it through the air, exhilarated at the way it seemed to come alive and nestle into his palm. After closing the cabinet, he carried his prize tight behind his back and started up the south tower stairs.

The climb was arduous. With each step a battle raged between the voices in his head. One voice, tiny but persistent, said that what he was about to do was evil. But the other, his mother's voice, was strong and commanding, all but drowning out the first.

"Go on, my son. So that we can be together."

The memory of his mother's cold embrace was like a black hole in his mind, sucking all thoughts of rebellion deep into its dark core. In the hidden room, she had tried to pull him close, enticing him with the promise of warm, ripe lips. Her hands had been soft and incredibly strong, but when he got close enough to see the soulless depths of those bloodred eyes, he had tried to pull away. But that had been as futile as fighting the laws of gravity. She had used her silky voice to allay his fears until all at once her pendulous breasts had pressed against his chest. Their touch was a caress that burned like fire. Then her hands had moved over his chest and down between his legs to fondle him in a way that his father had warned him about. Yet what could he have done? She was his mother! It had made him feel strange—feverish and excited, yet bad and dirty. And when she had kissed him, the last vestiges of his opposition had been swallowed by the cold vacuum of her being.

Q reached the second floor landing. What he was about to do was playing in his head like a video on fast forward—cutting, slashing, stabbing. Blood, gray lumps of tissue, pink and red organs. Slippery ropes of red and tan things. It was a horror movie. The boy shuddered, but when he looked down his hand was turning the knob.

Adar had just returned from the shower. She was sitting on the bed with a towel wrapped around her body, humming a soft tune and vigorously drying her hair. Q's grip on the knife tightened and he felt it respond to the embrace. He took a tentative step into the room.

Below the open window came the sound of an automobile engine racing up the driveway followed by the squeal of brakes. Adar jumped up and went to look out.

"Wait!" the voice in his head shouted, and Q stepped quietly back into the hall and closed the door.

Okata had a car waiting at Kahului Airport and surprised Quinn by offering him a ride. He tossed his bag into the trunk next to the tools of her trade: a 12-gage shotgun, a bullet-proof vest, boxes of ammunition and two cellophane bags. One had a police sergeant's dress uniform and the other an airy, pleated dress with tiny blue and pink flowers.

The drive started out in silence. The gruesome

business with the little girl seemed to have forced them deep into their own thoughts.

Back at the abandoned house, Quinn had picked out a dry rock at the water's edge to wait while Okata took the jeep back to call the state police barracks. There was a timelessness about the place, a still beauty that was so at odds with the direction his life was taking. Death had become a mongrel dog nipping at his heels and yet, as he'd run his fingers through the cool water, he'd felt a kind of peace. His thoughts had been so lost in the calm pool that he hadn't realized Okata had returned until he'd felt her hand on his shoulder.

"I sent a car to your house. It'll stay there till we get back."

The last thing he'd wanted right then was sympathy and understanding from her. Up until that moment, she had been the perfect target for his anger and frustration: the smart-ass woman cop who had the unmitigated gall to think she was as good a cop as he had been.

"Aw, shit," he muttered.

"You're welcome."

Okata had been on top of this thing from the start. God, how he hated to admit that to himself. But even as they raced back to his house, Quinn had to wonder if all her efforts would be enough to help.

He banged his shoulder on the door as the car leaned into the first curve on the Hana Highway. "I hate this fucking road."

"Everybody hates this road. You should have seen it before they widened it," Okata said; then added, "I owe you an apology. I checked you out. I found out about your wife and about the guy who killed her."

Quinn shrugged. "Shit happens."

Okata returned a sad grin. "Why don't you cut the macho bullshit?"

Quinn laughed. "Then I wouldn't know how to act."

"You ever decide to try, give me a call."

Quinn saw a small, sleek animal disappear in the bushes at the side of the road.

"What are those things anyway, weasels?"

"Mongoose."

"No kidding."

They passed the first in a long series of waterfalls. It didn't help their mood.

"You ever been married?" Quinn asked.

"Nope. Funny, men don't seem to find women who carry guns appealing. And I have yet to meet a guy who appreciates my clientele."

"Most women don't like men with guns any better."

"Your wife didn't like guns?"

"She was a cop."

"So you like liberated women?" Okata asked with a shy grin.

"Especially liberated women who can shoot straight."

They laughed. It felt good and a small chunk of the ice in his chest melted.

"You're so full of shit," Okata said.

An hour and thirty minutes later they turned into Quinn's driveway and parked beside a black-and-white cruiser. Okata reached for the door handle, but Quinn's hand stopped her.

"Gail, what the hell's going on?"

She put her back against the door and faced him. "This whole thing's beyond me."

"Come on, Sarge. Your gut feeling?"

She studied her lap for a moment. "I really don't know, but my feeling is it's bad. And it's just starting."

Adar was in the kitchen plying two state cops with milk and cake. "I'm glad you're back," she said when Quinn and Okata walked in. "Ben and Harry won't tell me what's going on."

She gave them a mock stern look and they actually blushed.

"It was nothing, really. Where's Q?" Quinn said.

"In the pool, doing his laps."

"I want to keep him close for a few days, okay?"

Adar touched the amulet through the thin fabric of her blouse. "What is it?"

Quinn looked at Okata, who said, "She has a right to know."

The cops looked curious too, so omitting the grislier details, Quinn told them the whole story. When he finished, the cops were visibly shaken, but Adar, although lost in thought, didn't seem surprised. Okata noticed her calmness too.

"Your reaction isn't exactly what I expected," Okata said.

Adar snapped out of her reverie. "I'm shocked. I was just giving thanks for your deliverance."

The patrolmen finished their cake and excused themselves.

"Stay here until relieved," Okata told them as they left.

"You can't keep them here forever," Quinn said, then grinned. "What I need is a security specialist."

"But this place already has an alarm doesn't it?"

"That isn't exactly what I meant."

The woman faced her daughter across the glass top of the patio table. "Marcus's idiots failed."

No visible emotion crossed the younger woman's face. "I said as much. This man Quinn is not his uncle."

The mother's face betrayed dark humor. "You sound almost pleased, daughter."

"Pleased? No, intrigued might be a better word. I sense strange forces at work here."

"From Ramsey? Don't make me laugh."

"I'm not sure. His mind and will are strong. He could be a worthy opponent."

"Ha!"

The daughter rose from the chaise lounge with the fluid grace of a cheetah. Her gown billowed about her sleek form like a royal cape. When she turned from the penthouse rail, her eyes were cold. "You would do well not to laugh at my perspicacity."

The mother's face flamed, but she held her tongue.

"Maybe there is another way to get what we need," the daughter said, softening her tone.

"Enlighten me."

"Every father has a built-in Achilles's heel."

Chapter Six

Ten Days Before Christmas

At the ringing of the bell, Adar ran to answer the front door, but Quinn cut her off in the hall.

"Hold on," he said, jacking a round into the chamber of the nine-mm automatic.

He had been in the library studying another of his uncle's cabalistic comic books when the bell sounded. Now, he peeked out the side window, laughed and opened the door.

"It's about time."

Most people totally underestimated Timothy Wolinsky. Because he was a Pole and had the irrepressible smile of a Bible salesman and ran off a steady stream of off-color jokes, it was easy to miss the lightning reflexes and ice-blue eyes. His hair was blond, long and combed straight back like a Southern politician's. Even his body was deceptive. He was only five seven and usually wore loose-fitting clothing, but underneath, his arms and chest looked as if they had been sculpted by Weider.

"Hey, stud," Tim said. "I climbed out of a sick bed to get here. But I think she'll recover."

Tim dropped his suitcase, dusted his hands on a pair of white sailcloth slacks, then tried to crush Quinn in a bear hug. He noticed Adar and quickly sobered.

"Tim," Quinn said, "this is Adar. Adar, this is Tim Wolinsky."

All smiles, Tim reached out and vigorously shook her hand. "Adar? What is that? Greek?"

"Hebrew."

"Well, it's a real pleasure to meet you."

Adar wasn't most people. She saw at once that the man's manners were a front; calculating eyes belied the false charm.

"This all you brought?" Quinn asked, pointing at the suitcase.

"Son, you know better than that. Come see."

Adar trailed the men to Tim's rental van. Tim opened the back door and began unloading bulky wooden and plastic crates, rapidly stacking the heavy containers as if they were so many Lincoln Logs.

"Tim is a very special person, Adar," Quinn said and laughed. "He's something of a security expert. Kerry and I met Tim on numerous occasions as he was—what is the politically correct term now?"

"Alternate shopping," Tim said.

"After-hours shopping would be more accurate.

We busted him three times coming out the back of Palm Beach's finest electronics stores."

"None of which stuck," Tim reminded Quinn for Adar's benefit. He looked around the front of the house. "Where are all the servants? I heard you had more money than God."

The men lugged the crates into the garage while Adar took Tim's bag to the ground-floor bedroom in the south tower. Quinn couldn't bring himself to give Tim the room that had belonged to Kerry. Kerry's things were still where he'd left them. As they deposited the last crate on top of the stack, Tim began checking the contents.

"How'd you get all this stuff past the airlines?" Quinn asked.

"You're kidding, right? How long do you think I'd stay in business if I had to send everything through the regular airlines? Anyway, what's with the cops down by the gate? I was afraid they were going to search me."

"A courtesy from one of the state cops."

Tim opened a crate and pulled out a 12 pound piece of dull black steel that looked like a blaster from a science-fiction movie.

"What the fuck is that?" Quinn asked.

"Twelve-gage automatic shotgun. MPs use them."

"No wonder you were nervous about the cops."

"You ain't seen nothing yet."

When Tim opened a pair of rectangular, olive-green boxes, Quinn noted the black paint smeared over the original lettering on the sides. "What's that?"

Tim stood up and opened his palms. "Grenades and LAWs rockets."

Quinn's eyes almost popped out of his head. He crossed the floor in two strides, staring into the boxes. "Jesus Christ, Tim. I said I was having trouble with a Japanese syndicate, not the fucking IRA."

"I took that to mean Yackuza. What are you so upset about? You were a Marine. You ever hear of anybody getting screwed because they had too much firepower?"

"No, but I heard of somebody getting ten to fifteen for having this kind of stuff. Where'd you get it? It's hot, isn't it?"

"Ask me no questions, I'll tell you no lies," Tim replied in a singsong voice. "Besides, you rich guys never get caught. It's always us poor entrepreneurs."

"How much did this stuff set you back?" Quinn asked as he hefted one of the grenades.

"Me, nothing. You, a bundle. I got these on what you might call consignment."

Quinn couldn't help but laugh. Tim Wolinsky skimmed through life on an edge thinner than an Olympic ice skater.

"Where's my godnephew?" Wolinsky asked.

Quinn peeked into one of the other crates and winced. "I don't know. He's around somewhere."

"Why do you say it like that? You two have always been so tight."

Quinn picked up an infrared night scope and turned it over in his hands. "We were until recently. I think he's going through early puberty. Every time we look at each other we practically bare our fangs."

"Yeah, kids. You can't live with 'em, can't shoot 'em in the head," Tim said sagely.

"I thought that was your philosophy about women?"

"Works the same way. Women and kids. I never understood either of them."

"How is Myra?"

"That bitch! Gone again. I should stick a homing device in her cunt. She spends more time on her back than an Aamco mechanic. You were lucky. You found the right woman and stuck with her, and you knew if you fucked around, she'd shoot you in the balls. The only way anyone'll ever keep Myra's legs together is to slap a pair of handcuffs on her ankles."

"Well I don't understand Q anymore. He even seems to hate Adar and they started out as good friends."

"Can't be puberty then. Man, what a set of knockers. How is she?"

Quinn put the scope down and lifted the lid on another crate in which he found a parabolic microphone and recorder. "She's my son's tutor, Tim. That's how she is."

"And that's supposed to mean you two aren't playing park the pickle?"

Quinn dropped the lid with a bang and gave his friend a look. Tim tried to ward off the glare with the palms of his hands. "Okay, okay. But just because she's your son's teacher doesn't mean that I can't try my luck, does it?"

"Tim, an Abrams battle tank couldn't stop you from trying."

Later that night Quinn was back in his favorite recliner reading a book called *The Booke of Secretes* that had been written in 1560 by Albertus Magnus. In the past few days, Quinn had just about made himself ill by wading through volume after volume of occult lore from his late uncle's library: *De Praestigis Daemonum* by Wier, 1563; *The Discoverie of Witchcraft* by Scot, 1655; *Daemonologie* by King James I of England, 1597, and *The Compleat History of Magick. Sorcery, and Witchcraft* by Boulton, which was practically hot off the presses, having been published in 1715. Quinn had learned about blood rites and magic potions, demons and saints, and he'd read the passage on the sacrifice of prepubescent children with particular interest. The description of ritual disembowelment closely resembled the wounds suffered by the little girl in the swimming pool. Many of the illustrations were so graphic that no sane human being could ever have put them down on paper.

As the clock struck ten, Quinn puzzled through incantations and spells for everything from making a woman hot for a man's body to summoning imps and demons. He'd dog-eared the page on love potions for later study. Another interesting item was the report of a mythical spirit that could be summoned by a witch to keep her dwelling clean. Quinn looked around the library. There wasn't a speck of dust on the yellowed books, no dust bunnies, no smudges on the desk or windows. It gave new meaning to the term dust devil.

Christ! he thought. Necromancy, demonology, witchcraft, sorcery, voodoo. His uncle had been one sick puppy. No wonder the man had never married. Then he flipped back to the chapter on succubi. The

133

pages were covered with handwritten notes in Bernard Ramsey's shorthand.

Maybe the old bird hadn't needed a wife, Quinn mused. If he'd really had a spirit to clean and a demoness for sex, all he would have needed was a hobgoblin to cook and he'd have been as happy as a pig in shit.

"But I bet the old boy would have chucked it all for a meaningful relationship."

When his eyes began to burn, Quinn laid the books aside and removed his glasses, massaging the bridge of his nose. The more he tried to concentrate on the exotic phrases and terms, the more he realized it wasn't his eyes that were the problem. It was his boy.

Tim had invited everyone into town for a late dinner. Quinn had begged off, but when he told Q that Tim was taking them out, the kid had thrown one whale of a tantrum. Naturally, being the adult, Quinn had countered this outburst with calm and reason. He had threatened to pack the kid's clothes and send him off to a military academy the next morning. The look in the boy's eyes had been enough to freeze Quinn's heart—such pure, unadulterated hatred. Q had stomped off to the waiting van without another word, sitting with his arms folded over his chest and his eyes focused straight ahead. Quinn would bet the three of them were having a jolly old time.

When he couldn't sit still any longer, Quinn got up and paced around the room, pausing in front of the windows. He thought it funny how the world always looked sinister when he was upset. His leafy lawn menagerie looked especially creepy, as if it were waiting in the dark for some unsuspecting clod to deliver a pizza.

"Being a parent sucks. Why the hell didn't they give us owners' manuals?"

Tired of being depressed, he padded down the hall to the kitchen. He had on a pair of cutoffs and a black T-shirt over that stupid leather pouch that Adar had given him. Rather than chance hurting her feelings, he kept wearing it even though it had rubbed a raw spot on his chest.

While he put together a turkey sandwich, piling on the Swiss cheese and hot mustard, he wondered how he'd look in one of those silk smoking jackets.

"Like a dick."

As he chewed, he looked around the kitchen. It was too clean. The place was starting to give him the willies. As he was making these observations, he was hopping back and forth on his bare feet.

"And on top of everything else, I'm freezing to death on a fucking tropical island."

He made two more sandwiches, slapping the mustard on thick, and grabbed another couple of beers.

"I wonder if everybody talks to themselves or just ex-cops," he mumbled as he went down the hall.

Slipping his feet into the pair of old tennis shoes he kept by the front door, Quinn took the food and started down the driveway. The house was getting to him and he decided to bribe his way into the cop car with free eats and then sit a while and swap war stories with the boys. It was dark. A quarter moon provided more shadow than light and the breeze off the ocean was soft and filled with floral perfume. After the frigid air of the house, his skin breathed a sigh of relief.

His tennis shoes made soft squishing noises as he made the curve in the driveway and saw the red 911 bumper sticker. "Okay guys, wake up. Dinner's—"

They weren't asleep—they were dead. Their heads were thrown back and their chests ripped open like a couple of butchered hogs. Their faces were swollen and black, and their eyes wide and horrible with disbelief. There was little blood in the car or on the ground and no sign at all of the missing organs.

Quinn dropped the food, jerked the door open and pulled the radio microphone to his mouth. "Dispatch, code 30, repeat code 30. Two officers down at the stakeout on Nanualele Point. Send backup and ambulance."

He let the microphone spring back into the car and felt the driver's hand. It was as limp and rubbery as a surgical glove, but still warm. The shotgun was right there, so he yanked it from the rack and jacked a shell into the breach.

Except for anemic moonlight and a lonely 40-watt bulb burning beside the mailbox, the area was dark as pitch. Quinn swept the barrel of the riot gun in a 360-degree circle. Anything could be hiding in the tangled jungle of underbrush that grew next to the road, and he felt as exposed as a duck in the middle of a pond on the first day of hunting season. Staying by the car would only expose him to the same fate that befell the cops, yet the idea of hiking back up that long shadowy driveway, past all those creepy hedge animals didn't exactly fill his heart with joy either. He peeked around the gate. The house looked as if it were a mile away.

"What the hell," he muttered.

First, making sure the safety on the shotgun was on, Quinn ducked into the hibiscus hedges at the side of the driveway and ran as quietly as possible behind a curtain of giant ferns. He couldn't see a damned thing so he moved in a crouch, staying close to trees and stopping every few feet to listen. Directly across from the entrance to the house was a massive Koa tree in the midst of a patch of thick ferns and Bird-of-Paradise plants. By running from hedge to tree, and crawling occasionally, he was able to make it into that nest of fragrant ferns, flopping down on his belly and sighting down the barrel of the shotgun at the front steps.

"Okay," he whispered in a voice so low that even the ants he had landed on couldn't hear. "You're surrounded. Come on out with your hands up and I promise not to shoot."

He lay there without moving, hardly breathing, for what felt like an hour. Twenty minutes into the stakeout, the bush by his head rattled softly, and when he moved the shotgun to cover it, a long green Iguana walked out and stared at him. It stopped and rolled its eyes, apparently irritated to find an armed and sweaty human lying in the middle of its living room.

"Don't look so smug," he whispered as he slapped angry ants. "You might be surprised at the things you'll do when you're scared."

Just as he looked back at the house, a man in a dark suit stepped out of the bushes at the north end.

"Ah! There you are." Quinn smiled and moved the shotgun slightly.

The man walked clumsily, as if the suit that hung so loosely on his bony frame was catching every twig. After looking around, the man motioned with the gun in his hand and a second man came out of the brush.

Quinn was lining up the little bead on the end of the barrel with the chest of the armed man when the leather pouch around his neck began to burn into his chest like a hot coal.

Then the men reached back and parted the bushes, and a huge, hairy creature shuffled out and sniffed the air. It grunted softly and drooled and kept opening and closing massive jaws. Quinn remembered seeing something just as ugly in one of his uncle's books. He forgot what it was called, but it resembled an orangutan with claws and a serious overbite.

The men, who didn't seem very comfortable around the thing, were constantly glancing from the windows to the creature and keeping their distance. As for the thing, it lumbered along behind them like a pet gorilla, its claws digging furrows in the ground and a cloud of insects swarming around its matted head. As they reached the front steps, the distant wail of a police siren brought them to a halt. The suits exchanged frightened looks and did a very strange thing. They looked into the nearest window and made some kind of sign in the air with their hands. A heartbeat later the creature began to dissolve.

Quinn took his finger off the trigger and stared. "Holy shit!"

While he'd walked down his share of dark alleys

and kicked in more than one crack-house door, Quinn never considered himself an exceptionally brave man. The week Kathy had been killed, he'd spent every night sucking on a bottle and staring at his pistol, wondering if he had the nerve to go on. Those times, he pulled a chair into his son's bedroom and stared at the boy until the sun came up. But as he watched that grotesque creature crumble into a mound of brown sludge, Quinn knew he had never been truly afraid before.

But as the men turned to leave, Quinn put aside his fear, pushed to his knees and aimed. Before he could yell to them to stop, a ghastly white face appeared in the library window. It looked like a woman with a mop of stringy hair and a pair of deep-set eyes that glowed like laser drills. The men paused, staring at her for several moments, then whirled and began firing wildly into the trees above his head. Quinn shouted for them to surrender, then ran out with the shotgun tucked tight against his hip, his hands working the slide and trigger. One of the men was hit in the arm and dropped his gun. The other went to one knee, aimed and fired. The bullet missed Quinn's ear by inches, but it threw him off stride enough so that his next blast trimmed a limb above the man's head. The shooter grabbed his companion and disappeared around the side of the house.

Quinn crossed the driveway on the dead run and was almost run down as the first of the reinforcements came screeching up in a flurry of flashing lights and smoking tires. The cruiser slammed to a stop and two uniformed policemen jumped out, leveling their guns at the first living thing they saw—Quinn.

He dropped the shotgun and raised his hands. "Don't shoot!"

Okata's unmarked Plymouth roared up the drive. Two more cars and a van rolled up, spilling men with body armor and shotguns, automatic and bolt-action rifles. Okata ran up with her gun drawn.

"They ran toward the beach," Quinn yelled and four of the cops from the van tore through the bushes.

"Are you okay?" Okata asked. When he nodded, she said, "What happened?"

He gave it to her quick and mean, minus the part about the dissolving creature. When he finished, they walked down to inspect the murder scene. The medics were just pulling the first body from the cruiser. The man's arm fell and his hand hit the side of the car with the dull thud of a rubber hammer.

"Shit!" the paramedic swore.

"What went on here?" asked a tall man dressed in plain clothes and alligator-skin boots.

"Capt. Benson, this is Mr. Ramsey. I'll let him explain."

Quinn repeated the story while the second cop was forced into a separate body bag.

"Goddamn it! It looks like they ran into a buzz saw," Benson said. "And all you saw were two men?"

Two members of the Special Weapons Team came jogging down the hill, their hobnail boots tapping in unison on the driveway. "One of them's hit, but they managed to make it to a boat, Captain. We put out a call to the Marine Patrol."

"Okay," Benson replied. "We'd better check out the house."

Remembering the hideous face he'd seen in the window, Quinn quickly acquiesced. Then, as they started up the driveway, he remembered something else and pulled Okata aside.

"Keep them out of the garage, okay?" Quinn said and Okata raised an eyebrow. "Please! I'll explain later."

Quinn muttered as the police filed into his home. "I'll be damned if I'm going to spend Christmas in jail because of Tim's toys."

The police went through the house from top to bottom, but didn't find a living soul. Okata took up a position by the door to the garage and every time one of the cops came close said, "I checked in here."

Tim, Adar and Q came home at two a.m., just as the van with the Special Weapons Team drove away. Two burly cops tried to stop Tim at the door, but luckily Quinn arrived before the fur began to fly.

Q immediately ran up the stairs to his room, but Adar wandered through the house with a stricken look on her face. Capt. Benson paced the hall with his charcoal sport coat open so everyone could see the matching chrome-and-black .38 on his hip. He seemed anxious to be somewhere else.

Finally, when the house was pronounced clear, Benson said, "I'm stationing a car at the end of the drive and another at the front door."

Quinn glanced at Tim. "That's nice of you, Captain, but I have help now."

Benson cast a skeptical eye in Tim's direction. "It's

your house, Mr. Ramsey, but if I were you, I'd want all the help I could get. We've been questioning that lawyer of yours about the Japanese investment group, but so far he hasn't been very cooperative. I tend to agree with Sgt. Okata. There's a good chance we're dealing with the Japanese Mafia, and if they want something of yours, they won't be discouraged easily."

Benson stopped to exchange a few words with Okata, then climbed into a big Chrysler with about a dozen antennae. She waited patiently until Quinn and Tim finished whispering and Quinn turned to say good night to Adar.

"You don't look well," Quinn said.

"I'm okay." Adar sighed. "I just need some sleep."

"Listen, Dar," Quinn said as he walked her to the bottom of the stairs, "I hope this stuff doesn't make you want to quit or anything."

She was so pale under her tan that her freckles stood out like a rash. "Don't worry."

"I wouldn't much blame you. But now that Tim's here, things should get better."

She smiled wanly, kissed him on the cheek, then slowly climbed the stairs.

"Yeah, well, Gail, you have to eat sometime," Tim said to Sgt. Okata as Quinn approached them. "How about dinner tomorrow night. You can show me around the island."

"Mr. Wolinsky, I don't think that would be a good idea."

"Why not? I'm a nice guy. Ask anybody."

"I don't date people I meet in the line of duty. It's one of my rules."

"Give her a break, Tim," Quinn said.

Okata smiled her thanks, but quickly turned serious. "How 'bout we take a look in the garage now?"

"Just cars, Sarge," Tim said.

"It's okay, Tim. Come on, Gail."

"Holy shit!" Tim muttered when Quinn opened the garage door and turned on the light.

The walls, the cars, the ceiling, even the boxes and cases were covered with pictures and obscene symbols drawn in blood: five-pointed stars, alien words, the head of a goat drawn by the hand of a madman. Blood had run down the walls, coagulating in foul puddles on the concrete and the place smelled like an abattoir.

"Well, now we know where all that blood went." Okata picked her way between the cars, holding her arms close to her body. She paused beside the first of Tim's crates, drumming her fingers on the lid.

"I'm not sure I want to know what's in here."

"Maybe we should—"

"Leave it alone, Tim," Quinn snapped. "It's guns, Gail. Automatic weapons."

She gave a bitter laugh. "Now why doesn't that surprise me?" She raised the lid, then let it slam and staggered back.

Tim and Quinn ran to the box and lifted the lid. A cold human heart was nestled comfortably on top of the M-16s.

Chapter Seven

One Week Before Christmas

Quinn walked into the solarium, his hands deep in the pockets of his hiking shorts and depression shading his face like a five-o'clock shadow. "Come on. We're gonna blow this place for a while."

Q looked up from his studies and frowned, but Adar smiled quizzically and asked, "Where are we going?"

"Swimming."

While Adar made sandwiches and Tim and Quinn loaded the jeep, Q stood in front of the garage swinging his dive mask and muttering like an Italian grandmother. They drove to the other side of the island, past Kaanapali, the luxury hotels on the highway and an ancient railroad that still ferried sugarcane, then down to a secluded stretch of road near Makaluapuna

Point. It was one of those days when the sun was white-hot, but the air was cool and salt collected on skin like scales. The grass on the links had been nitrogen fixed so many times it was almost blue, and fat men and trim women dressed in outfits that would have looked ridiculous at Mardi Gras chased golf balls over sculpted hills. Past the high rises, the road narrowed and the weeds grew tall and close.

"Okata told me about a place," Quinn said as he slowed down. "There!"

He pushed the nose of the jeep through a small gap in the grass and followed an eroded trail down through a grove of wind-stunted candlenut trees. The road ended at a fallen tree, where they piled out and ferried the gear down to a beach that was so smooth and black it looked like an asphalt parking lot. Although the cove was only a few dozen yards from the highway, the thick growth of vegetation cut the noise to nothing and allowed them the illusion of solitude.

When Quinn ran back for the beer, Q slipped out of his cutoffs and stepped into his swim fins. He spat into the mask, rinsed it out with ice water and pulled it over his face.

"Is he going to be okay by himself?" Adar asked Tim.

"Qujo? Hell, yes. He swims like a fish."

The boy backed into the surf, turned and knifed headfirst into an oncoming wave. Quinn came back a few minutes later and deposited the cooler next to their blanket.

"Thank God!" Tim said, pulling a frosty bottle from the ice.

145

The men stripped down to their trunks and Adar slipped out of her robe. She would have been hard-pressed to tell which man had abused his body more. Tim was very muscular, but he had the precursor of a beer gut stretching the elastic of his trunks and several old, red scars on his shoulders. Quinn was trim and well proportioned, but his biceps and right thigh bore the white puckered marks of old bullet wounds.

When Quinn saw her look, he said, "I forgot to duck."

Snatching up his snorkel gear, Quinn trotted down to the water. In a few moments, the tops of two tubes could be seen moving side by side through the waves.

"Quinn swims pretty good too," Tim said.

"Don't you like to swim?" Adar asked.

Tim drained the bottle, tossed it aside and opened another. "Don't have much use for water."

When Adar fingered her amulet and scanned the trees, he said, "What's wrong?"

"I'm not sure." She stood so still that the gentle wind seemed to whistle around her. "Probably nothing."

In a moment, she pulled the charm over her head and dropped it on the robe, then picked up the extra snorkel outfit and headed for the ocean.

Tim watched her swim through water as clear as blue ice; then he settled back and closed his eyes, letting the warmth of the winter sun work its magic on his body. Even if he'd been watching, Tim couldn't have seen the dark blue sedan that parked in the turn out at the north end of the cove.

* * *

Marcus Peterson peered down at the beach through a pair of oversize German binoculars.

"You sure we should be doing this?" the man behind the wheel asked.

"At the rate Tammy is going, we'll die of old age before we get our hands on that land."

The driver was a big man with a handsome, if somewhat cruel, face and blue reptile-scale tattoos all over his body. "Maybe, but you sure you know what you're doing?"

Marcus shot the man a withering glance. He put the binoculars down and picked up a brown wooden box from the floor of the car. The sides of the box were covered with strange lettering, the top with colored feathers and beads.

"I borrowed this from Tammy. It should do the trick"—Marcus opened the box and stared at the contents for a moment, his fleshy features twisting with revulsion—"if our little swimming friends don't work. If they don't, I've always got you."

It was like free falling through mountain air. The water was a comfortable 82 degrees and visibility could be measured in hundreds of feet. The bottom sloped gently, and it was littered with lava boulders that, from the surface, resembled shiny petroleum nodules. Q was so busy pointing out the schools of multicolored Moorish idols and triggerfish that neither he nor Quinn noticed Adar until she streaked underneath them. Quinn was envious of the tutor's grace and agility, the way she seemed to skim over the bottom as effortlessly as a seal.

In a moment she joined them at the surface, scissoring her legs languidly as she removed the snorkel from her mouth. "Come on down. I think I saw a lobster."

Quinn spat out a mouthful of salty water. "We can't take anything. This is a marine preserve."

"I don't want to eat it. Just come look. It's beautiful."

Q grinned and shrugged. The boy had been withdrawn on the trip, but the beauty of the ocean had put a serious dent in his shell of indifference.

"Last one to the bottom!" Quinn said, then pulled his mask down and dove for the reefs.

Adar led them through a maze of ebony rock guarded by castles of coral and towers of cylindrical tube sponges. Every inch of the bottom was alive with color: gardens of flowerlike plume worms, delicate lavender and pink variegated sea anemones and gangly gold-striped arrow crabs stalking the slippery rocks like surefooted little men on stilts. At about 15 feet, Adar held on to a piece of coral and pointed under a rocky porte cochere. Quinn saw the whiplike antennae and the black, red and gold bands of a Hawaiian rock lobster. Q kicked harder, trying to get down for a better look at the shy crustacean, but just as his faceplate pulled even with the ledge, something long and willowy darted out of the crevice, smashed into the side of his mask, then slithered under the nearest rock. Q's mask started to leak, but the boy didn't panic; he just glanced all around trying to find what had attacked him.

Quinn tried to reach his son, but Adar had his flipper, jerking it like a rip cord and pointing frantically toward the surface. When he turned his head, he saw the huge black mass that had stopped directly over their heads, cutting them off from the surface and air.

Until he felt the coolness of the shadow, Tim never suspected anyone was within a mile of the place.

" 'Lo, Sarge. You move kinda quiet for a flatfoot."

Okata had on a bikini top, cutoffs, sneakers and an ankle holster. "You people are out of your fucking minds."

Tim propped up on his elbow. "Nice to see you too."

She shaded her eyes and searched the water. "Where are they?"

"Snorkeling."

"I should have known when Quinn asked me about this place." She cast a black look in Tim's direction. "From you I'd expect something dumb like this."

Tim lifted the corner of the blanket, showed her the Italian shotgun and arched his eyebrows.

"Lot of good that would have done a minute ago," Okata snapped. "What if I had been someone else? He could have splattered all five of your functioning brain cells before you opened your eyes." She turned around and scanned the waves. "Where the heck are they?"

A seething swarm of venomous sea snakes had blocked the path to the surface, hovering in the water like a huge black cloud that eclipsed the sun for yards in every direction. Thousands of tiny heads and sleek, striped bodies squirmed all over each other like a bucket filled with slippery earthworms. The snakes were extremely poisonous and very aggressive. To prove the reputation well earned, eight or ten serpents slithered away from the herd and made a beeline for the trio of divers.

There was no time for deliberation. At best, they had a few seconds of air left in their lungs. Quinn glanced at Adar and Q and made a follow-me motion with his hands. Then he launched himself straight up into the scaly underbelly of the school. The reptiles reacted immediately, striking at his naked flesh with their tiny, needle-sharp fangs. With every inch he gained toward the surface, Quinn expected to feel the snakes' sharp kisses, but somehow he kept going. He clawed and kicked a narrow tunnel for Adar and his son, the way a man might dig his way out of a shallow grave. Just as his lungs were about to implode, Quinn broke the surface, paused long enough to make sure Q and Adar were behind him, then swam for the beach with everything he had. When he finally felt sand under his feet, he staggered out of reach of the surf and collapsed. A moment later, Q lay down beside him and Adar dropped heavily a few feet away, all of them panting like greyhounds.

"Have a good swim?" Tim asked.

Tim and Okata were standing over Quinn, but he couldn't reply.

"Aren't you a little old to be racing around in the water like that?" Okata asked.

"Snakes," Adar said with a gasp.

"Snakes?" Okata said, looking about her feet. "What about them?"

"We were surrounded by a school of sea snakes."

Okata shook her head. "Sea snakes don't school."

"Somebody forgot to tell them," Quinn muttered.

Okata glanced from face to face. "You're serious?"

"As a heart attack," Quinn replied.

Adar crawled over to her robe and slipped the necklace over her head.

"That's really weird," Okata said. "What'd you do?"

"I don't think I've ever seen anything like it," Adar said. "Quinn pushed them aside as if they were nothing and swam right through."

"Why'd you do a dumb thing like that?" Tim asked.

"Didn't have the air to go around," Quinn replied sheepishly.

"Well, you're one lucky son of a bitch," Okata said. "Sea snakes are deadly but they have tiny little mouths. If you'd tried to ease through them or swim around, they probably would have had you for lunch. By charging right through, you didn't give them a chance to get a hold on you."

Rubbing a dark bruise on the side of his head, Q said, "When I first saw them, I thought they were eels." He tossed a jagged piece of lava on the blanket.

"What's that?" Adar asked.

"A rock I picked up. I'm going to send it to Larry Pierce back in Florida."

"No!" Adar and Okata shouted in unison.

When Quinn and Tim stared, the women blushed. "It's bad luck." Adar said.

Quinn grinned. "Don't tell me—Pele, right?"

"The way things are going," Okata said, "you think you want to take a chance on any more bad luck?"

"But I just—" the boy muttered, but Okata shook her head sternly. He picked up the lava and threw it as far as he could, then turned and stalked back to the jeep.

At the turn off on the hill, the dark car drove away.

*   *   *

"I can hardly wait." Tim said dryly.

Tim, Adar and Q were seated around the dining table. They had changed for dinner: Adar, into bone-colored slacks and a black, long-sleeve Polo shirt; Tim, into black Duckhead slacks and a red flannel shirt; and Q into khaki hiking shorts and an MTV T-shirt. The chill that permeated the house didn't seem to bother him. They could hear Quinn slamming drawers and pans in the kitchen.

"Can he cook?" Adar asked.

"We never exactly swapped recipes, but I'd guess a TV dinner is a stretch for him," Tim said.

The dining room was a mishmash of opulent cabinets for china, porcelain and overly ornate lighting fixtures, but the overall impression was dark: dark wood, a dark tablecloth and dark wallpaper with a pattern of small red fleur-de-lis that looked like tiny drops of blood. Q kept looking at the big wooden cuckoo clock on the wall. Every 15 minutes a werewolf would come out and chase a blonde-haired girl in pigtails from one opening to another.

"You gotta give the guy one thing," Tim said. "Life's never dull when he's around."

Adar's smile was wry. "True."

Quinn came through the door, cradling a large Pyrex cooking dish between oven mitts. He deposited the dish on the hot plate on the table. "Okay, soup's on."

Tim raised half out of his chair and sniffed. "What is it?"

Q wrinkled his nose and sighed. "Chili-tamale casserole. It's the only thing he knows how to make."

Adar distributed the plates and opened a jar of applesauce and a box of club crackers. "It smells delicious."

Quinn beamed. "Chili, tamales, Monterey Jack and cheddar cheese. Quit crabbing," he said to Q. "It beats TV dinners."

Tim took a forkful, swallowed and grabbed his beer, draining the bottle in five gulps. "You forgot to mention the cayenne pepper."

"Oh, yeah, and Cayenne pepper. Too hot?"

"Aw, hell, no. We can sell the leftovers to the navy to stoke their boilers," Tim said. When Q spooned applesauce on top of the casserole and crumbled crackers over the top, Tim asked, "You're not actually going to eat that?"

The boy cut a hefty slice of tamale with his fork and shoved it in his mouth with a look of contempt. He didn't even break a sweat.

"That's it!" Tim said. "Tomorrow I find us a cook before my stomach lining is gone."

At ten that night, Q went to bed. The adults sat around the solarium, trying to make heads or tails out of the sea snake attack.

"Gail said she had never heard of sea snakes schooling," Adar said. "I think she's right."

"Tell her about the migrating lobsters, Quinn," Tim said.

"Every few years, usually in the spring or late summer, spiny lobsters begin to congregate somewhere in the southeastern Caribbean. Then thousands of them start marching over the sea floor. The line is yards wide and several miles long. Nobody knows why they do it. Nobody knows where they go. The environmentalist—"

"Bunch of old maids left over from the sixties," Tim said.

"—go nuts because every fisherman from Bermuda to the windward passage shows up and starts netting bugs."

"And the lobsters are too stupid even to change direction," Tim added.

"Anyway!" Quinn said with a sour look at his friend, "Washington finally stuck its nose in. Had the coast guard run off the Bahamian and Haitian fishermen as soon as the bugs walked into U.S. waters. Some of the fishermen were refugees living in Little Haiti and they were less than thrilled. These guys took lobster for a living and they figured the guard was taking food out of their kids' mouths."

"So first they started butchering and eating manatees," Tim said, breaking in again. "Can you believe it? Those fat, slow-moving sea cows? Then tell her what they did."

"I will, if you'll let me." Quinn took a sip of soda. "The fishermen went to the local paranormal practitioner—"

"Also known as the witchdoctor." Tim chuckled.

"And he cast a spell."

"And the coast guard started dropping like flies?" Adar grinned, really getting into the story.

"Nope. The next year the lobsters marched right up the gulf stream till they got within twelve miles of the coast and hung a right. The fishing boats followed them all the way up to North Carolina, with the guard and Greenpeace having fits, but they couldn't do a thing to stop them."

"I think the lobsters must have had a Loran receiver." Tim chuckled. "Only way they could have known where the twelve-mile limit was."

"I don't know." Adar yawned. "With that many antennae, they probably bounced a beam off the GPS satellites. Night, fellas." She got up and disappeared down the hall.

"I think my story did her in," Quinn muttered.

"I think your casserole did her in."

"You want another beer?"

Tim pursed his lips and stared at the ceiling for a moment. "Hell, why not?"

Outside the solarium, a man with binoculars watched Quinn and Tim from the cover of trees at the top of the cliffs. Dressed in black from a knit ski mask to combat boots, he carried a knife in his webbed belt that Rambo would have envied, a Yuppie catalogue crossbow in one hand and a silenced nine-mm automatic in a special shoulder holster. Underneath the army surplus ninja suit, his body was covered with blue reptile-scale tattoos.

The man had floated in on the tide with the motor to his craft off. He'd beached his boat down below, then climbed the flight of wooden steps and found the perfect vantage point, waiting patiently for Quinn's friends to go to bed. However, shortly after Adar left the room, the man started hearing things. First, it was the bushes behind him rustling when there wasn't enough wind to blow out a match. He put that down to a mongoose or a lizard. Then, every insect on the peninsula had shut up at the same instant and it was so quiet he could hear himself sweat.

The man decided not to wait on Tim Wolinsky getting sleepy. He was lining up his shot when his nose picked up a distressingly sour, burning odor through the nylon ski mask. The scope on the crossbow said Quinn was well within range. One tug on the release and the steel bolt would put an end to Quinn for good.

Suddenly, steely fingers seized the man's shoulders, lifting him up off the ground and spinning him around like a Kewpie doll. He fired the steel bolt point-blank into his assailant's dark robe, but the crushing pressure did not diminish. When he opened his mouth to scream, a hand released his shoulder and gripped his throat.

"Who sent you?" The voice was a whisper. Sexless, cold, deadly.

The man grinned and shook his head. "No one." His whisper was as low, but without conviction.

Eyes inside the cavernous hood began to glow like radiant marble chips. The pressure on his throat increased as the interloper said, "Who sent you?"

"Who are you?" the man rasped.

"I guard this place. Last chance—who sent you?"

"Fuck you. The devil made me do it."

The man was hurled from the top of the cliff and landed on the hard packed sand. He lay there stunned, broken, but still breathing. After an instant of his anguish, the cloaked figure was carrying him to the boat. On the long bench seat, the robed figure pressed something into the man's hand—something hard and rough. The man had just enough strength left to unfurl his fingers, revealing a piece of black rock. Powerful hands closed around his and squeezed until the bones popped like dry twigs in a campfire.

"No! Please let me go."

"All right."

The boat was propelled backward against the tide with such force that water spilled over the transom and filled the splash well. The boat did not lose way until it reached the rough water on the other side of the small barrier reef.

The man lay on his back, gazing up at a sky full of indifferent stars, rocking back and forth in agony and wondering how badly he was injured. It felt like every bone in his body was broken and a cold wetness was spreading through his chest. A moment later he felt soothing heat fill his hand. That sensation soon became searing pain that blackened his broken fingers, spread to his arm and shoulders and eventually to the padded seat.

On the beach, the hooded figure watched the fire spread until it consumed the boat. The blaze flared briefly, a blue teardrop against a sea sparkling black with pinpoints of reflected starlight. When the hulk finally slipped beneath the inky water, the figure turned and stared at the house atop the cliff.

"Hello, who's this?" Quinn asked.

After his all-night bout with heartburn, Tim had driven into town to find a cook and housekeeper. His candidate was a diminutive Asian woman in her forties with her gray hair in a tight bun, a wrinkle-free face and calm eyes. He ushered her into the room and introduced her with pride.

"This is Sharon."

"Sharon?" Quinn and Adar said in unison.

Tim nodded. "Sharon."

The woman bowed and said, "*Tamiekiko*."

"As I said—Sharon." Tim hustled the woman off to show her the kitchen and in a short time could be heard explaining to his protege how to make a Polish pizza.

As the afternoon passed, Adar took Q through his paces on Algebra and Latin, a language he suddenly found infinitely fascinating, while Tim lifted weights and Quinn showed Sharon the house.

"You won't have much cleaning to do, but we eat like horses."

She bowed, and he showed her the pantry and where the cleaning supplies were kept. She opened the door to the cellar and peered down the dark stairway.

"You don't have to worry about down there. It's a little dusty." Quinn suddenly wondered why the cellar had dust when the rest of the house was practically dirt free. "Anyway, we hardly ever go down there."

After bowing again, the woman followed Quinn around with her hands tucked into the sleeves of her loose, red silk jacket with a green, gold and black dragon on the back. In the kitchen, he got her started on dinner, then went to the office to do some paperwork. At six, Adar summoned him to dinner.

Sharon had made two huge pizzas. One was covered with coconut shrimp and anchovies, the other with Canadian bacon, pepperoni and Polish sausage. Tim's grin almost cut his face in two, and he dug in like a thoracic surgeon who had sewn his gold Rolex inside a patient's chest. Q took a slice with the sausages and picked at it as if it were his science project. Adar laid a slice with the shrimp in the middle of her plate. After cutting it into precise, one-inch squares, as if she were being graded on neatness, she proceeded to eat one square at a time, carefully opening her mouth just enough to allow passage and then patting her lips with her napkin.

As for Quinn, he had a slice of each, chewing and swallowing like a man plugging nine-volt batteries into Robbie the Robot. While he ate, Tim rattled on about whatever popped into his head. After dinner, Quinn retreated to the library. Rain had fallen steadily all day and he had started a fire in an attempt to cut the chill that seemed to seep out of the walls. At ten o'clock, Adar wandered in and peeked at the title of the book he was reading.

"You're really getting into that stuff. What happened to accounting and law?"

Quinn invited her to take a seat. "Dar, the way things are going, I thought it would be a good idea to put the business on the back burner for the time being. I'm going to leave things in the hands of the management company."

"You mean things with Q?"

"I'm losing him fast. I kept trying to convince myself it was a phase, but now I think it's connected to the other things that have been happening."

Adar crossed her legs. During the afternoons, she abandoned the tailored suits in favor of slacks and blouses. On the nights she spent around the mansion, she preferred loose skirts and long-sleeve shirts. With the austere suits had gone the aloof demeanor, and after a relatively short time, Quinn felt they were becoming friends. When things calmed down, he hoped for more.

"Something's been bothering me and I'd like to ask you a rather personal question," Quinn said. "But if you don't want to answer, I'll understand."

Since Adar sat patiently without batting an eye, Quinn said, "Do you know anything about witchcraft?"

"Some."

His mind began racing and he popped out of the chair. "I knew it! The charms, Massachusetts. You watched me fumbling with these stupid books and didn't say a word. Why?"

She stared at him until he reclaimed his seat and made a sign with his hand that he had calmed down. "Quinn, have you ever heard of the Wicca?"

"Wicca? Isn't that the stuff they make furniture and handbags out of?"

It was a poor attempt at humor, but she smiled anyway. "In this case it is an ancient religion. Some people call its adherents witches."

"So why didn't you say something?"

"It's not the kind of thing one puts on a job application."

"And you belong to this religion?"

"Not exactly. You don't join the Wicca the same way you join the Methodists. You have to be born into it."

"Born?" Quinn asked, feeling exceedingly dense to keep repeating everything she said.

"My mother, her mother, her mother—you get the picture."

Quinn began to smell a rat and his suspicions must have showed in his face because Adar said, "I can see from your expression you're getting the wrong idea.

I'm not the source of your problems."

"Kind of a coincidence, isn't it? You show up and suddenly we're up to our armpits in black magic."

Adar was silent for a moment. "Why do you say black magic?"

"How 'bout answering my question first?"

"I didn't happen to come here, Quinn. I was sent."

"Sent?"

"Okay, for some time, my family has been receiving strong vibrations. These emanations, if you will, were coming from Hawaii and the disturbances were too powerful to be natural. So we began to investigate. Some of my cousins are adept at finding things. But the problem seemed to be coming from several places at once. The big island, here on Maui and on Oahu."

"Three places? What does that mean?" Quinn asked.

"Won't you please tell me why you said black magic a few minutes ago?"

Trust didn't come easy. Quinn knew he couldn't always rely on his feelings when it came to good-looking women. "It was not a great leap after what I saw the day those two cops were killed."

"What did you see?"

"Something big and hairy with long claws." He went to the bookcase, found the leather-bound volume he was looking for and placed it in her lap. "One of those."

"A basilisk?" Adar inspected the drawing closely. "But this creature usually takes the form of a serpent or lizard. I have never seen this drawing before."

"Whatever it was, I'm sure it killed the men in the patrol car," Quinn said with a shudder.

"What happened?"

"I was hiding in the bushes in front of the house. Two men and that thing came around the corner. When the men heard the police sirens, they waved their hands in the air and the thing dissolved."

"Where?"

"Right out in front of the house."

"Show me."

"Too late. Remember, it's been raining. I checked the spot this morning and there's nothing left."

"I wish—"

"But I got this," Quinn said, holding up a small glass jar of yellowish-brown powder.

"And that is—"

"Dried monster. I scraped it up after Okata left the other night."

Adar took the jar and held it up in front of the fire. "You didn't tell Gail?"

"Yeah, right. 'Say, Okata, I saw this hairy creature with claws and foot-long teeth dissolve in front of my house. What? Take a ride with you? Sure.'"

Adar put the jar on the table and said, "I'll be right back."

While Quinn waited for her to return, he lost himself in the flames of the fire. Every few seconds he glanced at the drawing in the book lying open on the table. There was something else he should tell her—something about red eyes. Then the room seemed to spin slowly in his head and he closed his eyes.

"I need a keeper," he mumbled. "I can't remember shit anymore."

Adar came back ten minutes later wrapped in a faded bathrobe and carrying a ragged cloth valise.

She had scrubbed what little makeup she wore from her face and combed her hair out until it floated around her head in a soft carnelian halo. After placing the bag carefully on the floor, she unfurled a four-foot red, gold and blue dhurrie in front of the fire. The rug looked old. It was covered with the signs of the zodiac and lined with archaic letters and symbols. Adar set several vials and pouches in a semicircle on the floor.

Quinn watched this procedure with fascination. Each time she bent over, the brass medallion popped out of the robe, and each time she tucked it back in he found he was jealous of the amulet. At last she appeared satisfied.

"What now?" he asked.

Adar took a deep breath. "One of the time-honored ways that knowledge is obtained in the black arts is for one practitioner to steal it from another. Your uncle was a very powerful witch. If the person who killed him was adept in the arts, he might have been able to usurp his powers."

"You sound as if power like this can be lifted the way you'd steal somebody's wallet."

"Not in the least. It takes extensive knowledge of the charms and incantations, but it is done. Anyway, when you inherited your uncle's property and moved in here—"

Quinn laughed and clapped his hands. "You thought I was a witch?"

"You have shown unusual interest in his books."

"Come on. It was just morbid curiosity. Later, when all the weird shit hit the fan, I began trying to find answers."

"Maybe. But there is a strange, latent power in you."

"Right," Quinn said acidly. "Me and Shirley MacLaine."

"Scoff, but we had to be sure."

"So now you're sure?"

"Now, Quinn, don't freak out on me, okay?"

He nodded and Adar let the robe fall to the floor. Other than her amulet, all that remained were yards of glorious freckled flesh. He made a valiant effort to keep his expression neutral, but the bored expression felt like a rubber mask. Far from being relaxed, his body was stretched as tight as a guitar string and starting to cramp.

"Uh, you're going to have to undress," Adar said, then quickly added, "But don't get the wrong idea. Sexual energy is important to the working of most charms and magic, but that doesn't mean the sex act."

Quinn didn't move for a minute while he tried desperately to think up an excuse that would let him keep his clothes on without making him look like a jellyfish. At last he croaked, "No problem."

Adar couldn't help laughing. "Come on."

His fingers worked the buttons on his shirt like an 80-year-old man's. When the shirt was off, he paused and went to the door, locked it, then continued to undress in slow motion. By the time Quinn got down to his jockey shorts, his face was the color of the flames in the fireplace.

"Please try to relax," Adar said. "You have a wonderful body. There is no need to be embarrassed."

His blush turned into a full-fledged rash, but he

managed to step out of his underwear without falling on his face.

"Now, come and kneel across from me," Adar said and positioned herself at one end of the rug.

It took two minutes for Quinn to twist himself into position on the floor—on his hip with his legs turned protectively to one side. Adar placed a small clay bowl between them and poured a few drops of white liquid from one of the opaque vials. The uncapped bottle released an aroma as sweet as Newark on a hot summer night.

"What the hell is that? Eau de putrefying corpse?"

She ignored him, muttered a few words under her breath, then added a drop of green liquid from another vial. What had been bad got infinitely worse.

"Come on, Dar. I can't breathe."

While she worked, Quinn made comments to keep his mind off all the glorious female flesh sitting on the other side of that tiny rug.

You've seen breasts before, he told himself. Quit acting like a nerd.

Adar finished her canticle and moved closer, holding the bowl in her hands. "We must anoint each other with the oil."

"Say what?"

She spoke slowly, the way someone might speak to a retarded child. "Quinn, we have to rub this oil over each other, every inch. Now you're going to become aroused, but that's okay. It's part of the ceremony. I will become aroused too. But you must use the heat that your body generates to help focus your mind. Let the oil seep into your skin and free your thoughts."

Her eyes roamed his body from head to foot, then she said, "Ready? Kneel."

He got up on his knees. She dipped her fingers into the bowl and reached for his chest.

"Wait a minute, I want to ask a question," Quinn said. Adar pulled back and held the fingers over the bowl. "Are you really a schoolteacher?"

Adar shook her head and sighed. "You really are the strangest man I ever met. Yes, it's one of the reasons I was selected to come here."

She reached out again, but he said, "Wait! You said one reason. What's the other?"

"Later," she replied and smeared the greenish-yellow fluid over his nipple.

Q listened to the stillness of the house and the pounding of the rain on the window. His chest felt as if it were encased in steel bands, and his body was bathed in a clammy sweat in an ice-cold room. Sleep, the thing his body craved more than anything, had become as elusive as a shadow. He was exhausted, but the voices gave him no peace. His mother's voice, other strange voices that babbled in languages he didn't understand and the tiny voice that he believed was that of his dying sanity—they bored into his head like carrion worms.

It was getting late. Each tick of the clock by his bedside was like a knife in his heart. The room filled with flickering light from the storm, and the shadows of his swimming trophies cavorted across the nautical chest of drawers like a troop of malignant trolls.

Each new explosion of light brought a whimper. It was as inevitable as decay. She was coming. Coming to hover in the corner of the room with those awful dead eyes that seared his soul like red-hot pokers and the voice that sounded as if it came from a bleeding throat, demanding over and over, "Why does that woman still live?"

Then she would descend a few agonizing inches at a time—until she enveloped him and ripped his mind from him like a small tree being pulled up by its roots.

He'd tried to explain, tried to make her understand. "Things have changed. Something put her on guard. She locks her door. When we have class, she sits apart and never lets me out of her sight."

But his excuses never mattered. First, she gave that chilling smile, then she would float down. He wouldn't move, couldn't move. He was a fly trapped in a web of terror, watching helplessly as the spider dropped down from her silken tunnel, feeling those ice cold lips, those burning claws caress his body.

The night spoke again, a rumble of thunder that shook the walls.

Q looked at the clock. He was so tired. If he could only sleep, just for a little while, maybe she wouldn't come tonight. Maybe.

"What is that stuff? Ben Gay?"

Quinn's blood was on fire. Adar's oil filled his pores like hot soup and smelled worse than a medicine cabinet.

"Shush," she said softly. Her fingers were steel probes.

He closed his eyes and tried to think pure thoughts of his white-haired mother. Actually his mother had dyed her hair jet black right up to the day she keeled over during the fifth race at the dog track in North Miami. So he tried the American flag, then baseball.

Nothing worked. His penis was so stiff that he was afraid a strong breeze might shatter it.

"Relax," Adar said soothingly. "Just relax. Let your mind roam. Let it float."

All his mind could think of were those magic fingers. She applied the potion to his arms, smoothing it into his skin. Quinn screwed his eyes shut, afraid if he so much as looked at her he'd explode. She moved around him on her knees, spreading liquid desire over his neck and down his spine. He began to relax. He was still more aroused than he could ever remember being, but awareness of his body was fading like a morning mist in the high sun.

She moved to his buttocks and whispered, "Stand."

He did, like the scarecrow in a hailstorm. The room, the fire and the furniture had lost their harsh outlines. Everything seemed to be surrounded by a strange orange aura.

"I'm stoned." He giggled. "If Okata shows up, we're busted."

"Shh!"

When Adar finished the backs of his legs, she moved around to his front to complete the erotic paint job. Fortunately, when she applied the potion to his testicles, Quinn's mind was floating so high that he barely noticed.

"Your turn," she said as she rose to her feet.

Quinn went to his knees and scooped the liquid into his palms, rubbing it between his hands until it warmed. "We ought to bottle this stuff," he said. "We'd be rich."

"You're already rich."

"Oh, yeah. Well, we'd be famous then. Like the guy who makes those chocolate-chip cookies. Famous Adar's Sex Wax."

As he applied the potion to her legs and ankles, his mind began to balloon inside his head. He could feel the room and the books; the dust motes crashing into the windowsills sounded like falling meteors. The air in the room pressed down upon his body as gently as a truckload of feathers. His hands went up and over the curve of her buttocks and he massaged the small of her back. Adar sighed. It came out as a long drawn-out purr.

"That's wonderful," she said as he finished the back of her neck and went around to her front.

To Quinn's engorged pupils, her pores looked as large as the dimples in a golfball. He started on her toes and worked his way up, really getting into the massage, each hand dipping and spreading of its own volition, making little designs on her skin. The lotion expanded his mind until he could hear and feel the rotation of the earth and the movement of the planets.

When he reached her breasts, he came crashing back to earth. "Oh, God."

"Hurry," she said. "Finish."

They were breathing like a pair of marathon runners. He couldn't move. As his hands pressed against her nipples, the surrounding skin pebbled, raising a rash of goose flesh that felt like sandpaper to his supersensitive palms.

"Quinn!" she growled deep in her throat. She had her own gravitational field. Her lips appeared as wet and ripe as iced strawberries. "Quinn, we must not. Use your mind. Turn it outward."

"Couldn't we, you know, just for a second?"

"No!"

He completed the application by smoothing the lotion over her face, carefully avoiding her eyes.

"Now kneel," she said. "And face me."

He put the bowl in the middle of the rug and stared at his knees.

"Look at me."

"Wow."

Adar's eyes were glowing rings of green fire. She took the glass jar with the powder and held it between both hands. "Surround my hands with yours."

Quinn did as she instructed and she spoke in a low voice, carefully pronouncing words that were impossible to pronounce.

"I see it," she whispered. "It has not yet formed. Just a mass of malignant energy that floats. It moves through the dense brush beside the ocean." Her face was twisted with concentration, her eyes open wide. "It moves to the car. The policemen cannot suspect. They are laughing. The men who guard the beast are afraid of it. Their fear stinks like rotting flesh; it drips from their pores. The two could never have conjured up such a monster.

"One man walks out of the trees and goes to the open window. The policemen are not laughing now. They are alert. The man tells the officers that his car is broken and he is lost. He reaches into his pocket and takes out a glass vial. The police relax. One policeman reaches for the microphone, the other asks what the man has in his hand.

" 'Something for my asthma,' he tells them. Then he opens it and spills the contents inside the car.

" 'Hey, buddy!' the cop says. 'Be careful.'

"The energy can now take form. It uses the elements in the vial. First teeth, gleaming white and sharp, then claws. The hair seethes like a hundred worms on the floor of the back seat, forming a ball, then a nest, finally the body. The driver looks in the mirror and screams."

Adar shuddered violently and closed her eyes. "They are approaching the house now. The basilisk seeks your smell, but he cannot find it. I think the charm on your body masks it. They circle the house. The men are carrying something white—a handkerchief. They give it to the beast and it brings it to its snout. They round the corner and near the front door.

"Wait! A noise. They are confused. What to do? A voice speaks to them. An incredibly powerful voice. They make the sign of dissolution and the basilisk loses its cohesion. Its energy dissipates and its body returns to the elements. They are about to leave. The voice speaks again, warns them.

" 'He is behind you!' " Adar screamed. "I can see a face!"

Then she screamed as if her soul had touched the coals of hell.

Out of a sound sleep, the boy suddenly popped his eyes open, his heart threatening to burst through his chest like the metallic fetus in *Alien*. Her round, grinning face loomed over him like some hellish moon, and Q pulled the covers to his chin, knowing full well that cotton and down were no protection against what was coming.

"I am here my darling." The diaphanous form descended from its perch near the ceiling. "The whore still lives, my son. I am afraid I will have to discipline you."

Her grin turned into a snarl, baring a mouth full of black, razor-sharp teeth. The boy tried to cry out, to move, but he could not. All he could do was sob silently.

"Mama, please," he managed to whisper. "Please don't."

His mother's features rippled with pleasure. "That's right. Beg. Beg!"

As the creature's foul breath bathed Q's face, his overburdened nervous system loosed a stream of hot urine that ran unnoticed down his leg. The child closed his eyes.

When the shrill scream echoed through the corridors of the mansion, Q thought at first that he had finally found his voice. Yet when he opened his eyes, his jaw was still tightly clamped and the woman had stopped dead still in the air over his bed. Her face shifted and ran like quicksilver, and just for an instant, the boy caught a glimmer of something else—something with slitted red eyes and scales; something that snarled in frustration before it vanished, leaving behind an odor of cold putrefaction.

Quinn found a strong pulse in Adar's neck. He had just eased her onto her back when he heard another gut-wrenching howl from somewhere deep in the house. "Jesus, what now?"

A moment later, someone started pounding on the locked door, yammering in Japanese.

"Oh, shit!"

Still half looped from the potion, naked and standing over an equally naked and unconscious woman, Quinn didn't know what to do.

"Mr. Ramzie, Mr. Ramzie!" the cook called through the door. "Mr. Tim said come quick."

Adar's eyelids fluttered and he lifted her head into his lap. "Are you all right?"

She blinked rapidly, her eyes shiny and wide like the eyes of a deer. The cook was still yelling at the top of her lungs.

"Something's up. I'll be back. Will you be all right?"

Adar pushed herself into a sitting position and held her head for a second. "Yes, go ahead."

Quinn jumped into his clothing, darkened the room and squeaked through the door, pulling it closed behind him.

"Mr. Tim say come quick. Your son."

When Quinn reached Q's room, he found Tim trying to restrain the hysterical boy.

"What happened?" Quinn demanded.

"I don't know," Tim replied, giving him a quizzical glance. "I was in the kitchen and heard screaming in the library."

"Uh, Adar saw a mouse." Quinn tried to bite the offending tongue, but it was too damned slippery.

"Mouse? Right. Anyway, a split second later, Q started screaming. When I got here, he was shaking like a leaf, bawling and babbling nonsense."

Quinn got down on his knees beside the bed. "What's the matter, son?"

The boy was white. His eyes were red, swollen and wild, and he was mumbling about his mother, teeth and snakes.

"Phew," Tim whispered. "What kind of aftershave are you wearing?"

"Q? Come on, talk to me."

The boy's forehead was as hot and dry as desert sand. Quinn turned Q's face to him and saw the boy's eyes had rolled back into his head.

"I think he's going into shock! Get his feet up."

Tim folded a blanket and pushed it under the boy's feet while Quinn got the spare quilt out of the closet.

"Help me get him out of these pajamas," Quinn said when he returned. "He's wet himself and soaked right through to the mattress."

When Quinn unbuttoned the boy's pajama top he drew back in horror. "What the fuck is that?"

The upper left side of Q's chest was covered by a round bruise. Inside the purpled flesh was a ring of tiny scabs.

Quinn turned to the Japanese cook. Her eyes were the size of manhole covers and she quickly crossed herself.

"Sharon, do you know how to call for an emergency?"

"Nine-un-un?"

"Go call. Tell them we need an ambulance. Tell—"

"Wait!" Adar pushed everyone out of the way and carefully touched the wound. "Get my bag. It's still in the library."

"But—"

"No time for buts, Quinn. Hurry!"

"Should I call?" Sharon asked.

Quinn glanced at Adar, who said, "No, we can't let him out of our sight."

"What's the matter with him?" Tim asked while Quinn thundered down the stairs. "How did he get that bruise?"

Adar ran gentle fingers over the round scars. "My aunt told me about something like this once. I hope I'm wrong."

Quinn came puffing back up the stairs with the valise. The boy was panting, his hairless, almost concave chest fighting to pull in oxygen. Adar pulled out a thin green bottle and turned to Tim. "Get everybody out of here." She motioned with her head at Quinn and Sharon. "Whatever happens, don't let anyone come in." Tim stared stupefied as her eyes began to glow. "It may get noisy, but you must trust me. More is at stake here than just his life."

"What?" Tim said.

"You must trust me!"

After Quinn maneuvered everyone into the hall, Adar closed and locked the door.

"I hope she knows what's she's doing," Quinn said.

"I hope you know what you're doing," Tim replied.

Chapter Eight

Six Days Before Christmas

When Sharon brought a tray of coffee and toast into the library and placed it on the table, Quinn smiled at her Mary Poppins housedress and fuzzy slippers. "Thanks, Sharon."

The woman bowed and backed out of the room.

The night had faded as slowly as continents drift. In the hours before dawn, the child's cries had rivaled the screams of damned souls and Tim had urged Quinn to break the door down. Instead, Quinn had turned and bolted down the stairs.

"Where the devil are you going?" Tim called as he ran after his friend, who had gone into the library. "Are you nuts? It sounds like she's ripping his little heart out."

Quinn picked up the leather-bound book and

stared at the drawing of the hairy beast. "Tim, you trusted me one time when every fiber in your body told you not to. What I'm about to tell you is going to sound totally insane, but I'm asking you to trust me again."

Quinn laid out the whole gruesome story: his uncle, the little girl in the swimming pool, the hairy beast. By the time the sun had cleared the brooding gray clouds on the horizon, Tim had run out of questions and it didn't appear that he liked any of the answers.

"I know you didn't sign on for this," Quinn said. "If you want to bail out, I won't blame you."

Tim stared at his cup of stale coffee, sipped it and sputtered, "Japs should stick to tea. This tastes like shit."

Quinn knew that was the only answer he'd get. A few minutes later Adar knocked on the door.

"He's out of danger for now."

Quinn's hands started shaking and he had to put the coffee cup down before spilling it all over the expensive rug.

"Here," Tim said as he reached for the coffeepot.

"No, thanks." Adar sank into the seat beside Tim and let her bag drop to the floor. "It was worse than I expected."

"Worse? What could be worse?" Quinn muttered. For a multimillionaire, Quinn looked remarkably like a beach bum. He hadn't shaved in two days, and he still wore the same jeans and T-shirt from the previous day. The only thing in his favor was that the odor of Adar's bitter herbs masked the smell of his unwashed body.

177

Adar had found time to slip on a long T-shirt under her robe. "I was sent here because something was weakening the defensive barriers that protect our world from the horrors of the next plane. I expected to find that some group of weekend witches had found one of the ancient manuscripts and was trifling with spells they didn't understand. I'm in over my head. I need help."

"I'm sorry. I don't understand a word of what you're saying." Quinn sighed.

"Quinn, listen to me! Q thought that thing that was feeding on him was his mother."

Quinn sat up in the chair. "Thing? What in God's name are you talking about?"

"As I examined that powder you collected, my mind brushed against something vile. It was incredibly cold and totally devoid of humanity. I believe it's something that your uncle either knowingly or unknowingly invited in from the dark recesses of the void."

"Are we talking ghosts here?"

"No, not a ghost. Until I have a chance to speak with my aunt, I can only guess, but I think we're up against one of the Old Ones."

"There you go again!" Tim said. "Old Ones! It sounds like we're being haunted by somebody's grandmother."

"Hardly. What I'm referring to is a powerful vampire life force that feeds off fear and blood."

"Is that so?" Quinn growled, pounding his fist on the arm of the chair. "Then I'll burn this fucking place down around its ears!"

"I'm sorry, Quinn. It would be wonderful if it were that simple."

He took a deep breath and let out a long, tired sigh. "Okay, give me the rest."

"That's what I'm trying to tell you. I don't know everything I need to know. I believe your uncle called this thing into existence, but he is dead and the creature is still here. Some person or group must be sustaining it."

"That's nuts," Tim said.

"Let me try to explain what little I know. All around us is a realm that exists apart but coexistent with ours. It's no big secret. Mankind has been aware of this alternate world for centuries. Did you think Lovecraft made it all up? Hundreds of cults and religions have worshiped these old gods because they have powers that can affect our world, but only as long as they are in our world.

"Okay, you don't believe it, but stay with me. It takes great talent and enormous power to pierce the barrier and bring one of these beings into this plane. And it takes even more power to keep it here. It's important to understand that these creatures are not natural to our world and you should thank whatever deity you worship that this is so. The best analogy I can make is that these things are like the north end of a powerful magnet and our world is the south end; they repel each other. To overcome this repulsive force takes an even greater power and that power must be maintained or the creature would be sucked back into its own world.

"Just look at what's required for something as simple as a fish in an aquarium. If the fish is to survive, an artificial environment must be prepared beforehand and then maintained. This environment has to have the right temperature. The water must be kept in the correct chemical balance. It needs a place to live and to feel safe."

"Couldn't Quinn's uncle have called this big guppy here and given it some kind of protective shield?" Tim asked.

"So help me, Tim," Quinn snapped. "One more dumb-ass question!"

"Sorry. I'm not trying to be funny, and I'm not saying I believe any of this stuff either," Tim said in a rush. "It's a hypothetical question."

"And a good one," Adar replied. "In the past that is just what was done. But from what I understand, the shield would have to be constantly maintained or the creature would have to expend a great deal of its own energy to remain. But trapped inside the shield it would be unable to feed, and as we have seen by the wound on Q's chest, this is not the case."

"What about that hairy thing Quinn told me about?" Tim asked. "You're sure it isn't the Old One?"

"The basilisk? No, it's a minor demon called forth from base elements. Any dilettante can create such a creature."

"Can you?" Quinn asked.

She pulled Quinn's mushroom jar from her bag. "Aconite, or wolf's bane, celandine, hellebore, hippomanes, the flesh from the head of a foal, the blood of a swine, and the ground scorched hooves of a tapir."

"Right!" Tim said. "Stuff anyone could pick up at the local supermarket."

"No, but they're not that hard to come by either. Don't forget, these are creations of the black arts. We refer to them as antilife because they are against the natural order of existence. No member of the Wicca would ever create one of these things."

"You keep saying Wicca," Quinn said. "If they're the good guys, who are the bad guys?"

"As I said before, the Wicca is an ancient religion, but by no means is it the only one. For every church out there that worships light, there is one that worships the dark forces. Many of these predate Christianity by thousands of years. For us, Wicca is a way of life. Where your modern religions speak of a supreme being, we dip our fingers daily into the fabric of the universe. We strive for harmony. The earth, the cosmos—they are our altars. Every time a factory dumps its poison into a river, we suffer. We follow a code as strict as any monk. The powers we deal with are just as real as electricity or nuclear fission, but remember, anyone with the knowledge can tap into this power. Just as you can plug into an outlet and watch television, another can murder a human being in an electric chair. These others I mentioned, their ways are old. Their methods, cruel. Power and evil, the pursuit of wealth and pleasure is their god."

"What can we do?" Quinn asked as he rubbed his bloodshot eyes.

"I've done what I can for now," Adar replied. "I've woven a spell of protection around his room. That's why I don't think we should move him. But someone must be with Q every minute. I sent Sharon up when I came in."

"What can she do?" Tim asked.

"She doesn't have to do anything except keep him in that room. Remember, in his current state, Q still believes this creature is his mother. If it succeeds in luring him out—"

"We're going to need more help," Tim said.

"Who?" Quinn asked.

"Leave it to me," Adar replied. "I need to make a long distance call to my family."

"Go ahead," Quinn said. "And, Adar, money isn't a problem."

"You're right, but not the way you expect."

"Great!" Tim said as soon as Adar closed the door behind her. "A bunch of dried-up old hags running around the place. You and I might as well move into the Y.M.C.A."

"What makes you think they're going to be hags? Even you'd have to admit Adar isn't too hard on the eyes."

"True. But didn't you ever read Macbeth? Would you be willing to give odds that the rest of 'em look like her?"

Marcus Peterson III's office was designed to impress people who didn't impress easily. In its center was a black lacquered desk that, under recessed track lighting, looked as big as an aircraft carrier. Its wood had been polished until you could hold the *Wall Street Journal* over it and read the stock quotations. The rest of the room was just as imposing; deep-cushioned wing chairs, thick carpeting, a lavish bar, art, a view of blue water.

Marcus Peterson III slammed his briefcase down

on top of the desk. "The gall of that ignorant cock-sucker!"

Opening the case, he took out the firm's folder on Quinn Ramsey and threw it open, peering through narrowed eyes at the eight-by-ten glossy of Quinn in uniform. Marcus had just come from a meeting with the partners, and he felt the need for the numbing solace of a strong drink. At the bar in the corner, he unlocked and opened the doors that protected his liquor. Grinning its cold welcome from the center shelf was a small crystal skull, a painful reminder of the fate that awaited him should he fail to obtain control of Ramsey's land on the big island.

The first three fingers of rye went down like warm milk. Marcus shivered, poured another two fingers, and shuffled back to his chair. One by one he arranged the file photos on the blotter like tarot cards. Some were aerial shots of lush green vegetation on the side of a volcano. One was a telephoto of a large white dog in high grass taken from a helicopter. The dog was staring up at the camera with bared fangs. One photo, a wide-angle view of the waterfall and derelict house, was particularly disturbing. Marcus placed it in front of him and stared, willing it to provide some clue as to why all of a sudden his life was going to hell.

It all started when, to everyone's astonishment, that greedy bastard Bernard Ramsey had succeeded in luring Moloch from the depths of the void. Instead of sharing that wealth of power, he had whisked the creature away and stashed him somewhere. Before the coven could get their hands on Bernard and pry the location out of Ramsey, he had been roasted alive and that nephew of his had come bumbling into the picture. What had Bernard been thinking of, leaving everything to that jerk? Was it revenge? Then just when it looked as if the coven might get things back under control, that idiot Stalkins had set himself on fire, and there was the fiasco at Ramsey's mansion.

But what had happened to that tattooed dummy who drove Marcus's car? Marcus had sent him out to do one simple little errand and the man had vanished! Marcus was surrounded by idiots. What was he supposed to do?

Then tonight everything had come to a head. The partners had threatened him—Marcus Peterson III—as if it were his fault that Quinn Ramsey had the luck of a six-legged rabbit.

Marcus downed the drink in two gulps and slammed the tumbler onto the desk hard enough to shatter a less sturdy glass. He started out of the chair to fix another and paused! He took a step and stopped short.

The hardwood floor in the outer office creaked as if someone had just walked across it. Marcus looked at his watch. It was ten-thirty at night. Who the devil could be running around at this hour? he fumed.

"Smythe, you sniveling geek!" Marcus stomped to the door and threw it open wide. "Smythe, quit skulking around out here like some fucking cur. If you want to know what I'm—"

The office was empty. Marcus stood in the doorway, looking out over a sea of faux walnut-and-steel desks, each with the blank screens of word processors staring sightlessly back. The only evidence that any human had ever set foot in the place was the photograph of his secretary's dreary family on her desk.

"You need another stiff one, old boy."

Back at the bar, Marcus demonstrated his restraint by pouring less than an inch of liquor into the glass. As he raised it to his lips, that noise came again. It was a funny kind of sound, like a Dutch girl walking slowly in wooden shoes. He chuckled at his own absurdity.

"Who the devil would be wearing wooden shoes in a law office?"

The alcohol was having its effect and speech was becoming a challenge. Marcus staggered to the door, almost dropping the glass, but now someone had turned off all the lights and the room was as black as a coal mine. And the smell!

"Who died out here?" He laughed, but stopped when a cloaked figure separated itself from the shadows.

"Who is that?" Marcus called, his throat suddenly dry in spite of the alcohol.

Slight and trim within the black cape, the form seemed to glide over the floor on golf cleats—hardly a figure to install fear. Since it was obviously someone sent by Smythe to make Marcus look foolish in the eyes of the others, Marcus decided to bluff it out.

"Want a drink?" he said holding out the glass.

A pale hand shot out of the loose sleeves and closed around the lawyer's wrist. Marcus yelped and tried to run, but it was as if his arm was caught in a fiery vise.

"Let go, you're hurting me!"

The hair on his wrist started to smoke, filling the room with the rank, sulfuric smell of burning flesh.

"Oh, God! Let me go!" The lawyer's suit began to smolder, adding the stench of burning silk to the air. "Who are you? Why are you hurting me?"

The specter remained impassive as Marcus's blood began to sizzle, and terrible, all-consuming fire spread inexorably through his veins. He screamed and jerked like a great wolf with its paw caught in a steel trap. Heat flowed into his chest, swelling his heart and lungs, making it all but impossible to breathe. Without warning, Marcus stumbled free and fell flat on his back. Stunned, he looked at the empty sleeve of his jacket, then at the spectral figure over him holding up his blazing arm like a torch.

Marcus's scream started dogs barking in alleys, his heels beat a drumroll on the floor as he thrashed back and forth on the carpet, smearing a snail's trail of blood, charred flesh and fabric over the flame-resistant fibers.

The grim figure looked on, neither enjoying nor sympathizing with the lawyer's torment until finally Marcus raised his head. The face was no longer recognizable. The man's watery blue eyes were running down his cheeks; his tongue was the color of eggplant. He opened his mouth to make one last plea for mercy and exploded into flames like a pile of gasoline-soaked rags.

The shrouded figure stood over the pyre until it had cooled to black bones, then tossed a single *ohelo* berry on the remains.

"Haole pau."

Chapter Nine

Four Days Before Christmas

Okata parked behind the second of two airport courtesy vans that were blocking the entrance to Quinn Ramsey's mansion. She climbed out and leaned on the open door with her arms, careful not to get grease on her black pantsuit. She watched as Tim and Quinn ferried suitcases, boxes and bags into the house.

On his next trip back to the van, Quinn spotted Okata and trotted over. "Hey, Sarge."

"Quinn, what's up? You taking in tourists now?"

He laughed nervously. In the 36 hours since Okata had last seen him, Quinn looked as if he'd dropped ten pounds. His face was clean shaven but haggard, and his eyes were hollow, as if he'd had a high fever. She reached up and removed a pin from the collar of his new flowered shirt.

"Oh, no. Adar's family is here for the holidays."

"All her relatives are female?"

Quinn gave her that self-conscious laugh again. "Well, no. The guys went on a golf vacation to Arizona. You know what insensitive pigs men can be."

Okata nodded and slammed the car door. Tim came trotting out and picked up another suitcase. He gave a dirty look to the taxi driver lounging against the side of the van. When Tim saw Okata coming toward him, he dropped the bag and raised his hands.

"Don't shoot, copper."

An old lady whom Okata had never seen before stepped out onto the front steps and called, "Mr. Wolinsky! I'm waiting for that suitcase." She had a head of thick snow-white hair and a no-nonsense attitude. "Take it right up to my room."

A sick smile spread over Tim's face, but he picked up the suitcase and ran off without a word. Another strange woman came out as Tim walked in. Her small size and distinctly Asian features made her stand out like a speckled egg in the sea of Caucasian faces.

"Who's that?" Okata asked.

Quinn followed her gaze. "Oh, that's our new housekeeper. Tim found her."

"Is she a local?"

"I'm not sure. Look. Are you just visiting or what?" Quinn asked.

"Relax. I just stopped by to check in with the stakeout. Hanson said you'd been invaded by a pack of sorority babes."

"Well, it's good to see you, but—"

"Quinn," she said, hoping to stop his retreat. "Have you talked to that lawyer of yours lately?"

Quinn paused. "Peterson? I think he's still pissed at me. He hasn't called in a week or so. Why?"

"His secretary found him in his office yesterday."

Quinn turned and retraced his steps, standing near enough to keep from being overheard. "What happened?"

"Another crispy critter. I'll never go to another luau"

Quinn shook his head sadly, but he seemed too tired to do more. "Gail, I'm sorry to hear that, but I'm kind of busy right now. Can we talk about this later?"

She noted the way his shoulders drooped and nodded. "Sure. Give me a call in the next couple of days. If you're lucky, I'll buy you lunch." She slid back behind the wheel of the car and drove away. Tim came back and they watched the Plymouth fade. "What did she want?"

"Just to bring me some more good news."

Tim and Quinn had fortified themselves with a couple of cold beers and retreated to the safety of the backyard. They stood at the edge of the cliff, watching three of Adar's cousins sunning on the beach in bathing suits that were much less conservative than Adar's. The sun was low and orange, bisected every now and then by hungry gulls dive-bombing a school of bluefish like angry kamikazes.

"I wish I'd taken you up on that bet." Quinn chuckled.

"Where are the rest of them?" Tim asked.

"One's outside Q's room and another is inside in a chair. The rest, who knows."

In all, 12 women had shown up. One was Adar's great-aunt Mildred and one was Aunt Mildred's mother, Anna.

"They don't look much like witches," Tim said, enjoying the way the bikinis exposed more than they covered. "No brooms, no peaked hats. They don't even have black cats."

"I'm afraid you bought into all those old Halloween stereotypes," Quinn said as he sipped the beer. He was trying to work up some enthusiasm about the women being there, but he wasn't having much luck. He felt like a man lost at sea; cut, bleeding and surrounded by sharks. He needed a lifejacket, but he'd been handed a bunch of bathing beauties. "They look like coeds, except for Aunt Mildred and the mother of course."

"Chaperons."

"No shit."

"Anna looks like she could've been in the welcoming committee when Columbus landed. And that aunt—wow! You think maybe she swallowed a barrel of sour pickles?"

"She's eighty-six," Adar said from behind them, and the men flinched as she stepped to the edge of the cliff.

"No offense," Tim said.

When she tried a smile, but achieved only a tired contraction of muscles, Quinn asked, "What's the plan?"

"Marsha and Penny are going to stay with Q tonight. It'll give the rest of us a chance to get some sleep. Tomorrow morning, we'll hold a convocation to see if we can locate the focus of the Old One. Then, if we're successful, we'll try to pinpoint the loci of the other activity."

Quinn put his hand on her shoulder. "I appreciate this."

This time her smile was genuine. "Don't relax just yet. His room is safe, but until we have a chance to extend the charm to the rest of the house, no place else is. I suggest we try not to be alone any time tonight."

"Okay," Tim said with a sigh. "I'll pitch in. See the girl with the auburn hair and black suit? I'm willing to let her stay with me tonight. For her protection, you understand."

"What a guy." Quinn chuckled.

"That's really nice of you, Tim," Adar said, smiling brightly. "But I'd be careful if I were you. Penny is an eighth-level adept. All she needs to progress to the ninth level is to eat the heart of a lover."

As Adar went back to the house, Tim stared at the woman on the beach. She turned over on her stomach and reached behind her back to unfasten the strap.

"Adar's kidding, right?" Tim asked.

"Of course she's kidding, idiot. That's her sister."

"Oh, right. She's just trying to scare me."

"And a fine job she did too."

The woman dashed across the plush Oriental rug and picked up the cordless phone on the third ring. She was naked, her skin radiating health like that of a Swedish volleyball star.

"Yes?" She frowned. "Hello, Mother. What's the matter now?"

The frown slipped and was replaced by a look of hellish wrath. "Who would dare such a thing?"

She began to pace, walking with willowy strides out to the patio and looking her rancor at the human ants milling about on the street below.

"Well don't try to tell me it was an accident this time! Marcus was too paranoid to set himself on fire."

The strident clamor of Honolulu's traffic reached her like the sound of distant battle; the haze of its exhaust, like the smoke of distant fires. She wondered how the average man on the street put up with his daily struggle to earn a paltry living.

"What group? I know they're here, but they just arrived. How could they be responsible for any of this? Yes, yes. Somebody's at the door," she said when the doorbell sounded.

The woman held the phone with her shoulder as she fumbled with the locks. "Don't be ridiculous, Mother. Who would dare challenge me?"

The door opened and a man in his sixties bustled into the room, wearing his anxiety like a club tie. "It's only Albert. I have to hang up now before he has a coronary."

Albert Smythe buzzed about the room, leaving a trail of nervous perspiration as potent as pheromones. That he was in the room with a gorgeous naked woman seemed to have escaped his notice.

"You heard about Marcus?" Smythe asked.

"Yes."

"What are we going to do?"

"Well, I'm going to move my trust account."

Smythe plopped down on the Danish modern sofa,

192

squeezing his knees together like a truant in the principal's office. Then he began twisting his Harvard class ring. "That's not funny. Somebody is after us."

The woman threw her head back and laughed. "Who, Albert? The government? The FBI? The boy scouts? Who?"

"What about that witch who lives at Ramsey's estate?"

The woman shook her head. "Give me a break."

"Then what about the rumors?"

"Rumors?" Her laugh set his teeth on edge. "You mean the curse? Stories spread by a bunch of old Hawaiian fishwives? You of all people should know that's a crock."

"Then what about Ramsey?"

"Which one? The dead one or the ex-flatfoot?"

"Make fun! All I know is this whole mess started when Bernard bought that land. We never should have begun this. We were doing so well."

The woman stalked over and backhanded the old man across the face hard enough to bloody his nose. "Stop your sniveling!"

She licked his blood from her hand and lowered her voice. "Just once, I'd like to have someone like Quinn on my side, instead of a bunch of half-wits and drunks. Don't you realize that land is going to make us powerful beyond imagining?" She pushed Smythe's hand away from his nose and caught the bloody snot on her finger. "Marcus was a creep and a cheat. He obviously crossed the wrong people somewhere down the line." She cleaned her fingers with her tongue.

"But, I thought we were—I mean your charms, I

thought they protected us."

"They do, idiot, from bad luck and the dark masters. But nothing can save you from your own stupidity!"

The heat from her body permeated the room. Cupping her hands behind the old lawyer's head, she scratched his ears like he was her pet Doberman.

"Let me worry about Marcus, okay?" Her voice had dropped to a level that hit Smythe right between his legs. The effect was immediate and, for a man his age, impressive.

"But Randall? And Bernard?"

She stood in front of him and spread her feet apart. "Everything is under control. Now, come on, Albert. Mommy will take care of you. How about taking care of me?"

She pulled his head forward, closed her eyes and thought about the photograph of the smiling man in the sheriff's uniform.

That evening, after Sharon had made pizza again for everyone and retired to clean the kitchen, and Quinn had gone up to talk to Adar's sister outside of his son's bedroom, Tim and Adar sat around the massive dining room table. Tim was in the process of polishing off his sixth beer. He watched Adar sip herbal tea and pick at the last few globs of cherry Jell-O with low-cal topping, the jewel in the Asian housekeeper's dessert crown.

"Have you known Quinn long?" Adar asked.

Tim looked down the opening of the long-neck bottom as if the question had come out from its bottom. " 'Bout ten years."

"How did you meet?"

"The first time, he and Kerry busted me behind a stereo store on Forest Hill Boulevard."

"And that's how you became friends?"

"Not exactly. About four years ago, right around this time of year, I broke into a pawn shop on Flagler to do my Christmas shopping. I had a really primo Sony VCR, and when I came out the back, Quinn and Carl were leaning on their patrol car. They had me, dead bang. The other times Quinn had popped me, it hadn't stuck, but this time I was staring at a long vacation in Raiford."

"So what happened?"

"He didn't arrest me."

"He didn't? Why not?"

"He was looking for a fight, so he beat the shit out of me instead. Hey, don't let that choirboy act of his fool you. Quinn and Kerry used to have a lot of perps fall down and break things on the way to lockup. When Quinn dropped his gun belt, Kerry stepped in front of him and tried to talk him out of it, but Quinn told him to get in the car and shut up. Then he hit me harder than I'd ever been hit in my life. I'm not bragging, but I was in pretty good shape at the time. I worked out at the gym and took boxing and other stuff, so I figured I was going to get a chance to clean this cop's clock, free of charge. On top of that, I could smell the whisky on his breath. He was half in the bag."

"So you beat him up and that made you friends?"

"No, like I said, he beat me to a bloody pulp. He went crazy. I hit him and he didn't feel it. I was in the hospital for five days."

Adar rolled her eyes. "Now I understand. He beat

you senseless and put you in the hospital. Naturally you became bosom buddies."

Tim chuckled and shook his head. "No, that wasn't it either. It was Q. I was going to sue the prick for everything he had. He'd broken my jaw and a couple of ribs with his fists. I think my pride was hurt as much as anything. So, anyway, there I was in the lockup at the hospital, stacks of money jumping hurdles in my head and in walked Carl Kerry. The big dork even had a fistful of daisies." Tim laughed at the memory. "They looked like weeds in his big mit. Anyway, I was so surprised I didn't yell for the nurse. Kerry pulled up a chair and asked how I was feeling. "How do you think I'm feeling?" I said. Then Kerry went into this long, drawn-out story about how Quinn's wife was killed by a psycho he'd arrested for DUI three times and how Quinn had been drinking and he didn't mean what he did.

" 'So he sent you to keep me from suing him," I yelled. But Kerry said, Quinn didn't even know he was there. He said Quinn didn't give a damn about me suing him, 'cause he didn't have anything anyway, but that he felt like shit about what he did.

"Well, naturally, I didn't believe a word of it. It was just one cop covering for another, right? But Kerry brought in Q. The kid didn't know me from Adam, didn't even know why he was there. He sat by my bed and asked a bunch of dumb kid questions: why is my head bandaged? Does it hurt? What are all those black marks on my face? That kinda stuff. So, naturally, me being the world's biggest pussy—excuse me." Adar just smiled and waved for him to go on. "Anyway, me being a sap, I said I wouldn't press charges and I'd say I fell down a flight of stairs. Then I forgot about it and concentrated on trying to get a date with the nurse.

"The day before I was supposed to be arraigned, Quinn walked in. The man still looked like shit— shaky and pale, like he fell off the wagon onto his head. He said Kerry had told him I wasn't pressing charges and he asked why. I told him this fairy tale about how I deserved it for being so careless and letting a couple of clods like him and Kerry catch me. I don't think he brought my lie, but he nodded like it made perfect sense. After a while he got up to leave, but before he went out, he stopped and said, 'Oh, by the way.' Real nonchalant. Butter wouldn't've melted in his mouth. 'Seems like Carl forgot to read you your rights, so the DA had to drop the charges.' And then he strolled out.

"I felt better right away. Hell, I'd take a beating over hard time in Raiford any day. The next morning I walked out of the hospital and Quinn was waiting for me in that old piece-of-shit Toyota of his. 'Get in,' he said. He drove me to a store over on Okeechobee with a big for-sale sign on it. Quinn said he heard that I was good with security systems, seeing as how I was always finding ways past them. He said all the suits on Palm Beach were paranoid as shit, and he thought I'd be pretty good at installing security systems. So I said with my sheet, nobody was going to lend me money. He offered to cosign and said he knew the old geezer who was selling and that the guy would hold the note. So in one week I was out of the hospital, out of jail, and into a new life."

"And that's exactly the way it happened?" Adar asked after a moment.

"Well," Tim replied with a laugh, "I might have skipped over the part where Kerry threatened to bury me in pieces in some orange grove if I pressed charges. But I swear, the rest is gospel."

At the same time Adar was in the dining room hearing the story of how Quinn and Tim Wolinsky became friends, Quinn was sitting on the floor outside Q's bedroom pumping Adar's sister for information.

At 23, Penny had the attitude of a nun. She acted as if she were on intimate terms with somebody you'd really like to know. She was a part-time student in Pennsylvania, majoring in, of all things, abnormal psychology. She had Adar's lustrous red hair, but she wore it long and loose around her shoulders. She also had the same freckles and upturned nose, but where Adar's eyes were a soft sea green, Penny's were ice blue and hard as a frozen lake. Penny could be personable and friendly, but her smile was guarded and often didn't go any farther than her lips. From Quinn's point of view the worst thing about Penny was that when it came to Adar she dispensed information as freely as a sphinx. Even casual questions were met with polite, carefully worded evasions.

"Aw, Penny," Quinn said, finally throwing up his hands in frustration. "I don't work for *Sixty Minutes*."

"I know that. It's just that we're very private people."

"Come on. What was she like as a little girl?"

"She didn't like *Bewitched* and once tried to make contact with *Casper, The Friendly Ghost*."

"Really?" Quinn asked with a wide grin.

"Maybe."

As they were talking, Adar's cousin Beth—a painfully shy girl with lustrous jet-black hair and pale blue eyes—came down the stairs in a bathrobe. "Do you mind if I go for a swim?"

"Of course not. You have the run of the place," Quinn said.

After she returned a meek smile and flopped down the stairs in her sandals, Quinn asked, "That was Beth, wasn't it? I'm terrible with names."

Penny nodded. "I guess we can be pretty intimidating when we come at you all at once."

"How did Adar get in touch with everyone so fast?"

"We were at the house in Massachusetts. We've been there ever since this business began."

"Penny, uh, are any of you married? Do you have boyfriends?"

The first chink appeared in Penny's armor. She took a deep breath and let it out slowly. "Well, mother was married."

Quinn blushed. "Gosh, I didn't mean—"

"No, I know that. I was just pulling your chain. Most of us date, but generally we don't go steady. As you can imagine, it takes a certain kind of man to accept who we are."

"I bet."

"No, Quinn, really. It's more than just the ceremonies and potions and healings. We are very close as a family. Some men would feel threatened by that closeness. They'd feel shut out."

"Don't men ever participate in your rites?"

"Sometimes, but it's rare. For some reason, women generally seem to inherit the power. We think it's because of the UTD."

"Okay, I know I'm going to regret this: What's the UTD?"

She punched his shoulder and lowered her voice conspiratorially, "It's a woman's secret weapon. The Uterine-Tracking Device. Every time Daddy lost something, like his keys or his wallet, he'd run around the house yelling for Mom. Then she'd get all mad and ask him why he always called her when he lost something. He said because a woman's uterus is a tracking device for lost objects. And the funny thing was, she usually did find whatever he'd lost."

"What about you?" Quinn asked. "Are you dating?"

She winked at him. "You bet. He's a real hunk. He coaches soccer at Boston College."

"What about Beth there?" he asked, nodding toward the pool, but Penny's smile disappeared. "She's a beautiful girl. I bet she has guys lined up."

"Beth is shy."

"But—"

"Why don't we get a bite to eat?" Penny said quickly. "I'll just stick my head in and see if Marsha wants something."

He reached out and touched her arm. "I didn't mean anything."

Penny hesitated, then nodded. "It's okay. Old habits die hard."

Quinn followed her into the bedroom while she took her cousin's order. Q was on the bed reading a comic book. He didn't come out from behind the colored pages, so Quinn just stood with his hands in his pockets feeling helpless.

Back on the landing, as they started down to the

kitchen, Penny asked, "You call Adar 'Dar'?"

"Yeah?"

"She was always so serious. She never had a nick-name."

"It's not much of a nickname," Quinn replied, "not like stinky or spike."

"Try spike on her if you like, but I'd steer clear of stinky."

They went into the kitchen to raid the icebox. They stacked bread, mustard, ham, cheese and roast beef on the counter. Penny put the kettle on for tea.

"Adar doesn't like her nickname?" Quinn asked.

"I think she does, but don't tell her I told you."

"Why not?"

"She might turn me into a toad."

Quinn laughed, but Penny didn't.

The pool area was a steamy room the size of a small gymnasium and it reeked of chlorine and mildew. The walls on three sides were made from glass bricks so that swimmers could pretend they were bathing in the rugged Pacific instead of a pool filled with water kept at a constant 89 degrees. In the far corner were a large hot tub, a redwood sauna cabinet for four and a padded massage table.

The outer door echoed hollowly when Beth closed and locked it, and the bottoms of her sandals squealed like mice as she padded across to the small changing room and dropped her robe on the bench. She stripped off her suit and the leather pouch that hung around her neck so that she could rinse off before entering the water. Swimming was Beth's passion, and she was looking forward to a good 50 laps.

Out of the shower spurted tepid water that smelled of sulfur, but she ignored the odor, closed her eyes and turned in a tight circle to let it run over her sleek body. When the shower cooled, she wrapped herself in a towel and went to collect her suit. As she walked in front of the wall mirror, Beth did something she rarely did. She stopped and examined her reflection; high breasts, wasp waist, smooth, flaring hips, all topped by a face that would have looked right at home on the cover of a fashion magazine. Opening the towel, she stared. It was still there!

In her fantasies, Beth allowed herself to believe that if she kept her body covered, if she didn't look at it or think about it, the horrible deformity would just vanish like a rain cloud in the desert. Hot tears came unbidden as she stared at the third nipple jutting from the side of her right breast—the witch's mark she bore as a chromosomal gift from some long dead ancestor.

Heredity, they said. Heredity! Her family threw the word out so casually, as if it could take away her shame or the sting of revulsion she saw in the eyes of her cousins. Aunt Mildred said in time Beth would be proud, that her feelings came from being the youngest in the family and as yet inexperienced in the arts. But that was easy for them to say. None of the others bore the mark. Look at Adar! she fumed. Alabaster complexion as fine and smooth as doeskin, not a blemish, not a scar. Sometimes Beth hated her cousin.

Cheer up, she told herself. Dry those bitter tears and live life to the fullest!

"Horse hockey!"

A sudden cool draft interrupted her self-pity. Shivering, Beth scurried back to the lockers. When she reached the bench, her sandals were still there, but the suit, robe and rawhide necklace had disappeared. Standing in the tiny room, she was too amazed at first to be concerned. She just couldn't imagine who could have taken her things. The family knew how sensitive she was about her body. None of them would ever do anything so mean.

Then she remembered the way Mr. Call-Me-Tim Wolinsky had looked at her with his hot eyes and daring smile. She could feel that insolent gaze down low in her belly. But of course he didn't know about the mark.

That had to be it, she decided. Somehow, he had let himself in while she was in the shower, and he had hidden her things as a prank. Maybe later she would cast a slime lizard into his underwear drawer and see how funny he thought that was. She smiled grimly to herself.

Then she was struck by a horrible thought! What if he had seen her in the shower?

"Oh, God," she moaned, mortified to her very core.

She ran to the lockers. Surely he'd put her things in one of them. Behind the first door she found a wrinkled and moldy pair of men's underwear.

"Ugh!" She slammed the door.

Behind her, the lock turned with a soft metallic click. Beth looked around, but she was alone and didn't pay any attention to the door. The second and third lockers were also empty.

Beth gathered the damp towel tightly about her body. She couldn't understand why anyone would keep a shower room so cold. Any possibility the situation had of being funny had disappeared when the goosebumps began to swell.

As Beth reached for the handle on the last locker, her budding extrasensory talents kicked in. She jerked her hand away and took an instinctive step back. Something inside scratched softly against the door.

She tried to convince herself that Tim had somehow squeezed his bulk into that narrow steel closet. After all, it was just the sort of juvenile stunt a man like that would pull. Then the nerve-racking scraping came again—slow and soft, like dozens of tiny feet scurrying over tinfoil. The sound sent slivers of ice down her spine.

"Mr. Wolinsky, I don't think you're funny."

At the sound of her voice the locker door began to vibrate as something with hundreds of leathery legs clawed frantically to get out of the locker. Out into the confines of that tiny room. Out at her!

Beth backed away, watching in horrified fascination as the door seemed to bulge as if pregnant with unspeakable life. At the very instant she turned to run, the door gave way and a solid black wall of four-and-five-inch scorpions spilled across the floor. Beth dropped the towel and ran for her life. She hit the door at full speed, but it was locked and it threw her back into the room. Her bare feet skidded on the wet tiles and she fell flat. When she looked back, the hellish spawn was flowing toward her in an unstoppable wave. She crossed her arms over her face and filled her lungs for one last scream, but the scorpions swarmed over her, filling her mouth, cutting her lips and eyes to ribbons with their scythelike pinchers, drowning her in segmented legs and sinking their dripping stingers into every inch of exposed flesh. In seconds, the potent poison swelled her tongue, cutting off her air. Unable to breathe, Beth fought like a wildcat, but long after she was dead, the scorpions continued their mindless pinching and stinging.

Quinn was in the library with one leg dangling over the arm of his favorite chair when Adar came in and asked. "Have you seen Beth?"

Adar had changed into a black jumpsuit open at the collar to frame her amulet. Penny was leaning on the door in a matching outfit.

"Last time I saw her, she was going for a swim."

"That's what Penny said, but that was three hours ago. I checked the pool. The door's locked and I didn't see anyone."

"That's odd," he replied, rising to his feet. "The key is in the office."

The women followed him to the office and then to the entrance to the pool. Quinn tried several keys before he found the right one and they stepped cautiously onto the slippery tiles.

"She's not here," Penny said.

"Maybe she went down to the beach," Quinn suggested.

Penny started around the pool, examining the bottom with a troubled expression.

"Not after dark," Adar replied.

"I guess we'd better check the grounds," Quinn said with a shrug.

"What's in there?" Penny asked.

"Shower, lockers."

At the changing room door, Penny skidded to halt

so fast that she almost toppled over. "Adar!"

Beth's body was a discolored mass of flesh that had swelled to twice its normal size; it was leaking viscous yellow fluid from a thousand tiny puncture wounds. Quinn pushed on the door, but it wouldn't budge. He tried to find the key to fit the lock, but dropped the ring twice before locating the right one.

Penny held Quinn's arm and pointed. Dozens of the black arachnids were hurling themselves against the glass. Several of the female scorpions had made a nest in Beth's hair, and their bellies were crawling with their brood. "What are those things?"

"Scorpions," Adar replied.

"Gross," Quinn said. "I didn't know there were scorpions on Maui."

"There aren't," Adar replied. "Not like those anyway."

"We can't just leave her in there," Quinn said.

"I'll get Mildred," Penny said.

Penny's tennis shoes squeaked as she ran across the tile. The only other sounds were the muted hum of the pool filter and Adar's sobbing.

Great-aunt Mildred had been preparing for bed when Penny pounded on her door, and she rushed into the pool area wearing a long flannel nightshirt with her hair up in a set of oversize rollers that made her look like a praying mantis. She stared at the body through the glass door.

"This is my fault," Mildred said. A lonely tear ran down the heavily wrinkled cheek. "I should have made sure the house was safe."

"You couldn't have known," Adar said.

"Can't we get her out of there?" Penny asked.

Mildred gave a curt bob of her head. "Get the others."

"Shouldn't we call someone?" Quinn asked. "Okata or an ambulance at least?"

Mildred grasped the beaded leather pouch underneath the flannel. "They can't help her now," she replied and began spitting out a string of guttural words.

The scorpions reacted as if they had just spotted an exterminator, scurrying toward the corners and beneath the lockers, but it didn't save them. One by one, they exploded into puffs of green light. In moments the room was clear, and Mildred and Adar went to their knees beside the girl's body.

"I was a fool to underestimate this creature," Mildred said. She brushed a matted lock of hair away from Beth's face.

After a moment, Quinn picked up the towel Beth had dropped and covered her face. He kept glancing over his shoulder, half expecting to see one of the segmented killers lurking back in the dark corners. "What are we going to do?"

Adar helped her great-aunt to her feet, and Mildred said, "Find out what we're up against."

Quinn's face was a mask of fury. "When we find this thing, we're going to kick its ass, I hope."

"Swallow that anger, Mr. Ramsey," Mildred snapped. "It won't help. Besides, you don't hate the wolf when it kills or a snake because it strikes. It is the nature of the beast."

"Maybe I wouldn't hate them," Quinn said. "But I sure as shit would blow the sons of bitches away."

The women wrapped Beth in a clean sheet, carried her to a ground-floor bedroom and said a few brief words over her. By the time they finished, the girl's body was back to its normal size and her face was smooth and almost relaxed. When the women had their tears under control, everyone congregated in the library. Quinn grabbed Tim before he had a chance to drink himself into a coma and sent him to guard Q. Quinn had wanted to watch the boy himself, but Mildred vetoed that idea.

"We have to have thirteen," she said. "Beth is dead, so you're elected."

"Me? Good grief, Mildred. I don't know anything about magic. What do you expect me to do?"

"Just sit in the circle and concentrate when we tell you. Anything less than thirteen would put all of us in jeopardy."

Quinn gave in and stood to the side as the family prepared the room. One pair of cousins got the fire going while another made the rounds of the windows and doors, weaving spells in a verbal hash of prehistoric tongues. Anna, Mildred's mother, sat in a leather chair and watched while Adar, Penny and the rest drew a five-pointed star on the floor in front of the fireplace and surrounded it with alien letters and symbols. Mildred acted as overseer, checking the strength of the protective charms and the accuracy of the diagrams. All those acrylics and jars of glitter dust reminded Quinn of his third-grade art class.

When Mildred was satisfied, she pulled the tiger skin that normally covered the floor by the desk and set it next to the drawing. Then she let down her hair and unzipped her jumpsuit. The others followed her lead. Even Anna shook out an impressive mass of silver curls and stepped out of her clothing.

When Quinn did a surreptitious moon walk toward the door, Mildred said, "Where do you think you're going? Get undressed and get over here."

"I'm not taking my clothes off."

"And why not? You think you've got something special to hide?"

It was like a nightmare in which Quinn inadvertently stumbled into the wrong dressing room. The more Quinn tried to find a safe place for his eyes, the more soft pink female flesh they landed on. He thought staring at Anna was the safest course, but when he looked into her eyes, she grinned at him, giving him a good look at all five teeth and yards of pink gums. With no other choice, he began unbuttoning his shirt.

"Okay, but nobody's rubbing any of that Ben Gay stuff on me," he said.

The situation was almost funny. One naked woman was erotic; a dozen were intimidating. They sat in a loose circle around the star. Mildred at one point with her back to the fire, then Adar on her right, Penny to her left. Quinn sat opposite, between Marsha, a Nordic giant with Wagnerian breasts, and Janice, a petite brunette with pencil-thin legs and enchanting tufts of soft down under her arms.

"Ladies," Mildred said, "any of you who thought this was going to be an all-expenses-paid vacation in Hawaii better get that idea out of your heads. This thing we're about to summon murdered Beth, and I guarantee you, if we give it half a chance, it'll do the same to us.

"Now empty your minds. Mr. Ramsey," Mildred said, "we are going to attempt to root out this entity and force it to answer some questions, but first you should know a few things. Just as in our physical world, the netherworld has its hierarchy. It has an emperor, a prince, a grand duke, a prime minister—right on down to the foot soldiers that slog about in the ether. In their world, these beings live without physical warmth or material existence, yet they live with a constant gnawing hunger. In a way, they are like dark flowers that must feed on dark emotions to blossom. Fear, envy, hatred, greed, anger and pain are their food. Just as the sun is the source of sustenance for flowers, the suffering of mankind is fodder for these beings.

"Now we have no idea which of the demonic spirits we are about to encounter. Pray that it's one of the lower creatures, an elemental such as Urieus or Egin; one of the inferiors, Bael or Forau, for instance; or one of the many subordinate spirits."

"But you don't think it's the devil?" Quinn asked.

Mildred let slip a bleak smile. "Hardly. Contrary to what you see in the movies, Lucifer and the superior spirits rarely get directly involved with mankind. In this case, that would be like using an atomic bomb to sink a row boat."

While Quinn wondered if he had just been insulted, Mildred said, "We are going to try to establish contact now."

"Wait!" Quinn said. "What if it doesn't feel like talking?"

"That's unlikely. As inhuman as these creatures are, they are like us in one respect. They have egos the size of Montana. Normally they jump at the chance to confront a human being, and they will try to instill maximum fear and loathing."

"So why aren't people tripping over these things every day?" Quinn asked, genuinely perplexed.

"A fair question. You see, only a few have the necessary power to enter this realm of their own volition. The others must be summoned by someone on this side that has both the knowledge and the power."

"What about those main spirits? Don't they have the power to come here?"

"The superior spirits? They rarely need to. To understand this you must understand the world they inhabit. One of the most powerful of the dark emotions is envy. Now try to picture a world where every being loathes every other, where the powerful demons sup on the envy and jealousy of their subordinates. The superiors—Lucifer, Beelzebub and Astaroth, the Grand Duke of the netherworld—can live indefinitely on the hateful emotions of the less powerful creatures. And the fact that their minions are aware of this only adds fuel to the fires of their hate."

"So what you're telling me is that we're being haunted by one of these less powerful hobgoblins?"

"Probably. But any of the inferiors is terrible enough to drive a man mad with a look. The reason we can't be sure is because of the power this one wields. To call forth those scorpions, to cast them into that dressing room and then to have them remain intact even after poor Beth was dead required enormous power. I believe—I hope—the power came from the human devils who called the creature into this world and not from the being itself."

"I don't mean to insult you, Mildred, but why don't we just get a priest to do an exorcism?"

She laughed. Her laugh sounded surprisingly girlish coming from her withered body. "I don't mind. But good luck finding a priest to do an exorcism. To be effective, the exorcist must believe he is in mortal combat with evil. The modern church thinks possession, demons and the devil are passe. The theologically correct preach possession is a symptom of a diseased mind, and even if you could get the church to agree, they'd send some old geezer who would just go through the motions because in his mind he would really be treating your delusions."

"This will keep us safe?" Quinn asked, touching the leather pouch hanging around his neck.

"Let's hope so. We had better get started." The white-haired woman deftly cracked her knuckles and wiggled each digit. "I will pronounce a short prayer of consecration and then we will join hands."

At that moment, more than anything else, Quinn wished he were back in the safety of his patrol car. As usual, his face gave him away.

"Mr. Ramsey, this is very important! Once we start, do not let go of the hands on either side of you. Do not attempt to leave the circle. I can promise you that, if this being materializes, it will take a form guaranteed to cause us the most distress, and it will be calculated to work on the weakest member of the circle."

She stared at him to make sure he took her meaning. "As long as we remain united, the attack will be on our minds, but if anyone should break the circle, the entity could swoop down and devour one or more of us."

"Hold the phone! I thought you said that these things were incorporeal, that they only fed on emotions," Quinn said as his body began to drip with sweat.

"I never said that. The spirits feed on emotions alone in their own world! When they come into our sphere, an inferior is powerful enough to grab you with its mind and squeeze every ounce of mental and physical energy from you the way you would wring water out of a washcloth. Your body might not be touched, but your soul, your very essence could be sucked out in the blink of an eye. And a superior could pick any one of us up and tear us apart, as if plucking feathers from a chicken. Do I make myself clear?"

Quinn felt nauseated and light-headed. "Damned if I do. Damned if I don't."

"No! I assure you, Mr. Ramsey. Damnation will be like a trip to Disney World compared to what will happen if you break the circle."

Quinn examined the women's faces. Each was tight with determination. Some of the eyes were blue, others green; a few were bright brown like new copper pennies, but all were fixed on him.

"Call me Quinn."

Chapter Ten

12:01 a.m.—Three Days Before Christmas

The women had closed their eyes, shutting out Quinn, the library, and, as far as he could tell, the earth, the moon and the heavens. The icy floor made his bare behind ache, and he cast an envious eye at the plush tiger skin Mildred was sitting on. In a moment, the women bowed their heads and Mildred's lips moved, but she uttered no sound. Quinn felt a surge like a sudden increase in air pressure, and he wondered if he should close his eyes and bow his head too.

Then Mildred looked up and told everyone to join hands. Quinn clasped hands with the women on either side. Their palms were smooth and dry; his were wet.

Mildred's milky-blue eyes were tinged with rings

of green fire. "Focus on your son, Quinn. Focus on the love you have for him—just that love. Let go your fear. Empty it onto the floor. Rid yourself of hate, greed, anger or anything that could help our enemy."

Then Mildred asked the women if they were ready to proceed with the ritual. One by one, the heads nodded. When Mildred's eyes reached Quinn, he felt like a hot can of beer that had been dropped from a second-story window, but he nodded anyway.

In the midst of all his tension and fear, Quinn was able to drift back to the day his wife Kathy had brought Q home for the first time. Quinn had spent weeks painting the spare room pink because Kathy had been sure their baby was going to be a girl. He remembered how Q's wrinkled little body had fit so perfectly into his arms and how he had promised his son to repaint the room blue before it scarred his tiny psyche.

"I conjure thee hateful spirit by the power of love and the creator of the universe," Mildred said, oblivious to Quinn's fond memories. "Appear to this circle to answer all questions put to thee."

Mildred continued in a language that resembled Latin, then switched to another that made her sound like a consumptive clearing her throat. The ritualistic susurration seemed to be endless. Quinn was conscious of the cold floor, his cramped legs and Adar sitting Indian fashion on the other side of the pentagram. He tried to control his thoughts as he had been instructed. He wrinkled his forehead and squinted to shut out all visual distractions. But he might as well have been trying to make snowballs out of tap water because his eyes were drawn to Adar's face.

The first indication that something was happening was a sudden chill. To Quinn's surprise, the fire had not gone out; if anything, it was blazing higher than before. The women on either side of him tightened their grips, and his mind swelled with rage.

They don't trust me! They think I'm gonna run from a draft of cold air. Fuck this! he fumed. Then he tried to pull away, but the girls' fingers were made of steel.

"Think!" Marsha said in a harsh whisper. "Fight!"

What was she babbling about? he wondered. Fight what? Fight all this ridiculous mumbo jumbo? I should get up and check on Q.

Quinn did not move although he could feel red fury goading him to some kind of action. From the other side of the pentagram, Adar sent crystals of ice into his fevered brain to cool the rage. It was then that he noticed his breath floating in front of his face and the light bulb of realization finally clicked on: Something was happening.

The flames in the hearth had taken on a cold blue tint, and they were crackling like icicles. In front of the fire, a thick mist poured out from the burning logs, swirling and condensing like boiling milk until it took the shape of a beautiful naked woman with red hair and eyes.

"Kathy!" Quinn whispered hoarsely.

The apparition smiled at Quinn, exposing a mouth full of obsidian-edged teeth. "Hello, Husband."

"Do not reply!" Mildred snapped.

"What's the matter, Husband? Cat got your tongue?"

Quinn couldn't have answered if he'd wanted to. His mind was spinning like a weather vane. Not ten feet from him stood a being that was a dead ringer for the woman he thought he'd lost forever. The apparition had the same hair, the same dusting of freckles across the cheeks and shoulders, the same loving face and the same body that he had known better than he knew his own. The only flaw in the doppelganger's otherwise perfect disguise was the pair of creepy red eyes whose gaze seemed to burn everything they touched.

"Maybe you do not recognize me?" the creature asked. "Perhaps this will help."

In the blink of an eye the creature's shape twisted into a body that had been battered, broken and drenched in blood. Splinters of white bone jutted through the torn legs and chest, and the angelic face had been reduced to raw strips of flesh by a shattered windshield. One red eye dangled from a spongy gray nerve fiber.

"Is this better?"

Quinn closed his eyes in hopes of shutting out both the horror in front of him and the renewed anguish of his wife's death.

"You're not Kathy, you slimy son of a bitch."

"No, but she and I are good friends." The fiend chuckled. "She's a great piece of ass."

The creature's oily laughter sent another wave of hot rage through Quinn's system. This time he dredged up the memory of his son standing in waist-deep water on a Florida beach. He had a dime-store diving mask pushed up on top of his head, a bloated puffer fish cupped in his hands, and an expression of infinite amazement on his seven-year-old face.

Quinn growled deep in his gut. "You won't beat me!"

When Quinn opened his eyes, Kathy was gone, only to be replaced by a green-skinned creature crouching toadlike in front of the fireplace. It had a long face tapering to a pointed chin, a mouth with triangular teeth, leathery wings that were folded tight against its back, claws on its hands and feet and short, nubby horns on a head covered with thick, wiry hair. The beast reminded Quinn of the gargoyles he had seen in photographs of Notre Dame Cathedral.

"Sorry, old bean. Nothing personal."

"Are you finished?" Mildred asked dryly.

The demon's booming laughter shook the walls. "What do you want, witch?"

"We have questions to put to you."

The creature's shape shifted again. This time it chose the form of a huge serpent and coiled in front of the fire. It bared foot-long fangs and flicked out a yard of forked black tongue.

"You dried up old cunt, why do you waste my energies on this? I have no desire to answer your questions."

"You have stolen a life from us! You wish to test the power of our vengeance?" Mildred barked.

The reptile hissed and uncoiled. It raised itself up to its full height and flared out into a huge condor with the pointed head of a crocodile. "Your vengeance is of no consequence to me," the demon replied, but its saurian features flickered and faded for a moment.

As Mildred spoke, the other women kept their heads down and whispered constantly. Quinn felt an undercurrent of power flowing through their hands to his. It was all he could do to keep his mind focused on Q.

"Why have you entered this dwelling?" Mildred asked.

"For my own purposes," the demon said.

"What could interest you here? There is little to feed your needs—no strife, no suffering to be savored."

In a lightning-quick shift of features, the demon became a naked dwarf with bloodred hair, the wrinkled face of a crone and a huge, engorged penis. The demon took the swollen member in one clawed hand and waved it at Mildred like a wand.

"You're wrong there, you dried-up hag." The demon continued to stroke the obscene member as it grinned. "The feasting has been excellent."

Although Mildred's expression never changed, two of the younger women blushed. Their embarrassment didn't escape the entity's notice either. The creature hopped down from the hearth and took a step toward Adar's youngest cousin, Pamela.

A bolt of green fire exploded from Mildred's eyes. The glow shot across the room and surrounded the entity in a shimmering net. Quinn turned his head against the glare, but for a brief moment, a huge black shape stood out against the background of cold flames. It looked like a lizard with shiny black scales running in ridges down its back. Its head and snout were covered with thick scutes, rapier-sharp teeth and red multifaceted eyes. An instant later, the demon was a tall Nubian with a shining bald head, a thick, muscular body and the same red piercing eyes.

"You want to test me again, yes?" Mildred hissed, but the old woman had paled under the flush of anger. Something had shaken her.

"I grow weary of this," the black giant replied. "I have nothing to fear from you."

The demon's form shifted to that of a charred-and-mangled Carl Kerry. He spoke to Quinn in a perfect imitation of Carl's voice. "You don't have much luck with cars, do you, sport?"

"Who called you forth?" Mildred said.

Carl's crushed face tried to grin, but the jaw swung loosely by a strip of skin. "Fuck you, old whore."

"We have the power to send you back to your sterile world, back to scrabbling for space among the inferiors, back to fighting for scraps from the table of your masters. Answer me or return to nothingness."

The creature's eyes flashed as it stood against the combined will of the coven. Finally, it laughed and waved a hand toward the bookshelves, and a serpent as thick and black as a fire hose oozed between the books and plopped to the carpet. A moment later, a second snake uncoiled from its perch around a statue on the top shelf and dropped onto the first. The snakes coiled sensuously about each other, hissing like faulty steam radiators and wiggling their tongues. Quinn felt a new wave of terror twist his guts. The shelves were alive with the slimy reptiles.

The first two serpents uncoiled and slithered toward the circle. They moved silently, slowly, until the first stopped just behind Marsha, raised its head and puffed out a scaly hood. It was a black King Cobra nearly eight feet long. Its mate kept going right across the woman's naked thigh, its black, lifeless eyes fixed on Quinn.

Mildred spat curses at the laughing demon in one of her antediluvian tongues. As she spoke, her voice and those of the others in the coven rose as one, filling the room with a wall of noise. The snakes stopped, frozen in time. The library was sealed from the elements, yet a wind as hot and desolate as any from the deep desert whipped around the circle, tossing the women's hair and stinging everyone's eyes. The searing gale battled the frigid waves radiating from the demon until, with a roar of frustration, the creature changed back into the giant Nubian. It crossed its arms in front of its face and sent a blazing ball of energy directly at Mildred's head. Inches from her face, the ray ran headlong into a burst of green defensive energy from the circle and exploded in a shower of sparks.

By the time Quinn's pupils returned to normal size, the demon and the snakes had vanished, leaving the room still, but stinking of decay and electrical discharge. Judging from the clock over the mantle, time either was as frozen as Quinn's rear end or the whole episode had taken place in just five minutes.

"Can I let go now?" he asked Mildred.

The old woman nodded and dropped her hands. Adar got to her feet and began to minister to her. Webs of tiny blue veins stood out against the tissue-thin skin of the old witch's face. The others climbed stiffly to their feet, stretched and began to dress. Quinn forgot he was naked; he was too exhausted to care.

"Is she all right?" he asked.

"I'm fine," Mildred said. Although she was shaking like a leaf, she made a visible effort to hide her fear. She allowed Penny and Adar to help her into her clothes, then took a seat on the nearest sofa. "We have major problems."

Marsha zipped up her jumpsuit and said, "I'll go check on Q."

"What was that thing? Some kind of chameleon?" Quinn asked as he pulled on his trousers.

"No, and it isn't one of the inferiors either," Mildred replied. "It tried to mask its identity by constantly shifting its shape, but it gave itself away when we surprised it with the energy shield."

"I'm sorry," Quinn said. "Things happened so fast. When did we do that?"

"When we attempted to surround it with that green wall of energy. Remember, just for a moment, it looked like a giant lizard?"

"Yeah, so?"

"My studies of the ancient parchments indicate the existence of an extremely unpleasant and bloodthirsty fellow who was worshiped by the ancient Phoenicians, Moabites and Ammonites. This entity had a particular fondness for children, fire and self-mutilation, and many Christian scholars believe it is the great evil referred to in the books of Ezekiel, Jeremiah and Leviticus. It was described as a giant tusked reptile."

Anna spoke up for the first time in a while. "You can't mean—"

Mildred nodded solemnly. "Moloch."

"Who?" Quinn asked.

"In the Old Testament," Anna said in her creaky voice, "King Solomon built a high place in the valley of Hinnom near Jerusalem. Some say it was a roundabout way to pay homage to the old gods, notably Chemosh and Moloch. Hundreds of Israelites dragged their children up there, built great pyres and threw their babies in alive. Thus the Hebrew *Ge Hinnom* became *Gehenna* which is synonymous with Hades."

"But Adar said it was one of the old gods all along. So why is everybody so upset?"

Mildred shook her head sadly. "I owe Adar an apology. When she told me, I thought she must be mistaken. A powerful inferior maybe, but one of the Old Ones?"

"I hope you don't mind me saying so," Quinn said dryly, "but you're scaring the shit out of me."

"You'd better be scared," Mildred said.

Coming in from the hall, Tim leaned against the doorframe and asked, "So what do we do now?"

The old woman seemed to be at a loss. She puckered her lips as she thought. "It would take something incredible to lure Moloch into our world. What is it these messages you keep getting tell you to do—the ones in blood?"

"You mean the ones about selling my land?"

"Yes. Why on earth would anyone connected to the netherworld care about a piece of property?"

Quinn knew from her tone that she was talking

more to herself than to him so he waited. At last Mildred said, "Maybe we'd better take a look at this land of yours."

Gail Okata had been sitting in the Plymouth down in Quinn Ramsey's driveway long enough to qualify for her pension. As she watched the shadows pass back and forth on the mansion's window shades, she wondered what Ramsey and his guests were doing in there. For people on vacation, they certainly didn't do much sightseeing. Capt. Benson had been bitching about tying up a patrol car, so she was tempted to invite herself in to find out what they were up to. With that nut case Wolinsky, it could be just about anything. Yet her instincts told her to be patient. Ramsey was the key to the whole case; and sooner or later he would lead her to her quarry. She just hoped he wasn't involved.

Okata popped a cherry lifesaver into her mouth. She was glad she wasn't addicted to donuts. She didn't smoke because she hated the way cigarettes made the car smell. She was glad she didn't have to do many stakeouts or she'd soon weigh two hundred pounds. In her opinion, the only thing men found less attractive than a woman cop was a fat woman cop.

The night was cool and the wind hissed through the foliage. She cut her eyes to the topiary zoo and chuckled. She knew she was bored because every time she glanced out the window those goofy shrub animals seemed to be closer than before. Anyway, why did people waste time and energy shaping hedges to look like dragons and gargoyles?

Finally, in frustration, she got out of the car and stretched. As she did, her body seemed to elongate in the light from the pale quarter moon.

"Hello, sister," she whispered, staring at the stars. Then she said to the moon, "Hello, Mother. So may stars, so many—"

All at once loneliness seemed to make the lifesaver taste like wormwood in her mouth. It seemed like centuries since she'd been out on a date. It had been months since she'd even gone out to a movie.

The thicket rustled, making a quick shuffling sound that seemed too sneaky to be mere wind. Okata cocked her ear and walked boldly back into the brush. It was dark, but she could see. A few feet in, she found herself surrounded by more topiary animals, and she stopped to listen. After a minute of stony silence, she smiled grimly. "A little over-zealous, are we?"

When she turned to go back to the car, she almost fell over a dragon shrub. The creature's mouth was open displaying a set of thorny fangs.

"Whoa there. Where did you come from? And baring your fangs at me? She gave the bush a playful karate chop on the snout. "Ow! Shit!"

Her hand was dripping black blood from a pair of jagged puncture wounds in her palm. Okata's eyes blazed but just as quickly cooled.

"Want to play rough, huh?"

She squeezed her palm and brought it to her mouth. The bleeding stopped. As she returned to her car, Okata gave the dragon a parting glare.

"If it were up to me, you'd be compost."

Bored of watching happy silhouettes on someone

else's window shades, she ground the Plymouth's starter and headed for home. In the garden, the shadows reclaimed dominion. A short while later, the roots at the base of the topiary dragon began to smolder and the leaves, so lovingly trimmed, began to shrivel and fall like hair off a mange-riddled dog.

Marsha, Anna and five of the cousins remained at the mansion with Q while Quinn, Tim and the rest of the family flew over to the big island. Quinn had chartered a twin-engine Cherokee for the short hop to Hilo, and as soon as everyone had stowed his gear in the back of the plane, Quinn claimed the vacant seat beside the pilot, hoping that the view on the way over might shake off some of his fatigue.

They'd been up all night. Quinn and Tim had followed the women from room to room as they wove protective spells like mother spiders carefully preparing their webs. Later, they all had taken a turn standing guard outside Q's room, trying to make some sense of what happened in the library.

"A demon, Quinn?" Tim had asked. "A real live demon with horns and a tail and everything?"

"Come on. Quit busting my balls. They called it an entity. One of the Old Ones. What do you want from me?"

"But you saw this thing?"

"Don't try to make it sound worse than it was. I saw something, like I told you."

"It looked like your wife, then Carl, then a snake, then a big black guy. But what was it?"

"Mildred says it was really some kind of big lizard from outer space."

226

Quinn laughed as he remembered Tim's reply: "I knew it! My grandmother in Gdansk told me about them. Their spaceships land in the swamps and they steal children." Quinn hadn't been sure whether or not Tim was serious until his friend had added, "My cousin Peytor! For ten thousand cash, he'll bag this thing and haul it out of here for you."

The water below the plane was a deep cobalt blue reflecting a hot December sun. The big green-and-black volcanoes of Hawaii sat on the horizon like the teeth of a dragon under a blanket of dirty white clouds. As the plane flew closer, Quinn saw a mosaic of red earth, green trees and black rock, dotted here and there with Spanish tile rooves and pineapple fields. He should have been enchanted, but he was too tired and depressed to care.

"You're a lucky man, Mr. Ramsey," the pilot said over the roar of the engines. The driver of the Cherokee was a man in his late twenties with thinning brown hair and thick mirrored aviator glasses that concealed his eyes as he glanced back into the cabin.

Shows how much you know, Quinn thought, but he said, "Right."

Quinn felt old and used up. How could some hotshot pilot—with his crew cut, muscular arms and green tattoos peeking out under the sleeve of his shirt—understand? What right did a kid like that have to be a pilot anyway?

Twenty minutes later they were on the ground in Hilo, climbing into a pair of rented Jeep station wagons. They pulled away from the airport immediately, so no one saw the pilot pick up the pay phone in the parking lot.

Quinn kept one eye on Mildred as the car bounced over the rutted road. The old lady seemed relaxed, even relieved as they drove away from the airport. She teased and exchanged insults with Tim. But once they turned off Saddle Road and started around the side of the volcano, she grew progressively quiet and edgy. As they passed through the wooden fence, Adar and Penny stopped responding to Tim's constant stream of chatter.

Quinn hit the brakes. "Okay, what's eating you three?"

Mildred's eyes roamed over the volcanic rubble under the gloomy umbrella of leaves. "This place—I feel incredible energy here."

"Me too," Adar said. "Ever since we passed that gate."

"Good energy, bad energy, what?" Tim asked as the car started again.

"Old energy," Mildred replied.

Tim and Quinn mulled her answer over until they stopped at the end of the track. Everyone piled out and gathered around Mildred. She noted the path of flattened grass and told the others to follow her. They wound through thick ferns with branches drooping like giant green centipedes, then around the flaky trunks of Koa trees to the clearing in front of the waterfall.

"This way," Quinn said, then started for the abandoned house.

Mildred stopped him. "No! Not there. I sense nothing but death over there. Go that way."

She pointed toward the waterfall and took off around the pool, pushing through the lush vegetation and picking her feet stiffly out of the sticky mud.

While Adar and the other women fell in right behind her, Tim and Quinn exchanged glances.

Tim circled his finger around the side of his head, but they followed the women through the damp weeds anyway, picking up burrs and soaking the legs of their jeans. Mildred kept going until she reached the base of the rock cliff. By the time Tim and Quinn caught up, the women were standing in a semicircle around her, staring at the falling water as if it were the fountain of youth.

"It's here," Mildred said and the others nodded in agreement.

"What's here?" Quinn asked, spreading his arms.

"This way." Mildred pointed to a treacherous-looking ledge almost buried under mounds of ferns and moss that eventually disappeared behind the wall of water.

The bushes beside the rock shelf parted and a large white dog stepped out and took a seat in the middle of the path. It was about the size of a German shepherd, but it didn't act aggressively. The animal just sat there daring anyone to pass.

"What's the matter, fella? You hungry?" Tim stuck his hand out, and the dog bared its teeth, then whined and wagged its tail. Tim laughed and took another step. "Talk about sending mixed signals."

The dog stood up on its hind legs, bared a set of very long fangs and pawed the air in front of Tim's face. Tim jumped back and jerked a nine-mm automatic out from under his Hawaiian print shirt.

"Wait!" Mildred commanded.

"It's a fucking werewolf!" Tim snapped.

Mildred gripped the pouch at her neck and closed her eyes.

"No, he belongs here."

The women closed ranks, each fingering a leather pouch, and Adar said, "The energy is incredible."

"Yes," Mildred said. "I have never felt anything like it."

When the animal remained on its hind legs, wagging its tail as if walking upright was perfectly natural, Tim muttered, "The damned thing's schizophrenic too."

Mildred carefully approached the animal and held her hand under its nose. At first the dog growled, but then it dropped back on all fours and licked her hand. "I will go on from here alone."

Adar and the cousins accepted Mildred's statement without question, but Quinn hurried to disagree. "You can't. What if you slip and fall? You don't know what's in there."

She smiled and patted his shoulder. "Don't worry. It's true that I do not know where the path leads, but I know that what's at the end will not harm me."

"How can you be so sure?" Quinn rolled his eyes to the heavens and threw up his hands in surrender. "Listen to me. I'm asking a woman who talks to ghosts how she knows something. Just be careful, will you?"

"Stay clear of that house, Adar," Mildred said, pointing a gnarled finger at the half-completed structure. "I feel the same violent emanations coming from there as I felt when we confronted the demon."

With that said, Mildred pushed past the dog and made her way to the ledge. After one last look at her family, she walked carefully along the slippery rock until she disappeared behind the silver curtain of water.

Sharon brought cups of hot herbal tea for Marsha and Anna to the solarium, then went to make sandwiches for the cousins sitting guard outside the boy's room. She made Q's favorite: ham and cheese on rye with hot mustard. After the cousins were sipping their tea, Sharon let herself into the room and placed the tray on the night table.

"You must eat," she said, but the boy glanced at the sandwich and shook his head. She picked up the sandwich and took it to the bed. "Your father say you eat."

Q was stretched atop the comforter in a pair of white hiking shorts and a red Polo shirt. He listlessly flipped the pages of a comic book. After a moment of being ignored, Sharon put the sandwich down and picked up the glass of milk. "Drink and I will not bother you."

Q let the book drop and huffed a sigh that would have blown out a forest fire. Staring at her over the rim, he gulped the milk down, wiping the white moustache on the back of his hand. "There! Happy?"

When Sharon bowed slightly and nodded her thanks, Q went back to his book. The woman let herself out, then stopped and gazed at the cousins' bodies, stretched out flat on the floor.

Mist from the falls naturally cooled the air and the thick foliage kept it clean. In all, the air was a pleasure to breathe. Every few minutes a bird landed in the shallow end of the pool for a drink, its beak spreading ripples that made reflected clouds shimmy like freshly washed sheets flapping in the late afternoon breeze. What is it about this place? Quinn thought. It's like a little Garden of Eden.

"You didn't by any chance phone Okata the last time I was over here, did you?" he asked Adar.

They sat side by side on a shiny rock at the water's edge. Tim stood behind them checking the clip in his gun, while the rest of the family milled about in the shade of the ohia lehua trees. Adar picked at a patch of bamboo shoots growing at her feet. Tiny tadpoles darted between the muddy roots and schools of pewter-colored fry combed the muck at the bottom like stadium sweepers after a twi-night doubleheader.

"I wondered how long it would take you to figure that out," Adar said.

"Okata said it was an old woman."

Adar grinned and said in a scratchy voice, "Quinn Ramsey is going to be turned into a toad tomorrow on the way to his property."

"I've heard better. How did you know?" Then he chuckled. "Never mind. Dumb question."

"It's been twenty minutes," Tim said. "Maybe we should go check on her."

When Mildred came out from behind the waterfall, the others waited until she joined them in the shade.

"Come on, Quinn," Mildred said waving her hand.

"What about us?" Adar asked.

"No, just Quinn."

"Uh, can't I tag along?" Tim said.

"No, Tim," Mildred said. "Stay here and protect the women."

The cousins giggled, but he ignored them, pulled up the right leg of his jeans, took a revolver from his ankle holster and held it out to Quinn.

"He won't need that," Mildred said. She took Quinn past the canine sentry. The dog only looked amused at the humans' antics.

"What's back there?" Quinn asked.

"A cave."

The walk was spongy with moss, yet slippery after aeons of constant spray, and the water had a heavy metallic odor. Quinn kept his eyes on his feet until they were safely inside the short tunnel behind the falls. The walls were as dank as a sewer, and the jagged ceiling dropped a steady stream of cold condensation on their heads. A few yards in, the passage widened, and Quinn was able to straighten up and comb the hair off his forehead. The inside of the cave was the color of outer space. He followed the sound of Mildred's footsteps because he couldn't see the tip of his nose.

"Jesus, a bat would get lost in here," he said. "What is this place?"

"You'll see in a minute."

Quinn followed the sound of her footsteps, bumbling around in the dark with his hands out in front until Mildred stopped moving. The place had the echoes of a vast warehouse, but what light filtered in from the opening at their backs concealed as much as it revealed.

"Hey!" Quinn called.

Mildred spoke a couple of harsh words and the

torches spaced at intervals around the cave burst into life. "I forget others can't see in the dark."

The second he'd stepped into the cave, Quinn had felt an intangible presence. Now, with the flames beating back the stygian gloom, he could see they were standing in the middle of a gigantic underground mausoleum that ran deep into the bowels of the volcano. The torches illuminated only about one tenth of the entire complex, yet he could see literally hundreds of narrow openings that had been chiseled out of the solid rock.

He went to the nearest sepulcher and moved aside a rotting palm frond. Underneath the leafy shroud was a yellowed skull and a few bones from a collapsed rib cage. The skull rocked gently, disturbed for the first time in centuries.

The next opening beckoned. In front were ancient bamboo spears and a shield made of a sea turtle shell. Quinn gently pried open the covering of dried grass and saw more dust and old bones. This skull had a garland of long-dead flowers ringing it like a halo.

How many tombs? Thousands? Tens of thousands? he wondered. In the meager light it was impossible to be certain.

"Any idea who these people were?" Quinn asked.

"Kings, priests, warriors—the elite of ancient Polynesian society."

Each grave had been lovingly prepared. Some bore ancient weapons: a favorite obsidian sword or sturdy spear. Others were padded with musty feathered cloaks in colors that had once rivaled the splendor of the rainbow. Some had seashell jewelry or pottery or just tiny statues hand fashioned from cooled lava. It was a gallery of respect from the wealth of a dead civilization.

"Is this what it's all about?" Quinn asked, picking up a string of Cowery shells. The leather gave way and the shells bounced and clattered around his feet and finally skittered away among the cracks.

"You can't feel it?"

"Feel what? Despair? Sadness? Loss? What else is there to feel in a graveyard?" Quinn shrugged off Mildred's sympathetic hand and stalked away. "I'm sorry. Being rich was supposed to be fun, but it's turning out to be a real drag."

"Quit feeling sorry for yourself," she replied, not unkindly. "You're looking with your eyes. Use your other senses. Let your mind reach out like it did last night. Become a receiver. Listen!"

He scowled and sighed, but tried to do as she asked. He willed his body to relax and emptied his head. Mildred was holding her leather necklace so he took his in the palm of his hand too.

"Repeat after me," he whispered under his breath. "I am not an idiot. I pray to God that I am not an idiot."

"I can hear you."

"Shit!"

Quinn waited, thankful for once that Tim wasn't there to see what a fool he was making of himself. He listened so hard that gray dots exploded behind his eyes. He could hear water dripping, the wind whistling through the mouth of the cave and the splash of the falls outside. And maybe he heard another sound coming from far away, like cloven hooves walking over rocks, but he could have imagined it. After what seemed like hours, he became aware of a strange tingling sensation. Not an itch exactly, more like ants crawling over his skin. He shrugged his shoulders and scratched his arms. Another few moments and his lungs began to labor, a claustrophobic reaction that sometimes hit him in crowded elevators or packed theaters. Quinn's eyes flew open and he searched the dark corners.

"Somebody's out there!" he said.

"Calm down. No one's there. No one alive anyway. But you felt them, didn't you?" Mildred asked.

"What was it?"

"Psychic energy."

The dark suddenly became more hostile. Quinn wanted to leave fast, but instead he strolled around inside the tight circle of torchlight, stopping every couple of steps to try to pierce the darkness with his eyes. The feeling of being watched was like a hand squeezing his heart. It was so much easier to believe that some living person was out there in the dark than the residual life forces of a people who had died centuries before he was born.

"Are all graveyards like this?" he asked.

"Not many. Usually the souls depart this plane shortly after the end of their physical existence. When they do, the life energy gradually dissipates. However, in some cases the dead cling to a person or a place, and their energy stays with them."

"Why?"

"We don't know exactly. If a belief in a local god or religion is strong enough, it might actually trap the psyche, keep it bound."

Quinn waved his hand at the honeycomb of graves. "What about these people?"

"I can only give you my gut feeling, that the early Polynesians had very firm ties to these islands. They worshiped elemental gods: the sea and the land, the sky, even the fiery volcano goddess filled their everyday lives. I believe that is why they picked this mountain for their mausoleum. It was sacred to them."

"You got all that from your gut?" Quinn asked, even as he noticed the opening of a deep black tunnel on the other side of the cavern. "But they're not ghosts, are they?"

Mildred chuckled. "Quinn, for a policeman, you surely are superstitious."

"Huh! Shows how many cops you know. Kerry wouldn't even take a leak without his rabbit's foot. Where does that tunnel go?" he asked to steer the conversation away from his nerves.

"Let's take a look."

Mildred found a torch, lit it with flames from another and handed it to Quinn. They strolled past endless tombs. As they went deeper into the volcanic mound, the ceiling gradually came down until they were in a long, low tube. Quinn ran his hand over the porous rock.

"Is this a lava chute?"

"I believe so," Mildred replied.

The ground was as smooth as a ballroom floor, beaten flat by the passage of time and a multitude of bare feet. As they followed the gently sloping path, the cool, damp air of the upper chamber was replaced by oppressive heat and the stench of igneous rock.

"Phew!" Quinn said. "What's that awful smell?"

Mildred wiped tears from her eyes. "True fire and brimstone."

A few moments later, the tunnel ended in a wide balcony that jutted out over the heart of the volcano. Quinn stuck his head out for a quick peek and was almost asphyxiated by the rising heat and poisonous gases. When he drew back, his face was the color of a brick. He took a deep breath.

"It's like looking into hell. The lava is churning and boiling like it's alive. It's at least a hundred-thirty degrees in here. I've gotta get out."

He stumbled back into the tunnel and stopped to marvel at the way the smooth walls reflected the unearthly red glow. "It's like being inside a beating heart. You think they sacrificed people down here?"

Mildred motioned for him to follow her back up to the cavern. "Maybe. They probably sacrificed animals, maybe a prisoner of war or two, but that was about it. As bloodthirsty savages go, the ancient Hawaiians were pretty mild."

"Compared to what?"

"Oh, say, your average high-school football team."

"Make that the parents of the average high-school football team and I'll agree with you." Then a rock turned somewhere ahead and Quinn whispered, "God, I hope we didn't wake somebody up."

A white form waited between a pair of conical stalagmites. It was pale and moved like patch fog. Mildred held the torch high and revealed a scrawny white mountain sheep that blinked dumbly at the intruders, its eyes reflecting red in the torch flame.

"She probably lives in these caves," Mildred said,

noticing Quinn's surprise. "The mountain is honey-combed with lava and steam vents."

Quinn held out his hand and the sheep came up shyly, flaring wide pink nostrils. He stroked the animal's fuzzy head. "She's pretty tame. The tourists must be feeding her. Don't worry, old girl. We won't hurt you."

A sticky tongue shot out and licked his hand. He laughed, ruffled the sheep's ears and let her go. Then they resumed their trek up to the main chamber with their four-legged friend tagging along behind, her thick hooves ticking over the rocks in four-four time.

"What's it all mean, Mildred? Has all this crap we've gone through been over this old graveyard? Is all the black magic, all the death over another tourist attraction? A photo opportunity for the woman's garden club?"

"No, Quinn. It's about power. The power you felt up there in the cave."

"I don't get it. That itchy feeling couldn't be worth anything to anybody. Certainly not worth killing for."

Mildred sighed. "You're so Madison Avenue. All you ask is what's the bottom line? How much is it worth?"

The mouth of the tunnel lay just ahead, the tiers of dusty bones waited with eternal patience for the outcome of their discussion.

"Hey, it comes from being a cop," Quinn said in his own defense. "When somebody gets popped, the first thing we look for is who gets rich or who inherits."

"But this isn't about money." Mildred went to the

center of the cave, holding up her flaming stick like a geriatric Lady Liberty. "Before man in his wisdom invented gunpowder and computers, he had to rely on Mother Nature for food, for medicine and for protection from hostile elements. Our ancestors lived in caves like this one. Everyone lived with his tribe, which was really just an extended family, and in each family one member was chosen to be the shaman. These men were combination witch doctors, healers and storytellers. The history of the tribe was in their stories."

Mildred handed Quinn the torch and took a seat on a flat rock that looked as if it had been placed there for just that purpose. She massaged her knees as she spoke. "These ancient witches could heal more people with herbs and the powers of the mind than a hospital full of medical doctors or an entire pharmaceutical company. But they also understood the powers that drove the universe."

"You mean the gods?"

"I'm not talking religion here. The universe is balance: every positive has a negative. Good and evil are two sides of the same coin. Power comes from the source of all good, but the netherworld is inhabited by beings that cannot create power so they must steal it from the living. They cannot make life, so they feast on death.

"Take our friends here. Their love for each other and for these islands has bound them to this place. Their energy is still alive in this volcano. It permeates the rocks, radiating like a uranium core."

"I'm sorry. You lost me."

"Think of it this way. The mountain is like a giant

battery; it's been charged with emotions: the loves, hates and desires of thousands of people over untold centuries. I believe our adversaries want to control this battery, and use it for some unspeakable purpose."

Quinn's face in the flickering light showed his revulsion. "That's horrible! You think this bunch of Japs—"

"I hardly think a group of Japanese businessmen is what we're up against. Whoever these people are, they work in conjunction with the Old Ones, of which Moloch is the most vile."

"So what do I do? Keep fighting something I can't see. I've turned my home into a fortress. I'm afraid to go out for a bag of doughnuts. My son is a prisoner in his room. What am I supposed to do?"

"Only you can answer that Quinn. I know only one thing, ignoring the evil never makes it go away."

"Shit!" He went to the nearest crypt. It was empty except for a bed of dried leaves and dust. "Somebody didn't like the accommodations. Hey! What happened to the sheep?"

"I don't know," Mildred replied. "She went back to her hole in the wall, I guess."

"Funny to think about her roaming around down here, like she's keeping all these people company."

They doused the torches from behind the falls and walked out into the blinding sunlight. Tim and the girls were lying in the grass at the base of the trees and hopped to their feet when they saw them emerge. The white dog was still on guard at the end of the rock shelf. When the dog saw them, it turned and ran past Quinn into the cave.

241

*   *   *

On the ride back to the airport the women hardly uttered a word. Quinn fended off Tim's questions by promising to fill him in on the details later. He had to have time to think.

They dropped Tim off at the rental desk to take care of the paperwork on the cars while Quinn went to find the plane. It was parked next to a gas truck on the far side of the runway, but there was no sign of the pilot. Quinn approached the gas jockey and a tall, fleshy guy with a ponytail and chinos.

"Where's the pilot?" Quinn said.

"Mr. Ramsey?" the kid with the ponytail asked.

"Yeah."

"I'm Frank Robbins. I work for the charter company. Eddie got sick and they called me to fly you back to Maui. I'm ready whenever you are."

"Okay. We'll be a few minutes."

Quinn found the women milling around the post-card and T-shirt racks in the airport gift shop. Mildred was trying on a huge straw hat in front of a tiny mirror; the price tag dangled beside her right ear. Adar and Penny were holding up shirts against each other, trying to decide what to send home. Shopping seemed to be bringing the women out of the dol-drums, so Quinn got a soda from the cooler and thumbed through a true-crime magazine to give them time to relax.

"I'll see you at the plane," Mildred said.

Quinn glanced up from the book. "Pay for that hat before you leave, Minnie Pearl. I'd hate to see you get arrested."

"I did pay for it!" Mildred said, and Quinn ripped

the price tag from the hat. "I suppose you're happy now."

Adar came over to ask why Quinn was laughing and held up a black T-shirt with a silkscreen of an erupting volcano. "What do you think?"

"Who's it for?"

"My nephew. He's ten."

"Penny has a kid?" Quinn asked, looking over at the freckle-faced woman. He would have said she was too young to have a ten-year-old kid.

"No, Fran. One of my older sisters."

"How many sisters do you have?"

"Six."

"Geez." He studied the shirt. It had flames and smoke, roiling lava, and Hawaii printed in large letters across the bottom. Just the thing for a boy that age. "He'll love it. You got any brothers?"

"One, Randy. He's twelve."

"Big family."

Adar went back into conference with her family. T-shirts and paperweights began piling up beside the cash register. A few minutes later, Mildred marched back into the shop and came over to Quinn.

"There's something wrong with the plane."

He had been looking at a *Playboy* and it took a second for him to mentally shift gears. "What?"

"Something's not right."

"Come on. Show me."

They all trooped out to the airplane, the women sporting their spoils like a platoon just back from the shopping wars. Each woman had a bag of clothing, jewelry, postcards or other tourist junk.

"Frank, what's wrong with the plane?" Quinn asked.

The pilot lifted his regulation sun glasses and his eyebrows. "Who said anything was wrong with the plane?"

Quinn turned to the old woman in her coolie hat. "Mildred?"

"Something isn't right. I don't know what else to tell you."

The plane looked okay to Quinn. Someone had given it a bath and washed the windows; the fold-down ladder was in place, waiting. He pulled on his lower lip. Adar and Mildred huddled for a few moments, exchanging urgent whispers.

"We can't go on that plane, Quinn," Adar said at last.

He opened his mouth to argue. After all, here he was standing in front of another hotshot pilot, and he wasn't about to let any old woman and her great-niece tell him what to do. Then he stopped himself cold. He kept forgetting whom he was dealing with.

The women stood in a semicircle staring at him. Except for Mildred and her funny hat, they looked like a bunch of coeds on vacation, with their Bermuda shorts, cotton shells and sunburns. It would be hard for anyone to really grasp that they were members of an ancient sect.

"Sorry, Frank, we can't go with you," he said at last.

"But, Mr. Ramsey, you've already paid for the trip. The company won't refund the money." Robbins slapped his hand on the cowling. "There's nothing wrong with her, I promise you. She had her hundred-hour physical just yesterday."

Quinn took a 50-dollar bill out of his wallet and tucked it into the pocket of the kid's shirt. "We'll catch another plane."

"But I have to fly back to Maui anyway. This is silly."

"Young man, don't fly that plane," Mildred said.

They argued back and forth for ten minutes. Mildred couldn't tell Robbins exactly what was wrong with the plane, only that it felt wrong. At the end of that time, the kid threw up his hands.

"I have no choice, ma'am. If I don't fly the plane back, I'll lose my job." The boy glanced at the aviator's watch on his wrist. "I should have been in the air five minutes ago."

With that, he climbed up the steps and began to pull up the ladder.

"Do something!" Adar snapped.

"What do you suggest I do? Arrest him?"

Adar grabbed the bottom of the steps. "Mr. Robbins, if you'll come down from there and fly back to Maui with us on another plane, Mr. Ramsey will give you a job as his personal pilot."

When the kid's face lit up, Quinn grabbed Adar's arm and took her aside. "What are you doing?"

"If you let that boy fly that plane, it will be the same as murder."

"What kind of plane do you have?" Frank asked.

Quinn knew he'd been outmaneuvered. "I don't know yet."

"But I have to ferry this one back to Maui for the company," Robbins said.

"The deal is," Adar said, "now or never."

Robbins let the ladder fall and disappeared into the cabin for a moment. He returned with his flight kit, an honest-to-God leather fighter pilot's jacket and log book. "They're gonna raise a stink over this."

"Okay, fine," Quinn said. "Find us another plane so we can get home."

Quinn was beginning to feel as if he were back in the Marines. The whole party marched back to the airport office and he went to stare out the window at the runway. Robbins was on the phone, trying to find another plane and to contact his old boss to give him the bad news.

"I didn't know you wanted a plane," Tim said.

"Neither did I."

That was when the Cherokee and the gas truck next to it exploded, turning the gas jockey and the hanger into a raging inferno.

Chapter Eleven

1:20 a.m.—Two Days Before Christmas

"Is she still back there?" Quinn asked.

Cousin Pam, the baby of the clan, had agreed to drive from the airport on Maui to the house. After their near miss with the airplane, Quinn was in no shape to chance sitting behind the wheel. He had climbed into the back of the van beside Tim Wolinsky. They were weaving down the Hana Highway, trying not to lose Frank Robbins, who was following in the jeep.

Pam glanced in the rearview mirror. "The lady cop? Yeah, she's back there behind the jeep."

"Why doesn't she give me a break?" Quinn moaned.

"Come on, buddy," Tim said. "Don't blame Gail. Ever since you set foot on this island it's been one disaster after another. I'm surprised they haven't put the National Guard on alert."

"Hey! What about my uncle? People were dying long before I got here."

"I'm not saying it's all your fault. All I'm saying is Gail is just doing her job. A friggin' airplane blew up right in front of a whole busload of Rotarians, for God's sake. What's she supposed to do, pretend it didn't happen?"

"Oh, so now it's Gail. If a cop has boobs, she can do no wrong. Am I right?" Quinn said, and Tim made a rude noise in response.

"Can you imagine what this road was like before they fixed it?" Quinn asked, hoping to ease the tension.

"So what do we do now?" Tim asked.

Quinn leaned over and whispered, "I tell you what I'm going to do. Tonight I'm going into town and buying the biggest fucking Christmas tree I can find. One big enough to make the environmental freaks picket my house. Then I'm gonna wrap all of Q's presents and stick them under it. Then I'm going to find some of those old-fashioned stockings for him and all the women and hang 'em up on the fireplace in the library."

"Yeah," Tim replied quietly, "I know the kind you mean. The long knit ones with the stripes."

"I hate those cheap felt things. Anyway, what with me running back and forth to Honolulu, Q didn't have much of a Thanksgiving, so I'm gonna see if Sharon can whip up a goose for Christmas dinner."

"Goose?" Tim chuckled. "What do you know from goose? I bet in your whole life you never had goose, unless it was a McGoose sandwich from Mickey D's."

"Yeah? Well, Q's gonna have it better than I did."

Adar stuck her face close behind Quinn's head and said, "What are you two whispering about?"

The men exchanged conspiratorial winks before Tim said, "Me, I'm so tired I could sleep till the Republicans balance the budget."

"You're not going to tell me. Is that it?"

Quinn chuckled, looking over his shoulder at Mildred snoring on the rear bench seat. He put his finger to his lips and then put two fingers in his ears.

Adar grinned, but only halfheartedly. Her eyes were red and swollen, and she looked as if she would fall asleep any second.

"How is Mildred?" Quinn whispered.

"She's beat. The way she acts, it's easy to forget she's not a kid anymore."

"Yeah, you're right. Full of piss and vinegar as my grandmother used to say."

"She's been that way as long as I can remember. Mildred took over the family when my parents died. She managed to get all of us educated and keep us together."

The old woman snorted and wiped her nose on her bare arm. A moment later she was sawing logs again. Then Adar said, "You know, she's traveled all over the world by herself. Started when she was in her teens, something unheard of back then. She's been to the Sudan, Iraq, the Congo. She spent a whole year in Uganda, living in mud huts, studying with the local Hungans."

"Which are?"

"The witch doctors. Word is, even Amin was scared of her."

"You're kidding."

"We know a family in England, members of the Wicca over there. They told me that, when he killed that old woman after the Israelis freed the hostages from the airport, Mildred got so mad that she went out into the bush with a copper pot, a bar of black soap and her herbs. Two days after she came back, Amin was on the run from the rebels."

"Copper pot? Black soap? I don't get it?" Quinn said.

"Effigies, Quinn. Melt the soap, mold it, place a piece of hair or clothing from the person—"

"I thought that was voodoo."

Adar sighed, reached forward and tapped him lightly on the top of his head. "All magic comes from the same source. There isn't one magic for Africa and another for New York City. Voodoo for Haiti and Tarot for New Orleans. It's all the same. It's very much like modern medicine. Physicians specialize, right? One guy saws bones, another reads x-rays. Well, the world of supernatural arts is like that. There are hundreds of disciplines, thousands of entities, but only one source of power."

"Are you impressed, Tim? I can sit here, as cool as a frog in frozen yogurt discussing voodoo and hexes with a witch from Massachusetts."

The van passed the fork in the road just inside the city limits and Quinn turned to see if Okata would stop at the police station. But the battered Plymouth stayed right behind the jeep.

"Crap!"

"Did it ever cross your mind that Gail might be concerned about our safety?" Adar asked. "Besides, I think she kind of likes you."

"Get real," Quinn said.

"What about me?" Tim sputtered.

"Well, of course, she likes you, Tim. Who wouldn't?"

The caravan made the last turn to the estate, slowing automatically as they approached the front gate, but Pam slammed on the brakes when she saw the gate standing open.

"Go on!" Quinn barked.

The van coasted slowly up the drive. No sooner had it stopped rolling than Quinn was out and sprinting for the front door.

"Wait!" Okata yelled. She beat him to the entrance, approaching the door warily with her gun pointed in the air until she slowed to a halt at the bottom step. A ragged piece of human flesh dangled from the Christmas wreath on the front door. It took a moment before she realized it was a woman's breast. The stones on the stoop were spotted with bloody footprints.

Quinn groaned deeply in his chest and closed his eyes. "Please, please let them be all right."

Mildred tried to push past Okata, but the policewoman stopped her. "Where do you think you're going?"

"That's not a calling card from the welcome wagon up there," the old woman snapped. "It's a challenge. There could be other things waiting inside."

Mildred took a vial of glittery powder from her bag, uncapped it and scattered the contents over the porch. She muttered a few words under her breath and started up the steps.

"Don't go in there!" Okata called.

Tim pulled his automatic from the glove compartment of the van and ran after Mildred. Okata tried again to stop Mildred, but Quinn grabbed her arm and said, "The old woman knows what she's doing. Let her take point."

Gail shook off his hand. "Are you out of your mind? There's no telling who's in there."

"Who or what. But I'm begging you to stay with us on this. Mildred knows what she's doing."

Gail looked at the torn skin hanging on the door and said, "Dammit, Quinn. You had better be right."

Okata trailed Mildred, watching with incredulous eyes as the old woman worked her way into the house with her powders and charms. "What is she, some kind of witch?"

"Yes," Quinn said.

"You're not serious?"

"Yeah, I am, and don't look at me like that. You know the weird shit we've been going through. And don't give me any bull about the Japanese Mafia either."

"But, Quinn, ghosts and goblins? Please!" The policewoman pointed at Mildred's back. "What's one funny old woman going to do? Chase off the bogeyman with that sneezing powder?"

He grabbed Okata's arm and pulled her close, saying under his breath, "Let me tell you something. If it hadn't been for that funny old woman, our ashes would be blowing all over the tarmac on Hawaii right now."

Frank Robbins eased up to Quinn, his eyes on the dripping piece of flesh, and his long hair standing out as stiff as the tail of a fox. "Uh, Mr. Ramsey, what do you want me to do?"

Quinn spoke without taking his eyes from Okata's face. "Stay out here, Frank."

Quinn trotted back to the van and grabbed another gun for Robbins. "Here, keep an eye on the girls."

Robbins swallowed audibly and held the pistol the way he would a snake.

"Come on, Gail," Quinn said, and they went up the steps and into the foyer.

"Is that kid going to be all right out there?" she asked.

Quinn's laugh was weary and without a trace of humor. "Sure, the girls will keep him out of trouble. Come on."

The house was deathly quiet, the air unnaturally cold and so still and hard it stung like a slap in the face. When they walked over the granular substance Mildred was spreading, their soles crunched as if they were walking on eggshells.

"I guess we won't be taking anyone by surprise," Okata sneered.

Quinn's old friend, the stench of blood and excrement, reached him before Gail and he were halfway down the hall. He froze, forcing Gail to walk around him. She stopped beside Mildred at the door of the library. Then Quinn said, "I'm not going in there."

But naturally he had to, only to find five bodies lying on blankets of their own blood. They had been ripped and clawed so that an autopsy would be the only way determining whether the bodies had belonged to men or women—except for the corpse of Mildred's mother. Anna's frail body had been hacked into six parts and arranged with chilling precision. The head, with its tiny pearl earrings still in place,

was resting on the stump of its neck at the top of the
pentagram on the floor. An arm or leg had been
placed on each of the other points. Her shriveled
torso, minus one withered breast, was in the center.
The butchers had carved a message to Quinn in the
flesh of the old woman's stomach:

LAST CHANCE—SELL!

After that night, Quinn was never sure how long
he stood there staring. What seemed like hours was
probably only minutes, but only the sound of Adar's
sobbing brought him back to reality. When he came
to his senses, Okata was slumped against the doorframe with the gun hanging down at her side. Tim
had run back into the hall and gotten sick. Mildred
stood rock still in the midst of her dead relatives,
swallowing over and over.

All at once Quinn cried his son's name. He raced
for the north tower, taking the stairs two at a time.
At the landing, he stumbled over Marsha's remains.
Her clothing had been cut away, and she was covered with the same blue-black wounds that had been
found earlier on Q's chest. He paused to check for a
pulse, then gave up when he saw the gaping eye sockets.

Inside Q's room, a head with a tangle of brown
curls rested on a nest of pillows in the middle of the
bed. A piece of yellow legal paper had been stuffed
between its lips. Quinn frantically searched the clos-
ets and under the bed. He finally collapsed into the
rocking chair in the corner, put his head in his hands
and tried to hold on to his sanity.

When Okata burst in with her pistol, he didn't bother hiding the tears. She stepped around the bed and carefully removed the note.

"It says to get the papers ready and they'll contact you. Otherwise, they'll send your son back a piece at a time. I believe them."

"How did they get in?" Quinn asked.

"They couldn't have," Adar replied as she entered the room. "The house was sealed. It had to come from inside. We can't find the housekeeper."

"Sharon?" Quinn asked.

"Everyone else is accounted for," Adar said.

"All dead," Quinn said in a monotone. "All dead."

The woman whom Tim called Sharon marched into the penthouse ahead of two men carrying the unconscious body of Quinn Ramsey Junior. Their blood-splattered coveralls left a trail of red on the antiseptically white tiles.

"What did you bring him here for?" Albert Smythe whined.

"Would you rather I took him to your office? Maybe we could stick the little brat in your safe."

"No need to get upset Tammy."

"Where is my daughter?"

"On the terrace."

Tammy strode through the sliding-glass doors to the landscaped patio. The cloaked figure was standing at the rail gazing down at Waikiki. From the balcony, the lights of the shopping district spread out like the stars of the Milky Way.

"We have the boy."

The daughter was taller than the mother, missing six

feet by no more than four inches. She wore the robes that her talents had earned for her, bloodred with a hood that covered thick, waist-length black hair.

"Good. Put him in the spare room and keep him drugged."

"His father will give in now?"

The woman turned to face her biological mother. Her eyes were shaped like almonds, and they had stunning emerald-green irises. They were wild and seemed out of place above such well-formed, delicate cheekbones and the small, straight nose. Even twisted into a cruel smile, her lips were full and her teeth almost too perfect.

"Oh, Ramsey's group of Halloween hags will try to locate the boy. They will contact their feeble-spirit friends and consult their crystal balls, but in the end, he will have no choice."

The daughter turned back to the storm that was approaching from the sea. She watched the lightning dance in the thunderheads.

"I feel the power of the Old Ones burning my skin like heat from an open flame. When our pact is complete, no power on this planet will be able to stop us."

The mother knelt and kissed the hem of the red cloak.

Quinn sat on the top step of the long flight that led down to the beach. The wood was still wet from the previous night's rain, and the water had soaked through his cutoffs. Lost as he was in an agony of self-pity and self-loathing, he only pretended to watch the surf pounding the sand.

"Okata called the FBI," Adar said as she eased up behind him.

"The Federal Bureau of the Inept? Oh, goody. Tell her thanks, but I don't need my phones tapped."

Adar squeezed Quinn's shoulders, and Quinn climbed stiffly to his feet. "Come on."

He took her hand and led the way down to the beach. Then they walked just beyond the reach of the receding tide to a place where the rubble at the base of the cliffs formed a pocket of privacy.

"What have you been doing out here all by yourself?" Adar asked.

"I've been talking to the ocean and we've hit upon the secret of the universe."

"Which is?"

"No matter where you go, there you are." After another moment, he said, "Sorry. I'm acting like an idiot. You lost half of your family. You should be the one sitting out here being morose."

She hugged him and then held him at arm's length. "Yes, I did lose a lot of my family. But Q is all of your family."

"What are we going to do? Tim's cleaning and loading his guns. I guess if the Libyan Navy took Q, we'll be ready. And Robocop Robbins has locked himself in one of the guest rooms. I think he's under the bed."

"That's better," Adar said. "That's the cynical Quinn Ramsey we all know and love."

They still had on the soiled clothing from the day before and Quinn's jaw was itchy with day-old beard. Adar's cotton jumpsuit had stiff perspiration rings under the arms.

"Maybe I'll go take a shower," she said.

"What about—"

Adar nodded. "The girls are cleaning up."

"They don't have to do that," he said.

Adar gave him a sad smile. "Yes, they do. It's their way of paying respect."

She turned to go, but Quinn caught her hand and she turned around with a question in her eyes. He started to speak, then pulled her slowly against him.

"Maybe this isn't exactly the right time, but—"

Adar kissed him gently, her lips soft and warm. Quinn didn't press, savoring her feel and flavor: salt and toothpaste and her slightly gamy odor too. They kissed until his body began to quiver; then she pulled away. He kept his eyes closed for another moment, reluctant to acknowledge the world that waited back at the house.

"That was nice," she said. "I was beginning to wonder if there was something wrong with me."

"Not that I've noticed."

"Can I ask a personal question? Are you attracted to me because I remind you of your wife? I saw her photograph on your desk. There is a resemblance, but I'm not her."

"I know. I was confused. I wanted to make sure the attraction wasn't just the red hair."

"And now you're sure? Why all of a sudden?"

Quinn gave her a lopsided grin. "Kathy could be difficult at times, but she wasn't a witch."

"You bastard," Adar said and punched him lightly on the arm.

He pulled her against him again, this time crushing his mouth against hers. Adar pulled herself tight into the curve of his body and allowed his tongue to ignite a fire in their blood. When his fingers closed over her breast, she pushed back. "Whew!"

His blood was still boiling and he tried to pull her back, but she kept a stiff arm against his chest.

"Down, boy. I need a shower."

"You look fine to me."

She laughed again, this time it sounded genuine. "I don't want to play *From Here to Eternity* on your beach. Let's take it one step at a time, okay?"

"I'm sorry."

"Don't be. Violent death has a way of making the living terribly horny."

Quinn heard his name being called, and he peered around the boulder at the top of the cliff. Tim and Gail Okata were there. Tim waved for them to come up.

"Deja vu. I should a left him in jail when I had the chance."

"This better be good," Quinn said as he reached the top step.

"The Feds are here," Tim replied. "They brought some woman reporter with them."

"In God's name, why?" Quinn snapped.

Okata stepped in. "It's S.O.P. in cases like this. They want to get your boy's photo out as soon as possible. Someone might see him, might call in."

Quinn snorted. "There are no cases like this. How much did you tell them?"

"Kidnapping by a group of terrorists."

"Thanks."

"Don't thank me. You think I want to look like an idiot to those suits? As soon as they walked in, the big blond dork asked me to get him a cup of coffee."

"Next time he asks, tell me," Adar said. "I'll fix something to keep him awake."

They filed into the house through the solarium, passing from prickly heat and the stiflingly sweet aroma of tropical flowers to an artificially cooled environment with the stale hospitallike fetor of antiseptics and death.

"I'm going to check on Mildred," Adar said and peeled off toward the guest wing.

Leading Quinn past men in dark suits who were examining the bloody writing on the walls, Okata said "They think it's Chinese."

Tim stopped to give advice to the men collecting the blood samples. Quinn and Okata found the reporter examining the gallery of paintings near the office.

"Quinn Ramsey, this is Ann Pakula of the Honolulu Register."

The islands were full of beautiful women, but even in Hawaii, she stood out like a jade figurine in a coal bin. She was tall and obviously Polynesian, dressed in a form-fitting, two-piece suit that was so understated it had to cost a fortune. She carried a matching shoulder bag over the tweed jacket and a bodice that made it plain to anyone with eyes that she was female. Her thick black hair was twisted into a French braid and pinned at her neck. When they shook hands, Quinn experienced a visceral reaction that momentarily stunned him.

"I'm sorry we have to meet like this, Mr. Ramsey."

Her voice was light and musical, betraying just a hint of the Orient. Quinn showed her to the office, and he sorted through the drawers for the most recent photograph of his boy—a school photo taken eight months earlier. His eyes lingered on it for a second before handing it over.

Ann glanced at the picture, then tucked it out of sight in her purse. "May I ask a few questions?"

Before he could reply, one of the federal agents came to the door looking for Okata. She nodded to Quinn and slipped out of the room.

The reporter's question had gone right out of his head. The old familiar worm had begun gnawing at his stomach. His eyes wandered to the bottle of Scotch on the middle shelf of the bookcase and he wondered if the woman would be insulted if he offered her a drink.

Ann followed his eyes, got up and went to the bookcase. She took the bottle in one hand and two tumblers in the other, fumbling for a moment with the glasses, then came back to the desk. She poured an inch of Scotch in one glass and stopped just shy of the rim on the other.

Quinn took the full glass reverently to his lips. Thanks, I needed that," he said as he leaned back.

"I can see that," Ann said, reclaiming her seat and crossing her legs. She put on a pair of horn-rimmed glasses that somehow made her look even more sexy and propped a spiral notebook on her knee.

"Mr. Ramsey, what happened last night? I mean, I have the FBI's statement: Terrorists broke in, killed several of your houseguests and abducted your son. But that doesn't explain all the blood and the writing on the walls. Have you been contacted by the kidnappers yet?"

The liquor hit his system like an embolus. After so long without sleep, it shifted his brain into low gear and made him as edgy as a cat. "No, not yet."

"But you expect to to receive a ransom demand?"

His eyes were drawn to the knee supporting the blue spiral notebook. "Sure."

She jotted a few notes using a yellow pencil, then nibbled daintily on the eraser as she considered her next question. "But why do you think you were singled out? I mean, there are lots of people with money on this island. A lot of celebrities too."

She recrossed her legs, allowing Quinn a peek at the dark tops of her stockings. She wasn't making it easy, he thought as he ran his hand over the stubble on his chin. His skin felt hot and feverish. It was all catching up with him—no food, no sleep, no sex.

"Ms. Pakula, could we do this another time? I haven't had any sleep and I'm not at my best."

Ann's smile was wry as she nodded and put the notebook away. When her legs uncrossed, the skirt climbed to midthigh and caused a catch in his breathing. She leaned on the desk with her suit clinging like cellophane to the soft curves of her body, the top two buttons on her blouse undone. Her green eyes complemented her olive skin.

"Why don't we go for a ride, Mr. Ramsey? Some fresh air might clear your head."

Quinn licked his lips again and looked at the empty glass. Where had all the Scotch gone? He needed another drink a lot more than air, but he said, "Sure, why the hell not?"

Standing was a challenge, but with Ann's help he made it to her car, a rented Toyota, and climbed into the passenger seat. When the car's engine turned over, Adar came to the door and waved, then trotted down the steps and came to his window.

"Where are you going?" she asked, eyeing Ann's exposed thighs under the steering wheel.

"For a ride," Quinn replied dully.

"Quinn, you can't leave now," Adar said with a smile. "Gail is having fits with those Federal people."

"It's what she gets paid for." Even to his ears, the words sounded as if they came out sideways. "I need to get away for a while."

"But what if the kidnappers call? You can't just—"

Quinn's head snapped up and his eyes blazed like a rabid animal. "Quit nagging! I said I'd be back later."

When Ann drove around the fountain and disappeared down the drive, Adar stumbled up the steps, running headlong into Tim Wolinsky.

"Whoa, there. What's the matter? Where'd Quinn go?"

"I don't give a damn where he went!" Adar said with fat tears racing each other down her cheeks. "The creep can rot in hell for all I care."

She pushed him out of the way and ran inside to find her great-aunt.

Ann bypassed the taverns in Hana and drove to a bar across from the airport in Kahului. Along the way, Quinn sat with his forehead pressed against the passenger window to keep from completely losing control. He had never been so turned on by a woman in his life and it scared the crap out of him.

"Come on," she said when she opened his door. "You need a drink."

The bar was cool and dark, full of thirsty tourists and

sleepy flight attendants downing their liquid wake-up calls. The walls were decorated with an endearing mix of faux coral and plastic seashells. They took a booth in the darkest corner, sliding over black Naugahyde gone gray by the passage of many trouser seats.

"Beer," Quinn told the waitress with the short plastic grass skirt.

"And two Scotches," Ann added. "Doubles."

Quinn couldn't exactly remember why he was there. His head felt as if it were on the receiving end of a pile driver, and he was sweating and shivering like a man with malaria. Her strange perfume didn't help much either. It made him thirsty.

"Why don't you tell me what's going on?" Ann said.

The waitress put the drinks in the center of the table. Ann pushed the bottle of beer and one of the Scotches across to him and picked up the other glass, draining it in one gulp. Quinn pushed the beer to the side and used both hands to bring the glass to his lips.

"You'd think being rich was a piece of cake, right?" He eased the glass down as if it were made of cobwebs. When Ann shrugged and nodded for him to continue, Quinn told her about his uncle, about inheriting the estate and about the offer to buy the land.

"So why not just sell?"

He marveled at the way the third and fourth buttons on her blouse had miraculously popped open, exposing acres of creamy flesh above black lace. "Can't."

"Why not?"

Something was burning his chest and his hand went to the pouch under his navy Polo shirt. He shook his head slowly, trying to clear it. "I just can't."

Ann's eyes locked on the lump under his shirt, but she leaned over and patted his other hand, the one that was clinging to the glass like it was a lifeline. It made the blouse gape even more. "I'm staying at the motel across the street. Why don't we pick up a bottle and go over there? It's more relaxing."

"Okay." He tossed some bills on the table and followed the bouncing bodice to the exit. As he held the door, Ann leaned up and lapped the alcohol residue from his lips with the tip of her tongue.

That did it. He didn't care where they were. He let go of the door and made a clumsy lunge at Ann, but she laughed and skipped lightly out of reach. He stumbled out into the parking lot and almost collided with Gail Okata.

"What the hell do you think you're doing?" Okata demanded, waving a hand in front of her face. "Christ, you smell like a brewery. Get in the fucking car."

"We were just going for a bite to eat," Ann said.

"He's going back to Hana." Okata jerked Quinn around and pinned him with angry eyes. "Get in the car before I cuff you and run you in for being drunk in public and a world-class pain in the ass."

She grabbed his collar and dragged him to the police car and shoved him into the front seat.

"I don't feel good," he moaned.

"Good!" She slammed the door.

Ann gritted her teeth and watched them drive away. For a moment she had considered stepping in and putting that bitch cop in her place, but then, she had another thought.

* * *

Tim dogged Adar's heels as she practically ran through the house searching for Mildred. He was dying to find out what had happened between Quinn and Adar, but he was careful to keep his distance. Adar stomped into the library, went directly to the bar and poured herself a stiff jolt of soda, throwing it back and patting her lips on a cocktail napkin.

"Men!" Tim said. "They'll drive you to drink."

"Don't try to be funny."

"What's going on? Where's Quinn? Where'd Okata run off to? I feel like the retarded nephew. I'm always the last one to find out anything."

"Quinn went hunting and Gail took off after him. The Feds are having a ball gathering dust bunnies and fingernail clippings, and my sisters are bawling their eyes out in their bedrooms. Satisfied?"

"Hunting?" Tim muttered. "I don't think Quinn hunts. Are you sure?"

Adar slammed the glass down on the bar, held out her hand and recited an ancient spell. A three-inch cockroach appeared in the palm of her hand. "Tim, have you ever thought what it would feel like to go through life as a cockroach?"

He made a face as the bug crawled over her hand. The way its little antennae waved around made him queasy. "I hope that's a rhetorical question."

Before she could reply, Mildred came in and saved him. "I've arranged a charter for late this evening. Frank is going to fly the girls to California for the trip back home. Quinn was nice enough to pay for everything."

Adar nodded and closed her fist. When she opened it, the roach was gone. "Yeah, he's a peach."

Mildred had turned to leave, but Adar's tone gave her pause. "What's wrong?"

"That's what I want to know," Tim said.

"Timothy, go play with your guns," Mildred said, taking a seat at the bar.

"But—"

"Timothy!"

He shrugged and left the room, muttering, "Tim do this. Tim do that. Nobody ever tells me anything."

Mildred waited for the sound of his footsteps to recede, then said, "What is it dear?"

After Adar told her great-aunt about Quinn's rude behavior and his abrupt departure, Mildred said, "That doesn't sound like Quinn. But remember we're all under a great deal of stress. We lost loved ones and his son is in the hands of fiends. That would make anyone testy."

"Testy? Testy explains why he went running off with some bimbo?"

"He did what?"

"That's right. He drove off with that woman reporter. Left me standing in the driveway like an idiot."

"What woman?"

"Aunt Mildred, weren't you listening to me? I just said he drove away with this woman. He said he was going for a ride. I told him he couldn't. What would happen if the kidnappers called?"

"This woman—what did she look like?"

Adar rolled her eyes and took a sip of soda. "Expensive suit, but the dress was too short. Nice shoes, expensive handbag. I think she had long hair, but it was done in a braid and pinned. She had a pretty face, but too much makeup."

"What did her eyes look like?" Mildred asked with an exasperated sigh.

Adar pursed her lips. "I don't remember. She had on a pair of tacky eyeglasses."

Mildred made a tent with her fingers and tapped the peak against her lips. "Calm down. Quinn has enough on his mind without you sniping at him. We have to make arrangements to get to the airport. I'll find young master Wolinsky."

An hour later, Okata drove up. Quinn climbed out and staggered up the steps. Adar waited by his desk for him to stop and offer an apology, but when he saw her, he dropped his eyes to his feet and hurried past.

Mildred blocked the bottom of the stairs. "Are you all right? We have to go to the airport this evening. The medical examiner has released the bodies for the flight home. Can you spare Mr. Wolinsky to drive the van? You don't look well."

After Quinn nodded, Mildred smiled kindly and touched his arm. "You had better get some sleep."

He nodded again and stepped around her, taking the stairs as if each was a mile high.

Albert Smythe drove well for a man in his late sixties. His hands and feet worked the pedals in perfect sync with the tachometer. He enjoyed driving fast, but not recklessly. Albert had taken the mountainous Pali Highway, on his way to a dinner with a client in Kaneohe when he noticed the temperature gage on the Porsche was in the red zone.

The malfunction was inconvenient as all hell, but he let up on the gas and took the first exit ramp up to a deserted parking lot that overlooked the lush green valley on the eastern side of the Koolau Mountain Range. Albert punched the buttons on the car's cellular phone and told his client he was going to be late. Then he placed a call to the auto club, venting his spleen at the dispatcher when she told him how long it was going to take to get a repair truck.

"You twit! I told you I was late for an appointment, and it's getting dark."

"I'm very sorry, sir, but that's the best we can do." The girl's tone made it clear that she was anything but sorry.

"Did I tell you I'm an attorney with the biggest law firm in Honolulu?"

"I'll be sure to tell the driver. He'll be impressed."

Albert crushed the off button with his thumb and banged his head against the back of the seat. "Goddamned, cocksucking, two-bit cunt!"

With nothing better to do, Albert watched the shadows of the mountains reaching out like giant tongues to lap at the cool blue of the Pacific. In the mountains, once the sun made up its mind to set, darkness and cold came in a hurry. And those woods? Hadn't he just read a story about packs of wild dogs running around in the woods? A tourist had been bitten, his hand nearly chewed off.

"Why me?"

He stroked the soft pouch of the fetish under his shirt and peered through the dark-tinted glass. It wasn't really that dark yet—just dark enough to make every shadow look like some cur dog crawling on its belly at the edge of the forest. Life was turning out to be a bucket of sour lemons. He had an 80,000-

dollar sports car, and all it was good for was a unheated recliner.

"This is fucking ridiculous!"

Albert climbed out of the car, slammed the door and stalked over to the rail that kept the tourists from plunging a few thousand feet into the valley. Oblivious to the setting sun's golden overtones on the emerald-and-black mountains, he stared petulantly at his watch. It was bad enough to miss dinner with a rich client, but the delay would undoubtedly keep him from his regular date with Marla, his favorite slinky Scandinavian stewardess who worked part-time for one of the Island's better escort services.

When Albert turned to kick the Porsche, he saw the cloaked figure of a woman standing a few yards away. Her head was bowed as if she were awestruck by the beauty of the volcanic mountains that ringed the valley. Immediately on guard, Albert scanned the narrow lot for other cars, but there were none. Then he looked for the woman's companions, but she was alone. Since he was an attorney, his first concern was robbery, but the woman didn't appear threatening. Her build was slight, and unless she had a weapon hidden in the folds of the cloak, she wasn't armed. Most of all, she didn't seem very interested in him.

Well, what cloud was without its silver lining? Albert thought as he straightened his paisley tie and walked toward the mystery woman.

"That's a view worth flying all the way from Cleveland to see. Or is it Osaka?" he added when he noted the dusky hue of the skin of her wrist.

The woman didn't turn or utter a word. In fact, she didn't seem to have heard him at all.

Demon Fire

"Madam, I applaud your reticence. A young woman alone in the mountains can't be too careful. But I assure you, I have no evil intentions. My car broke down."

Albert took another careful step, mindful not to startle the woman should she suddenly look around. After all, sexual harassment suits were going around like the flu. "I'm an attorney and since we are stuck here together, I thought—"

"What is your name?" the woman asked in perfect, unaccented English.

Albert smiled disarmingly. Women always perked up when they heard the word, attorney. "Albert Smythe. I—"

Albert's senses were suddenly assailed by a thick sulfurous stench. Sure that his car was on fire, he spun around in a panic, but it was just as he'd left it. When he turned back, the woman was facing him. Albert caught a hint of high cheekbones, a lovely nose and eyes that glowed strangely under the shadow of the cowl. Then the woman threw back the hood and Albert stopped dead in his tracks.

"What—"

The car was too far away, so he ran for the woods. His feet turned on loose rocks and giant pine cones. Low-hanging tree branches as thin as guitar strings tore his face, yet he kept going, deeper and deeper into the forest until the edge of the cliff and the years of good living finally brought him to a halt. Albert stopped with his back against a giant Koa tree, wheezing like a geriatric race horse.

"Lucifer help me. Those eyes!"

Albert had seen his death in the eyes of a beautiful

woman, and now he clung to his fetish as if it were the holy grail. His mind roiled as he tried to remember the words of a charm of protection.

"Great Astaroth, grant me—" No, that was for wealth.

"Begone foul demon. As I drain thy blood, I curse—" A bug flew into his mouth. He spat it out and opened his eyes.

A swarm of fireflies had come down from the trees to bedevil him, swirling around his head and flashing their lights in his eyes. The bugs landed in his hair, and he could feel them crawling over his scalp. Albert tried to wave them away with his hand, but there were so many it was like trying to chase away air. The more he fanned, the faster their segmented bellies blinked. Soon they were crawling into his ears and mouth. Albert pushed away from the tree, sputtering and slapping at his face. He had to be careful. It was almost dark and he was only a few feet from the precipice.

Now the bugs were in his eyes, swimming in his tears, and they scurried up to clog his nostrils so that he couldn't breathe. He vigorously rubbed his face, but he only crushed the insects and smeared their light-producing bioenzymes into his eyes. Then Albert stumbled, smashed his knee on a jagged rock and howled like a mad wolf.

All at once, his scalp started to tingle. Albert scratched at it until it began to burn. Then a searing pain rushed over his face to his eyes. His screams rocked the forest, chasing owls from their lookouts and sending forest mice deep into their burrows. Totally blinded and limping, Albert fell over the edge of the cliff and tumbled into space. A thousand feet later, his body burst into flames. He completed his journey to oblivion by streaking through the night like a fiery meteor.

Savage dreams chased away any chance Quinn had for sleep. Instead, he lay on the bed, listening to the whoosh of air coming out of the air-conditioning vent and sweating the alcohol overdose out of his blood. Adar and what was left of her family had gone to see the bodies of their relatives loaded aboard a charter flight for a final trip home. Guilt ate at him like acid.

Of course, he knew he had treated her badly. Any halfway decent human being would have gone with them to the airport, if not to show appreciation, at least to show respect. Those women had died trying to help him. He rolled to the side of the bed and let his feet touch the floor.

The room was cold. Quinn went to the window. The sea mirrored his restlessness: Churning white-caps and angry rollers beat the shore like a frustrated child. The sound of his fist on the window frame was lost in the roar of wind and surf. He put his hot fore-head against the cool glass. The alcohol tapeworm began feasting again on his gut. He needed a drink, but his head already felt like a punching bag.

Maybe take a shower? His soiled denim shorts and rank black shirt felt like a suit of salt-encrusted ar-mor. The idea of cool water caressing his body was appealing, but just seemed too damn much trouble.

The stairs were almost too much, but by hanging on to the banister, Quinn made it to the ground floor without breaking his neck. He walked slowly into the solarium, stopping in front of his late uncle's stereo system. The sound of a human voice would be nice, and he wished Adar were around so they could talk. But since she wasn't, he rifled through the plastic CD cases. He ignored the classical CDs, which didn't fit his dour mood. At the bottom of the stack he came across four black faces glowing with indignation. It was one of Q's rap albums.

Even though he despised rap music, he put the disc on the player, stood in front of the speaker and let the pent-up frustration pour out of him. Each brutal beat of the music matched the pounding in his head. He found himself slapping his hand hard against his side. It wasn't until he realized that the gonging inside his brain was off tempo that it dawned on him someone was ringing the front bell. When he opened the door, Ann Pakula smiled shyly and handed him a bottle of Dewar's. She did a little pirouette to show off her slinky black dress. The lower part billowed about her ankles, but the front was cut low enough to cause vertigo.

"Hi, I thought I'd drop by to see if you were still among the living."

She pushed past him while he was trying to form a response and went directly to what Tim referred to as the Rod Serling Night Gallery.

"I really like this," she said, pointing to the representation of witches grappling on the ground.

"Uh, Ann, look. I'm not feeling very well—"

"No kidding. You look like shit."

"Hey, don't pull any punches. Go right ahead and tell me what you really think."

She pointed to the bottle. "Something for what ails you."

Just the feel of the cool glass set the dogs to barking in his stomach. "Thanks, but I think this is what's ailing me. Look, Ann, I appreciate—"

Her lips stopped his protest. "You haven't eaten, have you? Where's the kitchen?"

She took off like a shot, ducking through the formal dinning room and homing in on the swinging door to the kitchen. "Wow! Nice kitchen."

"Ann, really—"

"Don't expect gourmet cooking. I can do scrambled eggs pretty well, but that's about it."

"Ann, you don't have to do this."

She pushed him over to a tall stool at the end of the cooking island. "Sit. It'll only take a couple of minutes. Then I'll be on my way. I can see you're not well."

It took three skillets, two bowls, a measuring cup and two plates, but at the end of 20 minutes, Ann proudly set a plate of runny yellow eggs and two pieces of slightly charred toast in front of him. She stood hunched over the sink for a moment, then handed him a tall glass of milk.

"Here, this will help settle your stomach."

Looking at the yellow mess swimming on the plate, Quinn would have rather eaten road kill, but he couldn't figure a way around it. He picked up the fork and started shoveling the food in as fast as he could.

"Don't forget the milk," she said.

The milk tasted funny. Quinn held it up to the light, thinking it might have gone bad, but he wasn't about to complain.

"There," she said when he finished. "Feel better?"

The funny thing was, he did feel better. His head was clear and his stomach had ceased its revolt. As a matter of fact, he felt downright jovial. He decided a cold beer couldn't hurt. So he took two bottles from the icebox and followed Ann into the library. Ann pushed him down on the couch in front of the fireplace.

"Just sit there a minute while I get the fire going."

The cushions felt soft, and he closed his eyes for just a second. When he opened them, the fire was roaring.

"Wow, you have a way with wood."

"Thank you." She did a little curtsy, then took the cushion next to him. "I give good fire."

"You may not want to get too close," he said running his hand over his chin. "I need a bath."

She took a sip of beer, turned sideways and pointed her legs toward him. "How's this?"

"Save your olfactory nerves."

She laughed the way she knew he expected. Quinn noted the hem of the dress was well above her knees.

"So, tell me about yourself," he said. "How'd you get into reporting? Why not get an honest job?"

She laughed again and he discovered the sound was almost as intoxicating as liquor. Her eyes held him as she slowly kicked off the pumps and crossed her legs. He was enthralled by the little dark cap of hose over her toes.

"Not much to tell. I grew up in the islands, one of the smaller ones, Nihau. Went to school on Kauai, then to UC Berkeley. I came back after graduation and got a job with the newspaper here on Maui. They paid crap, so a few years later, I moved on to *The Register* in Honolulu."

"What about family?"

"Died while I was away at school."

"Sorry." Quinn was beginning to feel very relaxed. Lack of sleep felt like a bag of warm sand being poured over his head. Her toes massaged the sore muscles of his legs like a pair of plump caterpillars inching their way up his thigh. "Ummm. So how come a woman with your looks isn't married or living with someone?"

"The job mostly. I'm in my apartment maybe two days a week. I haven't been out on a real date, sat down at a real table with flowers and candles since"—her eyes misted over for a moment, then cleared—"Hawaii became a state."

"You travel a lot?"

His words were beginning to come out thick and slow, and his eyelids felt like barbells. Ann deposited her beer bottle on the end table, scooted over next to him and tilted his face up.

"I'm the one who's supposed to ask all the questions." She kissed him firmly, penetrating his defenses with a very active tongue.

"Ann, I'm pretty rank," he said, drawing back.

"I don't care." She slipped the straps of her dress from her shoulders and let the top fall. His eyes explored the bounty of her body. Her breasts were not huge, but firm and tipped with dark olive nipples that responded to the air conditioning. He felt a surge of unmitigated lust and began pawing and biting her breasts.

Ann's head dropped back and she shook her hair free. "Yes!"

A minute ago he was about to pass out; now he

had completely lost control. He sucked a fat nipple into his mouth, nipping it with his teeth.

"Harder! Suck!"

He tasted blood and it seemed to ignite a fire in his brain. The urge to rend and tear possessed his blood. She shoved his head back and stood, letting the dress gather around her waist. Then she knelt in front of him and began fumbling with his belt buckle. Something inside told him to stop, but that part was buried under waves of heat spreading like wildfire through his groin. After he raised is hips, she jerked his shorts down, took him in her hand and surrounded him with her mouth. And then he passed out.

"Not yet!" She heaved a sigh of frustration, but continued to stroke and coax. Finally she sat back on her heels, then looked down at his shrinking member and kissed the tip tenderly.

The blood was still singing in her ears as she climbed to her feet. Strange, she thought as she stared at his face. He was a good-looking man. His features were too craggy for commercials, but they were compelling. He was very different from the fleshy men she was use to. Ann had not lied about one thing: She was not turned off by the musky odor of his sweat. After the perfumed, limp-wristed men of her coven, Quinn Ramsey's earthy smell was most welcome.

She brushed the hair from his forehead and let her hand trail down to his lips. Why couldn't this one have had the power instead of his vile uncle? she mused. One finger caressed his bottom lip, feeling its resiliency. She explored the curve of his neck and unbuttoned his shirt to touch his hairy nipples.

All at once her hand stopped! Just below Quinn's right nipple was a tiny bump, larger than a pimple, but smaller than a pea. Her eyes widened. A third nipple! For the first time in her life, she felt honest emotion stirring in her belly and it was such a novel sensation that she couldn't handle it right then. The tiny gold watch on her wrist said she was running out of time. Later, she thought. She'd think about these feelings later. Then she stepped out of the dress, bent over and kissed his lips.

"Maybe there is a way."

With her purse and shoes under one arm, Ann strode to the hall, draped the dress over the table and pulled her amulet from her purse, slipping it into its proper place around her neck. Then, still naked as the day she was born, she went to the door of the wine cellar and tiptoed down the icy steps.

Adar watched until the blinking lights on the airplane's wings were swallowed up by low-hanging clouds. After waving her good-byes, she turned and walked behind the others to the parking lot, where Mildred waited with the van. Tim Wolinsky was strolling beside Penny, talking in low tones, trying to coax a smile. But no one felt like smiling. What had gone wrong? Again and again that question kept tormenting her.

No housekeeper, not even one trained in the arts, should have been able to defeat the family's charms. Mildred had overseen each placement, every sign, every seal, and Adar had double-checked each, going to the four corners of the mansion—even that icebox Quinn called a wine cellar.

Adar suddenly stopped, her eyes staring blindly at her sister's back. "The cellar."

Penny stopped and raised her hands as if to say, "What's up?"

Adar shook her head. Something was buzzing around in the back of her head—something about the cellar, about it being so cold. She remembered when she recited the charm of protection that her breath had hung in the air in front of her face, practically raining ice crystals as she pronounced the words.

Okata's beat-up Plymouth was parked behind the van. Both blocked the yellow curb. The policewoman was in a heated discussion with one of the airport cops. She pulled the leather badge case from the back pocket of her jeans. "Give me any more shit and you'll be busting hookers in Waikiki."

"The van's illegally parked, Sergeant. I'm just doing my job."

"So go do it someplace else."

The cop slammed his citation book closed and stomped off muttering about PMS and women in the police department.

"Thank you," Mildred said.

"Hello, Gail," Adar said. "I thought you were watching the mansion."

Okata's face fell. "Quinn isn't here?"

The sudden chill Adar felt couldn't be explained by the night wind. "No, he wasn't feeling well."

"But I got a call that he was having some kind of problem out at the airport and—" Okata's whole demeanor changed before their eyes. One moment she seemed merely perplexed; the next her face underwent a sinister metamorphosis. Her eyes narrowed into angry red slits as she shouted, "Shit! Get in the van and follow me."

Penny and Tim helped throw the seat belts around Mildred. Then Adar got behind the wheel and followed the Plymouth's flashing blue light. Fat drops of rain smeared the windshield as they roared out of the parking lot.

The only way Ann Pakula was able to survive the climb up the stairs from the wine cellar was by shutting down all her sense and her feelings and placing one foot in front of the other. After carefully closing the door behind her, she put her back against it to make sure it remained shut.

She was a mess. Her hair was wild and stringy, her body was covered with raw red scratches, and she had a nasty black-and-blue wound over her heart. Mustering the strength to move was hard, but she limped to the hall, where it took her three tries to climb into her dress.

On the drive back to the airport, Ann was oblivious to the lights of the oncoming traffic. It took all of her considerable concentration to keep from screaming.

It had been childishly easy for her to find Bernard's secret chamber. Once inside, Ann cast her eyes over the room and decided that his contrived ornamentations smacked of a B horror movie. The place had been cold enough to freeze air, but she was comfortable in her nudity, warmed by great excitement and anticipation. She had come to negotiate.

"I, who am the servant of the most high Astaroth do, by the power of his holy name, invoke thy presence, great Moloch. I compel thee by the power of the living Lucifer, by the grace of his crown prince Beelzebub and by the majesty of Lucifuge Rofocale. Take form! Appear before me to hear my petition."

Halfway through the invocation, the hokey star on the back wall had started to glow, and a few seconds later a pair of huge catlike orbs had opened in the nothingness before the makeshift altar. The pupils had been angry vertical slits floating in a red sea. The voice, when it came, had been calculated to disarm. A low whisper like the rasp of tumbleweed pushed by the wind said, "Why do you summon me?"

Ann's confidence had zoomed. "Great Moloch, will you not appear so that I may do you honor?"

The eyes stared without blinking for a time, then disappeared behind a curtain of mist. Inside the cloud, dark things twisted and churned like a deformed fetus trying to break out of its womb. Intense cold radiated from the cloud as Ann fought her impatience. When at last the cloud dissipated, a dark horrific figure crouched atop the altar, studying the naked witch with evident curiosity.

Moloch had chosen his gargoyle persona. The body was roughly humanoid, but it sported leathery wings and wicked-looking claws on its hands and feet. Its skin was the color of scorched copper.

"I am here," Moloch said simply.

Ann was still human enough to be unnerved by such an awesome display and shrewd enough not to let her response show. She took three tiny steps forward. "Lord, why do you dwell in this place?"

Moloch flicked out a thin black tongue that vibrated in the air between them. The tip was forked and pointed. "Why do you ask?"

She took another tentative step. "This place is cheap and theatrical. Hardly an abode for a creature of your lofty stature. My coven has been calling upon you for many years. We seek to enshrine you in a magnificent temple that we have built in your honor."

The creature gave up all pretense of whispering and emitted a great, booming laugh. "Enshrine? You mean imprison, like that accursed Ramsey."

Ann winced, but did not attempt to cover her ears. "No, we would never do that."

But, indeed, that was exactly what she planned.

At one time, everyone had thought Bernard Ramsey was just another occult groupie. He had attended all the black Shabbats, where drugs and liquor flowed like water, and oral sex was used as a greeting more often than shaking hands. He had kept to himself, watching, learning. He was a good listener, an educated man, a wizard with numbers and computers. Finally, mostly due to Ann's mother's vanity, the man had wormed his way into their confidence, and Tammy had entrusted their most important books and manuscripts to his care.

The coven—especially Ann, her mother, and the two high priests, Peterson and Smythe—had been working for years trying to unlock the secrets of the Old Ones. Of particular interest was Moloch, the primeval Ammonite god reputed to bestow wealth and eternal life in return for the sacrifice of human children. They had spent almost three years translating ancient manuscripts from Assyria and Iraq. Ann had traveled to the Congo, paddling up crocodile-infested rivers, to bring back codices handwritten in faded blood on parchments made from human skins.

Their studies had revealed that to lure Moloch into the physical realm would require a sacrifice of souls on the scale of the Nazi holocaust—far too many to escape notice if they had to rely on living beings.

Somehow Bernard had stumbled upon the answer: trapped souls, souls such as those of the ancient Polynesians bound to the cave under Mauna Kea. That had been just what the witch doctor ordered.

Ann had to give Bernard his due. The man had been as devious as a snake, but he had been able to locate the cave using powers that no one suspected he possessed. He had pulled strings to purchase the land secretly, spending millions of dollars of his own money. Then, to top everything else, he had stolen the manuscripts and translations and scurried back to his bunker, where, all alone, he had enticed Moloch with the promise of thousands of long-dead souls.

"It is true," Ann said, "that we seek your favor. We long for the gift of eternal youth and untold riches, but we are willing to repay you handsomely."

"With these fictitious souls that Ramsey claimed to control?"

"They are not fictitious, lord. They exist. And we control them."

The grotesque being laughed again, his eyes blazing like windblown coals. "Woman, why do I not believe you?"

"But it's true! If you agree to take the throne in your temple, we will shower you with power the likes of which you have only dreamed about."

Moloch eyed Ann's shivering form. With the creature's weird, feline eyes, it was impossible to tell what was going through his mind. "After Ramsey, how am I supposed to trust you?"

Ann wasn't sure what the thing would believe. She would have given anything to know how Bernard had trapped the damned demon in the first place. At last, in desperation, she turned her back to the creature for a moment, and when she faced it again, his eyes had gone wide with revelation.

"Because I am one of you," she said at last.

Moloch's grin was terrible to behold. His mouth was full of teeth like black punji sticks. His wings rustled and he dropped to the floor, rising to full height so that his horned head barely cleared the eight-foot ceiling.

Ann experienced her first pang of real fear when he crossed the distance between them and lifted her amulet with one finger. The claws on his toes left shallow furrows in the concrete floor. When the entity loomed over her, Ann noticed for the first time that the creature was more anatomically correct than the average gargoyle. He took hold of her shoulder and started to pull her to him.

"No!" she said in a panic.

"You seek my trust?" The creature's touch was like ice, burning to the marrow of her bones.

"Yes. You have no reason to distrust me."

Moloch flicked her right nipple painfully with one of those razor-sharp claws. She tried to escape his grasp, but his black tongue snaked out and wrapped around her neck like a noose. She fought like a tiger, raking the scales around his eyes with her fingernails and pounding the leering face with her fists, but she might as well have been throwing baseballs at a Sherman tank. Moloch jerked her off her feet had carted her back to the stone table.

"I will soon know if I can trust you."

Further resistance was futile. The creature shack-led Ann's hands and feet and positioned himself between her legs. He stroked the top of her thigh with a thorny hand.

"Humans are so warm."

Plump tears of terror trailed down her cheeks. She wanted to say something, but what? The creature climbed up between her legs, wagging his erect black member between bony thighs.

"No. Please," she moaned.

A wide grin split Moloch's saurian features. As he lowered himself onto her, he whispered, "Yes, beg. Who knows? Maybe it will help."

Ann's eyes felt incredibly heavy. Every muscle in her body was screaming. When she opened her eyes, she had to cut the wheel sharply to avoid a head-on with a van coming in the other direction, and she shook her head to clear it before returning to her dark musing.

So this was what it was like to be the sacrificial lamb. It wasn't the sex. Hell, she'd fucked just about every living creature with a heartbeat. No, that thing in the cellar had raped her mind and spirit as well as her body.

Maybe her spirit was polluted, but Moloch had done something to her, something that left her feeling as if maggots were crawling around in her gut. So what now? Should she run home and tell her loving mother? Then what? Before that night, Ann had been a juggernaut, her powers smashing anything that got in her way. She had always had almost everything she'd wanted. Suddenly the one thing she wanted more than anything was a fresh start, a new identity, a new life.

Ann had never known a real home. They'd had plenty of money, food, booze, drugs and jewelry. What would cooking on a stove be like? Baking a cake for someone? Lots of women did it. She'd heard some even liked it. Maybe it was too late for all that sentimental slop, but what about living in a normal house with a garden? She could do it! And what about shopping and movies? Ann had never bought a dress or a pair of shoes for herself. The coven had been her life, and now, suddenly, it struck her how much she had missed.

In the lights of an oncoming car she saw a vision: a little girl smiling up at her from the top of the makeshift altar at the penthouse.

Ann hit her high beams and forced the other car onto the narrow shoulder. "Who am I trying to fool?" she muttered bitterly.

Still, with help and the right person, who knew what could happen?

"Wasn't that what's her name's car, the reporter?" Adar said as a Toyota whizzed past the van.

"Looked like her," Tim replied.

Okata slowed to take the series of curves just before Quinn's driveway. A couple of minutes later, they parked and Okata lead the charge into the house with her pistol ready. Tim was a step behind her with a sawed-off, pump shotgun.

When they entered the front hall, Okata whispered to Adar, "Stay here."

Adar shook her head. "If he's hurt, he's going to need me."

Mildred tried to restrain her niece, but Adar shrugged off the old woman's hand and stayed in Tim's shadow as they played hide and seek down the corridor. Okata pointed to a puddle of blood near the hall table and cocked her weapon.

"God, I'm sick of this hall," she said.

When they reached the library, Tim went in high and Okata low, sweeping the room with their guns. Okata saw the top of Quinn's head sticking up over the back of the couch and ran around to the front.

"Oh, my!"

Adar stopped at the door, fearing the worst, but when Tim started laughing, she crept around the couch. It took a long moment for her to comprehend what was staring her in the face. Quinn was asleep on the couch with his shirt unbuttoned and his shorts and underwear bunched around his ankles. She watched in disbelief as he snorted, turned on his side and pulled his legs up under him.

"You bastard!"

Chapter Twelve

Christmas Eve

"Get up, shithead," Tim said.

Quinn opened his eyes slowly against the morning glare. "What time z'it?"

"Time for you to get up and take your medicine."

Quinn rolled to a sitting position and cradled his head in shaking hands. "Stop shouting."

"Let me warn you," Tim said. "You have a lot of questions to answer. Adar is really pissed."

"Adar? What's she mad about?"

"Take a shower and come down. The jury awaits."

After a quick shave and a long hot shower, Quinn came downstairs and eased into his chair at the end of the long dining table. Pouring coffee, he said, "Morning."

Adar was hiding behind the morning paper, and

the others were either watching him with sly grins or hard stares. Only Mildred returned his greeting.

"Good morning, Quinn. How do you feel?"

"Okay, I guess. Kind of sleepy. What time did you all get back?"

"About midnight. You don't remember?"

"No, I guess I fell asleep."

"When Adar slammed the paper down on the table, Mildred asked, "Do you remember being downstairs last night?"

The cup stopped just in front of his lips. "No."

"I don't suppose you remember having a visitor either?" Adar asked sarcastically.

"Visitor? Who?"

Adar made a rude sound with her lips, and Mildred said, "Honey, I told you this might be the case."

"Why do you always take his side?"

"Because I believe him."

"Then how did she get in?" Adar said, almost turning her chair over in her hurry to get to her feet.

"How did who get in?" Quinn said.

"That reporter," Mildred said. "We passed her on the way back from the airport."

"Ann?"

"Yes! Ann!" Adar snapped.

"Ann was here?"

"Someone was here," Mildred said before Adar could jump in. "Our spells had been broken. You remember we told you the spells would keep others out, but not if you opened the door and invited them in."

Quinn stared down at the cup and shook his head. "Ann was here?"

"If you say that one more time, I'm gonna brain you," Adar yelled.

Tim turned to Penny and whispered loud enough to be heard at the end of the table. "They ought to get married."

"I remember some music," Quinn said. Then his face turned the color of tomato juice as he recalled the dream he'd had about Ann Pakula—a dream of creamy breasts and a mouth like hot butter.

"Tell me," Mildred said.

"I don't remember," he replied quickly.

"Quinn," Penny said, "we found dishes in the sink. And we found traces of a potion in one of the glasses. Did you come down to eat?"

"I really don't remember."

"Well, there's something you need to see," Mildred said. "Come with us."

She got up and led the way along the hall, through the door to the wine cellar and down the stairs. The sound of shoes rang off the metal steps and echoed like dull bells in the confined space. Mildred went to the far wall and pulled the release lever, waiting for the wall to slide open and then pushed past the heavy curtains into the hidden chamber.

Quinn stood just inside the opening and stared. "Why is it so cold? What is this place?"

"Until last night, it was the cage of the demon," Mildred replied.

Quinn walked slowly around the room. When he came to the altar, he paused. If it were possible for solid rock to store and replay evil like a psychic CD this one did. He ran his hand gingerly over the rough stone and his fingers came away sticky.

"Blood," Mildred said.

"Moloch is gone," Adar said, "and we don't know why or, more importantly, where."

"Thank God," Quinn said.

"Maybe you should," Mildred said. "Maybe not."

"Can we get out of here?" he asked. "This place makes me want to throw up."

Back in the library, Quinn made a beeline for the bar. He had the shakes and his tongue felt like an angora sweater. Penny gently stayed his hand on the crystal decanter.

"Maybe you should keep a clear head," she said kindly.

"Tonight is Christmas Eve," Mildred said. "It's a major Christian holiday. It is also the feast night of Belial, a Great Shabbat to the Druids and a night of sacrifice to the Old Ones. If the kidnappers still need you to secure access to the volcano, fine. But if not, Q could be in danger."

Sour fear settled in the pit of Quinn's stomach. "What can we do?"

"Gail is trying to trace Ms. Pakula's movements. We know she checked out of her motel yesterday, and we're trying to find out where she went. That's our only hope."

"But I thought you had people who could locate things."

"We did," Adar replied. "Beth."

"So we just sit and wait for Okata to call?"

"Well, Penny has shown some talent in location," Mildred replied. "We are going to the cellar to see what we can do. Other than that, we wait."

"I'll be ready," Tim said.

"What I suggest is," Mildred said, "we try to get more rest. Get whatever it was that woman gave you out of your system so that your head will be clear when we move."

"You really don't remember last night?" Adar asked when the other women had left the room.

"No, I really don't. What happened?"

"Ask Tim." She followed the others into the corridor.

"Well, buddy, you were out cold on the couch in the library," Tim said. "Your shirt was unbuttoned and your pants were down around your feet."

"Oh, shit!"

"That wasn't the worst of it."

"What could be worse than that?"

"You had this big, goofy grin on your face."

Quinn tried closing the drapes and stretching out on his bed, but he couldn't sleep. He wanted to sleep, but every time he closed his eyes, he saw Q's face superimposed on the butchered bodies of Adar's family. A liquid sedative might have helped, but there was a good chance that if he picked up a bottle, he wouldn't be able to put it down. He had been to AA, was a graduate of the twenty-four step program . . . the twelve steps . . . twice, yet when they'd taken his boy, his first thought had been, what a perfect excuse to get drunk.

After an hour of rearranging his limbs on the bed, he went down stairs. Voices were coming from the solarium, but it was only Tim and two of the cousins. Mildred, Penny and Adar were missing. He went to the other tower, up the stairs to Adar's room and knocked. She opened the door in a pair of loose black silk shorts and a plaid blouse.

"Hi," he said lamely.

"Feeling better?" she asked. She sat on the bed and crossed her legs Indian fashion.

"Some. Look. I swear I don't remember what happened last night. And I don't know why I took off like that yesterday."

"So why tell me?"

"Come on, Adar. Don't beat me to death. I thought we made a good start."

One corner of her mouth turned up. "Start? Are we going somewhere?"

"You're not going to make this easy are you?"

"Nope."

He laughed and looked out the window. After several days of gloom the sun had finally appeared and the ocean was almost painfully blue. A quarter of a mile away, the barnacle-crusted mound of a humpback whale broke the surface. A moment later, its huge fluke slapped the water and splashed gallons of white foam high into the air.

"When this is over, what are you going to do?" he asked.

"I don't know. Go back home. Teach, I guess."

This was as hard for him as anything he had ever done. Fighting with felons, wrestling with drunks and arguing with hookers—that was easy. Hanging his feelings out for everyone to take potshots at was a fucking nightmare.

"I thought you might want to stay—and keep working with Q."

"I suppose you'll give me a raise."

"Of course."

"And benefits?"

"Sure. Medical, dental."

He caught her mocking tone and went with it. When she spoke the next time, she was standing right behind him. "And is that the only reason you want me to stay? To teach Q?"

Quinn turned and there she was. His arms went around her waist and pulled her close. "No, there's more—much more."

He held on. Her warmth flowed into the tips of his fingers; her eyes, green and alive, sparkled with promise. When they kissed, it was like stepping off a precipice with his eyes closed. The desire he felt was natural, but it was more than that. Her lips fit. Each curve and dip of her mouth seemed to find its match in his. Her arms reached all the right places, her tongue danced with his as if they had done so many times before. It was as if he had been walking through the world blind and had just opened his eyes. In a few moments, they parted, but clung to each other.

"Wow," she said breathlessly. "You've done that before."

He shook his head slowly. "Not for a long time."

She smiled and let her arms drop. "I suppose you've been studying for the priesthood since your wife died?"

"No, I dated a few times. But they—no, that's not fair. I was about to say they weren't right, but it wasn't them. I was the problem. A couple were really nice. One worked in the district attorney's office. I think she would have been good for me, but I just couldn't let go. The first time I had sex after Kathy died, it was just like scratching an itch. She knew it and it hurt her. I didn't see her again."

"So how do you know you're over it now?"

"I can feel you inside here." He pointed to his chest. "For a long time, I thought everything in there was dead—except for my love for Q. I thought that all my feelings had been buried along with Kathy. The other day on the beach, I felt them come alive again."

Her silence made him notice again how quiet the house was. He could hear the surf way down on the beach and the wind through the frangipani trees, but the house was no more than an abandoned museum.

"So how's that itch now?" Adar asked.

Ann Pakula brushed past the burly guard and opened the door to the dark bedroom. The square of light revealed Q stretched out on top of the bed, his slack features making him stand out like a phantom against a navy-blue comforter.

Before coming in, Ann had soaked in her oversize bathtub for a solid hour. The water had been hot enough to cook her skin as red as a lobster, but she still didn't feel clean. She recalled things she had done during her rise to power: sacrifices, first animal and later human; necromantic rituals in which she had pried secrets from the steamy entrails of her enemies; orgies in which she had engaged in every form and combination of sexual perversion known to man. But the host of barbaric acts never scarred her as badly as what had happened in the cellar of Quinn Ramsey's mansion.

She steeled her mind against the memory and went to the side of the bed. The child had his father's dark good looks and high forehead. An ornate, French Provincial armchair was tucked into one corner of the room. She pulled it next to the bed and took a seat. It was warm in the dark. She had refrained from using the lights, preferring the artificial twilight eking through the thick drapes.

After eight long years, the coven was close to attaining its goal, and she hoped that the letdown she was feeling was just the normal relaxation of tension at the end of an arduous quest. Yet as she stared at the son, Ann was forced to face the possibility that it was something else. She couldn't seem to get the father out of her mind.

Quinn was so different from his uncle. The man dressed like a beach bum, and he was totally out of his depth trying to run that vast estate. Yet in spite of all that, he had touched some kernel of melancholy deep inside that Ann never suspected she possessed. Maybe it was his bumbling naivete or his dark good looks. To be honest, it was probably all that latent psychic power sitting like a storehouse of untapped uranium just below the surface of his mind. For Ann, power like that had always been more addicting than heroin. If her plans worked out, that power would come in handy, and all she had to do was fake the spell summoning Moloch in a way that would keep her mother in the dark.

But how could she get next to Quinn? How could she get control of all that raw power? Sex? More money?

The door opened and a second later her mother's

presence permeated the dark like unexpected bad luck. "What are you doing here, child? The ceremony is in a few hours. Should you not be preparing yourself?"

"There is plenty of time, mother."

"The boy still sleeps?" she asked, pointing to a vial of Demerol sitting on the night table.

"Yes."

"We must prepare him soon."

"Why must it be this boy? Why not one of the street children?"

The older woman's anger floated on the air. "You would offer Lord Moloch a filthy street urchin?"

"A life is a life," Ann replied defensively.

"You know better than that! What's gotten into you?"

Ann wondered if her mother would appreciate the irony of that question. But she didn't want to raise her mother's ire, so she said, "We may still need to negotiate with Ramsey for the well of souls. If the boy is sacrificed, what will we offer in trade?"

"Anna, with Moloch in our power, we can snuff Ramsey out like a match."

"Are you sure Moloch is in our power?"

"Of course. We have prepared the containment chamber and charms carefully."

"But we never recovered the manuscripts Bernard stole."

The older woman slapped a palm against her thigh in exasperation. "We used other sources. What's the matter with you?"

What was the matter with her? What an insane question! Ann's birth 34 years before had been the product of a rather unique union. As a young woman, Tammy had been a somewhat befuddled yet happy member of a California coven that was made up of drug-sodden malcontents and dropouts who turned to witchcraft as part of their back-to-nature bent. Somehow, one of these cretins had stumbled upon a dusty copy of the *Grand Grimoire* in a San Francisco curio shop, and the coven had retired to a mountaintop near Muir Woods to hold their first real shabbat. After casting aside their clothing and building a nice bonfire, they drew a pentagram in the dirt with sticks and sat around in a circle while their Latin scholar read the passage that promised to summon one of the lesser spirits.

While the naked young man with his long, oily hair read the strange words, the others sat around fondling each other in preparation for the group grope that always followed their ceremonies. But this time, things had turned out differently.

As soon as the blood from a carefully cut forearm had dripped over the ancient text, the wind, which only seconds before had been calm, began to howl like a banshee. Most of the coven thought that a night sky clawing at itself with jagged fingers of lightning was all part of their pharmacological light show, so they just sat staring straight up and giggling. A few thought the sky was falling and tried to hide under a wall of filthy jeans and ponchos; still others ran screaming for the cover of the trees. Ann's mother had been high on LSD and so lost in passionate embrace with the son of a wealthy Napa Valley vintner that she was oblivious to the whole thing.

Young and full of raging hormones, Tammy was sure theirs was a pure and undying love—right up until the boy's vacuous blue eyes abruptly turned bloodred, and he began raking her breasts with unnaturally long fingernails. Tammy had screamed and fought, but her brain was awash in chemicals and her struggles were quickly overcome. Believing Tammy was having another bad trip, her friends ignored her calls for help. For the next ten months the young girl from the good Polynesian family in Hawaii had tried to convince herself that was all it was—that is, until the night Anna was born.

Tammy had gone to an underground clinic on Haight Street in San Francisco to deliver the baby. Her pregnancy had been a nightmare. Nine-and-a-half months of vaginal bleeding, cramps like burning snakes, vomiting, headaches and bile-colored diarrhea. To fight the horrendous pain, she had resorted to more and more drugs. She'd smoked countless bags of cannabis and dropped enough acid to boost a car battery with two dead cells. When her time came, the burned-out unlicensed doctor refused to give her anything for the pain. He'd already lost his license for pushing pills, and he'd done a dime in the joint for performing illegal abortions. He wasn't about to risk another stint for overdosing an obviously zoned-out acid freak.

The nurse, a fat black woman who had learned compassion while dispensing Thorazine at San Fran General, strapped Tammy to a table in the back and let her scream until bloody froth flew from her lips. When Anna came out, the nurse had passed out cold on the floor.

300

But the baby wasn't horribly disfigured. If anything Anna had been an exceptionally beautiful little girl, with her soft green, almond-shaped eyes, cute little button nose and creamy olive complexion. It was the tiny scale-covered tail that protruded a good half inch from the end of her sacrum that had caused the hardened old nurse to drop to the tile in a stupor.

The doctor was even more horrified. The last thing that man wanted was notoriety. To buy Tammy's silence, he had crammed all of his personal street narcotics into Tammy's ragged purse and hustled the mother and child out as fast as he could get them ready to travel.

But all that was ancient history. The important thing to Ann now was to keep Q alive. If she played the boy right, he just might be the key to the father. Ann had to stall.

"Mother, tell me again about the night father visited us."

Tammy laughed. "You never tire of hearing that story, do you?"

Ann's mother moved to a chair in the darkest corner of the room, and she put a flame to the end of a cheroot, blowing a fragrant cloud of invisible smoke toward the ceiling.

"It was three months after you were born. I was waiting tables in the Mission District, near San Francisco Hospital and dancing in one of the bars at night. I had just picked you up from the home of the old Mexican woman who watched you for two bucks a day. I was heating your bottle and a can of soup on the beat-up old hot plate we had in our apartment. You don't remember that place, do you?"

"No," Ann replied softly. She did remember roaches the size of armored personnel carriers and rats that wore catskin coats.

"Of course not, you were a baby. It was the pits. We had a toilet at the end of the hall, a bathtub that smelled like shit, and rats as big as bicycles. I had to tiptoe around used needles.

"Anyway, I was making dinner when the lights in the apartment went out. I thought it was another brown out until I saw the hall light under the door. Then I saw his eyes. They were like a pair of neon beams. He spoke to me and his voice was rough silk. It sent shivers down my spine. He said we were special. He had mated with many humans over the centuries but you were the first to survive. I remember thinking that it was probably the drugs.

"He told me that our lives were about to change, that we would have money and power, clothes and food. He told me about many things: places to go to find answers, people who would help us. Then he lifted me and took me to the floor.

"He didn't use hands, you understand, just the power of his mind. But my baggy dress was ripped off and he entered me. It wasn't like the first time when he'd used another's body. I thought I was going to lose my mind."

"When it was over, I lay on the floor covered in gallons of semen that burned like acid. I couldn't move for two days. I was afraid you would starve because I couldn't even get up to heat your bottle. But you didn't. If anything, you seemed healthier after that and he kept all his promises. The money flowed. I found the secret places and the forbidden books. I started your education before you could walk. And today, the world is ours."

"Yes, I owe everything I am to you, Mother."

"And I never saw anything except those eyes," Tammy whispered as the cheroot winked out. "Enough reminiscing. We must prepare for the final step. You have to bathe and anoint your body; then we have to make the pilgrimage to the place of ceremony."

"I will," Ann replied. "Just give me another minute."

Tammy vanished into the bright corridor, closing the door firmly behind. Ann gazed down at the unconscious boy and caressed his face.

"Unbelievable," Quinn whispered.

Adar's head was nestled in the hollow of his shoulder as he stroked her body with the tips of his fingers. His touch caused her skin to break out in a rash of lust and her breath to catch in her throat.

"Stop it." She sighed, pushing his hand away. "You're driving me crazy."

But he couldn't stop. He tried, but as soon as they went back to their whispered conversation, his hand would sneak over to cup her breast or walk down the flat plains of her stomach to explore the smooth texture of the skin on her hip. She finally held his hand, intertwining her fingers with his.

"I believe you," she said.

"About what?"

"About not making love in a long time." During their heated coupling, Adar had discovered Quinn's developing third nipple. Its significance was not lost on her, so she asked, "How much do you know about your family tree?"

"My family? Not much. We were never a close-knit bunch, but I don't think we ever had anyone hanged for stealing horses, if that's what you're worried about."

"How about burned at the stake?"

Quinn propped his chin on her stomach. "You're kidding, right? Come on. Just because Uncle Bernard liked to play Mr. Wizard doesn't mean I'm some kind of sorcerer's apprentice."

"Maybe."

He pulled a case off one of the pillows and wrapped it around his head in a loose turban. "Look at me, Ma." He wiggled both his eyebrows and his fingers at the flower pot on the nightstand. "Seem-seem-sala-beam. I command you to rise, oh flower vase."

They laughed easily together, but fell silent when they heard someone pounding up the stairs. Quinn jumped out of bed and began pulling on clothes.

"It's not the sheriff." Adar laughed and decided to shelve the discussion of Quinn's hereditary powers for the time being. Whether he believed or not wasn't that important anyway.

Penny knocked on the door. "Adar, is Quinn in there?"

"Whose reputation are you worried about?" She giggled when Quinn blushed violently and shook his head from side to side. "Yes! Come on in!"

Penny opened the door as Quinn finished with the last button on his shirt. Adar lay back on the pillow, but covered herself with the sheet.

"Gail is on the phone, Quinn. Are you going to stay there all day, girl?"

Quinn hurried to the door, picking up his shoes on the way. As he whisked past, Penny said, "What are you so red in the face about? You should be proud my sister has feelings for you."

"I am," he sputtered.

"Then kiss her good-bye and get to the phone."

A few minutes later Quinn picked up the phone in his office. "Yeah, Gail, what have you got?"

"What have you been doing? Jogging? I got lucky. I couldn't find any record of a woman matching Ann Pakula's description leaving on any of the commercial flights. But I found one of the charter agents that remembered her. Pakula hired a private jet to fly her to Oahu, and she paid for the flight with a credit card. I checked the card and it belongs to *The Honolulu Register* all right, but I dug a little deeper. I called a friend in the hall of records to trace the ownership of the paper since I thought it was strange that a mere reporter could hire a private jet to fly between islands.

"*The Register* is owned by a corporation called Magus Enterprises. I found out Magus is a privately held corporation with two major stockholders, Ann and Tamara Pakula."

Okata waited for a response, and when she didn't receive one, she continued. "So that got me thinking. I called the office of your late friend Peterson and asked to speak to one of the partners, but the funny thing is, none of them is around. The secretaries said they all went to some conference over on the big island. So I told them I was in the middle of the investigation into Peterson's murder and needed some information. They danced me around for a while but the head secretary admitted that Magus was one of Peterson's biggest clients."

"So where does that leave us?" Quinn asked.

"That depends on you. With what I have, my boss wouldn't authorize a flight across the street, much less over to Oahu. He won't give me any help either."

"And why not? I don't pay enough taxes?"

"No offense, Quinn, but even you aren't in Magus's league when it comes to pull."

"Thank you for the reality check."

"But you have a pilot."

"Yeah, I do. When do you want to leave?"

"How soon can we?"

"Wait." Quinn put the phone down and ran through the house yelling for Tim.

"He's down on the beach hitting on my sister," one of the cousins said. "I'll get him."

"What about Frank Robbins? Is he back?"

"Not yet, but he should be at the airport in an hour or so"

Quinn picked up the extension. "Gail? We can be ready as soon as I can arrange for a plane. Frank's returning in about an hour. What about you?"

"I have to get a few things. I'll call you back in twenty minutes. Will that give you enough time?"

"You bet. And, Gail, watch yourself."

Quinn replaced the telephone and searched the house for Mildred. He found her in the observatory. She had one eye glued to the lens of the telescope. After repeating Okata's story, he asked, "Where do you think they could be?"

"Penny thinks they're somewhere in Waikiki right now, but I wouldn't bet that's where they'll be later on."

"Where in Waikiki? Okata can send the SWAT team."

"It's not that exact, Quinn. Location is a feeling of spatial displacement, not like looking something up in a phone book."

"Spatial displacement, huh? Well, as soon as Tim gets ready, we're heading to the airport to meet Frank. When he gets back and refuels, we're flying to Oahu."

Mildred let her eyes trail over the occult graffiti and planetary symbols. "Your uncle was a powerful witch."

"Gee, I wish I'd known him," Quinn replied with as much sarcasm as he could muster.

"No, I mean very powerful," Mildred said more forcefully. "He was able to imprison a major demon. But the man was paranoid. I found evidence of a very elaborate defensive spell that he had cast over the house."

"Didn't do him much good, did it?"

"True. But, Quinn, he even drew runes on the rafters in the attic."

"Attic? What attic?"

Mildred went to the bookcase built into the north wall and gave the crystal skull on the middle shelf a counterclockwise twist. The heavy bookcase moved silently to the right.

"This place is beginning to give me the creeps," Quinn said as he dipped his head and stepped into the darkness.

Like any attic, the flooring was shaky. The room was hot and smelled of dust and fiberglass insulation—and something else. Mildred pulled the chain on a hanging bulb and flooded the room with sickly yellow light. There wasn't much to see: bare-roof supports and a few boxes. At the edge of the floored area was a steamer trunk, the kind with brass fittings and stickers from faraway places. As old and dented as it was, it was sealed with a heavy padlock.

"What's in there?" Quinn asked.

"I don't know."

Quinn threw up his hands and went outside to the workbench next to the telescope. After fumbling through the drawers, the best he could come up with was a pair of blunt scissors. When he went back into the attic, the lock was hanging open. He looked his exasperation at the old woman.

"I didn't say I couldn't open it."

With the trunk open, Quinn wasn't so sure he wanted to see what was inside. "You picked the lock," he said. "You look."

"What do you think is in there?"

"I don't know, but I don't think I'm going to like it."

"You sense something?"

He did sense something, and it made his skin crawl. "No, I just don't want to open it."

Mildred removed the lock and raised the lid. Underneath a protective Styrofoam sheet was a rotting feathered cloak, and at the bottom of the trunk lay a jumble of yellowed bones and tarnished jewelry. The skull was covered with strange letters and splotches of what looked like dried blood. Some of the bones had soot caked on one end. Despite his revulsion, Quinn reached in and lifted the skull up to the light. It was light and the bone was eggshell thin. The jaw had been wired in place and it swung open like it was laughing at some cosmic joke.

"Is there no end to the man's depravity?" Mildred hissed.

Gazing into the empty sockets made Quinn dizzy. "What?"

"Necromancy!"

"I don't know what that is."

"It's a form of divination. In this case, I think your uncle conjured up the soul of this poor dead creature and offered it up to Moloch."

Quinn's head filled with a sudden explosion of light. He was in a procession, marching with hundreds of gaily dressed people up the side of a smoking volcano. At the top of the rise, a brown man in a feathered cloak and tall headdress beckoned the throng onward. He felt a wellspring of pride and religious fervor. Suddenly, he fell into an inky vortex that spun him through a black universe. The loneliness was horrible. His friends, his family—everything was gone. He sensed a pinpoint of light and something monstrous that waited at the end of the dark tunnel.

"What do you see?"

Quinn snapped back to the attic. "What?"

"What did you see?" Mildred asked.

"Nothing." He quickly replaced the skull and slammed the trunk.

"I should have warned you that the spell might still

be active, but sooner or later, you are going to have to accept what you are."

"I'm a father whose son has been taken by psychopaths. That's all I am."

Mildred shrugged and pointed toward the roof. The beams were covered with lines of squiggly stickmen.

"Okay, other than the fact that Uncle Bernie robbed graves and had a mania for hidden rooms, what does that tell you?"

Mildred restored the crystal skull to its proper orientation and the opening was sealed. "He took those remains to lure the beast to this house."

Quinn ran his hand over his face. "Yeah, that's what I thought you meant."

"More importantly, he was scared. Scared enough to draw protective runes on every single roof beam. And he was powerful. Those runes are incredibly old, and although they look amateurish, they are perfectly rendered.

"If we had time," Mildred said almost to herself, "I'd try to figure out what it would take to lure a man as paranoid as your uncle out of this fortress."

"Mildred!"

"Okay. The man was obsessive. Anybody who would go to these lengths in his own home would probably do the same thing anywhere he went."

"Probably. But why is that important?"

"Because in addition to keeping things out, those runes would also keep them in. And regardless of how they were able to free Moloch, our enemies will need another place of confinement. A place that had been meticulously prepared beforehand."

Quinn paused to let her message sink in; then he went back to the bookcase and gave the skull another turn. Inside, he pulled the light close to the nearest beam and studied the runes. When he turned to leave, he saw they also surrounded the exit.

"Would this place have to be complete? I mean, would it need solid walls and a roof?"

"No," Mildred replied. "The construction of the place of containment is immaterial. Bricks and mortar won't stop Moloch, but the runes will."

"The abandoned house! The one beside the waterfall. It has the same drawings."

Mildred nodded approvingly. "Now you're using your head. It's also right next to the burial chamber, which would provide a very powerful attraction for the demon. But it almost seems too easy. Your uncle has other properties, doesn't he? It could be any of them."

"Okay, I admit it's a long shot, but Gail found out this group is somehow connected to that bunch of shysters at Peterson's law firm and the secretary over there told her they were all attending some powwow on the big island tonight. What do you think? Coincidence?"

Mildred smiled broadly. "Not likely."

The sun rested atop Mauna Loa's crater like a scoop of cool orange sherbet in a sugar cone. Below, a caravan of vans and sleek limousines rolled to a stop as close to the abandoned house as possible. Ann stepped out of the lead automobile and checked her watch. The red robe she had draped around her shoulders and the afternoon humidity immediately

311

brought a light sheen of perspiration to her face.

"Garth, put everything in the house," she said to the driver. "Tell the others to get the candles going and Mother will show them how to reinforce the charms."

After the driver, a man as wide and intelligent as a garage door, grunted once and went to the trunk to remove the coven's occult paraphernalia, Ann strolled through the high grass. The untapped energy inside the cave drew her to the edge of the pond, where she paused to ponder the falling water. At the side of the rock ledge, the tall grass moved. There was little humor in her smile as the triangular head of the white dog poked through the weeds. The animal caught her smell and bared its fangs, but did not leave its post. This act of defiance brought a red mist of rage to her mind.

"I will deal with you," Ann whispered, baring her teeth in reply. "I'll keep you alive while I strangle you with your own intestines."

Tammy's voice sounded behind her. The old woman was not happy. She spoke in clipped tones to the pack of idiot lawyers that stalked her shadow in their hot, silk-lined black robes.

"If you had done your jobs, we could have performed this rite weeks ago."

"But, Tammy," one man whined. "What could we have done? First Stalkins was murdered, then Peterson, then Albert. The police were all over us like flies."

Tammy strode by, resplendent in a flowing flowered pantsuit. Her attention and her wrath focused on the sweating lawyers, who trembled in her wake. A green van pulled up and two men unloaded the stretcher with Quinn's son. As they followed the path to the house, Ann stepped in front of them.

"Put him in the back bedroom. There is little air in this glade. It's cooler."

"Tammy said to wake him," a tall man said. He was dressed in the white short-sleeved robe of a neophyte. An old scar ran through his right eye, turning the dead orb the color of blue marble. His nose was flat and he had the type of pallor that increased under artificial gymnasium lights.

"Do not wake him," Ann said. "Let him sleep."

"But Tammy said the brat's supposed to be alert for the ceremony."

Ann narrowed her eyes. The second man, young and skinny with thinning brown hair, was the latest of her mother's lotharios.

"If you don't want to be the centerpiece of the next shabbat, I suggest that you do what I tell you."

The man's face clouded and he pushed forward, almost knocking his companion over. Ann followed, pausing at the entrance to study the runes around the door.

She had finally broken Bernard's magic. The runes no longer had any effect on her. But the cost was great. It had been less than 24 hours, yet the stirrings of dark life were growing in the pit of her belly. With the onset of the gnawing pains, she had at last understood why she had been so special to her father: Ann was to be the gate.

Since the dawn of time, the envious Old Ones had sought a permanent foothold in the earthly realm—a way to bask incessantly in the warmth of the yellow sun, away from the sterile, frigid regions of the netherworld. Over the centuries, they had mated with thousands of human women, but they had either been unable to produce or the act of carrying the monstrous offspring had killed the mothers before the end of their pregnancies. But Ann's birth had changed all that. She was different, a freak hybrid born of a demon father and a drug-crazed mother.

Ann walked all the way through the house to the bedroom in the back. She went to one knee beside the stretcher and put her hand on the boy's forehead as she continued to ponder her situation.

The worst of it was her mother must have known. Tammy had sent her to Ramsey's house to entice Moloch. In her naivete, Ann had thought Tammy wanted her to use her powers to lure the creature, but it was obvious that Moloch was only interested in her body. After all, she thought bitterly to herself, she had bartered her soul away years ago.

A terrible fate spread out on the screen of her mind: she was to be a vessel to carry dozens of monsters to the promised land. Ahead lay years of pain and terror. And then what? She could watch all her alien children go through the same thing. There were hundreds, maybe thousands of Old Ones waiting in the void, licking their thorny lips and fangs. Ann could not bare them all. It would take generations, but they would come. Then the earth would become hell.

"Why is he so chipper?" Adar asked.

Tim Wolinsky was whistling as he loaded crates into the waiting airplane. Every time he put a crate down, Tim did a little two-step shuffle and James Brown spin.

"He thinks he's finally going to get to shoot something," Quinn replied.

The van and jeep were parked in a private hanger so that Tim, Frank and Quinn could transfer their contents to the waiting jet. Frank stopped at the door of the plane, his back bowed under the weight of a heavy container.

"What the devil's in here?" Frank asked Quinn.

"Frank, you're a nice boy. Trust me. You don't want to know."

Frank's guileless blue eyes flinched. "Come on, Mr. Ramsey. Just tell me it isn't drugs."

"It isn't drugs."

"Okay, what's the game plan?" Tim asked as he made way for Frank's return trip to the plane.

"It's not a game," Adar said coldly.

Tim shrugged. "Lighten up Adar. We're going to get Q back and kick some occult butt."

Quinn stepped in. "You, Frank, Adar and I are flying to the big island. We'll load up the van we have waiting over there and go to the cave."

"So what if Q's not there?"

"If Q is there, we grab him and get the hell out. If not, we call Mildred back at the house. Then she and the rest of the family will hold one of their ceremonies to try to pinpoint his location."

"I don't understand." Frank Robbins said from the loading hatch. "How are they going to locate your son from Hana?"

"Just warm up the engines. We want to be away in fifteen minutes," Quinn said.

Tim cast an apologetic glance at Adar and said, "I don't get it. Shouldn't Mildred go with us?"

"Not going to hide behind some old lady's skirts, are you, Tim?" Adar smiled.

"Heck, no! I was just wondering."

"It's a fair question, Tim. Somehow Q has been surrounded with shielding spells that cloak his aura. If he isn't at the abandoned house, it's going to take all our resources to try to locate him. We'll already be shorthanded, and Mildred is the most experienced."

"Besides," Quinn said, "Dar can handle anything those bozos throw at us. Right, Dar?"

She smiled and shook her head. "I wish I had your confidence."

Frank cleared his throat. "Uh, Mr. Ramsey. Please just tell me once more we're not doing anything illegal."

Quinn grinned at the boy's honest anxiety. The kid had on jeans, a denim shirt and a camouflage vest. With his long hair and sandals, he looked like a Mormon missionary trying to pass as a mercenary.

Okata's copper-colored Plymouth stopped behind the van. It sputtered, choked and died in a cloud of blue smoke. She climbed out wearing jeans, a plaid shirt and a healthy supply of body armor. Her hair was carefully tucked up under a black baseball cap with the letters SWAT stitched in white across the front. She threw a sawed-off, nickel-plated shotgun over her shoulder and walked up to Quinn.

"Frank, you remember Sgt. Okata, don't you?" Quinn asked. "Why don't you ask her your question?"

"Hi, Sarge," Tim said as Frank ducked back into

the plane. "What are you doing here?"

"Quinn invited me. Don't you remember?"

"Whooie," Tim said, fingering the bright finish on the shotgun. "This what the girls in the department are sporting these days?"

Okata didn't take her eyes off Quinn. "Hey, Tim, take a day off. You don't have to be an asshole every day."

"What flew up your nose?"

"Tim, help Frank," Quinn said, then waited until his friend was out of earshot. "I know you were invited, Gail, but I changed my mind. We're just going for a little ride."

"Then you won't mind another passenger."

He took her arm and walked her to the hanger door. "Look. We think we know where my boy is and we're going to get him."

"I can help. I'll call ahead and get the special-weapons team ready."

"We have no evidence, no probable cause. You said so yourself. They won't give us shit. Besides, even if they did believe us, they'd go in like cops—by the book. Well, the book doesn't mean shit in this case."

"Quinn, you break the law, and son or no son, I'll have to arrest you."

"Last time I heard, flying from one island to another wasn't against the law."

Okata put her hand in the middle of Tim's chest as he tried to sneak past with one of his crates. She flipped the carton open and pulled out a fully automatic M-16. "I suppose you have a tax stamp for this?"

Quinn looked murder at Tim and snapped, "It's at the house."

"Well, then, we can just run back and get it."

Quinn threw up his hands. "We don't have time for that."

"All right then, here's the deal: I go or you don't."

Quinn did a slow ten count in his head while running through a few mental scenarios: handcuff Okata to her car, dope her coffee on the plane, kick her out of the plane over the ocean.

Adar walked up and stood at the policewoman's side. "If Gail wasn't a woman, would you be giving her such a hard time?"

"I don't know. You're going, but I admit I'm not happy about that either."

"I can take care of myself," Okata said.

Quinn cast a wary eye at the flack jacket and baseball cap, the shiny shotgun and the Glock on her hip. She had even found a pair of shiny combat boots— and her lipstick was perfect.

"Let her come," Adar said. "It'll make me feel better."

"Yeah," Tim said. "Let her come. She's so cute in that getup the bad guys'll take one look and die laughing."

After Wolinsky scurried back into the hanger, Quinn stopped pacing, turned to Okata and shrugged. "Okay, I just hope you know what you're letting yourself in for. This isn't a raid on some teenage crack house."

He stalked off as the jet engines began to turn. A few minutes later they were in the air.

Chapter Thirteen

6:22 p.m.—Christmas Eve.

"Why is the brat still asleep?" Tammy Pakula demanded.

"I told Alan to let him be," Ann replied. She hated it when her mother took that snippy tone with her.

Tammy had changed into her black robe, and she had thrown back the hood. In her hair was a golden tiara with a five-pointed star outlined in half-caret emeralds. The old woman's right wrist was wrapped with a golden-serpent bracelet that coiled up to the elbow.

"I don't know what's gotten into you, Ann, but you had better get your head out of your ass. Now come on. We have to inspect the preparations."

Tammy turned to go, then paused. "Remember one thing. Those people out there are a bunch of sheep. Half of them come to these shindigs for a free fuck. The others to get high. But don't ever under-estimate them. One hint of weakness from you and they'll turn into a pack of wolves and tear us apart."

"And the great lord Moloch won't?" Ann said calmly.

Tammy's hand shot out and slapped her daughter sharply across the face. Ann's head snapped back, but she refused to make a sound. She wiped blood on the back of her hand and stared into Tammy's eyes as she licked it off.

"Have you forgotten what's at stake here? We are close to controlling one of the elemental powers of the universe. Do I have to remind you we're talking about immortality? If you do anything to screw this up, I'll strap you to that altar myself and slit you open from your well-used cunt to your chin."

"Somehow, Mother, I don't think so."

Ann closed the red robe over her high, pointed breasts and marched down the hall and through the door to the swimming pool.

The best the rental company could provide on short notice was a rickety, four-wheel-drive panel truck. Undaunted, Quinn and Frank piled into the back with the guns and ammo while Tim drove. Gail and Adar squeezed into the front seat. Quinn left the rear door open so they wouldn't die of the exhaust fumes as the truck bucked and shuddered over the rutted highway.

"Who bombed the road?" Frank yelled over the screeching universal joint.

"Your tax dollars at work," Quinn said.

They thought Saddle Road was bad, but when the truck turned off onto the dirt road, the racket brought all conversation to a halt. It was all they could do to keep themselves and the crates from bouncing out into the mud. Twenty minutes later, they reached the split-rail fence. Quinn and Frank jumped down and met the others at the cab.

"Look at all those tracks," Okata said pointing to the churned-up mud. "And the gate's open."

"I think we had better hide the truck and go on from here on foot," Tim said.

Okata nodded and Tim pulled the truck behind a stand of thick palms, where they unpacked the crates. Tim had come prepared with fully automatic rifles and military shotguns. Frank watched wide-eyed as the weapons were checked. Tim hauled out some LAWs rockets while Okata shoved deer slugs into the bottom of her sawed-off shotgun and checked the spare clips for the Glock.

"I should have skipped band and taken ROTC," Frank muttered.

"Don't worry, Frank. You're staying with the truck," Quinn said.

Okata slapped the clip into the bottom of the pistol and shoved the pistol tight into her shoulder holster. She pulled a business card from her top pocket and held it out to the boy pilot. "If we're not back in an hour, call that number and tell them where we are."

"Wait a minute! I can shoot a gun. I think Ms. Sydelle should stay with the truck," Frank said blushing furiously.

"Our hero," Okata mumbled.

Quinn was tempted to agree with Frank. In her black jumpsuit and black high-top Reeboks, Adar looked as if she were on a shopping safari, not on the trail of homicidal witches.

"No," Quinn said, "we need Adar. But I promise you can go on the next raid."

Then Tim started shoving hand grenades into his pockets and looping the antitank rockets over his shoulder, and Okata finally blew her top.

"No way. I draw the line at rockets and grenades."

"You don't know what we're gonna find down that road," Tim said.

"I know what we're not gonna find. We're not going to find the Iraqi Republican Guards or even the Hawaiian National Guard."

"But—"

"But what? You're not going in there tossing grenades like Sergeant Rock of Easy Company or firing off rockets as long as Quinn's kid is in there."

Tim managed to look embarrassed and pissed off at the same time, but Okata just checked her digital Casio. "Let's move. It's getting late."

Frank stood in the road beside the gate and watched the others file down the side of the road, keeping to the overcast provided by low-hanging trees.

With the approach of night, gray shadows had taken over the forest and the bushes and tree limbs looked like skeletal arms stretching out to grasp the unwary. Each blowing limb had become the scrape of a clawed foot; every mud puddle, a quicksand trap. They walked single file. Tim Wolinsky, by virtue of toting the most lethal combination of weaponry, took the lead. But when he stopped three times in the first few hundred yards to sweep the forest with the barrel of his automatic rifle, Quinn went up to join him.

"Isn't this the place where I'm supposed to say, 'It's too quiet,' " Quinn said, trying to sound like Boris Karloff.

Tim jumped as if he'd been goosed. "It is too quiet. It's a fucking jungle. Where are all the birds and shit?"

"That why you're stopping every two feet? Looking for wildlife?"

Tim started walking again. "You remember that park off Flagler, over near Good Sam Hospital? Needle Park?"

"Yeah. Junkie heaven."

"One night about five years ago, I broke into that pawn shop on Spruce during one of our mini-hurricanes and one of your fat comrades in blue chased me into that hellhole. It was just about midnight."

"Brave son of a bitch."

"I didn't know. I should have guessed when Serpico stopped under the streetlight and started laughing, but I was running too fast."

"So what happened?"

"I hid in the mud under a palmetto palm. After about five minutes, when my heart stopped pounding, I figured the blue knight would call for backup and they'd be waiting for me on the way out."

Quinn kept his eyes glued to the dark green wall of trees. Behind them, Adar and Okata dodged the muddy potholes.

"When I caught my breath," Tim said. "I started hearing things. You know, twigs popping like they do when somebody walks through the bushes, and weird breathing. After a couple of minutes of that, a nice dry cell started looking pretty good. So I buried the swag, put my hands in the air and ran out like a wop war hero. But the cop was long gone. I ran to my car and drove back to Delray like the parish priest."

"That's a really nice story, Tim. Thanks for sharing it."

"I'm going somewhere, asshole. Be patient."

They rounded a curve, where the heavy canopy of branches made the road a tunnel. The leaves blocked the breeze, and even in the cool of the evening, their sweat spotted the ground at their feet.

"By morning I was laughing at myself for almost getting caught and for being such a pussy. I drove back to the park to dig up my buried treasure." Tim clicked the safety on the gun and seemed to relax. It was too dark now to see the shadows and that helped. "Less than ten yards from where I had been hiding, I found a fire pit, a bunch of blackened bones, some weird beads and seashells. The place was covered with dried blood and chicken feathers."

"Big deal," Quinn said. "A bunch of Haitians who couldn't afford the Colonel."

Tim chuckled without much humor. "Yeah, that's what I thought too, until I found the little girl's finger."

Quinn slapped his forehead. "Mary Margaret Duffy!"

"That's right."

"You made the call?"

"After I stopped shaking. You found her body, didn't you?"

Quinn looked over his shoulder to make sure Adar and Okata were close enough. "Yeah, what there was of it. We found part of her floating out in Loxahatchee. No arms, no legs, no head. Her father identified her by the birthmark on her back."

"The minute I started down this road, it reminded me of that park," Tim whispered.

"All the palm trees," Quinn said.

"Probably."

It had become totally dark, and the men had to follow the ruts in the road with their feet. Five minutes later they came upon the first of the luxury cars, a silver stretch Mercedes with mud up to its windows.

The cars and vans were lined up on both sides of the road and parked haphazardly between the trees. Ahead, through the forest, bright lights blazed, showing the abandoned house's wooden roof beams like the ribs of a decomposing corpse. Tim and Quinn ducked behind a black Lincoln limo until the women caught up. Tim released the safety on the M-16 and Quinn checked the clip on his Tarus nine mm while Okata unholstered the Glock and Adar kept a death grip on the medallion around her neck.

"More people than I anticipated," Adar said.

"Will they be armed?" Gail asked.

"Guns? Maybe. Some of the neophytes."

"Which ones are the neophytes?" Quinn asked.

"The ones in the white robes," Adar said.

"I say we keep it simple," Tim said as he pulled back the charging handle on the rifle. "We go in and tell them to freeze. If they breathe, we wax 'em."

Okata gave Tim a sour look and walked to the edge of the trees where she had a clear view of the house and the falls. Suddenly, she waved her hand frantically to get their attention; then she put a finger to her lips. The others picked their way through the shrubs and thick creeper vines. She pointed toward the edge of the pond.

Three people were taking advantage of the full moon and the idyllic setting to engage in a little recreational sex. The man on his back appeared to be in his late fifties; he had a head of silver hair and a heavy, hairy stomach. Riding hard on his waist, like a cowgirl in a barrel race, was a young girl with long brown hair. In a display of amazing balance, she was simultaneously fellating a black man in his early thirties.

"That son of a bitch!" Okata hissed.

"Shhhh!" Quinn whispered. "She doesn't look like she minds."

"Aside from the fact that the girl is underage, that fat bastard on the ground is Federal Judge Harold Wilkinson."

Holding back a laugh, Tim put his lips next to Quinn's ear and said, "I think he's interrogating a witness."

"Maybe he's voir direing her," Quinn suggested.

"I bet if I were to make a comment about the size of those boobs, the ladies would brand me an MCP for life."

Adar put her head just behind Quinn's and whispered, "If you two can tear yourselves away, I think I see a way out of our problem."

In the course of four short months, Angie Templeton's new boyfriend, Harry Wilkinson, had introduced her to the joys of physical love, cocaine, Satanism and group sex. They had become regulars at the shabbats, and this night, as soon as they had cleared the entrance to the dilapidated house, they had started cramming coke up their noses while Harry made the rounds, shaking hands and slapping backs as if he were running for reelection. Quickly bored, Angie attached herself to the first new face she'd seen: a young black lawyer named Jerome.

For his part, Jerome had been amazed when the mousy brunette with the mammoth breasts and crooked teeth turned out to be the main squeeze of the judge who had made his reputation by sentencing young black men to long vacations in the Graybar Hotel. One thing had led to another, and they had gone outside to cement their new friendship in a more friendly manner.

Angie had tried to talk her friend Sally Pendergrass into making it a foursome, but Sally was busy nursing her five-week-old son and basking in the glow of her newfound prominence in the coven. Tammy Pakula herself had been talking to Sally and stroking the baby's head.

Out in the bushes, Angie was doing her best to keep Harry hard, which was no mean feat the way the old guy was flying on crack. Her hips were going like a rocking horse while her hands and mouth were busy keeping Jerome happy. Jerome had just grabbed the back of her head and started quivering like a bowl of jelly when a beautiful Polynesian woman in a funny vest walked calmly up and hit him across the back of the head with a gun, then placed the barrel in the center of Harry's forehead.

"Hello, Your Honor. One word and I'm going to seriously violate your constitutional rights."

Harry's prick went down like the Hindenberg, and Angie slipped to the ground. A man appeared and snapped a pair of handcuffs on Jerome and hustled him off to the trees while a second man stood Harry up and cuffed him. Angie noticed the way the short man with the white-blond hair kept staring at her chest. She thought he was kind of cute and gave him a little smile. He smiled back, but before anything could develop, the other man came back and led Angie into the woods.

"I hope she doesn't waste him," Quinn whispered to Tim as they linked the girl to the young guy, then cuffed them both around the trunk of a palm tree.

"I don't think she'd do that," Tim replied. "Beat him to death maybe, but she wouldn't fire a shot and give us away."

In a moment Okata pushed the naked judge under the tree. "Get down on your knees!"

"Sergeant, I—"

"I suggest you have a seat, Judge," Quinn said. "You wouldn't be the first man to die because of a raging case of PMS."

"And who are you, sir?"

Okata kicked Harold Wilkinson behind his knee hard enough to make it crack and he went down. She flicked out one hand and snapped the steel restraints on his wrists then joined him to his friends.

Adar stood just outside the cover of the fronds, ignoring the drama under the trees. Her mind was focused on the brightly lit house.

Once the three were secure, Okata squatted on her heels with the Glock pointing in the general direction of the judge's scrotum. "It's Christmas Eve, and there is nothing I would like more than to hang your balls on my tree, Judge. If any of you make any noise, I will come back and remove your nuts with a nine-millimeter scalpel. Do we understand each other?"

The old man opened his mouth, noted Okata's expression, then just nodded.

Okata turned to the girl. "Are you all right?"

Angie nodded, but she was actually coming down from the high and beginning to feel both cold and sick to her stomach.

"If you have any pull with this old creep, keep him quiet, and I'll see what I can do to get you out of this."

Angie looked at the serious faces around her and nodded. "Who are you?"

"I'm a cop."

"You can do that? Keep my parents from finding out?"

Okata nodded. "How'd you get involved in this?"

Angie shrugged. "I baby-sat his grandkids. Harry took me home a few times. He's kinda neat."

"Right! How old are you?"

"I'll be sixteen in two weeks."

Okata pushed herself to her feet and glared at the judge. "Make some noise—please."

When Gail was done with the three prisoners, Adar went back to the line of cars and threw a robe to Quinn and Tim. "Put these on."

"Where's mine?" Okata asked.

"You're going to have to stay back and cover us."

"We can grab another one of these geeks and get one for me."

Adar squeezed the cop's arm. "We'll be safer if we're not all in there at the same time."

"What are you going to do?"

"If we're lucky, slip in, save Q and get out. If we're not lucky, hope these people are all weekend witches and don't know how to conjure up a bad cold."

Okata shook her head slowly. "You don't believe that any more than I do."

Adar gazed across the pond at the curtain of water. The moon had turned the falls into liquid diamonds and the surrounding swamp into a pewter diorama out of *Field and Stream*.

"We have no choice. The evil is spreading and it has to be stopped."

The men slipped into the robes. Tim's dragged the ground and Quinn's came down to his shins. They hurriedly exchanged garments and closed them over the weapons. Adar's robe stopped just above her ankles. Her sneakers showed, but they didn't seem to violate the dress code.

Tim tucked the butt of the rifle under his armpit and walked with a stiff, shuffling gait. "How's it look?"

"Like you sat on a corn cob." Quinn chuckled.

"It'll have to do," Adar said.

They started down the road, but slipped into the trees again as another limo skidded to a stop in the muddy field. Four more covenites brandishing champagne bottles climbed out of the back seat. Their black robes were loose, and it was obvious that there was nothing but bare skin underneath. To be safe, Quinn's group fell in step a few yards behind the revelers, but the hooded figures were so drunk and absorbed in each other's wit that it was unlikely they would have noticed a marching band behind them. Suddenly, the witches stopped to pass around a vial of white powder, and Adar dropped to her knee and pretended to tie her boot. The other group was close to the house, and the lights made carnival masks of their lax features.

Okata stepped behind Quinn and whispered; "It's Captain Benson!"

"Shit!" Tim said. "Does everybody in the whole fucking state belong to this voodoo club?"

Okata crouched behind the bumper of the closest car and whispered, "Go ahead. I'll keep you in sight."

Quinn lifted his hood and whispered to Tim, "Act drunk. I believe you've had the necessary training."

The men flanked Adar, giggled loudly and began walking with exaggerated stiffness. The back of the house was crawling with robes, black robes mostly, but a few white robes. Through the window, Quinn caught a glimpse of a red robe moving in front of the fire. The participants had gathered in small groups to chat, pausing now and then to inhale from a glass pipe or take a sip from a long-stem, plastic wineglass.

"Where's the freaking D.E.A. when you need them?" Tim muttered.

Quinn steered them to the side of the porch near the tall weeds, where he could keep an eye on the entrance and still see through the shattered windows.

"Where do you think they're holding Q?" Adar whispered.

A woman with long blonde hair ran up to Tim and offered him a smoldering marijuana cigarette the size of a Cuban cigar. Her white robe was open, exposing pendulous breasts and yards of exotic tattoos. Tim accepted the joint with a smile, and the woman rubbed herself all over him, smearing his mouth with scarlet lipstick as she ran her hands under his robe.

"You're dressed?" she said.

"I'm very shy." Tim smiled and took a long pull on the cigarette.

"Party pooper." The blonde laughed and ran off to accost the next man.

When Tim took another drag from the joint, Quinn snatched it out of his hand and threw it behind a bush. "What's the matter with you, Tim? You won't be much good to anybody stoned."

"Me?" Tim demanded as he turned to face Quinn. "I'll have you know that I can pick a lock, open a safe or hot-wire a Mercedes better stoned than sober."

Quinn put the tip of his nose an inch from Tim's. "So why was it every time Carl and I busted you you couldn't stand up?"

Tim dropped his eyes. "Bad luck."

Adar stepped between them and whispered, "People are watching."

She slipped her hand behind Quinn's neck and pulled his mouth down. He pecked at her lips while scanning the crowd to see who might have noticed them.

"You can do better than that," Adar said.

Quinn ignored the insanity around him for a moment and gazed down into her eyes. They were glowing with that same shimmering green fire that in the past had made him uneasy. He kissed her hard, wrapping one arm around her waist and pulling her up on her toes. When he released her, they were both breathing hard.

She kept her head on his shoulder and asked again, "Where do you think they're keeping Q?"

Quinn searched the crowd. Behind Adar's back,

Tim made a kissing motion with his lips and fluttered his eyelids.

"You stupid prick," Quinn said. Then he scanned the front room with its massive stone fireplace. The place was full of smoke and people and Q could have been anywhere. "One of the back bedrooms is the best bet."

"Through a window?" Tim asked.

Quinn shook his head imperceptibly. "All the windows in the back were boarded up."

"Then I guess we go in and get him."

Quinn went first, using his shoulders as a wedge as he mounted the steps and paused at the door to search for the red robe. He wiggled past two women drinking beer from cans. He felt like a man stepping into an open grave, and the press of sweaty, naked flesh was almost suffocating.

"They must have saved all the deodorant for the virgins," Tim whispered.

"Shh!"

One of the revelers had brought a portable CD player, and it was pounding out an eerie drum-and-flute melody that made the people wave their arms in the air with abandon and caused Quinn's teeth to itch. Robes flapped like the wings of giant raptors, revealing skin covered with intricate tattoos and runes that glistened in the light from the fire. All the while, the unwashed enthusiasm of the coven did little to improve the quality of the air.

It was hard for Quinn to believe that such diabolical expressions could belong to human beings. Jazzed up as those people were on crack or booze or crystal meth, and whipped into a frenzy by that insane tune, their faces were feral, their eyes as black and lifeless as midnight, their mouths slack and drooling. Their dance was the spasm of electrocution, and their howls meaningless drivel screamed in time to that awful music.

Working slowly toward the rear of the house, Quinn tried to match his expression to those of the people around him. The music was giving him a headache, but he nodded and snapped his fingers and used the cottony taste of fear in his mouth to keep focused. Adar, Tim, and he were on their own. It would take a miracle for Okata to cover their retreat if the need arose.

Rather than dwell on the hopelessness of the situation, he used mind games from his days in the patrol cars to keep his body under control. He drew pictures in his head: the beach, the Corvette he'd always wanted, Kathy's face. But her features kept changing into the likeness of the redheaded woman behind him. He made a promise to himself that if they got out alive, he would take Q and Adar on a long vacation. They would fly to the mainland, rent a car and drive until they found a place where the people had never heard of Hawaii, a cold place, with white snow and purple mountains.

The hall was less crowded. A few robed shadows moved back and forth like ghosts. Quinn went to the right, away from the pool, leading Tim and Adar down the dark corridor, past empty rooms with walls full of grime and bloody runes. At the corner, two men were leaning with their backs to the wall, sharing a joint.

"Wrong way bro," one of the men said.

"Bathroom," Quinn mumbled as he continued shuffling toward them.

"Outside man."

"My lady's sick." Quinn smiled.

As the guard examined Adar's angelic expression and hesitated, the flat edge of Quinn's hand crushed his larynx. The second man spat out the cigarette, but before he could open his mouth, Quinn turned and shoved four stiff fingers up under his sternum, then clipped the man behind the ear with his pistol. After a quick look over his shoulder, Quinn barged into the bedroom.

It took a few seconds for his eyes to adjust, and by that time, Adar and Tim had dragged the guards into the room and dumped them unceremoniously in the corner. Q was lying on his side on a bed made of a stretcher and a pair of sawhorses. His knees were drawn up to his chin, and his young face was as white as the robe draped over him. Quinn put his hand on the boy's forehead. It was burning.

"Somebody's coming," Adar said from the doorway.

Tim had the rifle out and pointed at the door in less than a heartbeat, and Quinn whispered, "Who?"

Adar was still for a moment, lost in the touch of her medallion. "I'm not sure, but it isn't good."

"I vote we boogie while we can," Tim said.

"I'll carry Q," Quinn said to Adar. "You may need your hands free to do whatever it is you do."

"They aren't going to sit still while we stroll out of here," Tim said.

"No, but between the M-16 and Adar's tricks, maybe we can convince them it's smarter to let us go."

The door opened and Tim pulled the trigger, but

nothing happened, not even the click of a faulty firing pin.

Ann Pakula filled the door in her red robe. "It won't work, Mr. Wolinsky."

Adar reached for her necklace, but Ann was faster. Her eyes sparked like tiny green suns. Adar bounced off the wall and fell to her knees. Throwing aside the robe, Adar came off the floor with her amulet held out in front of her like a shield. It cast a bright red beam of energy directly at Ann's face. The witch ducked and the doorframe where her head had been a split second before splintered, leaving a smoldering eight-inch hole. Ann countered by clenching her fists and holding them stiffly in front of her body, then flexing her fingers outward. A half-inch sheet of plywood ripped from the window with a loud, splintering crack and smashed into the back of Adar's head. Adar was down again, but far from out. She jumped up spitting alien phrases that dripped off her tongue like venom and waving intricate patterns in the air with her hands. Ann responded with her own string of verbal gibberish and matched each movement of Adar's hands with one of her own. They looked like a pair of prizefighters shadowboxing across a dark ring.

Quinn threw himself over Q to shield the boy from flying splinters while Tim ducked behind the makeshift bed, frantically working the charging handle on the useless M-16. Then Adar marched across the room, her face a mask of determination. With each step, the brilliance of the gossamer web of energy that she was weaving blossomed. Against this onslaught of concentrated sorcery, Ann Pakula began to give ground, backing grudgingly through the open door into the hall. Ann stumbled over the exposed doorsill and would have gone down except, at that moment, Tamara Pakula unexpectedly jumped into the fray.

The diminutive Polynesian woman proved to be a virtual dynamo of metaphysical power. A red-gold oval of glowing energy surrounded her like an invisible egg. Her face was bathed in perspiration and her heavily painted lips split into a mirthless grimace as she put out her hand like a cop stopping traffic. When the room exploded with golden light, Quinn and Tim covered their eyes and Adar blinked. Then the battle was over.

Adar was facedown on the floor in a room that smelled like an electrical machine shop. Quinn ran to her side, turning her carefully and checking her pulse.

"She is not dead, although she easily could have been," Ann said.

Quinn looked up with his raw hatred barely contained. Ann pushed past her mother and stood over her fallen opponent. Tim raised the rifle over his head like a baseball bat and Tammy curled her hand into a claw.

"No, Mother!" Ann faced Tim. "Do you want to die? Put the rifle down and you won't be hurt."

Tim hesitated until Quinn said, "Put it down, Tim."

Tammy motioned and two guards came in and took Tim's arms. At Ann's bidding, they marched Tim out, and a moment later, with a quizzical look at her daughter, Tammy Pakula followed.

"So she's your mother, huh?" Quinn asked, smoothing his hand over Adar's face.

"Yes."

"Why'd you take my son?"

"I believe you know why."

"The cave?"

She nodded. "The well of souls."

"Why?"

Ann stood close enough for him to feel the power coursing through her body. She gazed down at his face and didn't answer. Instead she said, "Our shabbat is about to begin. Why don't you join us?"

Quinn couldn't believe his ears. If not for his son lying unconscious ten feet away, he would gladly have strangled the woman. "Lady, you're some piece of work. You act like we crashed your tea party and now you're playing the gracious hostess."

Ann laughed softly. "A pretty good analogy."

"And what about my boy?"

Ann was silent for the space of five heart beats, then replied, "I don't want to hurt him—or your friends either."

"That's awfully good of you," Quinn replied with a snort.

"Believe it or not, I'm walking a tightrope here. During our shabbat tonight, we shall summon Moloch, and that requires a proper sacrifice."

"Q?" Quinn's voice was as dead as his dwindling hopes.

"That was the plan."

Quinn picked up the note of uncertainty in her voice. "Was?"

The robe swayed rhythmically as Ann paced the room. She went to the guards, nudged them with her toe, then went down on one knee and checked to make sure they were unconscious. "Maybe there is another way."

"What do you want?"

She gave him a sly sideways glance, watching his expression carefully in the dim room. "I sense latent power in you."

Quinn tried to keep the exasperation out of his voice. "Is everybody around here nuts? Come on, I've got about as much power as the vice president of the United States."

"Your uncle was very powerful and shrewd. He was able to conceal his powers from us while he lured Moloch to his mansion."

"That was my uncle."

"These things tend to run in families," Ann replied, holding out her hand toward Adar. "Just look at your friend and her family."

Quinn decided to stall. Sooner or later Okata or Frank Robbins would realize they were in trouble and bring help.

"So what?"

Ann stood with one leg cocked so that a smooth knee peeked between the folds in the robe. "You could be useful to me."

It would be a lie to say Quinn felt nothing. But he kept his eyes steady and steeled his mind, using Adar's hand as his lifeline.

"Come on," Ann said. "The festivities are about to begin."

"And if I don't feel sociable?"

"Quinn, be reasonable. We have you. We have your son, your friend, and"—Ann nodded contemptuously at Adar—"your pet sorceress. If you work with me, I will try to save them. If you refuse, you will all be sacrificed."

Ann held out her hand and said, "Come on. She

will be unconscious for hours."

"What about Q?"

"He will stay here until we need him. If we need him. That depends on you."

"All right."

"You will have to undress."

Ann reached out and pulled the tie on his robe. She saw the guns strapped to his body, the knife in his belt and the hand grenade hanging from his top pocket. She raised an eyebrow.

Quinn shrugged and began dropping the weapons in a pile. "I feel like one of the Chippendale dancers. Ever since I moved to these fucking islands, somebody has been asking me to take my clothes off."

The last time Quinn saw the pool area, it had been empty except for the mutilated body of a little girl. Now, the concrete floor was carpeted with blankets and mats, a huge stone altar had been erected over the deep end and the walls were covered with tapestries that showed black goats raping screaming women, signs of the zodiac and misshapen monsters with horned heads and scale-covered hides.

"You made some changes," Quinn said.

The witches had congregated in groups of two, three and four, drinking, smoking and fondling each other with abandon. After years of acting as referee for the wealthy scions of Palm Beach, Quinn had thought of himself as shockproof. But before his eyes, men were kissing women; men were fondling men; women were running around kissing everybody. Over in one corner, two middle age men had their hands under the robe of a nine-year-old girl. Quinn was much too cynical to be religious, but he decided that any god who allowed something like this to take place owed Sodom and Gomorrah a serious apology. He was sick to the core, but he did what he always did when he felt like crying: He made a joke.

"Looks like the fraternity parties we used to bust at PBJC."

Several of the celebrants reached out to touch the high priestess's robe as she worked her way through the labyrinth of panting bodies. "Loosen up and stop looking down your nose. You think you're so much better than these people? Many of those here are judges, lawyers and doctors."

"So this is just another kind of professional association?"

Ann stopped at the wall behind the altar and laughed in his face. "That is one of the things that first attracted me to you. Your warped sense of humor."

Quinn watched as muscular young men went from group to group, trying to break up the rutting couples. "Where's Hugh Heffner?"

"Who?"

"So what's on the menu tonight?"

Ann's tone was bored, but her breathing betrayed her excitement. "I was able to free Lord Moloch from his prison so that he could return to his own realm. Before he departed, he gave me his promise to return tonight if we offered the proper incentives."

Another pair of burly young men quick stepped a bound figure through the tangle of sprawled bodies. The man's face was covered by a mask made from the hollowed-out head of a large pig, and he kept tripping over the extended limbs. The guards forced him down onto the altar, securing his wrists and feet with shackles. Throughout the drama, the crowd continued to drink, laugh and shout as if the pig-headed man were invisible.

"You don't really expect me to stand here while you kill that man, do you? For all I know, that could be Tim."

Ann's fingernails bit into Quinn's arm. "It isn't Mr. Wolinsky. "Remember! If you want your friends to survive the night, you must do as I say."

Ann nodded and the executioner raised the evil-looking de Laval dagger, its black blade glinting hungrily in the powerful artificial lights. At the site of the exposed blade, the mob perked up and silence spread through the room like a lethal fog. On the altar, the victim began to thrash and moan, rattling chains and twisting from side to side. Inside the porcine mask, the man's eyes bulged as eternity suddenly became his reality. He picked Quinn's somber expression out of the sea of drunken faces and pleaded silently with him to do something. Quinn started to throw off Ann's restraining hand, then froze.

A man stepped through the door at the back of the room. He had a lump behind one ear and pitiless eyes. In one hand was Quinn's son, held tight against the man's chest; in the other was a rusty machete. Q was still unconscious, but the warning was clear.

Ann raised a hand and one of the roving attendants brought over an ornate silver chalice. The girl was young and pretty with long cornsilk hair held in check by a garland of flowers. When the girl held out the cup to Quinn she mouthed, "I love you."

"Drink, Ann said. "You will feel better."

Quinn's eyes never left the man holding his son. No matter what else happened, Quinn swore that man would never see the sun come up.

"Drink!"

He downed the bitter liquid without comment. As it slowly spread fire through his veins, Quinn discovered that he was turned on, yet he felt distant, as if he were watching the whole ridiculous circus on a giant-screen TV. Ann nodded to her mother, and the old woman grinned and returned the gesture. A moment later, the sacrificial knife moved. The man in the mask squealed like a pig having its throat cut. Blood blossomed like liquid rose petals, gushing over the altar and flowing down the sides of the swimming pool, and the crowd went wild.

"It isn't real. It isn't real," Quinn whispered over and over. But when the two black-robed priests dipped their bare arms into the dead man's abdomen, he turned away.

In a voice just loud enough to be heard over the howls of delight from her pack, Ann said, "You do not understand. We are not unnecessarily cruel. Once you feel the rush, you will be with us."

She couldn't be right, could she? Quinn's befuddled brain protested. Was there a part of him that longed for the freedom of absolute power? Look how quickly he'd gotten used to the money, the house, the fancy cars, as if some part of him insisted that he was born for it. And what was this latent power everyone kept talking about? It was as if he carried some freak combination of nucleic acids deep in his DNA that sat there like a festering virus waiting for the right moment to infect him with terminal greed.

Was it preordained that one morning he'd wake up, look in the mirror and see the face of Bernard Ramsey staring back at him?

Quinn turned back in time to see the butchers loop the man's intestines around their necks and prance around the altar. Suddenly, his body convulsed, sending stream after stream of steaming vomit against the wall until he was too exhausted to stand.

Ann knelt beside him, offering a glass of amber liquid. When he tried to push it away, she whispered, "It's just wine."

The wine killed the sour taste of bile, but couldn't wash away the self-loathing Quinn felt—for himself, for Ann, for the human race. She turned his face toward her, kissed him and ran her hand up his thigh. He tried to push her away, but she held on with surprising strength.

"Don't fight, Quinn. Let it happen."

Her fingers ignited little fires inside his brain. Quinn knew he had to resist, knew part of what he was feeling was that witch's brew. But knowing didn't help. What she was doing felt too good.

"Not yet, daughter," Tammy said as she stood looking down with flinty amusement sparkling her cold eyes. "We have a long way to go before the fun begins."

The crowd was on its feet, parting for a young girl bringing her nursing baby to the deep end of the pool. Blood from the altar had run down the tile, forming a viscous puddle around the drain. The girl stopped beside the blood, gazing at Ann with raw adoration. She pulled the baby away from the warm breast and held it aloft. Denied its meal, the child began to wail.

Demon Fire

"Mistress, I offer my boy child as sacrifice to hasten the arrival of Lord Moloch."

Ann nodded and bestowed an angelic smile on the young mother. The girl gently placed the screaming infant on its back next to the blood. She threw off her white robe and accepted a dagger from one of the guards.

"That's not really her baby," Quinn whispered and his body began to tremble.

"Yes, it is." Ann's soft breath was in his ear. "If she wants to do this, why should you care?"

"What time is it?" he asked.

"It is almost midnight."

Midnight! Had he been there so long? Frank must surely have gone for help by now. He had to stall.

"Listen, Ann—'"

The infant's cries suddenly stopped. Quinn turned pale and refused to look down into the concrete abyss. Instead he took another glass from a nearby tray, downing the contents in three gulps.

The crowd's cheers rivaled the raucous din of a professional football game, shaking the rafters and boring into his brain like hungry worms. Quinn hardly noticed as the young mother, covered in gore from head to foot, walked back up to the shallow end of the pool and climbed the steps. She faced Ann and raised her arms in salute. Her mouth was smeared with blood. Two of the guards took the white robe and covered the girl with a new black one. She hugged it tightly around her, then turned to bestow a wet kiss on the attendants. The mind deadening-music started again and girls with serving trays swept through the crowd.

"Dante was wrong," Quinn mumbled.

"What?" Ann cried.

"God didn't make hell. Man did," Quinn said. "What is this, half time?"

"Come on, Quinn. You have to feel something."

Did he? Did he feel anything? He felt revulsion. He felt sorry for the dead man and for the tiny baby. He even felt a kind of sick compassion for the crazy woman who had murdered her child. But mainly he felt a growing sense of unreality.

"You must feel it," Ann said. "He is near. The offerings we have made draw him to us. His love rolls before him like waves before the storm."

The coven was rapidly losing control. Robes were coming off, hair was coming down and the mob was falling to the floor in a frenzy of passion. Quinn didn't know whether they felt Moloch's approach or just felt the effects of too much dope and booze. But it was turning into one hell of an orgy.

"Here," Ann said, pushing the silver goblet at him again.

Quinn put out his hand to ward it off. "Ann, I don't know what you want from me, but knocking me out with drugs isn't going to do you much good."

"It isn't dope. Just a little something that allows us to break down those artificial barriers that society and its fatuous churches have developed to enslave us. The things you feel are what're bottled up inside. This just frees them."

Quinn eyed the liquid as if it were poison, wondering again if Ann were lying to him or if it mattered. If the stuff knocked him out, wouldn't he be better off? He took another swallow and the oily warmth raced to his groin. Ann jerked the cup from his hands, drank deeply, then tossed it aside and threw her arms around his neck.

"Tell me now that you don't feel anything."

Quinn was as hard as a rock and wondered if that was what Ann meant. She kissed him hungrily, her tongue probing his mouth like a moist finger. Her hands clawed at his chest.

"Not yet!" Tammy hissed. "You're losing control of the shabbat! Moloch will not be pleased."

Ann released Quinn and turned on her mother. "I don't care! This is for me. Don't you understand? All my life it's been what you wanted. You! You! You! I've been the one living in a sea of blood and pain. Is it too much to ask for something for me?"

Tammy backhanded her daughter across the face. "You stupid bitch! You think he wants you? Do you think if we weren't holding his son, he would be here right now?"

"No! He is one of us. He has power and it is strong! I feel it."

"What kind of power?" the old witch demanded, curling her hand into a fist in her daughter's face. "The power of Moloch? The dark power that bends the forces of nature to our will? Or the power of that pack of hags who he brought here? They're a bunch of weak-kneed earth mothers sucking on the tits of impotent elemental spirits."

The members of the coven were oblivious to the battle of wills taking place between their leaders. The shabbat had degenerated into a sea of writhing bodies and sucking mouths. Ann seemed caught up in the sexual tension that vibrated through the room.

She threw off her robe, standing naked before the world. Her body was well proportioned, with high pointed breasts and slim hips. She turned to the side and Quinn's eyes bulged with shock and horror.

Ann's belly was slightly rounded, already beginning to throb with malevolent life. But what drew his astonished eyes was the scaly, foot-long appendage that hung down like the tail of a lizard between the rounded swells of her buttocks.

"This is what I am! A brood cow for the beast masters of the netherworld!" Ann threw her hands out wide and screamed. She cupped her hands under her breasts and walked toward Quinn. Then she dropped her hands and grabbed the de Laval athame from the altar, holding it high in her right hand. "Accept me. Love me as I am, and I will give you the universe. Or watch your son precede you across the river of death."

Tammy grabbed her daughter's arm and spun her around. "You would throw away everything for this man? I will cast your soul—"

Ann never found out where Tammy planned to send her soul. Ann ripped the fetish from her mother's neck with her free hand, spat out a hurried incantation, then plunged the dagger up to its hilt into Tammy's black heart. The old woman stared at her daughter with wide, horrified eyes. Her mouth worked soundless as she fought with Ann for control of the knife.

"Who has the power now, you pathetic old sow?"

Ann pronounced the spell that would send her mother's soul down into everlasting fire. Then she gave the knife's pommel one final vicious twist, watching with evident satisfaction as the life faded from Tammy's eyes. Mother and daughter stood together for several seconds, weaving like two dancers locked in a waltz of death. Then Ann jerked the knife free, stepped back and let the dead body fall. In the deafening silence, Ann stared in sudden confusion at her hands, amazed to find that they were once more covered with blood. She turned to face Quinn and her congregation, the blade still dripping in her hand.

The revelers were standing shakily but they were up on two legs. It wasn't the untimely death of their high priestess's mother, however, that had brought them to their feet. It was the cold mist that had formed in the night sky above the roofless swimming pool, blotting out the stars and moon.

The coven waited to see what would happen, and the fog pulsed, impervious to the capricious breezes that whipped through the glade. Then the fog filtered down through the exposed rafters, scattering the squealing crowd with chunks of condensed ice. The cloud hovered for a moment over the partially devoured remains of the baby, then it dropped the rest of the way into the pit, completely whiting out the deep end of the pool.

"Moloch," Ann whispered.

Chapter Fourteen

12:22 a.m.—Christmas Day

Little by little, wisps of the concealing vapor drifted away until all that remained was a black gargoyle. He stood alone in the deep end of the pool. The baby's corpse and the puddle of gore had vanished.

"Mr. Ramsey, what a surprise. I had expected to meet your son." The creature turned its attention on Ann. "Ah, I see your mother's tiresome nagging finally got the better of you."

Ann backed up until stopped by the concrete wall. "I didn't summon you."

Moloch laughed, exposing his horrible teeth. The members of the coven were stoned, yet amazed that an honest-to-God demon had appeared in their midst.

"Oh, but you did, my dear, and most eloquently.

You surely must have realized I would hear your mother's screaming soul as it entered my domain. What more congenial invitation than her lifeblood there on your hands?"

Ann gasped, and the bloody dagger clattered to the tile.

"You honestly thought I was under your control?" Moloch spread his arm out to the night sky as if performing for an unseen celestial audience. He walked in a wide circle, enjoying the sight of the cowering bodies.

"Why are you here then?" Ann called out.

Quinn was frantically searching for help: Adar, Okata, Tim, the eighty-second Airborne. He moved his feet in a crablike shuffle to put distance between himself and the suddenly pale witch.

In front of Quinn, Moloch took the form of a dark-haired man with a flowing beard and a cheap white robe. His thin face was etched with deep lines of indescribable sadness as he stood with his hands out wide at his sides.

"You do not know what day this is? This is the birthday of that inept carpenter from Nazareth. And since I am not without a sense of irony, I decided that my child would arrive today."

Ann crossed her hands protectively over her stomach. "I don't know what you mean."

In a flash, Moloch became Tammy, detailed down to the black robe and the fountain of blood gushing from her heart. "Honey, you didn't practice safe sex. You should have kept your legs crossed."

Quinn saw the way Ann's hands covered her belly and the sweat that poured down her face. He felt sick to his soul. In the meantime, the shocking physical appearance of their long-awaited lord had sobered the coven. They avoided each other's eyes as they hurried to gather their robes and make their way to the exit.

Moloch laughed and waved one hand. One second there was a door, the next, a solid brick wall appeared. Several people screamed and pounded the blocks with their fists.

"It's rude to leave a party early. You would all miss the blessed event," Moloch said.

Moloch changed again. He became a seven-foot-tall hairless ape with razor-sharp claws and arms that hung down to the ground. He walked at a leisurely pace to the shallow end of the pool, then up the concrete steps. The covenites drew back in terror, trying to hide behind their flimsy robes. Moloch paused before the young mother, leaned over so that she could smell the hot, stale stench of death on his breath and whispered, "How did he taste?"

When the girl buried her face in the crook of her arm and began to sob, the ape grabbed a fistful of her hair and lifted her clear off the floor. "Answer me, bitch!"

The girl was too terrified to do anything but scissor her legs and scream. The creature snorted in disgust and sank its fangs into her chest. The survivors decided it was a good time to panic, but the pandemonium they raised accomplished little more than masking the horrible slurping sounds the demon made as he fed. They trampled each other trying to cram themselves into the corners of the room. Several panicked members were knocked into the deep end of the pool by their colleagues, breaking legs, and ribs and, in one case, splattering a man's skull.

In moments, Moloch sighed and tossed the corpse aside, as if it were no more than an empty soft drink can. "What's the matter with all of you? Isn't this what you wanted? Isn't this what gives meaning to your pitiful lives?"

The creature took two quick steps and grabbed a grossly overnourished black man by the back of his neck. He shook the man the way a dog shakes an old sock. The man's neck snapped like a stick, and Moloch took his other hand and ripped the head from the body, fastening his mouth to the gushing stump. In seconds, the flaccid remains joined the discarded body of the girl. The creature wiped his mouth on the back of its hairy arm and changed again. This time he became a naked human male with an average build and dark brown hair. Quinn had to look twice to recognize himself.

"Is this what you want, daughter?" The demon beat his hollow chest. "For this, you would give up immortality?"

Ann's skin was as gray as the concrete wall she was using for support. Her eyes bounced back and forth between the two Quinns. The inhuman Quinn grinned and changed back to the gargoyle.

"Come, daughter. Embrace your father."

"Please?" she said and reached out one hand to Quinn.

Moloch grabbed her arm and pulled her to him, resting a gnarled hand on her abdomen. "That's right. Beg. It might help."

Without changing his expression, the demon

opened Ann's stomach with one flick of his wrist and deftly scooped out the fully developed fetus, as if plucking a pearl from an oyster. Ann never made a sound. She looked down at her insides oozing between her fingers as she tried to hold the ragged edges of her stomach together. In the end, she folded into a heap at the monster's feet.

Moloch held up the wiggling child like a trophy. It was red and pink. Covered with Ann's blood and placental tissue, it resembled a human infant, except for the chitinous scales on the shoulders and the ridges of its backbone and the waves of cold that came off it.

"My son, you must be hungry."

Moloch turned toward Quinn. He clutched the baby and the child's tiny claws popped out, red and ready. The baby gazed at Quinn as a starving man would look at a T-Bone steak. It grinned and its mouth was already brimming with tiny tusklike teeth. Quinn inched down the wall, probing the brick with his fingers in a vain effort to find a way out. He looked past the monster and stopped cold.

In the midst of all those naked bodies, the cloaked figure stood out like a bald eagle in a cage full of bald parakeets. As the gargoyle closed in, Quinn noted the figure's silent approach and tried to become part of the wall. It wasn't until the smell of sulfur overcame the creature's body odor that Moloch became aware of the mysterious presence. He turned just as the robe hit the floor.

"What's that?" Mildred shouted.

Mildred and the girls had been sitting for hours,

arranged in a tight semicircle around the library fireplace, holding hands and concentrating their energies on the abandoned house. She glanced at the clock ticking loudly over the mantle. It was almost one o'clock on Christmas morning.

For some time they had been getting clear indications that things were going badly. First, about an hour earlier, they had lost contact with Adar. Her aura had winked out like a candle in an open window. A few minutes later, a feeling of doom had swept over them and hit their collective consciousness like a blast of Arctic wind. Finally, as they were trying to reestablish contact, a blanket of dark energy had fallen over the entire area, cutting them off as effectively as a severed telephone cable.

But the girls refused to give up. Mildred sent out a psychic S.O.S. to every elemental spirit and every sympathetic soul they had ever heard of. And just now something had happened. It was as if the sun had gone nova on the dark side of the moon.

"What could it be?" Penny asked.

"Gail?" Quinn said. "What the hell are you doing?"

Okata had ditched the black cloak and all of her clothes and stood eyeing Moloch across the deep end of the pool. "You have no place here." Is she talking to me? Quinn wondered. He looked for the doorway but it was still a solid wall. How had she gotten in?

Moloch cradled his offspring lovingly against his chest. No human being could claim to read such a creature's expression, but if Quinn had to guess, he would have said Moloch was flabbergasted. For that matter, so was he. Given the choice, Quinn wouldn't have faced such a monster without a tank. But here was Okata, all 66 inches of her. No gun, no flack vest, not even a brassiere. Yet for all the concern that showed on her face, she could have been writing the eight-foot demon a ticket for overtime parking.

"Take that abomination and go back where you came from," Okata said.

"I sense something about you," Moloch replied. "What are you? An elemental? Another witch?"

Quinn wanted to shout, "She's a cop, asshole, and you're under arrest." But he decided it was a good time to exhibit his newfound respect for police-women and let her handle it.

The white dog's head appeared in a gap between the rafters. It dropped to the ground and stood at Okata's back as she said, "I guard this place."

Moloch scanned the room, his laugh was full of contempt. "This place is hardly worth dying for."

The air was becoming uncomfortably hot, and Quinn and several of the others began choking on sulfuric fumes that seemed to follow Okata.

"I order you one last time. Begone," Okata said.

Moloch changed into something that resembled a two-legged armadillo with a whip-thin tail and a long snout full of the same sharp teeth. The child did not move or make a sound, but continued to gaze at Quinn with a rapt expression. Moloch stretched out one armor-plated hand over Ann's body and it began to twitch. The skin of her belly parted and a black leech slithered out. It raised one end, located its target, then cut a circuitous route around the altar toward Okata. The thing's mouth was round and wet and full of tiny triangular teeth. Everywhere it went, it left a glistening trail of slime.

One worm followed another, then another until the floor was carpeted with humping blobs. Some were six or seven feet long and as thick as a man's thigh. Quinn couldn't decide which was more bizarre: the disgusting herd oozing toward Okata or the fact that she was just waiting for them. Either way, he tried to squeeze his body between the cracks in the corner.

The leaches fanned out around Okata, sliding over each other and coiling their bodies into tight knots, rearing up to expose their puckered mouths. Quinn could stand it no longer. "For Christ's sake, Gail. Run!"

Okata's face was a mask of loathing, but when she looked at Quinn, it softened and she seemed to make up her mind about something. When she turned her attention back again, Moloch's defeat shone in her eyes. She turned her palms up, curled her fingers into claws and held them about a foot apart. Moloch watched all this with a mixture of amusement and disbelief. In a moment, her eyes began to blaze with flames that spread down her arms to her palms and formed a roiling ball of white-hot fire. The circle of slugs tried to squirm away from the unexpected heat, but they were too slow. The fire leapt from her hands rolling across the floor in a tidal wave of heat that turned the leeches into six-foot charcoal briquettes. Once released, the flames became living scythes, cutting down the terrified covenites, turning their soft pink bodies into living torches that crumbled into heaps of ash in a matter of seconds. The flames encircled the dumfounded demon, licking his impenetrable hide as they crept up his body toward the squirming infant. For the first and last time, Ann's baby gave vent to its unearthly hate, bellowing out a promise of revenge in a voice that echoed through the room like the roar of a dragon. Then the flames consumed it.

Fire couldn't affect Moloch. In his rage, he tried to annihilate it by swatting and clawing at the flames that taunted his body. At last, he screamed in frustration and hurled the tiny charred corpse of his son into the soot-streaked swimming pool, then changed into a gross reptilian form.

"Why?" Moloch howled.

Okata didn't blink. "I guard this place."

Moloch's shape shifted over and over. He finally settled on the most familiar form, shook a massive fist at Okata, then went up in smoke. The last things to disappear were his malignant red eyes.

"I will see you again!"

At the onset of the fire, Quinn had dropped to the floor, covered his head and steeled himself for the agony which was sure to come. But when Moloch disappeared, the roar of the flames gave way to a room heavy with silence. He kept perfectly still, letting his ears do all the work while he waited for the other shoe to drop. Then something warm and wet licked his ear.

Quinn yelled like he'd been stabbed and rolled over. "Call him off, for Christ's sake!"

The dog was breathing its hot breath in Quinn's face. Okata had reclaimed the black cloak and was once more covered to her neck. Quinn got up and stared at the carnage. The heat had been so intense that the bricks were glazed. Even the pools of blood had boiled away and the bodies of the coven had become piles of drifting gray ash. Yet the flames had missed him completely, and across the room, his son slept soundly on a blanket of char.

Quinn tried to think of something clever to say, something that would sound good over a few beers at the local tavern. "Are you going to hurt me?"

Okata crossed the floor and stood beside the dog, looking at him with a solemn but steady gaze. "Why would I hurt you, Quinn?"

"Then maybe you'll tell me what just happened?"

She buttoned the cape. "Of course."

He brushed himself off. Okata's was the only robe that had survived the fire, so he had to stand with his legs together and his hands cupped over his genitals.

"Many hundreds of years ago, my people crossed the Pacific from the islands to the south and claimed this land for their own. I have been here since the dawn of time, alone except for the birds and turtles, and my heart longed for the feel of human feet upon my slopes and children to call my name."

"Time out!" Quinn said. "What are you telling me? Aren't you a witch? I mean every woman I've met since I came to these islands is a witch."

Okata smiled and reached out her hand. Quinn forced himself not to flinch as she brushed the hair out of his eyes. "No, I am Pele, a goddess to the people of these islands for thousands of years."

"Pele? You told me a story about Pele. She was the goddess of fire or something?"

"My spirit resides in the heat of the earth. My heart beat is the boiling lava of the volcanoes."

Quinn forgot he was nude and began waving his hands around for emphasis. "But you're a cop. You're Gail Okata."

"I take many forms."

To make her point, Okata's body shrunk down on all fours. Her ears sprouted and formed white hairy points, and in less than a second she had become a white mountain sheep. She licked his hand and then changed back.

In the past months, Quinn had seen so many fantastic things that a woman changing into a sheep didn't faze him. "You were in the cave."

"That's right. I had to know what you planned to do with the spirits of my people."

Quinn scratched his head as he started to pace. "What could I do?"

"Your uncle planned to trade them for power and wealth."

"Uncle Bernard? Yeah, no doubt about it. He was a worm." Quinn realized what he had said and glanced at the remains of the leeches. "Sorry."

"Yes," Okata said. "I had to stop him."

Quinn's eyes bulged. "You killed him?"

She nodded without expression. "I executed him and Stalkins, Peterson, Smythe—everyone who knew about the cavern."

Quinn developed an immediate sinking sensation in the pit of his stomach, but Okata said, "You have nothing to fear. You will respect my dead."

"Wow, I will. Thanks."

His hands went back over his groin. "But, Gail—I mean, Pele—"

"I am still Gail, Quinn. I have always been Gail just

as I have always been Pele."

"Uh, what happens now? Is Moloch dead? Is it over?"

"What never lived cannot die. As for it's being over, I have no answer. I have foiled a plan that the dark lords have been working on for many centuries. They may attempt revenge, but I will be ready."

"What are you going to do?"

"Do? As long as the earth remains, I will guard this place."

"No, I mean, will you go back to being Gail Okata? Will you still be a cop?"

Gail spread her hands out to her side. "I have used this form for many centuries. Since my first children landed on these shores. It is a good way to go about the islands."

She reached down and stroked the dog's head. The animal's hairy tail beat against her leg. "They are all gone now. To the new generations I am just a legend, a funny story to tell the tourists. But I remember them all. Fat, happy Kaahumanu: Opakau; the first chief: the good-natured warrior Kamehameha. They first came to me in fear of the wrath of my lava, but later they came out of love. Each night I roam the dark caverns and speak with their souls. They worshipped me, but now they are gone. I have not forgotten."

Quinn felt like crying. Okata smiled sadly. "I can't wait to tell Adar about you. Wow, a real goddess."

"I am truly sorry, Quinn, but I can't allow that." Then she lifted one hand and the white dog landed on Quinn's chest, pinning him to the concrete.

"Ugh! What have you been feeding him?" Quinn

asked, turning his head to the side.

Pele entered his mind. Her presence was a fire that carefully burned and cleansed certain cells. She filled him, squeezing his essence into a small corner. But there was no pain—only immense power and, just before he blacked out, a feeling of immeasurable time and vast loneliness.

EPILOGUE

"He's coming around," Adar said.

Quinn opened his eyes. Tim, Frank Robbins, and Gail Okata were standing over him; Adar was kneeling at his side. "What hit me?"

"We were hoping you could tell us," Adar said and pressed his hand between hers.

Quinn sat up only to be rewarded with a queasy stomach and a head that started spinning like a top. "Where's Q?"

"He's okay," Adar said. "It looks as if they shot him full of narcotics. He's still a little groggy."

Quinn held up his arm for Tim and Frank to help him up. He wrapped the blanket covering him closely around his body. "Has anyone seen my clothes?"

363

Okata had them balled up under her arm. Quinn turned slowly in place. Except for a few strange scorched marks, the room was almost antiseptically clean. Adar ran her hand over the scab on the side of his head.

"You have a nasty bump. You're going to need a medic."

Quinn smiled at his beautiful witch. "I might have someone in mind."

"Mr. Ramsey, the field out there is full of cars," Frank said. "Where did they come from?"

"I don't know." Adar and Tim braced Quinn as he hobbled to the door and asked, "Where did they come from Tim?"

"I don't know either. Frank and Gail found me in the back room, sleeping the sleep of the just. I have a headache and a blank space for all of last night."

"Nothing?"

"I remember coming here loaded for bear, then waking up in that bedroom."

Quinn turned to Adar. "What about you?"

Adar stared at Okata for a long moment, then said, "I don't remember anything either."

Okata trailed behind the trio, listening patiently to Frank Robbins yammering in her ear.

"The cops are on their way, but I bet you're wondering what took me so long. First, I got stuck in the mud. Then I got lost. Did I tell you I'm not from around here? Then I found this shack out in the middle of nowhere, and I banged on the door until this old guy came out. After twenty minutes of showing him every card in my wallet and swearing on every book I could lay my hands on, he finally believed I wasn't a Narc. Then he told me he didn't have a phone."

The rest of Frank's story was lost to Quinn as he ducked into one of the half-completed bathrooms to dress. Outside, he found his son stretched out on a blanket under a palm tree.

"How are you, kid?" he asked, touching the boy's arm.

"Okay, Dad."

Quinn started to squeeze the boy's hand, but there was something in it. He pried the boy's fingers open and found a piece of lava about the size of a walnut. "What's this?"

"I had a dream," Q said, his voice heavy with sleep. "I saw Mom. She wanted me to do something, but I can't remember what."

"Don't worry about it, sport. Just relax."

"I'm hungry. Do I have to study today?"

"Nope. It's Christmas."

"It's cold out here. Let's get him into the truck until the police arrive," Quinn said. "I could use a place to sit down myself."

Once Q was safely in the back of the panel truck, Quinn climbed stiffly into the passenger seat. He stared at the waterfall while Tim and Frank went to gather up Tim's artillery. Adar and Okata stood by the open door, and in the distance, they could just hear the sound of sirens.

Quinn looked at Okata and chuckled ruefully, "I guess I'll be seeing a lot of you." For some strange reason, he felt sorry for her. "Why don't you come by the house after all this is over? We're going to try to have some kind of Christmas dinner and open presents."

Gail smiled shyly. "Maybe. We'll see."

"Do come, Gail," Adar said.

"Maybe. I have to see some people."

Quinn's head felt like shit. "Say, Dar, you got any more of those leaves?"

Gail Okata waited until all the cars were towed, all the prints were taken and all the cops had left before returning to the tree. Okata had released the girl and the young lawyer before the police arrived. Now, she removed the gag from Judge Wilkinson's mouth. The man's body was bloated from insect bites.

"You must be out of your mind!" Wilkinson said. "Let me go right now, Sergeant, or I'll have you up on charges."

Okata had her handcuff key on a chain, and she twirled it around her finger as she turned her back. "Judge, before you were elected to the bench, I believe you were a partner in the firm of Block, Growe, Peterson, Smythe, & Rynd."

Wilkinson rattled the silver bracelets. "So what? Let me go!"

"Marcus Peterson's firm?"

The judge sighed as if he were speaking to an idiot. "Yes, Marcus and I were partners."

"And you helped Bernard Ramsey purchase this land. You pushed to change the restrictions in fact."

"If it is any of your business, yes!"

When she turned around, Okata was holding a ball of white flames in her hands. "Then you have Pele to pay for your crimes."